Howard Malcolm Jenkins

The family of William Penn, founder of Pennsylvania

Ancestry and Descendants

Howard Malcolm Jenkins

The family of William Penn, founder of Pennsylvania
Ancestry and Descendants

ISBN/EAN: 9783337060312

Printed in Europe, USA, Canada, Australia, Japan

Cover: Foto ©Raphael Reischuk / pixelio.de

More available books at **www.hansebooks.com**

The Family of
William Penn
Founder of Pennsylvania
Ancestry and Descendants

BY

HOWARD M. JENKINS ,

AUTHOR OF VOLUME ONE, MEMORIAL HISTORY OF PHILADELPHIA,
ETC., ETC.

1899
PHILADELPHIA, PENNSYLVANIA, U. S. A.
THE AUTHOR

LONDON, ENGLAND
HEADLEY BROTHERS, 14, BISHOPSGATE WITHOUT

PREFACE.

THE occasion of this volume is substantially, perhaps sufficiently, stated in the opening of the first chapter. To the
explanation there given a few particulars may be added.
There has always been, the author believes, a strong and very
reasonable interest in the personality of William Penn, as the
Founder of Pennsylvania, and as a worthy figure in the world's
history, and some of this interest attaches to the line of those who
have descended from him. The volume here prepared assumes
simply to deal with this Family subject. It is not a history nor
a biography. In one or two places, perhaps, the record has been
permitted an extension which could not be entirely justified by
the plan of the work, but excusing this by the special interest of
the subject at those points, the author thinks the book has been
fairly confined to its original and legitimate plan.

Some of the family letters, very possibly, may be regarded as
containing details too trivial for printing. The view adopted as
to such matters has been that the account is thus made more precise and distinct, and is invested with human interest.

Indeed, a book of this character must in part find its justifica-
tion as being a study, a picture, of social conditions in the period
to which it belongs, and such a study or picture is obviously of
little value unless it is presented with lines sufficiently distinct,
and details sufficiently definite, to make a positive impression on
the mind. While it has not been desired to dwell upon features
that are unpleasing, and not to reward a reader—if any such
there be—who comes in search of scandal, yet it has not been

thought proper to omit a candid, if brief, mention of whatever is essential to the completeness of the record.

One criticism to be reasonably made is that which must apply to nearly all such works,—that the treatment of individuals is unequal, that in cases where the claims are alike more is said of one and less of another. This is explained by the variation of materials,—in some cases they are abundant, in others scanty. Concerning some persons there survive letters and documents so numerous and so full that there is no difficulty in making a satisfactory account of them, while as to others only a few particulars remain, or are accessible.

Note.—The stock of unbound sheets of this work having been accidentally burned, in the fire at the establishment of the J. B. Lippincott Company, Philadelphia, the book has been reset, and copies printed to replace those burned.

TABLE OF CONTENTS.

LIST OF ILLUSTRATIONS.

vii

I.

The Origin of the Penn Family.

THE ancestry of William Penn, the Founder of Pennsylvania, has not been positively ascertained farther back than his great-great-grandfather, who bore the same name, and of whom I shall presently speak. But the evidence seems to me sufficient that his family was originally Welsh. The name itself is distinctly Welsh,—a word of common use in that language : *pen*, a head or highland. When a name was to be assigned to his newly granted province, in 1681, he himself chose, he says, " New Wales," but the King gave it the name of PENN-SYLVANIA, and the Secretary, Sir Leolin Jenkins,[1] a Welshman, could not be prevailed on to change it. Mentioning this, Penn (in his well-known letter to Robert Turner, March 5, 1680–81) explains the meaning of his own name, it being, he says, " Welsh for a *head*, as Penmanmoire in Wales, Penrith in Cumberland, and Penn in Buckinghamshire," etc.

The story in Watson is also well-known, that the Reverend Hugh David came over with William Penn " about 1700" (on the " Canterbury," of course, in 1699, if the story is true), and that in conversation on the ship Penn said, " Hugh, I am a Welshman myself," adding the explanation

---

[1] Hepworth Dixon, in his " Life of Penn," refers to the Secretary with whom Penn discussed this subject, as Blathwayte, but it is obvious it was Jenkins. Cf. the record in the " Breviate of the Boundary Case," " Pennsylvania Archives," Second Series, Vol. XVI. p. 355. There is a good sketch of Sir Leolin (or Llewelyn) Jenkins in the " Dictionary of National Biography."

that one of his ancestors had come from Wales into England.[1]

The arms borne by William Penn, the Founder, *Argent, on a fesse Sable three plates*, are the same as those of the Penns of Penn, in Buckinghamshire, according to the Heralds' Visitation of that county, 1575-1634. They are the same, also, as those of the Penne family of Shropshire, on the border of Wales, according to the Heralds' Visitation of that county, 1564-1620. This latter family, in a pedigree given in the Heralds' manuscript,[2] extending over fifteen generations, begins with Sir William Penne, Knight, Lord of the Bryn (hill), who married Joan, daughter of Ririd Voel of Lodfoll, and follows with his son, Sir Hugh Penne, Knight, who married Jane, daughter to Jer. Goch ap Bleddin ap Kinvan. The pedigree thus " bristles with Welsh names," and in the eighth generation from Sir Hugh Richard Penne married Lowry, daughter of David Lloyd ap Sir Griffith Vaughan, and Sionett Penne married Ievan ap Llewelyn ap Griffith,—all of which record, it need hardly be said, is thoroughly Welsh.

[1] "Annals," Vol. I. p. 219. While the account ascribed to Hugh David is obviously incorrect as to the point of William Penn's *grand-father* being " named John Tudor," other details in it are not in-credible, and some of them are supported by independent testimony. The Founder is reported as saying that his ancestor, John Tudor, " lived upon the top of a hill or mountain in Wales," and was generally called John *Pen*-munrith, or John on the top of the hill ; hence, ultimately, John Penn. This might have been. It is worth note that the Welsh Tu-dors, ancestors of Henry VII., are said to have come from Penrunydd, in Anglesea. And it is of record that Edward VI., grandson of Henry VII., in 1553 made a grant of land to David Penn, in consideration of the services of his wife, Sybil Penn, who was the nurse of Henry VIII.'s children, a near association of the Penns with the royal Tudors being thus suggested.

[2] Harleian MSS., British Museum, No. 1241, cited in *Quakeriana*. London, October, 1894. The Bucks Visitation is Harleian MSS. No. 1533.

Not only did the Penns of Penn, in Bucks, bear the same arms, *Argent, on a fesse Sable three plates*, as the Shropshire family and Penn the Founder, but they had among their family the names David and Griffith, distinctly Welsh. " How are we to account for the occurrence of these Welsh names in a family inhabiting a remote village in the heart of England, except by supposing it was of Welsh descent, and kept green the memory of its extraction?"[1]

An old manuscript, prepared in the middle of the seventeenth century by a member of the Penn family of Worcestershire, and preserved by Mr. Grazebook, a well-known English authority on heraldry, describes the arms, *Argent, on a fesse Sable three plates*, as belonging to the "main stem of the Penn family," and says,—

"As for our beginning I own it to proceed from the Britons, our estates lying amongst them, and in the Marches of the same, which anciently belonged to Penn-house, before that it was divided and scattered by many branches into several counties."[2]

On the tomb of Sir William Penn, father of the Founder, it is stated that he was son of Giles Penn, "of the Penns of Penns-Lodge in the county of Wilts, and those Penns of Penn, in the County of Bucks," and this inscription, it is fair to presume, was made with adequate knowledge. The author of it was doubtless William Penn, the Founder.[3] His intelligent acquaintance with his father's career, and devotion to his memory (shown afterwards in his " Vindication"), his ability in composition, and his rights as eldest

---

[1] Article in *Quakeriana*, already cited, October, 1894.

[2] Ibid. The "Marches" were the partly Welsh counties bordering on England, geographically and politically counted as part of England.

[3] The expression on the tablet, that the Admiral, "With a gentle and Even Gale, in much peace, arrived and anchored in his Last and Best Port," strongly suggests the style of William Penn, the Founder.

son, heir, and executor, make it unlikely that the work would be intrusted to any other hands.[1]

In the transcription of the monumental inscription to Admiral Penn, Mr. J. Henry Lea (*Penna. Mag.* Vol. XIV. p. 172) differs from all other authorities as to the language used in it, by omitting the words "and those Penns of Penn in the county of Bucks." These appear in the full inscription given in Granville Penn's "Memorials" of the Admiral, in Burke's "Commoners of England," and in Maria Webb's "Penns and Peningtons;" and Mr. W. H. Summers, author of the interesting and valuable "Memories of Jordans and the Chalfonts" (London, 1895), says, in a letter from Beaconsfield, October 3, 1895, to *Quakeriana*, London,—

"When in Bristol a few weeks ago, I entered St. Mary Redcliffe Church and examined Admiral Penn's monument. It certainly is very difficult to decipher the inscription, but I was able, even without a glass, to read the disputed words '*and those Penns of Penn in the County of Bucks.*'"

To this may be added that a photograph of the tablet, taken for the author of this volume, clearly shows the words in question, and in a visit to St. Mary Redcliffe, 1899, he was able to assure himself additionally, by personal inspection.

"Relation of kindred," says Granville Penn, in his "Memorials" of the Admiral (Vol. II. p. 575), "was always mutually claimed and acknowledged between the family of Sir William Penn and the Penns of Penn in Bucks, now represented by Earl Howe; but the genealogical connection does not appear on record." It is also true—though the fact may be of no great significance—that at Penn, in Bucks, in the parish church, where the Penn family of that place are buried, Thomas Penn, of Stoke Poges (son of the

[1] The Admiral's widow writes to her son (W. P., the Founder), October 9, 1670, "The man is returned from Bristol, and set up his monument very well," etc. (Foot-note to Granville Penn's "Memorials," Vol. II. p. 568.)

Founder), constructed a large family vault, in which the remains of six of his children, who died in infancy, 1753–60, were deposited and now remain.[1]

From these several pieces of evidence it seems to me reasonable: (1) that the ancestry of William Penn was originally Welsh; (2) that families of the name in several southern and southwestern counties of England, bearing the same arms, were of a common stock, derived from Wales; (3) that the Penns of Wiltshire and Bucks were nearly related, and when the lines shall be traced will prove to be common ancestors of the Founder.

[1] Letter of Rev. J. Grainger, M. A., vicar of Penn, to W. H. Summers, cited in *Quakeriana*, London, November, 1894.

II.

Admiral Penn's Progenitors.

COMING now from the probable to the certain, we begin the line of William Penn, the Founder, with his great-great-grandfather, who died 1591. Records from that date make it plain. This ancestor was " William Penn, of Myntie, in the County of Gloucester, Yeoman," whose will is recorded in the Prerogative Court of Canterbury, and has been printed in full in the *Pennsylvania Magazine*, by J. H. Lea (Vol. XIV. p. 58).[1]

" Minte, Minety, or Minty," says Britton's description of Wiltshire (London, 1814), "is a large parish, principally situated in a detached portion of the hundred of Crowthorn and Minety, which belongs politically to the County of Gloucester, though completely environed by Wiltshire." An earlier description (Atkyns's "Gloucestershire," pp. 346, 358) says " Minchy, now Minety, was always accounted a member of the manor of Cirencester, and gave the name to the hundred of Minety, now united to the hundred of Crowthorn ; it anciently was within the hundred of Cirencester. The parish church, the parsonage, the vicarage-house and a small hamlet called Wiltshire-row, lie in the hundred of Malmsbury, in Wiltshire ; the rest, and far the greater part of the parish, lies in the hundred of Crowthorn and Minety," in Gloucester.

Penn's Lodge, Clarkson says ("Life of Penn," p. 1), was near Minety, " on the edge of Bradon Forest, in the northwest part of the county of Wilts, or rather in Gloucester-

---

[1] Also by Coleman (London, 1871) in his "Pedigree of Penn."

shire, a small part of the latter being enclosed in the former county." [1] In Granville Penn's "Memorials" (Vol. II. p. 375) there is a letter from John Georges, a barrister-at-law, M.P. for Cirencester (then a man of seventy-three), dated at "Bawnton, near Cicester," January 27, 1665-66, to Sir William Penn, in which he urges him to repurchase the ancestral place at Minety. In this letter Mr. Georges says,—

"And now give me leave . . . to revive a former notion to you : that . . . you would redeem unto your name and family the lands in Myntie, which were your ancestors', the Penns, for many generations, worth about 100/ per ann., with a genteel ancient house upon it. I have heretofore made an overture of this my desire to Mr. Nicholas Pleydell, the present owner of it, and never found him averse to part with it," etc.

We fix, therefore, William Penn, of Minety, as a yeoman, living at Penn's Lodge, a "genteel, ancient house," in Gloucestershire, adjoining Wiltshire. His will, dated May 1, 1590, shows that he had had one son, William, whose wife's name was Margaret; that William was dead at the time of making this will, but Margaret surviving, with six children, George (explicitly named as the eldest son), Giles, William, Marie, Sara, and Susanna.[2] He directs that his "body be buried in the parish church, chancel, or churchyard of Minetie." It appears that it was so buried, and that a monumental stone in the chancel, near the south door of

---

[1] A large tract of country lying to the south and southeast of Minety is still distinguished by the name of Bradon Forest, though it is now almost entirely denuded of trees, and a great part of it is enclosed for cultivation." (Britton's "Wiltshire," p. 633, London, 1814.)

[2] The record of Marriage Bonds in the Diocesan Registry Office at Salisbury shows the bond of Richard Cusse, of Wooton Bassett, in Wilts, August, 2, 1633, to marry Susan Penn, of the parish of Brinkworth, spinster. Mr. Lea says she "is unquestionably the daughter of William and Margaret (Rastall) Penn, and the aunt of Admiral Penn ;" if so, she was at least forty-three years old, as she is named in her grandfather's will, 1590.

the church, bore the inscription, "William Penn, dyed the
12 of March in the year of our Lord 1591." The rector
of Minety, Rev. Mr. Edwards, in 1890 reported that the
stone had then—at the distance of three centuries—"quite
disappeared." [1]

The yeoman of Minety, though a man of moderate estate,
appears thus to have been a person of social distinction in his
neighborhood, entitled to sepulture and a memorial tablet
within the parish church. We pass now to his son William,
who, as the will shows, had predeceased him. The will
gives the name of the son's wife (Margaret) and the names
of their six children (stated above), but discloses little more
concerning him. But the letter, already partly cited, of the
barrister Georges to Admiral Penn presents something
further. He addresses the Admiral as "loving cousin,"
and claims a "share and interest" in him as one of his
"kinsfolk and near allies," and in explanation says,—

> "And to the end that you and yours may be truly informed . . .
> how I make my title to it, you may please to know that your grandfather,
> William Penn (whose name you bear) was by your great-grandfather
> (of the same name also) placed with my great uncle, Christopher
> Georges, then a counsellor-at-law, to be bred up by him, and with whom
> he lived many years as his chief clerk, till he married him to one of
> his sister Ann Georges' daughters by Mr. John Rastall, then one of the
> aldermen of Gloucester, . . . By which pedigree it may appear to you
> that your father and myself were cousin-germans but once removed." [2]

[1] Cf. J. Henry Lea, *Penna. Mag.* Vol. XIV. p. 57, foot-note.
Clarkson, in his "Life of Penn," says, "A flat grave-stone, which per-
petuates this event, is still remaining [he wrote about 1812]. It stands
in the passage between two pews in the chancel. It states, however,
only that he died on the 12th of March, 1591."

[2] The list of lay subsidies for Wiltshire, 1587, has a reference to William Penn, of Malmesbury, who Mr. Lea thinks was the law-clerk,
the son of the yeoman.

We pass now to the third generation. Of the six children of William, the law clerk, we have little knowledge,[1] except as to Giles, the second son. He was "a captain in the navy, and for many years a consul for the English trade in the Mediterranean," Granville Penn says, and the Admiral's mural tablet uses nearly the same words. The "Calendar of English State Papers," in 1635-39, shows a long correspondence between Giles Penn and the Government, in which he desires a commission to lead an expedition against the Sallee corsairs of Morocco, a commission which might or might not have been finally given him, except for the pressure of the then impending civil war. The Admiral's tablet says his mother, the wife of Giles, was of "the Gilberts in the County of Somerset, originally from Yorkshire," and the records of St. Mary Redcliffe, Bristol, show the marriage of "Giles Penne and Joan Gilbeart," on the 5th of November, 1600. That this was our Captain Giles is fairly certain, and makes an alteration in the customary Penn pedigrees, which give the name of Giles's wife as Margaret.[2] Granville Penn says, " Giles had two sons, between whose ages was a difference of twenty years." These two were George and William, the Admiral, and as the latter was born in 1621, it fixes George's

[1] Susan's marriage is probably noted (see foot-note preceding), and George, by an allusion in Admiral Penn's will, lived at Bradon Forest, Wilts (in succession to his grandfather), and had a son William. I am advised, as these sheets are passing through the press, by Mr. J. Henry Lea, that he is about to print some further facts, and I may avail myself of these, in a later chapter of the book,

[2] This error occurs in the Penn Pedigree, by Coleman (London, 1871). Coleman also has other errors : he confuses George Penn, uncle of the Admiral, with George, the Admiral's elder brother, and gives the year of William Penn of Minety's death as 1592 and his will 1591,—both dates a year too late. He says William the Founder "treated with the Indians 1681 and 1682," he being in England the whole of 1681. He spells William Aubrey's name Aubury, and Gulielma he uniformly prints Gulima.

birth as 1601, and corresponds appropriately with the date
1600 as that of the parents' marriage.

As to Giles Penn's children other than George and William, the records of St. Mary Redcliffe show the baptism
of "Rachell daughter to Gyles Penne," February 24, 1607,
and the death of "Eleanor the daughter of Mr. Giles
Penne," November 24, 1612. Two daughters of Giles Penn
must have grown up and married and had issue, or one
have married twice, for Admiral Penn, in his will, names
his "nephews, James and John Bradshaw, and William
and George Markham." He also names his "Cousin William Penn, son of George Penn, late of the Forest of Bray-
don, Co. Wilts, Gentleman, deceased," which indicates that
his uncle George, named executor in the will of the yeoman of Minety, dwelt in Wiltshire and closed his life there.
The nephew William Markham is of course well known
to us, the first cousin of the Founder, and many years Lieutenant-Governor of Pennsylvania.

George Penn, the elder son of Captain Giles and brother
of the Admiral, was "brought up to commerce," Granville
Penn says, "became an opulent merchant in Spain, and
resided many years at Seville." But this is a scanty and
somewhat vague outline of the experiences of George,
which appear to have been romantic and unfortunate to a
degree not here suggested. Mr. Conner, in his "Sir William Penn, Knight," says that "the elder [son] having
grown rich as a merchant in Spain, was pounced upon by
the Inquisition as heretic and sinner. Torn from wife and
fortune, tortured and expelled, he regained his native land
but to die." This affords us a fuller idea of the case, and
the whole story is given in documents and comments which
Granville Penn prints in the "Memorials." These are, first,
the minutes of the Committee of the Admiralty, at London,
in the time of the Commonwealth, when Captain (afterwards
Sir) William Penn was cruising on the coast of Ireland in
the 30-gun frigate "Assurance." Thus, the minutes :

"*Jan. 12, 1646-7.*—A Spanish gentleman, named Don Juan de Urbina, being taken by Captain Penn, on the coast of Munster, in a prize that came out of Waterford, did this day attend the Committee, (together with Sr. Bernardo, agent for the ambassador of his majesty of Spain . . .), and desire that he might be set at liberty, being a person of quality . . . he alleged that he came from Bilboa, was bound to Flanders, to be secretary to the governor thereof ; that the ship wherein he was embarked was cast away about Waterford in Ireland, at the end of June last. That he had been at Kilkenny, Ross, and other parts of Ireland . . . That . . . he had embarked himself for Bilboa in the *St. Patrick* of Waterford, which was after taken by Captain Penn, who did offer affronts to his person, stripping him naked, and putting him among the common mariners ; for which he therefore desired satisfaction and reparation in his honor," etc.

The committee, after an examination into the case, decided that there was no reason for the Don's detention, and directed "that he be delivered to Mr. Bernardo," the agent for the Spanish ambassador.

In Captain Penn's journal he had made this entry of the Don's capture :

"*13th December, 1646, Sunday.*—About eight of the clock in the morning we spied a sail, to whom we gave chase ; and about eleven we came up with her, and took her ; she belonging to Waterford, and was called the *Patrick* thereof, of burthen about 60 tons, laden with hides, salmon, and several other commodities, bound for Bilboa ; and had in her about 8 Spaniards, passengers."

No particular mention, however, is here made of the Don. Explanation of the case is plainly needed, and this Granville Penn, after these quotations, proceeds to supply. At the time, he says, that Captain Penn took the " St. Patrick," his brother George was a prisoner in the hands of the Spanish Inquisition, and had suffered the most cruel treatment ; the captain therefore regarded Don Juan "as a representative of the Spanish nation," and proposed " to repay to him a mollified portion of the severities and indignities which his brother was suffering at Seville. But his object was not merely to make a Spaniard suffer for his

brother; it was to do an act that should speak home to the
Spanish government, and provoke a public notoriety of the
outrage for which he could obtain no other redress; and for
that purpose he selected from amongst the captured Spaniards him who was of the highest quality to endure a vi-
carious chastisement for his nation. He did not apprehend
severity of censure from his employers, when the motive
of his conduct should be fully exposed; nor does any record of censure appear in the minutes of the Council. . . .
Shortly after this event, George Penn was dismissed from
the Inquisition; and it is not unreasonable to assume that
Urbina's report, on his return to Bilboa, of the fraternal
retaliation exercised upon his person by Penn determined
the liberation of the brother." [1]

As to this last statement we must express some doubt.
It seems unlikely that the Don was in such temper upon
his return to Spain as to expedite the enlargement of the
English heretic; he would have been more likely to urge
the inquisitors to give another turn to their screw. It
appears, too, by the further documents which Granville
Penn gives, that George Penn was finally discharged and
sent out of Spain, and that this must have taken place—
without apparent interference from outside influences—
fully as soon as the time of the Don's liberation at London.
In an appendix (C) to his first volume, Granville Penn
prints George Penn's own account of himself and his
troubles, drawn up for presentation to Cromwell. This
describes the time of his arrest as in 1643, and the whole
period of his detention as being three years, two months,
and six days. It is obvious from this that his enlargement could have been little if any later than the date of
Don Juan's appearance before the Admiralty Committee,
January 12, 1646-47. In his petition and statement to
the Protector, George Penn says that "after living many
years in Spain, that is to say, chiefly in Seville, Malaga,

[1] "Memorials," Vol. I. pp. 230-233.

Cales, and Sanlucar, in credit and estate," he was apprehended by officers of the Inquisition, at his house in Sanlucar, in the year 1643. They first executed the ceremony of excommunication, "body and soul," then broke open all his rooms and warehouses, and seized his property, "to a nail in the wall," and confiscated all debts due him, found by his "books, writings, and accounts." Then they took him to Seville, where he was placed in a "dungeon some eight feet in diameter, as dark as a grave," and left alone. An allowance of bread and water was given him every Monday, to last a week. Once a month he was tied to the dungeon-door and received fifty lashes with knotted whip-cords, fresh stripes usually arriving before the previous month's wounds had healed. All this lasted, he says, three years without any formal charge being made, "they intending by it to make me be my own accuser;" finally he was accused before seven inquisitors and put upon the rack for four hours, when, the torture being beyond endurance, he confessed "all their false accusations" *en bloc.* The accusations, he explains, were that he was "a most damnable heretic, by birth, breeding, and perseverance," that he had married a woman of the Catholic faith, a Spanish subject, born in Antwerp, had endeavored to pervert her and her sisters, and had intended to take them to England, "a land which of all others in the world overfloweth with all sorts of most damnable heresies and disobedience to the see of Rome," etc. Finally, upon his abjuring the Protestant faith, a public procession was formed in Seville, he was taken to the church, and his offences, confession, and sentence proclaimed "in the sight of thousands." His property was confiscated,—about ten thousand pounds' value, he declares,—he was ordered to leave Spain within three months, on pain of death; he was sentenced to be burned if he should be again under arrest and found to have renounced the Roman faith; lastly, his wife was divorced from him, and she was ordered to be married to a Spaniard "for her better safeguard from me and securing of her soul from my heretical suggestions."

The dates of this transaction, including the condemnation in the church of Seville, are wanting, and we can only infer them, but it seems to me most probable that the whole of the business was known to the young sea-captain, the brother of George Penn, when he caught the little ship with its "8 Spaniards" coming out of Waterford, in the winter of 1646, and that as he stripped and exposed the unhappy secretary of the governor of Flanders he was inflicting a retaliatory blow, and not expecting to propitiate the Inquisition at Seville, or hoping to secure the good offices of the humiliated Don Juan.

George Penn, at any rate, came back from Spain to England without his property, and presumably without his Flemish wife. He fortified his case with the deposition of twelve English traders who had known him in Spain, and who estimated his own loss at six thousand pounds, and the property seized in his hands belonging to others at "near as much more." He applied, or prepared to do so, to the Protector (probably Richard Cromwell, not Oliver), and subsequently renewed his effort with Charles II. The latter, it appears, considered his case favorably, for a presentation of a claim for damages was made by his nephew, William Penn the Founder, to Queen Anne, during the negotiations for the Peace of Utrecht in 1712–13, and in it the statement is made that the king (evidently in 1663 or 1664), "out of compassion and justice to Mr. George Penn, appointed him envoy to reside at the King of Spain's court in order to and with commands that he should, insist upon satisfaction from that king for his sufferings, loss, and damage. But Mr. George Penn," the petition adds, "being then about sixty-three years of age, was prevented of going thither by his sudden death." [1]

[1] Appendix C, No. 2, "Memorials" of Admiral Penn, I. 555. As to this petition, it is evident that it must have been prepared (if drawn

The veracious Samuel Pepys, in his Diary, says, August 1, 1664: "Last night I was waked with knocking at Sir W. Pen's door; and what was it but people's running up and down to bring him word that his brother, who hath been a good while, it seems, sick, is dead." This was obviously George Penn.

TABLE OF ADMIRAL PENN'S DESCENT.

1.—William Penn, of Minety, yeoman, *d.* 1591,⚊

2.—William Penn, law-clerk,⚊Margaret Rastall.

3.—(Six children, including) Giles Penn⚊Joan Gilbert.

4.—George, *b.* 1601,   WILLIAM   Four (?) daughters.
    d. 1664.   (Admiral).

by William Penn himself) early in the negotiations for the Peace of Utrecht, for he had his apoplectic seizure October 4, 1712.

III.

Admiral Sir William Penn.

COMING now to the Admiral, the great-grandson of the Yeoman, and father of the Founder, we may make selection among many personal details. Granville Penn, great-grandson of the Admiral, has gathered into his two volumes (London, 1833) the materials of a Memorial of his ancestor at once dignified and honorable. Contending with all the gibes and slurs of Mr. Samuel Pepys's Diary, and compelled to extract from that rich storehouse of history and spite the allusions to Sir William, he accomplishes the task with credit. We shall, in a moment, cite some of Pepys's paragraphs bearing upon the Admiral's family life and personal qualities. Many of them lie enfolded each in its own layer of backbiting, but this the reader can perhaps allow for. We present now the monumental inscription to the Admiral, placed in the church of St. Mary Redcliffe, at Bristol, where his mother, Joan Gilbert, had been buried earlier, and where, in pursuance of his will, he was himself buried, with full ceremony, September 30, 1670.[1]

We take the inscription as it is given by Granville Penn (Vol. II. p. 580), as follows :

> To the just Memory of Sr Will^M Penn, Kt., and sometimes
> Generall : Born at Bristoll An. 1621 : Son of Captain Giles
> Penn, severall yeares Consul for ye English in ye Mediterranean ;
> of the Penns of Penns Lodge in ye County of
> Wilts, and those Penns of Penn in ye C. of Bucks ; and by
> his Mother from the Gilberts in y^e County of Somerset,
> Originally from Yorkshire : Addicted from his

---

[1] Cf. letter from R. Ellsworth, Bristol, to Captain Challoner, *Lancaster Herald*, "Memorials," Vol. II. p. 567, describing the ceremony.

Vice Admiral of England
during the Interregnum
in the Victories obtained
over the Dutch in 1653 & 1654;
for which he was invested
with a Gold Chain and Medal;
took Jamaica and was chosen
Member for Weymouth in 1655.

SIR
WILLIAM PENN,
K.T.
B 1621. D 1670

Vice Admiral of England
in the Reign of King Charles II;
Great Captain Commander
under the Duke of York in the
Victory obtained over the Dutch in
1665. Commissioner of Adml & Navy,
&c. &c. &c.
chosen Member for Weymouth in 1660.

Youth to Maritime Affairs ; he was made Captain at
the yeares of 21 ; Rear-Admiral of Ireland at 23 ; Vice-
Admiral of Ireland at 25 ; Admiral to the Streights
at 29 ; Vice-Admiral of England at 31, and General
In the first Dutch Warres, at 32.   Whence retiring,
in A° 1655 he was chosen a Parliament man for the
Town of Weymouth, 1660 ; made Commissioner of
the Admiralty and Navy ; Governor of the Town and Fort
of King-sail ; Vice-Admiral of Munster, and a Member of
that Provincial Counseill ; and in Anno 1664, was
chosen Great Captain Commander under his
Royall Highnesse in y* Signall and most
evidently successful fight against the Dutch fleet.

Thus, He took leave of the Sea, his old Element ; But
continued still his other employs till 1669 ; at what
time, through Bodely Infirmities (contracted by y*
Care and fatigue of Publique Affairs),
                              He withdrew,
Prepared and made for his End ; and with a gentle and
Even Gale, in much peace, arrived and anchored in his
Last and Best Port, at Wanstead in y* County of Essex,
y* 16 Sept. 1670, Being then but 49 and 4 months old.
To whose Name and merit his surviving Lady
hath erected this remembrance.[1]

The Admiral, it has already been said, was born at Bristol
in 1621, twenty years later than his brother George.   He was
"baptized in the church of St. Thomas the Apostle, in that
city, on the 23d day of April," in that year.   His father edu-

---

[1] This inscription, as stated in the main text, is here taken from
Granville Penn's "Memorials" of the Admiral.   It varies at several
points, but not any essential one, from that given in Maria Webb's
"Penns and Peningtons."   In the latter the spelling is uniformly
modernized : "King-sail," above, is contracted to "Kinsale ;" the
first Dutch "warres" is made "war ;" "whence *retiring*" is made
"*returning* ;" it makes him chosen "Great Captain Commander" in
1665, not 1664, as above ; the word "evidently" before "successful,"
is omitted ; "*thus* he took leave" becomes "*then* he took leave ;" at
"*what* time " is made " at *which* time ;" the word "years" is inserted
after "49" (as the sense demands) ; "to *whose* name " is made "to *his*
name ;" and "*merit*" is made "*memory*."

cated him " with great care, under his own eye, for the sea-service ; causing him to be well grounded in all its branches, practical and scientific, as is shown by sundry elementary and tabular documents, nautical journals, draughts of lands, observations and calculations, which still survive." [1]   He served with his father, as a boy, " in various mercantile voyages to the northern seas, and to the Mediterranean, became a lieutenant in the royal navy," and "thenceforth passed the whole of his active life " in that service, under the Parliament, the Protector, and the Restoration.   He married " very early in life," says Granville Penn, and the biography of him by Professor J. K. Laughton, in the " National Dictionary of Biography," says "about 1639." If in that year, he was only eighteen years old.   But Hepworth Dixon has called attention [2] to an entry in Pepys's Diary which seems to fix the date of the marriage in 1643–44.   It says,—

"*Jan. 6, 1661–2.*—To dinner at Sir W. Pen's, it being a solemn feast day with him,—his wedding day, and we had, besides a good chine of beef and other good cheer, eighteen mince pies in a dish, the number of years that he hath been married."

Subtracting the eighteen pies from the date of this feast would fix the marriage January 6, 1643–44 ; and as William Penn the Founder, who has always been described as the first child, was born October 14, 1644, this date thus receives a reasonable confirmation.

Captain Penn's wife was Margaret Jasper, of Rotterdam, daughter of John Jasper.   And this is all that seems to be known of her family, though why our information is so meagre is not easily explained. [3]   John Jasper is generally described

[1] Granville Penn, " Memorials," Vol. I. p. 2.

[2] " Life of Penn," p. 16.

[3] Mr. Charles P. Keith, of Philadelphia, a distinguished genealogist, has informed me that he has seen in printed records, but precisely where he has not been able to recall, evidence that Margaret Jasper was a widow at the time of her marriage to Captain Penn, Jasper being her maiden name.

as a merchant, sometimes as an "opulent" one; by one authority he is named a burgomaster, and the editor of Lord Braybrooke's edition of Pepys calls him Sir John.   As to his daughter, we have little knowledge, except the pictures coarsly drawn by Pepys.   This one is well known :

"*Aug. 19, 1664.*—To Sir W. Pen's to see his lady the first time, who is a well-looked, fat, short old Dutchwoman, but one that has been heretofore pretty handsome, and is now very discreet, and I believe hath more wit than her husband.   Here we stayed talking a good while, and very well pleased I was with the old woman." [1]

The further allusions to Lady Penn by Pepys are not all in the same vein as this, though there are one or two that are not appropriate for reproduction.   If we were forced to judge of her discretion, or even her wit, by his stories, we should hardly place them high, at least not from our stand-point of manners.   The rompings and roisterings, the black-ing of faces and tumbling upon beds, which he describes—how truly is a question—do not sound nice, and it seems very evident that, after allowing for Pepys's own coarseness and habitual readiness to backbite, we must make a further large allowance for the times of the Restoration, within the influence of Charles II.'s court.   A few passages from Pepys, alluding to Lady Penn, may be given ; she is men-tioned also in others, to be cited in a moment, relating more particularly to her husband and daughter :

"*June 8, 1665.*— . . . then to my Lady Pen's, where they are all joyed, and not a little puffed up at the good success of their father [in the naval battle with the Dutch, June 3]; and good service indeed is said to have been done by him.   Had a great bonfire at the gate. . . . "

[1] It appears rather odd that, as Pepys now records, this was his first sight of Lady Penn, for he had been closely associated with her husband for four years, and he records, earlier than this, numerous occasions when he and his wife were in company with Margaret, the daughter.   What is still more odd is that he evidently did not see Lady Penn at her own house, at the time of the wedding-feast dinner, in 1661–62,—supposing his diary entries to be accurately set down.

"*June 6, 1666.*— . . . And so home to our church, it being the common Fast-day, and it was just before sermon ; but . . . how all the people in the church stared upon me to see me whisper to Sir John Minnes and my Lady Pen."

"*June 11, 1666.*—I with my Lady Pen and her daughter to see Harmon [Captain, afterwards Rear-Admiral, wounded in the naval battle] whom we found lame in bed."

It would be pleasant to wash the ill taste of Pepys out of one's mouth with something better ; but, as has been said, there is little information available concerning Lady Penn from other sources. The high regard of William Penn the Founder for his mother is generally asserted. Clarkson says[1] he had for her "the deepest filial affection. She had often interposed in his behalf when his father was angry with him for the dereliction of Church principles, and of the honors and fashions of the world, and she took him under her wing and supported him when he was turned out of doors for the same reason." In a letter written to a friend he speaks of "my sickness upon my mother's death." The biographical sketch prefixed to the collection of his "Select Works" says that at the time of his father's displeasure at his adoption of Quaker views he was "thus exposed to the charity of his friends, having no other subsistence, except what his mother privately sent him." Lady Penn died at the end of February or beginning of March, 1681–82, and was buried on the 4th of March, at Walthamstow, in Essex.

The will of Admiral Penn is printed nearly in full in Granville Penn's "Memorials," and an abstract of it is given in the *Pennsylvania Magazine*, Vol. XVI. It is dated January 20, 1669, and was proved October 6, 1670. He mentions in it his wife, Dame Margaret Penn ; son William Penn ; younger son Richard Penn ; daughter Margaret, wife of Anthony Lowther ; and the nephews Bradshaw and Markham, and cousin William Penn, previously referred to in

---

[1] " Life of Penn," p. 109.

these notes. He directs that the monument in the church
at Bristol shall be for himself and his mother, but Mr. J. H.
Lea says (1890) that, upon a visit there, he "found no
trace" of any such memorial to the mother; probably none
was erected.

The Admiral's public career cannot here be described.
The abstract on the church tablet will sufficiently serve.
His marriage has been mentioned. Some notices of him
by Pepys may be here introduced; he is alluded to in the
Diary many scores of times between 1660 and 1669:

"*Sept. 8, 1660.*—Drinking a glass of wine late, and discoursing with
Sir W. Pen. I find him to be a very sociable man, and an able man,
and very cunning."

"*Nov. 1, 1660.*—This morning Sir W. Pen and I were mounted
early, [to ride to Sir William Batten's] and had very merry discourse all
the way, he being very good company."

"*April 18, 1661.*— . . . Then, it raining hard, homewards again,
[from visiting Lady Sandwich, at Walthamstow] and in our way met
with two country fellows upon one horse, which I did, without much ado,
give the way to, but Sir W. Pen would not, but struck them, and they
him, and so passed away, but they, giving him some high words, he
went back again, and struck them off their horse, in a simple fury, and
without much honor, in my mind, and so come away."

These allusions have the air of truth. But the key-note
of Pepys's dislike for Sir William appears in an entry in the
summer of 1662. It seems that Pepys was interfered with
in his enjoyment of some of the "pickings" of the office.
His greediness could ill brook that:

"*June 3, 1662.*— . . . At the office, and Mr. Coventry brought his
patent and took his place with us this morning. Upon our making a
contract, I went, as I use to do, to draw the heads thereof, but Sir W.
Pen most basely told me that the Comptroller is to do it, and so begun
to employ Mr. Turner about it, at which I was much vexed, and begun
to dispute; and what with the letter of the Duke's orders, and Mr. Bar-
low's letter, and the practice of our predecessors, which Sir G. Carteret
knew best when he was Comptroller, it was ruled for me. What Sir J.
Minnes will do, when he comes, I knowe not, but Sir W. Pen did it like
a base raskall, and so I shall remember him while I live."

Probably this threat entered in heat in Pepys's secret cipher, was actually kept. His malice is shown many times. Thus :

"*July 5, 1662.*—At noon had Sir W. Penn who I hate with all my heart for his base treacherous tricks, but yet I think it not policy to declare it yet, and his son William, to my house to dinner . . . "

"*July 9, 1662.*—Sir W. Pen came to my office to take his leave of me, and, desiring a turn in the garden, did commit the care of his building to me, and offered all his services to me in all matters of mine. I did, God forgive me I promise him all my services and love, though the rogue knows he deserves none from me, nor do I intend to show him any ; but as he dissembles with me so must I with him."

"*July 1, 1666.*—(Lord's day.) Comes Sir W. Pen to town, which I little expected, having invited my Lady and her daughter Pegg to dine with me to-day ; which at noon they did, and Sir. W. Pen with them , and pretty merry we were. And though I do not love him, yet I find it necessary to keep in with him ; his good service at Shearnesse, in getting out the fleete, being much taken notice of, and reported to the King and Duke ; . . . therefore, I think it is discretion, great and necessary discretion, to keep in with him."

"*Feb. 21, 1666-7.*—To the office, where sat all the morning, and there a most furious conflict between Sir W. Pen and I, in few words, and on a sudden occasion, of no great moment, but very bitter and smart on one another, and so broke off, and to our business, my heart as full of spite as it could hold, for which God forgive me and him."

"*April 10, 1668.*—Meeting with Sir William Hooker, the Alderman, he did cry out mighty high against Sir W. Pen for his getting such an estate, and giving £15,000 with his daughter, which is more, by half, than ever he did give ; but this the world believes, and so let them."

A few other allusions, rather less unpleasing than these, may be added. The last, in June, 1668, approaches the end of the Admiral's active career :

April 18, 1666.—To Mr. Lilly's, the painter's [Lely, afterwards Sir Peter] ; and there saw the heads, some finished, and all begun, of the Flaggmen in the late great fight with the Duke of York against the Dutch. The Duke of York hath them done to hang in his chamber, and very finely they are done indeed. Here are the Prince's [etc.] and will be my Lord Sandwich's, Sir W. Pen's'' [etc.]

"*July 4, 1666.*— . . . In the evening Sir W. Pen came to me, and we walked together, and talked of the late fight. I find him very plain that the whole conduct of the late fight was ill" [etc., explaining at length its character, and his view of a proper system of naval attack]. "*May 27, 1668.*—To see Sir W. Pen, whom I find still very ill of gout, sitting in his great chair, made on purpose for persons sick of that disease, for their ease ; and this very chair, he tells me, was made for my Lady Lambert" [wife of General Lambert, the Parliamentary commander]. "*June 4.*— . . . and besides my Lord Brouncker is at this time ill, and Sir W. Pen." "*June 17.*—Saw Sir W. Pen, who is well again."

Admiral Penn had three children : William the Founder, Richard, and Margaret. By the will of the Admiral, Richard was to have had one hundred and twenty pounds a year until he was twenty-one, and then four thousand pounds, but he survived his father only three years. He died in April, 1673, and was buried at Walthamstow. There is a letter in Granville Penn's "Memorials" (pp. 559–60), addressed to "the Hon. Sir W. Penn, Knt., etc., at his house at Wanstead, near London." dated at Livorno (Italy), June 2, 1670, from William Poole, commanding the ship "Jersey," to which letter there is this postscript :

"My cousin Richard Penn, is very well, and goes to Florence with Sir Thomas Clutterbuck, to wait on the ambassador." [1]

This Richard Penn, Granville Penn says ("Memorials," foot-note, p. 560), was the younger son of whom we are speaking. It would seem that he had been on the "Jersey" with Captain Poole, and it is probable that he was designed by his father to be a seaman. Pepys makes one allusion to Richard, and not unkindly :

[1] The original of this letter is in possession of Isaac Sharp, custodian of the Friends' records at Devonshire House, London. Sir William Poole and Sir Richard Rooth, commanders in the English navy, were both, as it seems from allusions in Granville Penn's "Memorials," kinsmen, perhaps cousins in some degree, of Admiral Penn.

"*Feb. 14, 1664-5.*—This morning betimes comes Dicke Pen to be my wife's Valentine, and came to our bedside. By the same token, I had him brought to my side, thinking to make him kiss me, but he perceived me, and would not ; so went to his Valentine : a notable stout, witty boy."

Margaret Penn, the daughter, married Anthony Lowther, of Mask (or Marske) in Yorkshire. She is mentioned many times by Pepys, and often offensively. His dislike for her father he apparently conferred also upon her. Her husband is referred to more favorably. It would appear that he was a man of good character as well as good estate. In William Penn's " No Cross, no Crown," he quotes the dying expression of "Anthony Lowther, of Mask, a person of good sense, of a sweet temper, a just mind, and of a sober education," whom I presume to have been the father of Margaret's husband. I cite here some of the earlier allusions of Pepys to Margaret Penn :

"*July 28, 1661.*—To church, and then came home with us Sir W. Pen, and drank with us, and then went away, and my wife after him, to see his daughter that is lately come out of Ireland ; and whereas I expected she should have been a great beauty, she is a very plain girl."

"*Oct. 6, 1661.*—To church . . . There was also . . . Mrs. Margaret Pen, this day come to church, in a new flowered satin suit, that my wife helped her to buy the other day."

"*Dec. 11, 1661.*—My wife by coach to Clerkenwell, to see Mrs. Margaret Pen, who is at school there."

Margaret's school days appear to have been over by 1664, for then she seems to have devoted herself to fashionable occupations, and to have taken lessons in painting at her home. Pepys has these entries,—the last one characteristically spiteful :

"*Nov. 20, 1664.*—Up and with my wife to church, where Pegg Pen very fine in her new colored silk suit, laced with silver lace."

"*Jan. 13, 1664-5.*—To my Lady Batten's where I find Pegg Pen, the first time that I ever saw her to wear spots."

"*Aug. 7, 1665.*—Talking with Mrs. Pegg Pen, and looking over her pictures, and commended them ; but . . . so far short of my wife's as no comparison ! "

"*Sept. 3, 1665.*—I took my Lady Pen home, and her daughter Pegg ; and after dinner I made my wife show them her pictures, which did mad Pegg Pen, who learns of the same man."

The appearance of Mr. Lowther on the scene is recorded by Pepys :

"*Jan. 11, 1665-6.*—At noon to dinner all of us by invitation to Sir W. Pen's, and much company. Among others . . . his . . . [prospective] son-in-law Lowther, servant to Mrs. Margaret Pen."

"*April 12, 1666.*—My Lady Pen comes to me, and takes me into her house, where I find her daughter and a pretty lady of her acquaintance, one Mrs. Lowther, sister, I suppose, of her servant Lowther's. . . . Mrs. Margaret Pen grows mighty homely, and looks old."

"*Jan. 4, 1666-7.*—Comes our company to dinner; my Lord Brouncker, Sir W. Pen, his lady, and Pegg, and her servant Mr. Lowther. . . . Mr. Lowther a pretty gentleman, too good for Pegg."

The marriage seems to have been very quiet and decorous, and thus, sad to say, gave great offense to the virtuous Pepys :

"*Feb. 14, 1666-7.*—Pegg Pen is married this day privately ; no friends, but two or three relations of his and hers. Borrowed many things of my kitchen for dressing their dinner. This wedding private is imputed to its being just before Lent, and so in vain to make new clothes till Easter, that they might see the fashions as they are like to be this summer ; which is reason good enough. Mrs. Turner tells me she hears Sir W. Pen gives £4500 or £4000 with her." [1]

"*Feb. 20, 1666-7.*—To White Hall, by the way observing Sir W. Pen's carrying a favor to Sir W. Coventry, for his daughter's wedding, and saying there was others for us, when we will fetch them, which vexed me, and I am resolved not to wear it when he orders me one. His wedding hath been so poorly kept that I am ashamed of it ; for a fellow that makes such a flutter as he does."

"*Feb. 22, 1666-7.*—All of us, that is to say my Lord Brouncker, J. Minnes, W. Batten, T. Harvy, and myself, to Sir Pen's house, where

---

[1] See the reference by Pepys, April 20, 1668, to the report which greatly exaggerated this sum.

some other company. It is instead of a wedding dinner for his daughter,
whom I saw in pakterly clothes, nothing new but a bracelet that her
servant [now her husband] had given her, and ugly she is as heart can
wish. A sorry dinner, not anything handsome or clean, but some
silver plates they had borrowed of me. My wife was here too. We
had favors given us all, and we put them in our hats, I against my
will, but that my Lord and the rest did."

"*Feb. 27, 1666-7.*—To Sir W. Pen's, and sat with my Lady, and
the young couple (Sir William out of town) talking merrily ; but they
make a very sorry couple, methinks, though rich."

And not only did the marriage, the later dinner, and eke
the wedding favors dissatisfy the diarist, but he was further
offended by the fineness of her coach, and what he regarded
as the inadequacy of her wardrobe ; while later he was dis-
gusted at seeing her train borne by a page :

"*May 1, 1667.*—Thence [the King's playhouse] Sir W. Pen and I
in his coach, Tiburne way, into the Park, where a horrid dust and a
number of coaches. . . . But that which I did see and wonder at with
reason was to find Pegg Pen in a new coach, with only her husband's
pretty sister [Margaret Lowther, afterwards the wife of Sir John Holmes]
with her, both patched and very fine, and in much the finest coach in
the park, and I think that ever I did see one or other, for neatness and
richness in gold and everything that is noble . . . but to live in the
condition they do at home and be abroad in this coach astonishes me
. . . then home ; where we find the two young ladies come home and
their patches off ; I suppose Sir W. Pen do not allow of them in his
sight. Sir W. Pen did give me an account of his design of buying Sir
R. Brooke's fine house at Wamsted " [etc. The purchase was not
made].

"*June 28, 1667.*—To Sir W. Batten's, to see how he did. . . .
He told me how Mrs. Lowther had her train held up by a page, at his
house in the country ; which is ridiculous."

"*July 14*, (Lord's day.)— . . . and so towards Epsom [in a coach
and four, Pepys, his wife, and Mrs. Turner] talking all the way presently and particularly of the pride and ignorance of Mrs. Lowther, in
having of her train carried up."

"*Sept. 11, 1667.*—Come to dine with me Sir W. Batten and his lady,
. . . and Sir W. Pen and his lady, and Mrs. Lowther, who is grown,
either through pride or want of manners, a fool, having not a word to
say ; and, as a further mark of a beggarly, proud fool, hath a bracelet

of diamonds and rubies about her wrist, and a sixpenny necklace about her neck, and not one good rag of clothes upon her back."

Anthony and Margaret Lowther had issue. The birth of their first child, a girl, is noted by Pepys as occurring February 8, 1667–68, and he reviles "Pegg," as usual ; this time for the smallness of the company at the christening. Coleman's "Pedigree" names two children, Sir William Lowther, who married Catherine Preston, and Margaret Lowther, who married Benjamin Poole. Anthony Lowther was M.P. for Appleby in 1678 and 1679. He died in 1692, and was buried at Walthamstow. Margaret survived him many years. She is named in the will of her brother, William Penn the Founder, made in 1712, as one of the trustees to dispose of his proprietary rights in Pennsylvania. She died in 1718, and was buried, Granville Penn notes, at Walthamstow.[1] Anthony and Margaret's son William was created a baronet in 1697. In the next generation Sir Thomas Lowther, Bart., of Holker Hall, in Lancashire, married Lady Elizabeth, daughter of the Duke of Devonshire, and their son William dying unmarried in 1756, the baronetcy became extinct, and the Lowther property passed to the Cavendish family, and merged in the estates of the Dukes of Devonshire.

What property, if any, Admiral Penn received from his father, Captain Giles, is unknown. But in 1654, as he was preparing for the famous West India expedition with Venables, he prevailed upon Cromwell to make him a grant of forfeited lands in Ireland. An order of the Protector, dated December 4, 1654, is given in full in Granville Penn's "Memorials," Vol. I. p. 19. It is addressed to the Lord

---

[1] A letter from Hannah Penn, 9th of Third month (May), 1720, "to Rebecca Blackfan, at Pennsbury, or elsewhere in Pennsylvania," says, "I find several of my Letters to thee and others have miscarried, and therefore know not whether thou had acc't of ye Death of my dear Sister Lowther, who Died of a Lingering Fever & gradual decay about 5 months after her dear Brother,"—*i. e.*, in 1718, five months later than the Founder.—*MSS. in Collection Historical Society of Pennsylvania.*

Deputy and Council in Ireland, and directs "that lands of the value of £300 a year, in Ireland, as they were let in the year 1640, be settled on General Penn and his heirs," to be located in some place "where there is a castle or convenient house for habitation upon them, and near to some town or garrison." The grant was partly made "in consideration of the great losses sustained by General Pen and his wife by the rebellion in Ireland," and in the minute of Council upon which the Protector's order was based it is recited that the favor is extended "in consideration of his sufferings in an estate of his wife's in Ireland." What estate she had, if any, or where · it was situated, or how acquired, must remain, I presume, uncertain. But the grant made by Oliver to his sea-commander is readily identified. It lay in County Cork, "the castle and estate of Macromp," and "had been the ancient possession of Macarthy, Lord Muskerry," against whom Penn had been fighting a few years earlier (1646), Muskerry being then the commander of the royal (and Roman Catholic) forces in Ireland. Some other property in County Cork the Admiral seems to have bought, in 1657, of Lord Broghill, and in a letter to Henry Cromwell, Lord Deputy for Ireland, dated at Macromp, 9th November, 1657, Penn speaks of his property "in Macromp and Killerea."

In Ireland, at Macromp, it would appear the Admiral spent much, if not most, of his time between 1655, when he was released from his confinement in the Tower, after the return from Jamaica, and 1660, when he was among the company that repaired to Holland to bring the king back to England. Meantime Lord Muskerry had become, in 1658, by the king's favor, Earl of Clancarty, and at the Restoration he naturally lost no time in claiming of his royal master the restitution of the lands taken from him by the Protector. A document printed by Granville Penn, in his "Memorials,"[1] states that "Sir William Penn, upon the king's ordering the Earl of Clancarty to be immediately possessed of his

[1] Appendix N. Vol. II., p. 617.

ancient estate, did surrender the castle, town, and manor of Macromp, being a garrison wherein was constantly and conveniently quartered a foot company and a troop of horse; with many thousand acres of land contiguous; and the castle, town, and manor of Killcreagh, with several lands thereunto belonging, the whole amounting to £848 per annum, [etc.] unto the said Earl of Clancarty." In lieu of this surrendered property the king gave the Admiral some other "forfeited lands . . . in Imokilly;[1] namely Rostillon, Shangarry, and Inchy, with the lands joining thereunto." This gift the Admiral was able to hold, though he had to contend for it, in the courts and elsewhere, for several years,—at least as late as 1666,—the favor of the king being of importance to him at more than one juncture. The property was in County Cork, and yielded then, it appears, about one thousand pounds a year. Shangarry, in course of time, became familiar as one of the places with which the Penn name is most intimately associated.

In London the Admiral had his home, during most of the last ten years of his life (1660–70), the period of his service as Commissioner, etc., of the navy, in one of the houses attached to the Navy Office, provided as an official residence. It was here that he was the near neighbor of Pepys, who also had an official house. Gibson, an old seaman who had served under the Admiral, and who wrote to William Penn the Founder in March, 1711–12, giving him reminiscences of his father, says,[2] " I remember your honour very well, when you newly came out of France, and wore pantaloon breeches, at which time your late honoured father dwelt in the Navy Office, in that apartment the Lord Viscount Brouncker died in afterwards, which was on the north part of the Navy Office garden." And in the same letter Gib-

[1] This is elsewhere referred to, in a letter of the Admiral, as Eniskelly.

[2] Memorials," Appendix M, Vol. II., p. 612.

son says, "Your late honoured father was appointed general of the fleet, in 1655, to take St. Domingo; at which time he dwelt upon Great Tower-hill, on the east side, within a court adjoining to London-wall. And he frequently came upon the hill next his dwelling, to be applied to by persons under the degree of commanders. One day of which, I was presented to your late honored father by my late master Mr. John Carter, purser of the *Assurance* when your late honoured father commanded her," etc.

Pepys makes many allusions to the contiguity of his residence at the Navy .Office with that of the Penns. The enlargement, under official authority, of their houses is repeatedly referred to, and an allusion to it may be noted in the paragraph, July 9, 1662, already cited, where, walking in the garden with Penn, "the care of his building" was considered. At the time of the Great Fire of London, in September, 1666, Pepys records that he and Sir William "did dig another [pit in the garden] and did put our wine in it, and I my Parmesan cheese," etc. And on two or three nights at this time, distressed and alarmed by the fire, he slept in the Admiral's house. It was at the house on Great Tower Hill, described by Gibson as occupied by the Admiral in 1655, that William Penn the Founder is presumed by some writers to have been born, in 1644.

The portrait of the Admiral, painted by Lely for the Duke of York, as recorded by Pepys (April 18, 1666), is now in the hospital at Greenwich. A copy of it forms the frontispiece to Granville Penn's "Memorials." There has been in recent years a portrait found at Blackwell Grange, in Durham, which has been thought by some to be that of William Penn, the Founder, and a copy of it has been placed, under that supposition, in the National Museum collection in Independence Hall, Philadelphia. This, says the biographer of the Admiral in the "National Dictionary of Biography," Mr. J. M. Rigg, "is really the portrait of the

Admiral." It is very likely that Mr. Rigg is correct in this statement. The gold chain voted the Admiral by the Naval Council, in August, 1653, remains in the family of his descendants. In the Admiral's will he devised to his son William " my gold chain and medal, with the rest and residue of all my plate," etc. Of his personal appearance, the old seaman Gibson says, in the letter before cited, " Your late honoured father was fair-haired ; of a comely round visage, a mild spoken man ; no scoffer, nor flatterer ; easy of access, so as no man went away from him discontented."

The Admiral's " letters to his son in Ireland," says Granville Penn, " of which many remain, are almost wholly filled with instructions respecting his estates ; yet among these some few passages occur which tend to show his mind and disposition. . . I have now by me letters he [the son] received from his father in the years 1666, '67, '68, and '69, in all which I find but one passage expressive of offence." This (October 6, 1669) evidently refers to the son's adoption of the views of the Friends and his renunciation of a courtly career.

The " dying words " of the Admiral are familiar, being quoted by many writers. They come from William Penn the Founder's " No Cross, No Crown," originally written in 1668, while the Bishop of London had him imprisoned in the Tower for his tract, " The Sandy Foundation Shaken," these portions being added in the second edition, published 1681. They are of permanent interest in this connection, as showing the Admiral's reflections upon reviewing his career. " My father," says the son, " not long before his death, spoke to me in this manner :

" ' Son William, I am weary of the world ; I would not live over my days again, if I could command them with a wish ; for the snares of life are greater than the fear of

3

death. This troubles me, that I have offended a gracious God, that hath followed me to this day. Oh, have a care of sin ; that is the sting both of life and of death. Three things I commend unto you : First, let nothing in this world tempt you to wrong your conscience ; so you will keep peace at home, which will be a feast to you in a day of trouble. Secondly, whatever you design to do, lay it justly, and time it seasonably, for that gives security and dispatch. Lastly, be not troubled at disappointments ; for, if they may be recovered, do it ; if they can't, trouble is vain. If you could not have helped it, be content ; there is often peace and profit in submitting to Providence, for afflictions make wise. If you could have helped it, let not your trouble exceed your instruction for another time. These rules will carry you, with firmness and comfort, through this uncertain world. . . '

"Wearied to live, as well as near to die, he took his leave of us ; and of me, with this expression, and a most composed countenance : 'Son William, if you and your friends keep to your plain way of preaching, and keep to your plain way of living, you will make an end of the priests to the end of the world. Bury me by my mother : live all in love ; shun all manner of evil ; and I pray God to bless you all, and he will bless you.'"

IV.

William Penn: Childhood and Youth.

WILLIAM PENN, Founder of Pennsylvania, the son of Captain, afterwards Admiral, William Penn, was born in London on the 14th of October, 1644.

Captain Penn had just been appointed to the command of the " Fellowship," in the navy controlled by the Parliament. The extracts from his journal of his cruise in this ship, printed by Granville Penn in his " Memorials" of Admiral Penn, show that on Saturday, the 12th of October, he being on board, the ship, which had been lying in the Thames, left Deptford at six o'clock a. m. and dropped down the river. But the next entry is not made until the 4th of November, when she weighed anchor "and came into the Downs." The common, and no doubt a fair, presumption has been that she was delayed on her voyage to the Irish coast—where she subsequently took part in the operations against the royalists— by the stay of Captain Penn on shore, on account of the birth of his son, on the Monday following the start from Deptford.

It has been assumed by biographers of Penn[1] that Captain Penn, in October, 1644, at the time of the birth of his son, was living in the house described by the seaman Gibson (already cited) as the Admiral's residence in 1655, " upon Great Tower-hill." This may be correct, but there is narrow ground for the assumption. In the eleven years that intervened Captain Penn was much of the time at sea, and his

---

[1] Dr. Stoughton, in his "William Penn, Founder of Pennsylvania," London, 1882, and perhaps others.

family were living elsewhere. That the same house would be
occupied in 1644 and in 1655 is at least doubtful.

The biographical sketch of Penn prefixed to his "Select
Works" says he "was born in the parish called St. Katherine's,
near the Tower of London." The baptism register of
Allhallows Church, Barking (London), contains this entry :

"1644, October 23. William, son of William Penn, and
Margarett his wife, of the Tower Liberty."

Allhallows, Barking, is an interesting old church at the
east end of Great Tower Street, in the ward of that name,
dedicated to Allhallows and St. Mary, and said to be "the
most complete mediæval church remaining in London." Its
distinguishing title, Barking (for there are several Allhallows
churches in London), is derived from the fact that its vicarage
originally belonged to that of Barking, outside the city, in
Essex.[1]

The "Fellowship" having sailed, Margaret Penn presently
went with her child to Wanstead, in Essex, in the suburbs of
London, and that place, down to the time of the Admiral's
death there in 1670, becomes prominent in the family history.
In what house they stayed at Wanstead does not appear,
but a misconception of Captain Penn's worldly condition has
led some of the biographers of his son to say that they
resided at Wanstead, in "one of the country seats" belonging to the Captain. This is, of course, simply imaginative.

---

[1] The Great Fire of London, September, 1666, was stopped at this
point, at the church, its dial and porch being burned.

Pepys: September 5, 1666.—" . . . I find by the blowing up of
houses, and the greate helpe given by the workmen out of the King's
yards, sent up by Sir W. Pen, there is a good stop given to it [the Great
Fire] as well at Marke-lane end as ours ; it having only burned the
dyall of Barking Church, and part of the porch, and there quenched.
I up to the top of Barking steeple, and there saw the saddest sight of
desolation that I ever saw. . . . "

John Quincy Adams was married in this church (July 26, 1797).
Many of the state prisoners executed on Tower Hill were buried there.

Unless we are grossly misinformed concerning him, Captain Penn's circumstances at that time did not permit him the ownership of either town-house or country-seat.

Wanstead is close by Chigwell. At the latter place there were free schools, founded in 1629 by Harsnet, Archbishop of York.[1] To these young William Penn was sent. One of them was for instruction in English, the other a Latin school. The quaint and strictly framed rules of the arch-bishop's foundation give us a clue to the boy's education. Those of the school "for teaching the Greek and Latin tongues" required that the master should be "a good poet; of a sound religion, neither papal nor puritan; of a grave be-haviour; of a sober and honest conversation; no tipler or haunter of alehouses; no puffer of tobacco; and above all, apt to teach, and severe in his government." Waiving con-troversy upon the religious clause, it cannot be said but that these exacting specifications were likely to give a pronounced ·character to the school, and probably secure a teacher of some ability. It was directed also by the archbishop that the text-books in the higher school should be "Lilly's Latin and Cleonard's Greek grammar," that, for "phrase and style," the scholars should read "no other than Tully and Terence," that for poetry they should have "the ancient Greek and Latin, no novelties, nor conceited modern writers." As to the teacher of the English school, it was required that he write "fair secretary and Roman hands," "that he be skillful in ciphering and casting of accounts, and that he teach his scholars the same faculty."[2]

[1] Samuel Harsnet (1561–1631), vicar of Chigwell from 1597 to 1605, a pluralist of considerable scope, a vigorous polemic, inclined to high church, and charged with "papistical" views, was made archbishop under Charles I., 1629, owing his elevation, it is said, to Thomas Howard, Earl of Arundel. He was buried in the parish church at Chigwell, at the feet of his wife, in a tomb in the chancel floor, and there is a "fine brass," after a design of his own, in his memory, on the wall.

[2] Lyson's (Rev. Daniel) "Environs of London," 1796, Vol. IV. p. 128.

These schools at Chigwell the lad attended, it is said, until
he was twelve years old.[1]   That he acquired a good knowledge of Latin there is fairly certain, and as to Greek, the
foundation of his acquaintance with it may also have been
laid in this period.   His writings in later time show him to
have been a fair Greek scholar, and his copy of the Greek
Testament was sold at auction in London in 1872.

Without intending to speak minutely of any part of
Penn's life, it seems proper to dwell a moment at this point
on the surroundings of these early years, while living at
Wanstead and attending the Chigwell schools.   Dr. Stoughton devotes some pages to an intelligent and suggestive sketch
of them, pointing out that this part of Essex in those years
" was steeped in Puritanism," and that the conditions of
the boy's life there may well have influenced his subsequent
career.   Dr. Emanuel Utey, vicar of Chigwell, had been
ejected from his place for alleged ritualistic practices in church
in 1641, and in 1650 it was reported by commissioners that
there had been no settled minister there since his departure.
The disputes in the church at Wanstead, also, between Pres-
byterianism and Episcopacy began about 1642, and ran high.
A number of the people drew up and signed a celebrated
" Protest " against all " innovations " which, as they considered, would lead away from " the true reformed Protestant
religion."

His years in the country, in the midst of a community
of strenuously earnest advocates of religious change, attending a small and strictly administered school, hearing the
anxious discussion of great and serious events going on in
England, must have left their deep impression on William
Penn.   Adjacent to Wanstead and Chigwell there lay—until
1851, when it was disafforested—the woods known as Hainault
Forest, and in these, it may reasonably be supposed, the

---

[1] Clarkson, p. 3. Stoughton speaks of his life at Wanstead " for
about eleven years."

active, spirited boy rambled and played, acquiring that love
for nature and that acquaintance with it by which his subsequent career was marked.[1]   The region is still "very picturesque in parts, abounds in nightingales, and can show some
fine trees, although none so large nor so celebrated as the
Fairlop oak, which stood not far from Chigwell."[2]

Returning to London about 1655 or 1656, it is said that
Admiral Penn had a private tutor for the lad at the house on
Tower Hill.[3]   But this could have been only for a brief period,
if the account given by Granville Penn can be confidently
followed at this point.   He says that the Admiral, after his
release from the Tower, in 1655, took his family to Ireland,
and indicates that they practically remained there until
1660, when Charles II. returned from Holland and the
monarchy was restored.   It may thus be assumed that, until
he went to the University, Penn's education had been received
at Chigwell and at the hands of private tutors,—the latter for
a short time in London, and for a longer period at Macromp,
in Ireland.   In 1660, in October, he went to Oxford, and on

[1] Of the period of his youth in Ireland, say 1656–60, Hepworth
Dixon says, "In person he was tall and slender, but his limbs were
well knit, and he had a passionate fondness for field sports, boating,
and other manly exercises." ("Life of Penn," p. 26.)   Of his residence at Oxford, Anthony Wood says, "he delighted in manly sports
at times of recreation."   These recall the familiar story, derived from
Samuel Preston's grandmother, that Penn, when he met with the Indians in Pennsylvania, on his second visit, "walked with them, sat with
them on the ground, and ate with them of their roasted acorns and
hominy.   At this they expressed great delight, and soon began to show
how they could hop and jump ; at which exhibition, William Penn, to
cap the climax, sprang up and beat them all !"

[2] Citation in Stoughton, p. 6.   The Fairlop oak was one of the show-
trees of England until it fell, partly as the result of fire, in February,
1820.   Its girth at the ground was forty-eight feet, and three feet up
thirty-six feet.   Its branches covered a circumference of three hundred
feet.

[3] Clarkson, p. 3.

the 26th of that month was entered as a "gentleman commoner" at Christ Church College.[1]

Who his tutors were, or what the circumstances of his life in Ireland, is not disclosed by the biographies; but it seems quite plain that the lad of 1660 arrived at Oxford very much of a Puritan in his religious temper, and that his subsequent tribulations there were a not unnatural consequence of this disposition. In his own account of his second tour in Germany, 1677, he summarizes the narrative which he gave to Anna Maria von Schurmann, and the Somerdykes, in their house at Wiewerd, at the morning interview on the 13th of September, and unless we could take the view that he was a deceiving or self-deceived man, its significance must command our attention. He says:

"Here I began to let them know how, and when, the Lord first appeared unto me, which was about the twelfth year of my age, anno 1656. How at times betwixt that and the fifteenth, the Lord visited me, and the Divine impressions he gave me of himself; of my persecution at Oxford, and how the Lord sustained me in the midst of that hellish darkness and debauchery; of my being banished the college; the bitter usage I underwent when I returned to my father; whipping, beating, and turning out of doors in 1662. Of the Lord's dealings with me in France, and in the time of the Great Plague in London. In fine, the deep sense he gave me of the vanity of this world; of the *Irreligiousness* of the religions of it."

The biographic value of this passage is important. Granville Penn, with scant sympathy for the Quaker, but more for

---

[1] From the account in Janney it would be inferred that he went to Oxford in 1659, the expression of the former being that he did so "at the age of fifteen." This error occurs by following Clarkson, who uses substantially the same language. Foster's "Alumni Oxon." is cited by Mr. Rigg, in his article in the "Dictionary of National Biography," for the exact date,—that above, October 26, 1660.

the Admiral, in his memorial of the latter minimizes the bréach between father and son at the time of the Oxford troubles, but it is evident that he does so unduly; the impressive details above are too plain to be set aside.

Dr. Stoughton, pointing out the manner—not at all unfavorable—in which Anthony Wood, the minute and caustic annalist of Oxford University, describes Penn's stay there, questions the accuracy of the stories that he joined in tearing off the gowns of the students, etc., and even suggests a doubt whether he was expelled by the authorities. But as to the latter point his own expression above, "my being banished the college," appears conclusive. Anthony Wood describes the young man at some length, "enumerates a number of his works, and treats him with considerable civility."[1]

Paragraphs in Pepys, at this period, throw light on the situation. The following are of interest:

"Nov. 1, 1661.—At my house, Sir William sent for his son, Mr. William Pen, lately come from Oxford."[2]

"Jan. 1, 1661-2.— . . . Home again, and sent to young Mr. Pen and his sister to go anon with my wife and I to the theatre. That done, Mr. Pen came to me, and he and I walked out . . . so home again to dinner, and by and by came the two young Pens, and after we had eat a barrel of oysters, we went by coach to the play ["The Spanish Curate."] . . . From thence home, and they sat with us till late at night, at cards very merry, but the jest was Mr. Pen had left his sword in the coach, and so my boy and he run out after the coach, and by very great chance did at the Exchange meet with the coach, and got his sword again."

"Jan. 25, 1661-2.—At home. . . . Walking in the garden. . . . Sir W. Pen came to me, and did break a business to me about removing his son from Oxford to Cambridge to some private college. I proposed

---

[1] Cf. Stoughton, p. 36.

[2] This passage Hepworth Dixon cites ("Life of Penn," p. 31) as authority for the statement that he was then expelled from the University. But it is plain from Pepys's further entries that the expulsion was not at this time, but several months later.

Magdalene, but cannot name a tutor at present ; but I shall think and
write about it."

"*Feb. 1.*—I and Sir William Pen walked in the garden, talking about
his business of putting his son to Cambridge ; and to that end I intend
to write to-night to Fairebrother, to give me an account of Mr. Burton
of Magdalene."

"*March 16.*—Walking in the garden with Sir W. Pen : his son
William is at home, not well. But all things, I fear, do not go well
with them—they both look discontentedly, but I know not what ails
them."

"*April 28, 1662.*—[At Portsmouth] Sir W. Pen much troubled upon
letters came last night. Showed me one of Dr. Owen's to his son,
whereby it appears his son is much perverted in his opinion by him ;
which I now perceive is one thing that hath put Sir William so long off
the hookes."   .

With Penn's stay at Oxford the planting of Pennsylvania
is in some degree connected. Twenty years later, his letter,—
dated at Westminster, 12th of Second Month (April), 1681,
just after the grant had been made him by the King,—addressed to Robert Turner, Anthony Sharp, and Roger Roberts,
at Dublin, contained a passage which has been repeatedly
noted :

" For many are drawn forth to be concerned with me [in Pennsyl-
vania], and perhaps this way of satisfaction [for losses which he had
previously mentioned, due to his being a Quaker] has more of the hand
of God in it than a downright payment : this I can say that *I had an
opening of joy, as to these parts, in the year 1661, at Oxford, twenty
years since ;* and as my understanding and inclinations have been much
directed to observe and reprove mischiefs in government, so it is now
put in my power to settle one." [1]

What is signified in the expression "an opening of joy,"
etc., is somewhat uncertain, but Dr. F. D. Stone has pointed
out, in connection with it,[2] that as early as 1660, George Fox

[1] Letter in full in Janney, p. 163, and Vol. I., "Memoirs of the
Historical Society of Pennsylvania," p. 210.

[2] Winsor's "Narrative and Critical History of America," III. 475.

was thinking of forming a colony of Friends in the region subsequently granted to Penn, and corresponded with Josiah Coale, who was then in Maryland, on the subject.

Following upon his departure from Oxford, and a brief stay in London, came the tour in France, the studies under Moses Amyraut, the Protestant theologian,[1] at Saumur, and the excursion into Italy. Penn returned from Turin in the summer of 1664, being recalled by his father, who now expected active employment in the naval war with the Dutch. Pepys has these two allusions :

"*Aug. 26, 1664.*—Mr. Pen, Sir William's son, is come back from France, and come to visit my wife ; a most modish person, grown, she says, a fine gentleman."

"*30th.*—Comes Mr. Pen to visit me. I perceive something of learning he hath got, but a great deal, if not too much, of the vanity of the French garb, and affected manner of speech and gait. I fear all real profit he hath made of his travel will signify little." [2]

Upon which it may be remarked simply that Mr. Pepys had little prevision of the future, so far as young " Mr. Pen " was concerned.

[1] In the biographies Amyraut's name has suffered. Dr. Stoughton calls it Amyrant, and Janney's printers have made it Auryrault ! Amyraut, himself an interesting man, derives some addition of importance to us because of Penn's studies with him. He was "one of the most celebrated divines of the reformed church of France, during the 17th century," a modified Calvinist, charged by his enemies as holding doctrines that opened " a door to Arminianism, even to Pelagianism itself," but "repeatedly absolved," nevertheless, "from charges of heresy, by synods of his own church." He had been appointed to the church at Saumur, in 1626, and to the chair of theology in the university there in 1633 ; in the latter he remained till his death, in 1664, soon after Penn's stay with him at Saumur.

[2] We may recall the statement of the seaman, Gibson, already cited, " I remember your honour very well, when you newly came out of France, and wore pantaloon breeches."

"*Sept. 5, 1665.*—Home pretty betimes, and there found W. Pen, and he staid supper with us and mighty merry talking of his travells, and the French humours, etc., and so parted and to bed."

The events following the return from Italy down to the writing of "The Sandy Foundation Shaken," and his imprisonment in the Tower in 1668, are all interesting, but must be passed over without much detail. He began the study of law at Lincoln's Inn (February 7, 1664–65), was presented at court, attended upon his father, was on board the fleet,[1] and brought despatches to the King. Letters sent to his father at this time are worth reproduction, as showing the filial attitude of the writer. They are in Granville Penn's "Memorials," Vol. II., p. 318, and are also reproduced by Janney :

"From Harwich, 23d April, 1665.

"Honoured Father,—We could not arrive here sooner than this day, about twelve of the clock, by reason of the continued cross winds, and, as I thought, foul weather. I pray God, after all the foul weather and dangers you are exposed to, and shall be, that you come home as secure. And I bless God, my heart does not in any way fail, but firmly believe that if God has called you out to battle, he will cover your head in that smoky day. And, as I never knew what a father was till I had wisdom enough to prize him, so I can safely say, that now, of all times, your concerns are most dear to me. It's hard, meantime, to lose both a father and a friend. . . .   "W. P."

"Navy Office, 6th May, 1665.

"At my arrival at Harwich (which was about one of the clock on the Sabbath day, and where I staid till three), I took post for London, and was at London the next morning by almost daylight. I hasted to Whitehall, where, not finding the King up, I presented myself to my Lord of Arlington and Colonel Ashburnham.

"At his majesty's knocking, he was informed there was an express from the Duke ; at which, earnestly skipping out of his bed, he came only in his gown and slippers ; who, when he saw me, 'Oh ! is't you ? how is Sir William ?'

[1] *Pepys: April 25, 1665.*—"This afternoon, W. Pen, lately came from his father in the fleete, did give me an account how the fleete did sail, about 103 in all. . . . "

Remembering that formerly you made a motion for the giving up your Commission, and observing the readiness of your name, and observing the occasion of representing the late Mutiny among the Souldiers in this Garrison, I have thought fit to let you know that I am willing to place the Command of that Company in him, and desire you to send a resignation to that purpose. And so I remain ——

[Facsimile version]

"He asked how you did at three several times. He was glad to hear your message about Ka. [?] After interrogating me above half an hour, he bid me go about your business and mine too. As to the Duchess, he was pleased to ask several questions, and so dismissed me.

"I delivered all the letters given me. My mother was to see my Lady Lawson, and she was here.

"I pray God be with you, and be your armour in the day of controversy! May that power be your salvation, for his name's sake. And so will he wish and pray, that is with all true veneration, honored father, "Your obedient son and servant,

"WILLIAM PENN."

The naval battle with the Dutch, in which Admiral Penn was "Great Captain Commander," and in which he won a signal success, occurred June 3, 1665, and soon after the frightful increase of the plague in London drove Penn to the country. In the autumn of that year his father sent him to Ireland. There he remained for the most of two years. In this period occurred the episode of his military service, under Lord Arran (second son of the Duke of Ormond), at the siege of Carrickfergus, and about the time of this affair— May, 1666,—there was painted the "portrait in armor," of which the Historical Society of Pennsylvania possesses a copy, presented by Granville Penn in 1833. This is a half-length; the artist is unknown. It is doubtless the only portrait extant of William Penn painted from life, unless it be considered that the Blackwell Grange picture is really his, and not that of the Admiral. The portrait in armor is at Pennsylvania Castle, in the Isle of Portland, formerly the property of the Penns, now owned by J. Merrick Head, Esq., of Ardverness, Reigate, Surrey; a replica belongs to Captain William Dugald Stuart, of Tempsford Hall, Bedfordshire.[1]

[1] The portrait in armor is so familiar that it needs no particular description. Which of these pictures is the original I do not undertake to determine. The portrait has been engraved by S. A. Schoff, Boston, with the aid of a crayon reduction by William Hunt; by John Sartain, by W. G. Armstrong, and probably by others. The Schoff picture is

The incident of the attendance by Penn on Thomas Loe's preaching at Cork, his further and renewed convincement of the views of the Friends, and his arrest by officers at a Friends' meeting in that city now followed,—the arrest being upon September 3, 1667. He returned soon after that to London, then became openly and actively identified with the Friends,[1] and presently began to write and speak in their behalf.[2] In 1668 he published "The Sandy Foundation Shaken," and on the 12th of December of that year he was committed to the Tower on account of it. He had been, as he himself tells in the manuscript fragments of an "Apology,"[3] twice to court earlier in the year, once in company with George Whitehead, Josiah Coale, and Thomas Loe, and next time with Whitehead and Coale, to urge a relaxation of the persecution of the Friends. Their sufferings by "Stocks, Whips, Gaols, Dungeons, Præmunires, Fines, Sequestrations, and Banishment," compelled his deep sympathy, and they

in Winsor's History, Vol. III., p. 474 ; the Sartain in Watson's Annals, in Janney's "Life of Penn," and in the "Memorial History of Philadelphia," as a frontispiece to Vol. I. The three engravings vary somewhat in the expression of the face : that of Sartain makes it more mature and refined than either of the others ; the Armstrong engraving is a very satisfactory reproduction of the portrait.

[1] *Pepys : "Dec. 29, 1667.* (Lord's day.)—At night comes Mrs. Turner to see us ; and there among other talk, she tells me that Mr. William Pen, who is lately come over from Ireland, is a Quaker again, or some very melancholy thing ; that he cares for no company, nor comes into any ; which is a pleasant thing after his being abroad so long. . . . "

[2] According to Hepworth Dixon ("Life of Penn," p. 44), it was in 1668 that, after a painful interview, "the indignant Admiral turned him out of doors." There seems to be no good authority for this statement. Penn's own narrative to Anna Maria von Schurmann, already given, definitely mentions the "turning out of doors" as "in 1662." This date seems to have been overlooked by Dixon.

[3] "Memoirs of the Historical Society of Pennsylvania," III., Part 2.

were entitled, he thought, to better treatment. "Accordingly,"
he says, "I had formed a scheme to myself for that purpose.
But it so fell out that, towards the close of that year, I was
made incapable of prosecuting the resolution I had taken,
and the plan I had layd of this affair, by a long and close
imprisonment in the Tower[1] for a book I writ, called
[etc.][2] . . . I was committed the beginning of December,
and was not discharged till the Fall of the Leaf following ;
wanting about fourteen days of nine months. . . . Within six
weeks after my enlargement I was sent by my Father to settle
his Estate in Ireland," etc.

In the Tower he had written "No Cross, No Crown,"
which must be considered, no doubt, the most important of
his numerous religious writings.[3] The subject—a crown of
reward for the cross of suffering—sprang naturally from his
own situation. Hepworth Dixon says that, "considering
the shortness of time, and other untoward circumstances
under which it was produced, the reader is struck with the
grasp of thought, the power of reasoning, the lucid arrange-
ment of subject, and the extent of research displayed. Had
the style been more condensed, it would have been well
entitled to claim a high place in literature."[4]

[1] This imprisonment was a harsh one. He says ("Apology"),
"As I saw very few, so I saw them but seldom, except my own Father
and Dr. Stillingfleet, the present Bishop of Worcester. The one came
as my relation, the other at the King's command to endeavour my
change of judgment." Bishop Stillingfleet treated him considerately.
"I am glad," proceeds Penn, "I have the opportunity to own so publickly the great pains he took, and humanity he showed, and that to his
moderation, learning, and kindness I will ever hold myself obliged."

[2] *Pepys:* "*February 12, 1668–9.*—Got William Pen's book against
the Trinity, and I find it so well writ, as I think it is too good for him
to have writ it ; it is a serious sort of book, and not fit for everybody to
read."

[3] A second edition was issued in 1682, the twenty-fourth (English)
edition in 1857.

[4] "Life of Penn," p. 63.

His release from the Tower must have been, from his own account, near the end of August, 1669. On the 15th of September he left London, and on the 24th of October he sailed from Bristol for Cork, where he arrived on the 26th, to resume his charge of the Irish property. He found, as he tells us in his fragmentary "Apology," the Friends under "general persecution, and those of the City of Cork almost all in prison," so that he promptly "adjourned all private affairs," and hastened to Dublin to the authorities to intercede in their behalf. Rutty's "History of Friends in Ireland" says that "William Penn, who was here this year, did frequently visit his friends in prison, and hold meetings with them, omitting no opportunity he had with those in authority to solicit on their behalf; and as the Ninth month [November] national meeting was this year held at his lodgings in Dublin, an account of Friends' sufferings was then drawn up by way of address, which he presented to the Lord Lieutenant, (John, Lord Berkeley, Baron Stratton), whereupon an order of Council was obtained for the release of those that were imprisoned."[1]

Penn remained in Ireland until the summer of 1670. He resided at Cork and at Dublin, preached at the Friends' meetings, wrote religious pamphlets, appealed not only to the Lord Lieutenant, but to Lord Arran, the Lord Chancellor, and others, in behalf of the Friends, and attended meantime to the care of his father's property. In April, 1670, the Admiral wrote to him, "I wish you had well done

[1] This passage in Rutty's History (which is a continuation and enlargement of a brief account by Thomas Wight) is repeated almost verbatim by Gough in his "History of the Quakers," and is cited by Janney, p. 55. The release of the Friends was ordered June 4, 1670. In the "Life of Penn" prefixed to his "Select Works" it is stated that, "being arrived at Cork, he immediately visited his friends there, and the next day had a meeting with them . . . having tarried there some days, he went from thence to Dublin, and on the 5th of the 9th month was at the National Meeting of Friends, which was held at his lodgings."

all your business there, for I find myself to decline." Penn, therefore, presently returned to England, and joined his father at Wanstead. His sister Margaret, as we have seen, was married, and was living with her husband in Yorkshire; while Richard, in June, as appears from Captain Poole's letter, already cited, was in Italy. The Admiral's career was nearly closed. His son-in-law Lowther had written to him in April, recommending for his purchase an estate near his own in Yorkshire, but the time for that was past.

Penn, however, was to undergo one more remarkable experience before he parted from his father. On August 14, 1670, it being the first day of the week, he went with William Mead to the meeting of Friends in White Hart Court, Gracechurch Street. William Mead, a country gentleman of some estate in Essex, had been a captain in the Parliamentary service, and for a time, like John Gilpin, a "linen-draper bold" in the city. He was now one of those recently converted to the views of George Fox, and active in spreading "the Truth," as the Friends held it.[1] The meeting-house in Gracechurch Street had been, like the others in London, for some weeks closed under the operation of the "Conventicle Act,"[2] and guarded by sol-

[1] He married, in 1681, at the Devonshire House Friends' meeting, in London, Sarah Fell, one of the daughters of Margaret Fox by her first husband, Judge Fell, of Swarthmoor Hall, in Lancashire.

[2] The "Conventicle Act," passed by Parliament in 1664, embodied clauses contained in a previous harsh act of 1661. It was renewed in 1667, and in April, 1670, after quite a struggle in Parliament, was again enacted, to take effect May 10 of that year. It was one of the most oppressive of the long series of persecuting measures enacted in the Restoration period, levelled at the Dissenters, and fell heavily upon the Friends, who would not give up their meetings. It forbade the assembling of five persons or more, "besides those of the same household," in "any assembly, conventicle or meeting, under colour or pretence of any exercise of religion, in any other manner than according to the liturgy and practice of the Church of England," and imposed a ruinous

diers against use by the Friends, and on each Sabbath since
the law took effect (May 10) there had been some of them
arrested and imprisoned or fined.   On May 15, George
Fox was taken, in front of the meeting, but the informer
failed to appear against him, and he was released; later
John Burnyeat, George Whitehead, and others had fallen
victims to the sharp enforcement of the law by the lord
mayor, Sir Samuel Starling.   On this 14th of August the
Friends had repaired to their meeting-house (Gracechurch
Street), but had found it closed and guarded as before.
A group had remained outside in the street, and Penn,
removing his hat, had begun to address them, when in a
moment constables appeared, with a warrant from the lord
mayor, and arrested him and Mead; and being thereupon
haled before Sir Samuel in short order, and duly reviled
by him, they were committed for trial.   Penn's letter to his
father, dated next day, the 15th, from "the sign of the
Black Dog, in Newgate Market,"—"a wretched sponging-
house," Hepworth Dixon calls it,—informed the sick Admiral at Wanstead what had happened.

series of fines, part of the proceeds of which went to informers. "By
this law," says Sewel ("History of the Quakers"), "many an honest
family was impoverished ; for the Quakers did not leave off meeting together publicly. . . . At London, as well as at other places, many were
spoiled of their goods very unmercifully, and many times people of good
substance brought to mere poverty, seeing not only the shop goods of
some but also their household goods have been seized, insomuch that
the very sick have had their beds taken from under them, . . . nay,
they have been so cruel as to leave them nothing ; insomuch as when
the child's pap hath stood in a pannikin, they have thrown out the pap
to take the pannikin away."   Sewel adds, however, that the greed of
the informers was sometimes checked by humane magistrates.
     The text of the "Conventicle Act" of 1670 is given in full by Sewel ;
also by Besse, who gives, besides, the previous acts of 1661 and 1664.
The law of 1670, though capable of being made to work great hardship,
was less severe than that of 1664, which imposed heavier fines, and
added imprisonment and transportation.

The trial of Penn and Mead is a tempting theme. It forms an episode in English history at once dramatic and diverting. In its historical and legal aspects it is important, and as a picture of manners in London under Charles II. it has elements which Shakespeare would have made immortal. As to the chief actor, Penn, nothing in his extended life and varied activities better discloses his qualities.[1]

The trial began September 1, and was continued on the 3d, 4th, and 5th. Ten magistrates were upon the bench: the mayor, Sir Samuel Starling; the recorder, Sir John Howell; five aldermen, among them Sir John Robinson, the oppressive and persecuting lieutenant of the Tower; and three sheriffs. The browbeating and bullying from the court, especially from the recorder, the spirit, readiness, and wit of Penn's defense (and Mead, it must in justice be said, bore himself equally well), the courage and endurance of the jury, the ridiculous break-down of the whole proceeding,—though the court indulged its spitefulness to cover its mortification at the end,—make up a chapter which every biographer of Penn is irresistibly led to cite as fully as possible. Penn's promptly issued account of it, "The People's Ancient and Just Liberties Asserted," has been many times reprinted, and its simple and graphic details make it worthy of a place beside classics of Defoe or Bunyan.

The sequel of the trial, too,—the imprisonment of the jury in default of payment of forty marks fine for refusing to find a verdict of guilty, their release upon *habeas corpus* in a suit against the lord mayor and recorder for illegal imprisonment, the trial of the suit in the Court of Common

[1] The impression made by his conduct at this trial is suggested by Lafayette's toast at Philadelphia, at the dinner to Richard Rush, July 20, 1825. Lafayette gave: "The memories of Penn and Franklin—the one never greater than when arraigned before an English jury, or the other than before a British Parliament."

Pleas before a bench of twelve judges, the elaborate argu-
ment of the question by distinguished counsel, the unani-
mous decision that a jury is to judge of the facts and that
it cannot be coerced,—that the court may try " to open the
eyes of the jurors, but not to lead them by the nose,"—and
the ultimate triumphant discharge in open court of Edward
Bushel [1] and his eleven resolute companions,—is set down in
the law reports of England as a famous case. " It established a truth," says Hepworth Dixon, " which William
Penn never ceased to inculcate—that unjust laws are power-
less weapons, when used against an upright people."

Penn, with Mead, had been recommitted to Newgate
September 5, in default of the payment of fines for " con-
tempt of court " in declining to remove their hats during
the trial. Some one, however, paid their fines two days
later, and they were released.

The Admiral, at Wanstead, was now within a few days
of his close. Penn's discharge from Newgate took place
on the 7th of September, and it was but nine days later,
the 16th, that his father died.

SUMMARY : ADMIRAL PENN.

SIR WILLIAM PENN, KNIGHT, son of Captain Giles and
Joan Penn, born at Bristol ; baptized in the Church of St.

---

[1] The browbeating of Bushel by the court, all unavailing as it was,
is a notable feature of the trial. " Sir," said the recorder to him, when
the jury first reported they could not agree, " you are the cause of this
disturbance, and manifestly show yourself an abetter of faction ; I shall
set a mark upon you, sir !" " Sirrah," interjected the mayor a moment later, " you are an impudent fellow ; I will put a mark upon
you !" Again the mayor, infuriated at the verdict of not guilty as to
Mead, shouted, " What, will you be led by such a fellow as Bushel ?
an impudent, canting fellow ! I warrant you, you shall come upon no
more juries in haste !" Sheriff Bludworth declared he knew when he
saw Bushel on the jury there would be trouble, and the lord mayor
threatened, " I will cut his nose !"

Thomas the Apostle April 23, 1621 ; married, 1643–44,
Margaret, daughter of John Jasper, of Rotterdam. He
died September 16, 1670, at Wanstead, Essex, and was
buried September 30, at St. Mary's Redcliffe, Bristol. His
wife, born (?) ; died 1681–82, and was buried March 4 of
that year in the church at Walthamstow, Essex. Their
issue :

1. WILLIAM PENN, Founder of Pennsylvania.

2. Margaret, born (?) ; married, February 14, 1666–67,
Anthony Lowther, of Maske, Yorkshire, and left issue, a
son (and perhaps others) William, created a baronet in 1697.
Margaret died 1718, and was buried at Walthamstow. Her
husband died 1692, and was buried at Walthamstow, where
there is a " monument " to him. (In a letter, 9th of Third
month (May), 1720, to Rebecca Blackfan, at Pennsbury,
Pennsylvania, Hannah Penn said, "My cousin John Lowther is married, has one child, a daughter, and lives at
Mask, as yet. My cousin Sir Thomas, the heir of Sir William, is just returned from his travels in France and Flanders. He went out a very promising hopeful young man,
and I greatly hope is not worsted but improved by his
journey." It was this Sir Thomas Lowther, Bart., who
married Lady Elizabeth Cavendish.)

3. Richard, born (?) ; died without issue 1673. Extract
from Walthamstow parish register : " Richard Penn, gent.,
second son of Sir William Penn, Knight, from Rickmers-
worth, buried Ap'l 9, 1673."

V.

William Penn's First Marriage.

WILLIAM PENN, by the death of his father, " came into the possession of a very handsome estate, supposed to be worth at that time not less than fifteen hundred pounds per annum ; so that he became, in point of circumstances, not only an independent, but a rich man."

This statement, made by Clarkson,[1] has been followed by successive biographers ; Janney, Dixon, and probably others repeat it. The property which the son received was substantially that in Ireland, the Shangarry and adjoining estates ; if there was any other of importance that came into his possession from his father I have seen no account of it.

Penn's first marriage followed about a year and a half after the death of the Admiral. In the mean time he had been again imprisoned six months (1670–71), at first in the Tower and then in Newgate, for being at the Friends' meeting in Wheeler Street, London, and for refusing to take the oath of allegiance (tendered as a " snare" to the Friends, who would take no oaths) ; had written several more political and religious pamphlets ; and had made his first religious visit to Holland and Germany.

The years of his courtship and of his first marriage—as late, at least, as his first return from Pennsylvania—form the halcyon period of Penn's career. There is about these years an air of hopeful and buoyant cheerfulness. The accounts given of the Springetts by Mary Penington, and of

---

[1] " Life of Penn." p. 33.

54

WILLIAM PENN: BEVAN CARVING

the Peningtons by Thomas Ellwood, are at once romantic and idyllic. Upon these details it will always be pleasant, in the study of the Founder's varied experiences of sunshine and cloud, to linger.

Early in 1668, it is said, William Penn first met Gulielma Maria Springett.[1] She was then living in the family of her stepfather, Isaac Penington, with her mother, Mary Penington—previously the wife of Sir William Springett, her (Gulielma's) father,—at Bury House, near Amersham, in Buckinghamshire. Isaac Penington was the son of Alderman Isaac Penington, of London, sometime lieutenant of the Tower, Lord Mayor of London, and one of the judges who condemned Charles I. to death. In 1654, Isaac, the son, had married the widow, Mary Springett, and somewhat later both had joined the religious movement of which George Fox was the leader. In 1658 they had settled at the Grange, at Chalfont St. Peter's, in Bucks, which had been assigned as a residence (not conveyed) to Isaac by his father, and they continued to live in that part of the country, amid many vicissitudes, until their death and burial in the Friends' ground at Jordans, near Chalfont, where also William Penn and most of his family are buried.[2]

[1] This is the statement of Maria Webb, in the "Penns and Peningtons." In a document quoted in that work, a narrative said to have been given by William Penn to a certain Thomas Harvey, and by him repeated to the (unknown) writer, it is said that in 1668, after his return from Ireland, Penn had been visiting and speaking in the Friends' meetings in the country ; then, upon being summoned by his father to come to him, at Wanstead, he attended on his way a meeting in London, and after its close, "happening to be in the house of a Friend who resided in the neighborhood, Gulielma Maria Springett came in and was introduced to him ; this was in the year 1668, and was the first time he ever saw his future wife." The authority of this document in some respects appears dubious, but on this point it may be trustworthy.

[2] Isaac Penington died October 8, 1679, while he and his wife were on a visit at Goodenstone Court, a property belonging to her, in Kent.

Gulielma Maria Springett was the only child of Sir William Springett, Knight, who was a native of Sussex, born about 1620, and who died February 3, 1643-4, of a fever contracted at the siege of Arundel Castle, in Sussex, where he was commanding as a colonel in the Parliamentary army. His wife, Mary, afterwards Mary Penington, was the daughter of Sir John Proude, Knight, and was born about 1624.[1] She died at Worminghurst, in Sussex, September 18, 1682, a little more than a fortnight after the sailing of the "Welcome" for Pennsylvania (and a few months later than the death of William Penn's mother, the widow of the Admiral). Her daughter, Gulielma Maria, whose name thus represented those of both parents, was a posthumous child. She was born " a few weeks after the death of her father," Maria Webb says,[2] and as this occurred, as already said, February 3, 1643-4 her birth may have been either in the closing days of 1643, old style, or the beginning of 1644. Maria Webb says, " It may be presumed she was born in 1644, but we have no exact record of the date." She was thus some six or seven months older than William Penn.

The Peningtons continued to live at Chalfont Grange until 1666. The property had been confiscated in 1660, as belonging to the regicide alderman, but they had remained

His remains were brought to Jordans ground for interment. Mary Penington died (as also stated in the text), while on a visit to her daughter Penn, at Worminghurst, in Sussex, September 18, 1682, and was buried at Jordans.

[1] The narrative of her early life and first marriage, the death of her husband, her becoming a Friend, and her later experiences at Chalfont and Amersham, is given in Maria Webb's " Penns and Peningtons," and, as already suggested in the text, is a most interesting picture of real life. Many details concerning her and her family are given in that work, and also in W. H. Summers's " Memories of Jordans and the Chalfonts," published in London, 1895.

[2] " Penns and Peningtons."

there six years, apparently on sufferance by the Crown. To whom it went, on their ejectment in 1666, is not definitely stated; some of the alderman's town property was obtained by the Bishop of Worcester, and some in the country by the Duke of Grafton, illegitimate son of Charles II. by his mistress, the Duchess of Cleveland.[1] The Peningtons were repeatedly visited, while they remained at the Grange, by Thomas Ellwood, and for a time he resided there as tutor to their children. His description of them in his autobiography includes several references to the young girl, Gulielma, with whom, it was surmised, he had fallen in love, and whom, as his ill wishers suggested, he might carry off. He had, however, no such schemes; he admired her, but at a respectful distance. Of a visit to the Peningtons, at the Grange, about 1659, Ellwood says,—

" I mentioned before, that during my father's abode in London, in the time of the civil wars, he contracted a friendship with the Lady Springett, then a widow, and afterwards married to Isaac Penington, Esq., to continue which he sometimes visited them at their country lodgings, as at Datchet, and at Causham Lodge, near Reading. And having heard that they were come to live upon their own estate at Chalfont, in Buckinghamshire, about fifteen miles from Crowell [the home of the Ellwoods], he went one day to visit them there, and to return at night, taking me with him.

[1] "A local tradition asserts that the notorious George Jeffreys [Judge of the 'Bloody Assize'], who is credited with the erection of the Greyhound Inn at Chalfont St. Peter's, resided at the Grange before the erection of his house at Bulstrode. It is added that a portrait of the 'Unjust Judge' was long preserved at the Grange under peculiar circumstances. Jeffreys had given strict orders that it was never to be removed from the walls of the house. After his disgrace, accordingly, it was removed to the cellar, fastened to the wall, and bricked in. So says tradition; but tradition says many strange things." (Summers. "Jordans and the Chalfonts," p. 95.) Alderman Penington remained a prisoner in the Tower from his commitment in 1660 to his death, December, 1661. His jailer was that same Sir John Robinson whose acquaintance we made at the time of Penn and Mead's trial.

"But very much surprised we were when, being come hither, we first heard, then found, they were become Quakers ; a people we had no knowledge of, and a name we had till then scarce heard of.

"So great a change, from a free, debonair, and courtly sort of behavior, which we formerly had found them in, to so strict a gravity as they now received us with, did not a little amuse us, and disappoint our expectation of such a pleasant visit as we used to have, and now had promised ourselves. Nor could my father have any opportunity, by a private conference with them, to understand the ground or occasion of this change, there being some other strangers with them (related to Isaac Penington), who came that morning to visit them also.

"For my part I sought and at length found means to cast myself into the company of the daughter, whom I found gathering some flowers in the garden, attended by her maid, who was also a Quaker. But when I addressed myself to her after my accustomed manner, with intent to engage her in some discourse which might introduce conversation on the footing of our former acquaintance, though she treated me with a courteous mien, yet, as young as she was, the gravity of her look and behaviour struck such an awe upon me, that I found myself not so much master of myself as to pursue any further converse with her. Wherefore, asking pardon for my boldness for having intruded myself into her private walks, I withdrew, not without some disorder (as I thought at least) of mind."

Penn's courtship, if begun so early as 1668, progressed without undue haste. He is particularly said to have visited Guli, in Bucks, after the death of his father, in 1670, and upon his release from Newgate, in 1671. His pamphlet "A Seasonable Caveat against Popery," is dated at "Penn in Buckinghamshire," 23d of Eleventh month (February), 1670, a few months after his father's death, and as this was not far from the young lady's neighborhood, it may suggest calls upon her at that time.

The time of the marriage has been left by the biographers quite obscure. Janney mentions it briefly, without assigning any date. Dixon says, "the marriage was performed in the early spring of 1672, six or seven months after his liberation from Newgate." Maria Webb states that no family documents are forthcoming relative to this period in

Penn's life. But Summers, in his more careful investiga-
tion of local sources, supplies from contemporary documents
all the data that are needed to complete the account, and
the marriage certificate itself has been found of record, and
will be given in full below.

In the Jordans Friends' Monthly Meeting Book, under
date of 7th of Twelfth month, 1671 (February 7, 1671–2),
there is this minute :

"William Penn, of Walthamstow, in the County of Essex, and
Gulielma Maria Springett, of Tiler's End Green, in the County of
Bucks, proposed their intention of taking each other in marriage.
Whereupon it was referred to Daniel Zachary and Thomas Ellwood to
inquire into the clearness of their proceedings and give an account to
next meeting." [1]

These preliminary proceedings took place at a monthly
meeting held at the house of Thomas Ellwood. He had
married Mary Ellis in 1669, and had taken up his abode at
Hunger Hill, or Ongar Hill, not far from Beaconsfield, in
the Jordans and Chalfont region. In this house he lived

---

[1] "Jordans and the Chalfonts," p. 158.—Penn is described as "of
Walthamstow," and Mr. Summers suggests that Lady Penn's residence,
—that of the Admiral,—though always spoken of as at Wanstead, may
have been really in Walthamstow, the parish adjoining. But Mr. Summers is at a loss to explain why Gulielma is described as "of Tiler's
End Green." Her stepfather, Isaac Penington, was then in Reading
jail, on religious account, and her mother was engaged in building the
house at Woodside, near Amersham, five miles from Tyler's Green,
where the Peningtons subsequently lived. Mr. Summers suggests that
Gulielma was in lodgings at Tyler's Green, and that she may have
been staying with some of the Penn family. There were Penns in
Bucks who were then Quakers, for in the petition of the Quaker women
of the country (1659) for the abolition of tithes, there are among the
four hundred and seventeen signatures those of Anne and Elizabeth
Penn. It seems to me, however, a more reasonable suggestion that—
there being no clear evidence as to her residence elsewhere at this time
—Mary Penington was herself lodging at Tyler's Green, and her
daughter with her.

until his death in 1713. His poetical "Directions to my
Friend Inquiring the Way to My House" run thus:

> "Two miles from Beaconsfield, upon the road
> To Amersham, just where the way grows broad,
> A little spot there is called Larkin's Green,
> Where, on a bank, some fruit trees may be seen ;
> In midst of which, on the sinister hand,
> A little cottage covertly doth stand ;
> 'Soho!' the people out, and then inquire
> For Hunger Hill ; it lies a little higher,
> But if the people should from home be gone,
> Ride up the bank some twenty paces on,
> And at the orchard's end thou may'st perceive
> Two gates together hung. The nearest leave,
> The furthest take, and straight the hill ascend,
> That path leads to the house where dwells thy friend."

At the next monthly meeting, March 6, 1671–2, the
records show that "the consent and approbation of Friends"
was given to the marriage, and it duly followed on the 4th
of the following month, April, 1672. An old manuscript
volume, kept in that time by Rebekah Butterfield, a Friend,
at Stone Dean, a dwelling within sight of Jordans, is now
preserved by Mr. Steevens, of High Wycombe, Bucks, and
records thus :

"4th of 2nd Mo. 1672. They [W. P. and G. M. S.] took each
other in marriage at Charlewood, at a farmhouse called Kings, where
Friends meeting was yᵉ kept, being in yᵉ parish of Rickmansworth, in
yᵉ county of Hertford."

The certificate of marriage is as follows :

Whereas, William Penn, of Walthamstow, in the County of Essex, and Gulielma Maria Springett, of Penn, in the County of Bucks, having first obtained the goodwill and consent of their nearest friends & Relations, did in two publick Monthly Meetings of the people of God called Quakers, declare their intention to take each other in Marriage, & upon serious and due consideration, were fully approved of the said Meetings, as by several weighty testimonies did appear.

These are now to certifie al persons whom it doth or may concern that upon the fourth day of the second month in the year one thousand six hundred seventy two, the said WILLIAM PENN and GULIELMA MARIA SPRINGETT did, in a godly sort & manner (according to the good old Order and practise of the Church of Christ) in a publick Assembly of the People of the Lord at King's Charle-wood in the County of Hertford, solemnly and expressly take each other in marriage, mutually promising to be loving, true and faithful to each other in that Relation, so long as it shal please the Lord to continue their natural lives.

In testimony whereof we then present, have hereunto subscribed our names, the day and year afore written.

Margret Penn	Robt. Hodgson	Giles Child
Rich. Penn	John Jenner	Stephen Pewsey
Isaac Penington	Charles Harris	John Harvey
John Penington	Edward Man	Elizabeth Walmsly
Mary Penington	Sam : Hersent	Rebecca Zachary
Mary Penington Jun	Rich : Clipsham	Mary Ellwood
Elizabeth Springett	Robt. Jones	Jane Bullocke
Alexander Parker	Tho : Ellwood	Mary Odingsells
George Whitehead	Martin Mason	Elizabeth Murford
Sam : Newton	Tho : Dell	Mary Newton
Wm Welch	Edward Hoar	ffrances Cadwell
Geo : Roberts	John Puddivat	Helena Claypoole
Tho : Zachary	John Jigger Sen	Sarah Mathew
James Claypoole	Abraham Axtell	Sarah Welch
Tho : Rudyard	John Costard	Mary Welch
		Martha Blake

[Certified to be an Extract from the Register or Record numbered 168 Bucks, and entitled a Register of Marriages formerly kept by the Society of Friends at the Monthly Meeting of Upper Side.] [1]

[1] Copy furnished from the General Register Office, Somerset House, London, August 11, 1896.

TABLE, GULIELMA MARIA SPRINGETT.

| Herbert Springett, | Sir John Proude, |
| of Sussex. | *m.* Anne Fagge. |

| Sir William Springett, | Mary Proude, |
| *b. circa* 1620, *d.* 1643-4. | *b. circa* 1624, *d.* 1682. |

GULIELMA MARIA SPRINGETT

m.

WILLIAM PENN.

King's Farm, Chorley Wood, is still a well-known and readily identified place. Though in Hertfordshire, it is but half a mile from the Bucks line. The name of the place is said to be derived from its having once been a hunting-box of King John. "The present house," says Summers, "probably dates from the latter part of the fifteenth century. The front, which is timber framed, presents one feature of interest in a curious old window, and there is a large door of very similar style, which probably in Penn's time was the main entrance, but is now concealed from view by a modern structure used as a dairy. The back of the house, where the entrance door now is, seems rather newer than the front, but was probably built earlier than 1672. The large room to which the window just now mentioned belongs is probably the one in which the marriage took place, and presents an interesting farm-house interior. The house is very much hidden from view by an immense barn, solidly built, and strengthened by numerous buttresses. This is said to have been fortified by an outpost during the civil war, by which party does not appear, and the loop-holes then pierced in the wall, which were only bricked up a few years ago, are still distinctly visible from the interior. The old farm has not passed unnoticed by artists, but its historic interest seems to have hitherto been overlooked."

Following the marriage, Penn and his young wife went to live at a house he had rented (probably), Basing House, Rickmansworth. It also is in Herts, but near the line of Bucks. Here they made their home for about five years, going in 1677 to Worminghurst, in Sussex, a property of his wife. Basing House is still standing, but much changed in appearance. Mr. Summers says (1895) it "is so shut in by a high wall with a row of trees behind it that little can be seen of it from the street, while what little is visible is so modernized by stucco and other alterations that there is some difficulty in picturing its original appearance. The garden front is less changed, but a fine avenue of trees and an extensive lawn have disappeared." [1]

At Rickmansworth three children were born, all of whom died in infancy, while a fourth, Springett Penn, born at Walthamstow, Essex, lived to grow up. Quoting again Mr. Summers : "Towards the end of 1672 Penn became the father of a little girl, who was named Gulielma Maria. She only lived a few weeks, and was buried at Jordans. Next year a boy was born, and called William. He lived about a year, and was then laid to rest beside his sister." (This statement is also made, though not exactly in these words, in Maria Webb's book, and may be derived from it.) Later, according to Mr. Summers, a third child was born (a girl), of whom Penn speaks in a letter to George Fox, December 10, 1674 : " My wife is well, and child ; only teeth, she has one cut." This child was named Mary or Margaret. She died not long after this letter to Fox, and was buried at Jordans with her brother and sister.

[1] Maria Webb says (" Penns and Peningtons "), " The house at Rickmansworth .   . is more perfect than any other of his [Penn's] residences. The front has evidently been modernized, perhaps early in the present century ; the rear, opening on the garden, appears not to have been altered ; but the lawn, with the avenue of fine trees, no longer exists."

These statements, substantially true, are not quite exact. The two children, William and Mary (or Margaret), were twins, and were born February 28, 1673-4. The record of the births of all the four, as made by the Friends' Monthly Meeting for the Upper Side of Bucks, is as follows:

"1672, 11 mo. 23 : Gulielma Maria Penn, daughter of William & Gulielma Maria Penn, born at Rickmansworth, Herts.

"1673, 11 mo. 28 : William & Mary Penn, twins, children of William & Gulielma Maria Penn, born at Rickmansworth.

"1675, 11 mo. 25 : Springett Penn, son of William and Gulielma Maria Penn, born at Walthamstow, Essex, parish of Rickmansworth." [1]

The registry of the deaths of these children appears in the record of Friends' Meeting for the Upper Side of Bucks,[2] where the death of the first, Gulielma Maria, is stated to have occurred First month (March) 17, 1673 ; of William, Third month (May) 15, 1674 ; and of Margaret (Mary), Twelfth month (February) 24, 1674, this last being ("old style") nine months later than William's death, and not three months earlier, as it might appear at first glance.

Three children had thus been born and had died before the birth of Springett Penn. It is Springett who is referred to in Penn's account of his return from his religious tour in Holland and the Rhine country, in 1677, when he says, "The 5th of the next week [November 1] I went to Worminghurst, my house in Sussex, where I found my dear wife, child, and family all well." Worminghurst was part of the inheritance of Guli from her father; she and her husband appear to have removed to it from Rickmansworth early in the year 1677, for in describing his departure for the Continental journey, he says, "On the 22d of the Fifth month [July], 1677, being the first day of the week, I left my dear wife and family at Worminghurst in Sussex . . . and

[1] From Friends' records at Devonshire House, London, as given by Mr. J. Henry Lea, PENNA. MAGAZINE, Vol. XVI., p. 335.

[2] Cited in Coleman's "Pedigree," p. 8.

came well to London that night. The next day I employed myself on Friends' behalf that were in sufferings [in prison, etc.] till the evening, and then went to my own mother's in Essex." [1]

Three children of William Penn and his wife were living in 1682, when he sailed for Pennsylvania. These were Springett, born in 1675 at Walthamstow, as already mentioned, and Letitia and William, Jr., born at Worminghurst. The letter of counsel to his wife and children, written by Penn on his departure, is well known, and has been many times published. The warmth of his affection for his wife appears in one of the first paragraphs :

" My dear wife ! remember thou wast the love of my youth, and much the joy of my life ; the most beloved, as well as the most worthy of all my earthly comforts : and the reason of that love was more thy inward than thy outward excellencies, which yet were many. God knows, and thou knowest it, I can say it was a match of Providence's making ; and God's image in us both was the first thing, and the most amiable and engaging ornament in our eyes. Now I am to leave thee, and that without knowing whether I shall ever see thee more in this world, take my counsel into thy bosom and let it dwell with thee in my stead, while thou livest."

But the letter of which this is part was evidently not intended for the children, when written, but to be given them when they should become old enough to understand

---

[1] Worminghurst descended to William Penn, Jr., as an inheritance from his mother, upon her death in 1694. He sold it in 1707, and the subject will be more fully mentioned later. " The house," Maria Webb says, " was situated on an eminence overlooking the beautiful south downs of Sussex, and within a few miles of the sea. It was razed to the ground long since, and the Worminghurst estate absorbed in the domains of the Duke of Norfolk. Only the stables now [1867?] remain to mark the spot."

5

its import. Springett was then only seven years old, and
the others younger. There are in the collections of the
Historical Society of Pennsylvania the originals of three
letters written by Penn to the little children, in a juvenile
style adapted to their years,—missives of familiar parental
simplicity. These letters bear the date of August 19, 1682,
not quite a fortnight before the " Welcome " left the Downs.
They are all upon one sheet, and bear the superscription,
" For Springett Penn, at Worminghurst, Sussex.—By Arun-
dell Bagg." The letters are here given :

" MY DEAR SPRINGETT
  " Be good, learn to fear God, avoide evil, love thy book, be kind to
thy Brother and Sister & God will bless thee & I will exceedingly love
thee. farewell dear child
                                      "thy dear Father
    " 19ᵗʰ 6ᵐᵒ 82."   " Wᴹ PENN.

" DEAR LETITIA
  " I dearly love yᵉ & would have thee sober, learn thy book, & love
thy Brothers. I will send thee a pretty Book to learn in. ye Lord
bless thee & make a good woman of thee. farewell
                                      " Thy Dear Father
    " 19,ᵇ 6ᵐᵒ 82."   " Wᴹ PENN.

" DEAR BILLE
  " I love thee much, therefore be sober & quiet, & learn his book, I
will send him one, so yᵉ Lord bless yᵉ. Amen
                                      " Thy dear father
                                           " Wᴹ PENN."

One other child, Gulielma Maria, was buried at Jordans
in 1689, making the fourth then dead. The Surrey and
Sussex Friends' records (preserved in London) show that
she was born at Worminghurst, Ninth month (November)
17, 1685. The register of burials of the Upper Side of
Bucks Meeting of Friends shows that she died at Hammersmith, in Middlesex, Ninth month (November) 20,
1689.[1]

[1] Cited in Coleman's " Pedigree," p. 8.

Springett Penn died, as has already been mentioned, in 1696. The memorial of him prepared by his father, " Sorrow and Joy in the Loss and End of Springett Penn," is pathetic throughout, and in places beautiful,—one of the finest of many fine compositions from his hand. It discloses his sad sense of loss; it was upon this eldest of his then living children that he had evidently placed his hopes. There are many touching expressions in the memorial which might be quoted, but I confine myself to a few passages which suggest the character of the young man and relate to the circumstances of his death :

" My very dear child, and eldest son, Springett Penn, did from his childhood manifest a disposition to goodness, and gave me hope of a more than ordinary capacity ; and time satisfied me in both respects. For, besides a good share of learning and mathematical knowledge, he showed a judgment in the use and application of it much beyond his years. He had the seeds of many good qualities rising in him, that made him beloved and consequently lamented : but especially his humility, plainness and truth, with a tenderness and softness of nature, which, if I may say it, were an improvement upon his other good qualities. . . . He desired if he were not to live, that he might go home to die there, and we made preparation for it, being twenty miles from my house ; for so much stronger was his spirit than his body that he spoke of going next day, which was the morning he departed, and a symptom it was of his greater journey to his longer home. . . . Feeling himself decline apace . . . somebody fetched the doctor ; but, as soon as he came in, he said, ' Let my father speak to the doctor, and I'll go to sleep,' which he did and waked no more ; breathing his last upon my breast, the tenth day of the second month, between the hours of nine and ten in the morning, 1696, in his one and twentieth year. So ended

the life of my dear child and eldest son, much of my comfort and hope   .   .   .   in whom I lose all that a father could
lose in a child, and he was capable of anything that became
a sober young man, my friend and companion, as well as a
most affectionate and dutiful child."

Springett died at Lewes, on the south coast, where he
had been taken, no doubt, for more favorable air and surroundings.   He was buried at Jordans, making the fifth of
Penn's children then interred there.

Preceding Springett two years, his mother, Gulielma Maria
Penn, had died, February 23, 1693–4.   Her death occurred
at Hoddesdon, in Hertfordshire, to which place it would appear
Penn had gone after being acquitted before the King (William
III.) and Council, of Jacobite plotting, being thus enabled to quit
the seclusion which he had maintained for three years.   He
wrote from "Hodson" (Hoddesdon), on the 11th of Tenth
month (December), 1693, to Thomas Lloyd and others at Philadelphia, announcing his "enlargement" and the friendliness of
the King, and added, "From the Secretary, [Sir John Trench-
ard] I went to our meeting at the Bull and Mouth; thence
to visit the sanctuary of my solitude; and after that to see
my poor wife and children; the eldest [Springett] being with
me all this while.   My wife is yet weakly; but I am not
without hopes of her recovery, who is of the best of wives
and women."

In the memorial which he prepared of her, "An account
of the Blessed End of my Dear Wife, Gulielma Maria Penn,"
he says she "departed   .   .   .   in the fiftieth year of her
age; being sensible to the very last.   .   .   .   She did, at
several times, pray very sweetly, and in all her weakness
manifested the most quiet, undaunted, and resigned spirit, as
well as in all other respects.   She was an excellent person,
both as wife, child, mother, mistress, friend, and neighbor.
.   .   .   She quietly expired in my arms.   .   .   .   I hope I

may say she was a public as well as private loss ; for she was not only an excellent wife and mother, but an entire and constant friend, of a more than common capacity, and greater modesty and humility ; yet most equal and undaunted in danger ; religious as well as ingenuous, without affectation ; an easy mistress and a good neighbor, especially to the poor ; neither lavish nor penurious ; but an example of industry, as well as of other virtues : therefore our great loss, though her own eternal gain."

It would appear that her health had been for some time declining, but there seems to be no distinct evidence on this point. She was buried at Jordans ground, near her children. She had been nearly twenty-two years married. Four of her children were dead, three survived.[1]

Of these three surviving children, Springett, the oldest, who died two years later, has been fully mentioned. Letitia, next in age, lived to be an old woman. While a girl, she accompanied her father to Pennsylvania in 1699, and is often referred to in his letters as " Tishe,"—a two-syllabled diminutive of her name, more common in old times than now. She seems to have been a lively and probably a self-willed girl.

[1] A portrait of Gulielma Maria Penn, on glass, is described by Maria Webb (note following preface, " Penns and Peningtons ") as in the possession, 1867, of "the descendants of Henry Swan, of Holmwood, Dorking, who died 1796." This picture was engraved for Mrs. Webb's book, and its resemblance to the portrait of Hannah Middleton Gurney, wife of Joseph Gurney, of Norwich (great-grandparents of Joseph John Gurney), known as the " Fair Quakeress," was remarked. Mrs. Webb, however, pointed out that while the dresses are precisely alike in the two pictures, and there is other resemblance as to the figures, the faces differ, and she concluded that the portraits are genuine in each case, and that the engraver of the " Fair Quakeress " picture (Hannah Middleton Gurney), working about 1746, had copied the dress of Gulielma Maria Penn as a contemporary figure. The picture of Gulielma Maria Penn is given in the " Penns and Peningtons " (English edition) and that of Hannah Middleton Gurney in A. J. C. Hare's " Gurneys of Earlham " (London, 1896).

Her father, writing from Pennsbury to James Logan, in July, 1701, just before his final return to England, said, " I cannot prevail on my wife to stay, and still less with *Tishe*. I know not what to do. Samuel Carpenter seems to excuse her in it ; but to all that speak of it, say I shall have no need to stay, and a great interest to return." And there is the story of Watson "that when she was at Thomas Evans's place, at Gwynedd, seeing the men at threshing, she desired to try her hand at the use of the flail, which to her great surprise brought such a racket about her head and shoulders, that she was obliged to run into the house in tears, and expose her playful freak to her father ! "

Letitia Penn married William Aubrey. The marriage seems to have been arranged after her return to England with her father and step-mother in 1701. A letter from Penn to Logan, 3d February, 1701-2, written at Kensington, says, " My wife and little Johnne well at Bristol. Tishe with me." And, writing from London, 21st June, 1702, he says, " My wife hitherto is kept by her father [*i. e.*, detained with him on account of his illness] whence she is coming next week to Worminghurst on my daughter's account, in likelihood to marry." A few weeks later the arrangements were well forward, for William Penn, Jr., wrote to James Logan, from Worminghurst, August 18, " I was much surprised at what you told me about my sister's engagement to W. Masters, but we find little in it, for she has been at the meetings [of the Friends, to ask approval and oversight of the marriage, according to their rules of discipline] and he was here, but could prove no engagement, for it passed the meetings, and she is to be married the day after to-morrow."

The alleged engagement to William Masters (of Philadelphia) referred, no doubt, to some intimate acquaintance— of whatever degree—existing during Letitia's visit here. Upon her departure for England care had been taken to procure for her, from the monthly meeting of the Friends, a certificate that she had "behaved herself here very soberly and according to the good instructions which she hath received in the way of truth," etc., and that, as far as they knew, she was under no engagement of marriage.[1]

But Logan, who was evidently under the impression that Letitia had given William Masters reason to consider her pledged to him, wrote to Penn that though he supposed she had by that time "changed her name," yet he added, "I can not forbear informing thee of what has been too liberally discovered of her, and among the rest by some that signed the certificate, viz. : that she was under engagement of marriage, before she left this place, to William Masters ; the said signers, upon some unhappy information given them, lately expressed so great dissatisfaction at what they had done that it had been proposed to send over and contradict or retract it."

The marriage to William Aubrey took place on the 20th of August, 1702. A letter from Penn to Logan, dated at London, September 6, says, "My daughter is married next Fifth-day will be three weeks. We have brought her home, where I write, a noble house for the city, and other things, I hope, well. But S. Penington's, if not S. Harwood's, striving for William Masters, against faith, truth, and righteousness, will not be easily forgotten, though things came honorably off to his and the old envy's [? enemy's] confusion, his father's friends nobly testifying against the actions of both." And William Penn, Jr., in a letter of about the same time, wrote Logan, "My sister Letitia has, I believe, a very good sort of man, that makes a good husband. William Masters, whatever grounds he had for it in Pennsylvania, made a mighty noise here, but it lasted not long."

The Founder, among his other characteristics, had that which is not uncommon with great men, and also small, a decided dislike for having his plans crossed, and a strong con-

[1] See a fuller citation of the certificate in Watson's "Annals," Vol. II., p. 117.

fidence that whoever did so must surely deserve condemnation.
In this case it is probable that he would have done as well to
let Letitia's Philadelphia affair go forward, instead of nipping
it, as he doubtless did.   In all the subsequent history of the
Penn family, William Aubrey figures solely and entirely as an
exacting and unpleasant person.   His father-in-law's complaints
of his demands for money on that side, and poor Logan's
struggles to meet them on this, form a feature of the Penn-
Logan letters for years.   If it were the fact, as seems to be
suggested, that her father broke off the Philadelphia match
and arranged that in London, he must have had occasion
many times bitterly to rue at least the latter portion of the
performance.   In December, 1703, Penn wrote to Logan that
he had heretofore sent him "three several letters" about "son
Aubrey's affair," the payment to him of one hundred and
twenty pounds per annum.   September 2, 1704, he again
writes on the subject of "Son Aubrey's affairs," and adds,
"In the mean time both son and daughter clamor, she to quiet
him that is a scraping man, will count interest for a guinea
(this only to thyself), so that I would have thee fill his attorney's hands so full as thou canst."   In 1706, August 14,
Logan wrote to Penn, "I know not how to behave to W.
Aubrey and his wife; they have never wrote since their last
angry letter.   Please and keep it to thyself, for I still honour
my young mistress, and would by no means break with them."
In 1707, June 10, Penn writes, "But my son-in-law Aubrey
grows very troublesome, because he gets nothing thence
[Pennsylvania] about to an open break, did I not bear extremely."   Finally, a month later, when Logan was preparing
to come to England, Penn wrote, July 5, "All our loves are
to thee, but W. A. a tiger against thee for returns.   Come
not to him empty as thou valuest thy credit and comfort."

Which quotation will suffice, no doubt, for the subject ;
there are several such passages in the Penn-Logan letters.

William and Letitia Aubrey had no children.   She survived

him fifteen years. He died about May 21, 1731, as he was buried at Jordans May 23 of that year. April 6, 1746, Letitia's remains were also interred there. The stone marking her grave (placed there, with others, by Granville Penn, in the present century) bore for many years the name " Letitia Penn," instead of Letitia Aubrey.

There are letters from Letitia among the Penn manuscripts in the collection of the Historical Society of Pennsylvania, but none that need occupy much of our attention. The following, in 1734–5, to her half-brother, John Penn, who was then in Pennsylvania, is given as an example :

LETITIA AUBREY TO JOHN PENN.

" London ye 23 Jany 1734-5

" DEAR BROTHER

" I was very glad of yᵉ favour of thine, & to hear of your safe arival ; that thee found things better yᵉ expected ; yᵗ my Brother Thomas has put them upon a better footing yᵃ you heard before thee went. I heartily wish all may be settled to your & yᵉ whole familys Comfort ; am obliged to thee for thy kind expressions in thy Letter to serve me ; I have show'd my nephew what thee writes and believe he will send a Power to end yᵗ vexatious affaire of Mount Joye¹ by ye first shipe yᵗ it can be gott ready to go by ; J. Logan informs me yᵗ five thousand acres of Land taken up in Sr J. Faggs name, now mine, is settled upon intirely, yᵗ there is not enough left for one plantation, wch I think very strang there is no Law to hinder such things yᵗ every one may enjoye theire right ; if this be ye case yᵗ I cannot have my land there My request is yᵗ I may have it somewhere else, my circumstances will not permit my loseing it, also the other five he saith he dont know where to take it up yᵗ any will bye it, all wch I intreat thee to Consider

¹ The allusion here is to the manor of Mount Joy, part of what is now Upper Merion Township, Montgomery County. The manor was given Letitia by her father, October 24, 1701, being supposed to be seven thousand eight hundred acres, at a yearly rent of one beaver skin. On July 10, 1730, William and Letitia Aubrey sold the property to Sir Archibald Grant, " of that part of Great Britain called Scotland." (*Cf.* article " The Old Iron Forge—' Valley Forge,' " PENNA. MAG., Vol. XVII.) I am not able to explain why, if the sale was made to Sir Archibald Grant in 1730, there were still perplexities about it in 1734–5.

me in & make it thy own case y⁸ I hope for redress ; thee knows what
I have in England so leave it.   I am very glad to find yᵗ I may expect
my money so sone, altho' I cannot have it at better interest, nor
security any where, I am sencoable of : I must desier thy assistance in
yᵗ affaire of R. Ashton, who has never paide me, altho' his promises
from time to time to my brother ; & also to speak to my Brother about
proclamation money he wroot me of, wch would be very acceptable to
me to receive it ; I perceive thee finds it a plentifull & pleasant Country ;
but not beyond old England.   I am with sincere good wishes & Dear
Love

                               "Thy affect. Sister and true friend
                  •   " LAETITIA AUBREY
" Mary desiers her Respects may
be presented to thee."
    (Endorsed : "To John Penn Esq. Proprietor of ye Province of Pen-
silvania att Philadelphia, America.
                               "per CAPTIN RICHMAN.")

    Letitia Aubrey's will is dated July 20, 1744 ; she describes
herself as of London, widow.   At the time of her death she
lived at Christ Church, Spitalfields.   Her will contains several
specific legacies.   To her nephew William Penn, 3d, son of
her brother William, she gave a silver cup and salver, silver
teakettle, tortoise-shell cabinet, etc.   To others she left other
pieces of plate, etc., including "a broad piece of gold to
Eleanor Aubrey, now Clark, niece of my late husband, William
Aubrey."   Remembering her great-nieces and nephew, children of her niece Gulielma Maria (Penn) Fell (daughter of
William Penn, Jr.), she left forty pounds to Robert (Edward)
Fell ; fifty pounds to Mary Margaretta, who afterwards married
John Barron ; and forty pounds to Gulielma Maria Frances,
who afterwards married John Newcomb.   To her nephew
William Penn, 3d, she bequeathed all her American estate for
life ; after his death to his daughter Christiana Gulielma, who
afterwards married Peter Gaskell.   To the "poor women" of
Devonshire House Friends' Meeting, Bishopsgate Street,
London, she left fifty pounds,—the Friends about that time
being somewhat pressed in their undertaking to care for their

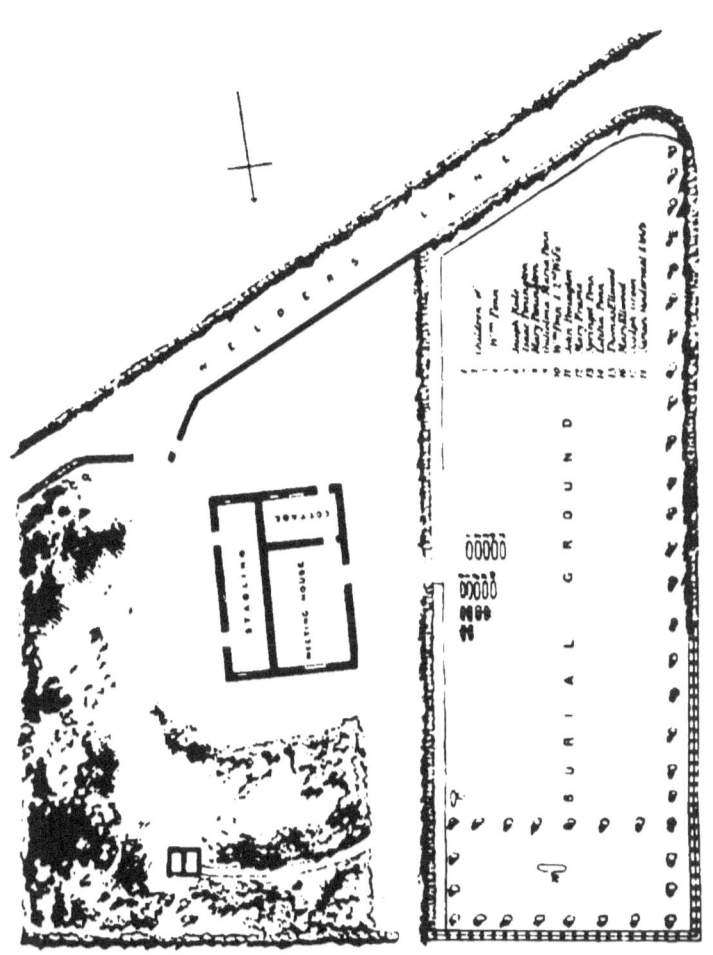

PLAN OF JORDANS GROUNDS

poor members. The residue of her estate she left to her nephew William Penn, 3d, and his daughter Christiana Gulielma.[1]

William Penn, Jr., deserves more full notice than would be appropriate in this part of the narrative. We shall consider him separately, after speaking of his father's second marriage.

SUMMARY : WILLIAM PENN'S CHILDREN BY HIS FIRST MARRIAGE.

WILLIAM PENN, Founder of Pennsylvania, married, first, at King's Farm, Chorley Wood, Hertfordshire, April 4, 1672, GULIELMA MARIA, daughter of Sir William Springett, Knight, and his wife Mary (daughter of Sir John Proude, Knight). GULIELMA MARIA PENN was born about the end of 1643 or beginning of 1644 (O. S.), and died at Hoddesdon, Herts, February 23, 1693–4. Her children by WILLIAM PENN were :

1. Gulielma Maria, born at Rickmansworth, Herts, January 23, 1672–3 ; died there March 17, 1673–4 ; buried at Jordans.

2. William, born February 28, 1673–4, at Rickmansworth ; died there May 15, 1674 ; buried at Jordans.

3. Mary, or Margaret, twin with William, born at Rickmansworth, February 28, 1673–4 ; died there February 24, 1674–5 ; buried at Jordans.

4. Springett, born at Walthamstow, January 23, 1675 ; died at Lewes, April 10, 1696 ; buried at Jordans ; unmarried.

5. Letitia, born at Worminghurst, Sussex, March 6, 1678 ; married, August 20, 1702, William Aubrey, of London ; died without issue, and was buried at Jordans, April 6, 1746. William Aubrey was buried at Jordans, May 23, 1731.

6. William, Jr., born at Worminghurst, March 14, 1680 ; married and had issue. See details later.

7. Gulielma Maria, born at Worminghurst, November 17, 1685 ; died at Hammersmith, Middlesex, November 20, 1689 ; buried at Jordans.

[1] These details are from Westcott's "Historic Mansions," pp. 32, 33.

VI.

William Penn's Second Marriage.

TWO years after the death of his wife, Penn married again. His second wife, Hannah Callowhill, was the daughter of Thomas Callowhill and the granddaughter of Dennis Hollister, both of Bristol, England, prosperous men of business and prominent Friends.[1] (Clarkson describes them as "eminent merchants," and Janney follows this.) A deed of June 26, 1661, shows the marriage of Thomas Callowhill and Hannah Hollister as about occurring, and describes him as a "button-maker, sonn and heir of John Callowhill, late of said city [Bristol] gent, deceased." Later, in 1682 and 1711, other deeds describe Thomas Callowhill as "linen draper," and this, no doubt, was his occupation during most of his business life.

Dennis Hollister was a grocer. He had four daughters, Hannah, Lydia, Mary, and Phebe. Hannah married Thomas Callowhill; Lydia married Thomas Jordan, a grocer; and Mary married Simon Clement, a merchant.

[1] Dennis Hollister was among the early Friends in Bristol. In 1660 their meeting was held at his house, and January 15 a party of soldiers arrested all present. He was subsequently imprisoned. Thomas Callowhill was taken from his house by soldiers, the same year, 1660, "for refusing to contribute to the charge of the City Militia," and suffered much in person and estate, later, as a Friend.

Dennis Hollister is mentioned in the marriage certificate of George Fox, 1669. After stating that George Fox and Margaret Fell had twice made known their intention of marriage at Broad Mead Meeting, Bristol, it says, "and the same intentions of Marriage being againe published by Dennis Hollister, at our public Meetinge place aforesaide, on the two and twentieth day of the month and year aforesaide," etc.

96

Penn, of course, was well acquainted with families of
Friends in all parts of England, and doubtless knew the
Callowhills. His courtship of Hannah,[1] as appears from letters
preserved among the Penn papers of the Pennsylvania Historical Society, was warmly pursued in the later months of
1695. It is probable, but is not clear from these letters, that
the engagement of marriage had then been made.[2]

The Bristol records of the Friends record the birth of
Hannah Callowhill, daughter of Thomas and Annah (*sic*), of
High Street, Bristol, Second month (April) 18, 1664. She
was, therefore, nearly thirty-two years old at the time of her
marriage.

ANCESTRY OF HANNAH CALLOWHILL.

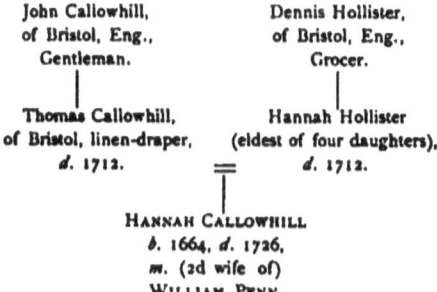

John Callowhill,   Dennis Hollister,
of Bristol, Eng.,   of Bristol, Eng.,
    Gentleman.   Grocer.

Thomas Callowhill,   Hannah Hollister
of Bristol, linen-draper,   (eldest of four daughters),
    d. 1712.   ⚌   *d.* 1712.

HANNAH CALLOWHILL
b. 1664, *d.* 1726,
m. (2d wife of)
WILLIAM PENN.

[1] Clarkson says, Penn "had long felt an extraordinary esteem" for
Hannah Callowhill.

[2] The letters preserved (of course by Hannah Callowhill) are some
ten in number ; one or two, though addressed on the outside to her
father, appear to be intended for her. They convey many ardent
representations of regard, and earnestly urge her not to delay the
marriage. Some passages suggest the thought that the wooer was more
in love than the lady, but we may reflect that he was a fluent letter-
writer. In one letter he says, "This is my eighth letter to thy fourth,
since I saw thee." A few days later, "This is my tenth letter to thy
fourth, which is a disproportion I might begin a little to reproach thee
for, but I do it so gently, and with so much affection that I hope it will

The marriage proceedings were regularly conducted according to the Friends' order, which, newly set up in 1672 when Penn was first married, had now become well settled and recognized. The intention of marriage was declared to the "men's meeting," at Bristol, November 11, 1695, and the meeting gave leave to proceed, February 24, 1695–6. On the 5th of March following the marriage took place.

The certificate of the marriage follows. I am not aware that it has heretofore been published. Penn's biographers generally refer to his second marriage, as they do to his first, quite indefinitely, most of them not giving the date : [1]

[The memorial or copie of the certificate of William Penn's and Hannah Callowhill's marriage the certificate itselfe being wrott on a pece of Parchment stampt with the five shillings stamp according to the statute.]

Whereas it doth appeare by the Memorialls of the mens meeting of the people called Quakers in the Citty of Bristoll that William Penn of Warminghurst in the County of Sussex Esq and Hannah Callowhill daughter of Thomas Callowhill of the Citty of Bristoll Linen drap did on the eleaventh day of the ninth month 1695 manifest their intentions of marriage. And whereas such their intentions were on the ffoure and twentieth day of the eleaventh month in the yeare aforesaid published in the publique meeting house of the said People in the psence of many people there congregated. Now forasmuch as there appeares noe just cause wherefore a marriage betwixt the said William Penn and Hannah Callowhill should not be consumated. We therefore whose names are hereunto subscribed are witnesses that on the day of the date hereof the said William Penn taking the said Hannah by the hand did declare that he did take the said Hannah Callowhill to be his wife. And that the said Hannah holding the said William by the hand did declare that she did take the said William Penn to be her husband.

prevail with thee to mend thy pace." One or two letters at the close of the series, just before the marriage, discuss details of house-keeping, the style and furnishing of a carriage, etc.

[1] It is another of the errors of Coleman's " Pedigree " that he states that this marriage occurred 1699. Dixon (" Life of Penn," p. 286) says the marriage occurred " in January."

And that also the said William Penn and Hannah Callowhill holding each other by the hand did mutually promise each to other to live
together husband and wife in love & faithfullnes according to God's
holy ordinance until by death they shall be separated. And also the
said William and Hannah as a further testimony of such their taking
each other & of such their promise to each other have hereunto with us
subscribed their names this fifth day of the first month in the yeare one
thousand six hundred ninety & five.

WILLIAM PENN
HANNAH PENN.

George Bowles	Joshua Mallet	Rich Sneade	Thomas Callowhill
Thomas Sturg	John Whiting	Charles Harford	Anna Callowhill
Alexander Pyot	John Clarke	Benja. Coole	Sp: Penn
Gilbert Thompson	Nathaniel Wade	Richard Vickris	Laetitia Penn
Thomas Bivin	James Stretter	John Field	Wm Penn Jur
John Corke	William Lickfold	Rogr Haydock	Thomas Harris
Henry Goldney	Thamazin Yeamans	John Boulton	Walter Duffeild
Mary Russel	Thomas Jordan	John Vaughton	Phebe Harris
Elizabeth Goldney	John Everard	John Tompkins	Mary Clement
Sarah Hersent	Abraham Jones	D. Wherly	John Lloyd
Lydia Gregory	John Harper	Margt Duffield	George Stephens
Paul Moon	Henr Dickinson	Briget Haynes	Hump: Crosley
Nicho Relst	J. Penington	Eliz. Penington	
Tho: Speed	W. Penington	George Diton	
Mary Speed	Mary Wherly	Robert Bound	
Tho Lewis	Sarah Jones	Tho Hicks	
Alce Cooper	Judith Dighton	John Clement	
Katherine Bound	Elizabeth Cooke	James Millard	

[Certified to be an Extract from the Register or Record numbered
116, and entitled a Register of Marriages of the Society of Friends.] [1]

This certificate suggests some remark. It will be noticed
that the contracting parties, the bridegroom and bride, sign
their names, preceding those of the witnesses. In 1672, as
will be seen by referring to the Penn-Springett certificate, this
was not the case, the witnesses only signing. In this certificate, also, for some peculiar reason, the record kept in London has the signature of Penn and his wife in *facsimile*,
and in the certified copy forwarded me the copyist has again
cleverly imitated the two signatures. Among the witnesses

[1] Copy furnished from the General Register Office, Somerset House,
London, July 4, 1896.

are William Penn's three children, Springett (then within a few weeks of his death), Letitia, and William, Jr. The bride's father and mother sign, she writing her name, it seems, Anna. Thomas Jordan appears, but not his wife Lydia, though deeds show her living as late as 1711. Mary Clement signs, but her husband Simon is absent. Henry Goldney, often referred to in Pennsylvania affairs, and one of the mortgagees of the Proprietorship later, is a signer. He was then living in London ; it was at his house in White Hart Court that George Fox died, January, 13, 1690–91.[1]

Penn is described in this certificate as of Worminghurst ; that continued to be his home, apparently, until 1697, when, his biographers say, he removed to Bristol. In 1699, on the 3d of September, almost precisely seventeen years after his first departure in the " Welcome," he sailed the second time for Pennsylvania, in the " Canterbury," accompanied by his wife and his daughter Letitia. They reached Chester at the end of November, and landed at Philadelphia December 3. " My passage was long, three months," Penn wrote in a letter to Secretary Vernon, March 10 following, " but merciful in that the northwesters had purged this town from a distemper that raged two or three months therein, brought as believed from Barbadoes, of which 215 died."

Going first to the large house of Edward Shippen, on Second Street, north of Spruce, afterwards called the " Governor's House," where they remained about a month, Penn and his family then took up their residence in the famous house of Samuel Carpenter, the " Slate-Roof House," on Second Street, south of Chestnut ; and here, on the 29th of January (1699–1700), the first child of the Founder, by his second marriage, was born,—John Penn, known usually as " the American," from the fact that he only, of all William Penn's children, was

---

[1] Henry Goldney himself died October 6, 1724.—*Breviate.*

born on this side of the Atlantic.[1] A letter from Isaac Norris
when the boy was past a year old, dated at Philadelphia,
March 6, 1700-1, says, " The Governor, wife and daughter
well. . . . Their little son is a comely, lovely babe, and
has much of his father's grace and air, and hope he will not
want a good portion of his mother's sweetness, who is a
woman extremely well beloved here, exemplary in her station,
and of excellent spirit." There are several allusions to the
child in his father's letters to James Logan, from England, after
the family had returned there.   They sailed, on the homeward
voyage, in the " Dolmahoy," November 3, 1701, and on the
4th of January, 1701-2, Penn wrote from Kensington
(London), " We had a swift passage—twenty six days from
the Cape to soundings, and thirty [to] Portsmouth. . . .
Tishe and Johnne after the first five days hearty and well, and
Johnne exceeding cheerful all the way." And in another letter
of the same date he says, " Wife and father and child are going
this week for Bristol." February 3 following (1701-2) he
says, " My wife and little Johnne well at Bristol." Again,
from London, June 21, 1702, " I bless the Lord mine were
lately well, my last son thriving much, and Johnne perpetually
busy in building or play otherwise but when he eats or sleeps,
as his mother informs me. I have not been with them but
seventeen days these five months." And a year and a half
later the little boy had been taught to remember the city of
his birth, for a letter from his father, written at London,
December 4, says, " My wife, Johnny, (who is still going to

[1] Foot-note in " Penn-Logan Correspondence," Vol. I., extract from
a letter : " Third-day, 31st 11th mo., 1699. Our Governor has a son,
born last First-day night, and all like to do well."   The title applied to
John was early used. *Vide* letter from Penn to Logan, London, March
10, 1703-4 : " Remember poor Johnnee, the little American, according
to what I writ, both of his grandfather's lot and land, and what I gave
him in my former letters."—" Penn-Logan Correspondence," Vol. I.,
p. 277.

6

Philadelphia in Pennsylvania), Tommy and Hannah, were also
pretty well last post."

The allusions just made, " my last son thriving much " and
" Tommy and Hannah," signify two more children.   They
were both born at Bristol, in the house of their grandfather
Callowhill.   The Friends' records of Bristol Meeting, preserved at Devonshire House, London, show these entries :

" 1701-2, 1 Mo. [March] 9—Thomas Penn born at dwelling-house
of Thomas Callowhill, son of William and Hannah Penn."

" 1703, 5 Mo. [July] 30—Hannah Margarita Penn born at Thomas
Callowhill's in James Parish, daughter of William and Hannah Penn." [1]

John Penn, the son born at Philadelphia, from these references of his father's and from such other evidence as we have
concerning him, seems to have been a lively and well-tempered
person.   Watson says he " was quite an amiable man," and
adds that in the estimation of James Logan he was " his
favorite of all the proprietor's children." [2]   We may note at
this point, since he died unmarried, the main facts concerning
him.   He was in his nineteenth year at his father's death, and
had spent much of his time, subsequently to his father's
apoplectic stroke in 1712, with his mother's relatives at Bristol. [3]

[1] Entries cited by J. H. Lea, PENNA. MAG., Vol. XVI., p. 334.—An
allusion is made in a letter of Penn to Logan, from London, June 6,
1703 : " . . . My poor wife going down to-morrow to Bristol to lie in."
Again, in a letter to Logan from Worminghurst, August 27, 1703 : " I
came from Bristol three weeks ago, and was there but about fourteen or
sixteen days, on occasion of my wife's lying in, who this day month
[four weeks] was brought to bed of a daughter, whom we call Hannah
Margarita.   They with my two sons were lately well, and so am I, bless
God at present."

[2] "Annals," Vol. I., p. 116.

[3] Watson says of John ("Annals," Vol. I. p. 116), " He had been
brought up in Bristol, in England, with a cousin, as a merchant in the
linen trade, a situation in which he gave his parents much satisfaction."
The latter clause of this statement could refer only to his mother, as he
was but twelve years old at the time of his father's disability.   There
are a number of references in Hannah Penn's letters, in 1716 and 1717,
to his being at Bristol.

Following the authority of his father's will, his mother, by "a deed of appointment," in November, 1718, "directed and appointed " that John should receive one-half of the Proprietary estate in Pennsylvania, the three lower counties, and "elsewhere in America." He seems to have taken his heirship, with the subsequent development of its great value, cheerfully and without appearance of pride, and to have borne himself kindly towards his younger brothers. He came to Pennsylvania in September, 1734, landing at Chester, in company with his sister Margaret and her husband Thomas Freame, and was ceremoniously welcomed at Philadelphia on the 20th of the month. He remained here a year, returning in September, 1735, to attend to the litigation with Lord Baltimore over the Maryland boundary. For some years before his visit here he had a country place at Feens, near Maidenhead, in Berkshire, and maintained there what seems to have been a modest bachelor establishment. His death occurred October 25, 1746. He was buried at Jordans. The journal of Rebekah Butterfield says,[1]—

" 5th of 9th month November 1746, Daniel Bell, Isaac Sharples, and Sarah Holland were at y⁰ burial of John Penn at Jordans. S. H. lodged at A. B. [Abraham Butterfield's]. Y⁰ rest went away. There was y⁰ Herse, seven Coches, and two Chaises. It was a large Meeting."

And in another part of her journal she had inserted an extract from a local newspaper, the *Oxford Flying Weekly Journal*, of November 1, 1746, as follows :

"On Tuesday night last, being the 25th of October, after a long and painful illness, which was borne with the greatest fortitude, resignation, and cheerfulness, died at Hitcham, in the County of Bucks, John Penn, Esq., the eldest of the surviving sons of William Penn, Esq., late Proprietary of the province of Pennsylvania ; a gentleman who, from his strict justice and integrity, the greatness of his mind, his universal benevolence to all mankind, and his many other amiable qualities, was a worthy successor to his great father. In his life he was highly esteemed

[1] Cited by Summers, " Jordans and the Chalfonts," p. 248.

Mr. Summers says, in his "Memories of Jordans and the Chalfonts" (p. 269), "In a plan of Jordans burying ground, made by John Wilkinson, of Wycombe, from the original by Rev. B. Anderson, Vicar of Penn (who obtained the information from Prince Butterfield in 1798), and now in possession of Mr. J. J. Green, it is distinctly stated that the grave opposite Isaac Pennington's is that of 'William Penn's son John,' not of John Pennington, as stated on the stone. This is confirmed in Wilson Armistead's 'Select Miscellanies,' 1851, Vol. VI., p. 160. It also states that Margaret Freame's son Thomas is buried in the same grave with his mother."

John Penn died unmarried, and left his one-half interest in Pennsylvania and the lower counties to his brother Thomas for life, giving Thomas thus a three-fourths interest. There is a portrait of John Penn, ascribed to Sir Godfrey Kneller, which, at the preparation of this work, (1899), is in the possession of Mrs. Admiral Lardner, of Philadelphia.[1]

Penn's residence, after his return from America, in 1701, was for a time in lodgings at Kensington, but his wife no doubt spent a good deal of her time at her father's house in Bristol. Leaving Kensington, the biographical sketch prefixed to his "Select Works" says "he removed to Knights-bridge, over against Hyde-Park corner, where he resided for some years.[2]

by all who knew him, and his death is as generally lamented. He dying without issue, his estate in Pennsylvania descends to his next brother, Thomas Penn., Esq., who for many years resided in that province for carrying on the settlement thereof, upon the foundation which was laid by their father."

[1] A copy, by James R. Lambdin, made 1859, is in the Philadelphia Library, and is described—erroneously—by numerous writers as the original by Kneller. It is lettered on the back "Thomas Penn," but this seems to be an error, as the portrait is in all probability that of John.

[2] Describing Norfolk Street, Strand, built about 1682 on part of old Arundel House, Wheatley and Cunningham's "London Past and Present" (London, 1891) cites (Vol. II., p. 601) the following from Hawkins's "Life of Johnson":

In the year 1706 he removed with his family to a convenient habitation, about a mile from Brentford, and eight from London, where he dwelt some years. . . . In the year 1710, the air near London not being agreeable to his declining constitution, he took a handsome seat at Rushcomb, near Twyford, in Buckinghamshire,[1] [*sic*] where he had his residence during the remainder of his life."

The fourth child of Penn by his second marriage was Margaret. The Bristol Friends' records show :

" 1704, 9th Mo. [November] 7, Margaret Penn, born at Thomas Callowhill's, in James Parish, daughter of William and Hannah Penn."

Margaret lived to grow up, and married Thomas Freame. There are extant lively letters from her to her brother Thomas, written a few years later, to which we must refer in a chapter on the family life at Ruscombe after Penn's disability. Just before Margaret's birth, in a letter of her father to Logan, dated at Bristol, October 7 (1704), he says, " Herself [the

" The last house at the south-west corner of the street was formerly the habitation of the famous William Penn, of whom it is well-known that his circumstances at a certain period of his life were so involved that it was not safe for him to go abroad. He chose the house as one from whence he might, upon occasion, slip out by water. In the entrance to it he had a peeping-hole, through which he could see any person that came to him. One of these who had sent in his name, having been made to wait more than a reasonable time, knocked for the servant, when he asked, ' Will not thy master see me ? ' ' Friend,' answered the servant, ' he has seen thee, but he does not like thee.' The fact was that Penn had, from his station, taken a view of him, and found him to be a creditor."

This story, if authentic at all, seems to me quite as likely to belong to the period, in 1691, after the accusation by the " informer " Fuller, when Penn found it most prudent to go into retirement. He remained in London much if not all of the time, and very likely declined to see troublesome visitors.

[1] Ruscombe was in Berks, about six miles from Reading. It is curious that a narrative of Penn's life, prepared not long after his death, should make the error of locating it in Buckinghamshire.

wife of William Penn, Jr.] and the three pretty children are
all pretty well, for aught I hear, as through the Lord's mercy
my three also are, and myself as well as my circumstances will
admit ; but my family increases apace, which I account a
mercy, and yet it sometimes makes me thoughtful when I
look forward."

The fifth child was Richard.   The Bristol Friends' records
show his birth at his grandfather's, in Bristol :

"1705-6, 11th Mo. [January] 17, Richard Penn, born at Thomas
Callowhill's, son of William and Hannah Penn."

The sixth child was Dennis. He was born at Ealing,
near London,—the residence spoken of above as "a mile
from Brentford." The Friends' records for London and
Middlesex show:

"1706-7, 12th Mo. [February] 26, Dennis Penn, born at Ealing,
county of Middlesex, son of William Penn, gent., and Hannah Penn,
of Worminghurst."

The six children, until the death of Hannah Margarita, a
year after Dennis's birth, were all living and doing well.
There are numerous allusions to them in the Penn-Logan
letters. Isaac Norris, writing from London, March 3, 1706-7,
says, "He [William Penn] had appointed a day for my
attendance, but did not come, being hindered by the birth
of another son, as I since hear, about Fourth-day last. She
[H. P.] lies in at Ealing, about eight miles off, and he's
there." Thomas Callowhill writes from Bristol, March 23,
1706-7, to James Logan, "I received letters this week from
both the Proprietor and my daughter. They are both and
their family in pretty good health—she scarce got out of her
confinement, for she was delivered of a son named Dennis,
not a full month since. She has now four sons and two
daughters—I bless God, healthy and hopeful. They are
living at a place called Ealing, near London."

Dennis Penn was named for his mother's grandfather,

Dennis Hollister, of Bristol. He survived his father, and was assigned by his mother, in her deed in 1719, a share of the Pennsylvania property. He died, however, in his minority, in January or February, 1722-3. The "Breviate" in the Boundary Case states [1] that his death occurred February 6, 1722. Rebekah Butterfield's journal gives the date of his burial at Jordans ground as January 8, 1722-3. One or the other account is wrong a month.

Hannah Margarita, the third child, born at Bristol (as above) July 30, 1703, died at Bristol in February or March, 1707-8, while her father was in prison in London. A letter from Isaac Norris to James Logan, dated at London, March 6, 1707-8, says, "Our Proprietor and Governor is still in the Fleet, good lodgings, has meetings there, is often visited, and lives comfortably enough for the circumstance. Their daughter Hannah is dead at Bristol." [2]

And not only the death of this favorite child, but the birth of one more, making seven children of his second marriage,—as there had been seven of the first,—occurred while Penn was still in confinement. This last child, named Hannah, for her mother, was born in London ; she lived but a few months. The Friends' records give both her birth and death. Those for London and Middlesex show :

"Hannah Penn, born Seventh mo. [September] 5, 1708, Parish of Ludgate, City of London, daughter of William, Esquire, and Hannah."

And the records for the Upper Side of Bucks show :

"Hannah Penn, daughter of William Penn, late of Worminghurst, in the County of Sussex, England, and Hannah, his wife, departed this life at Kensington, in the county of Middlesex, on the four and twentieth day of the eleventh month, one thousand seven hundred and eight, [January 24, 1708–9], and was buried at New Jordans, aforesaid." [3]

[1] "Pennsylvania Archives," 2d series, Vol. XVI., p. 440.

[2] *Cf.* foot-note by Deborah Logan, "Penn-Logan Correspondence," Vol. I., p. 206.

[3] Cited in Coleman's "Pedigree," p. 8.

A letter from Penn to Logan, sent over by Governor Gookin, and dated at London, September 29, 1708 (a few days before his release from the Fleet prison upon the compromise of the Ford claim), says, " My poor wife had a quick and easy time for her last child-bearing, almost a month since, and has a daughter of her own name, in the room of an excellent child [Hannah Margarita] that died last spring, the love and admiration of all that knew her." And a few weeks later, December 29, 1708, writing again to Logan, he says, "My poor wife is better, that has been ill to a dangerous circumstance. All mine by her are well, which are six in number, thro' mercy, and so is my son Penn now, though dubious a month ago, and my daughter Aubrey, but my son's wife is at present out of order."

The five children who survived, after the death of Hannah (as above) in January, 1708–9, were all living when their father died in 1718 : John, Thomas, Margaret, Richard, and Dennis. Of John we have already spoken. Thomas and his family must be treated of at length. Margaret, as heretofore mentioned, married Thomas Freame. The marriage took place in 1727. An allusion in the " Breviate" of the Boundary Case (" Pennsylvania Archives," 2d series, Vol. XVI., p. 443), where she is quoted as a party, July 5, 1727, to " a family deed of indenture sextipartite,"[1] says she joined in its execution with Thomas Freame, " whom she was then going to marry."

Among the Penn family letters in the collections of the Historical Society of Pennsylvania is one from London, May 7, 1723, from Thomas Freame to John Penn. It begins " Dear John," is deferential and polite in tone, and uses the Friendly expressions " thee," " thy," etc. The writer had apparently been visiting John Penn at his home in

[1] The six parties were John, Thomas, and Richard Penn, Margaret Penn (jointly with Thomas Freame), and two trustees, Joseph Wyeth and Sylvanus Bevan.

the country, and had been ill there. He says, " Pray give my
kind regards to thy sister Peggy." This may have been the
beginning of the courtship. Letters from Thomas Penn to
John Penn (Margaret's brothers), October 25 and 31, 1727,
refer to Thomas Freame as if married to Margaret, and in
May, 1728, a letter suggests the expectation of a child.

The Freames came to Philadelphia with John Penn in
September, 1734, and appear to have lived here for some
years. Thomas Freame's name appears in the list of the
captains of the seven companies raised in Pennsylvania in
1740 to take part in the expedition under Wentworth and
Vernon, which made the futile attack on Cartagena, in
Spanish South America, in March, 1741. A daughter of
the Freames, Philadelphia Hannah, was born in Philadelphia [1] in 1740, and married, May 8, 1770 (being his second
wife), Thomas Dawson, an Irish gentleman, who in 1770
was made Baron Dartrey, and in 1785 Viscount Cremorne,
both in the Irish peerage, the latter honor being "of Castle
Dawson, County Monaghan, Ireland." He died 1813, and
the viscounty expired with him, as he left no descendants.
The barony (Cremorne), however, was continued by a great-
nephew, Richard Dawson, created Earl of Dartrey, 1866.
He was a lord-in-waiting to the Queen 1857–58 and
1859–66. John Jay Smith spoke of him (1867) as a " nobleman of large income," and "in high favor." Viscount
Cremorne's wife (Philadelphia Hannah) died in 1826, Coleman's " Pedigree " says. The famous Cremorne Gardens,
in London, on the Thames, occupied a site which Viscount
Cremorne had owned, and where he had resided.[2] " There
was a lovely portrait of Philadelphia Hannah Penn, Lady

[1] John Jay Smith's address, November 18, 1867. Introduction to
" Penn-Logan Correspondence," Vol. I., p. 32.

[2] In 1825 the property belonged to Granville Penn.—Wheatley and
Cunningham's " London."

Cremorne, in the great north room of Stoke,[1] painted by Sir Joshua [Reynolds], and one of the last acts of the late Mr. [Granville John] Penn was the presentation of this portrait, and that of her husband, to Earl Dartrey. Some of the Cremorne furniture and china and plate was at Pennsylvania Castle in 1865."[2]

A child of the Freames (Thomas) was buried at Jordans August 2, 1746. Margaret Freame was buried there February 12, 1750–1. Rebekah Butterfield's journal contains these entries:

"2nd of 6th Month [August] 1746, Benjamin Holmes, Thomas Whitehead, and William Penton was at yᵉ burial of Thomas Freame, grandson to our friend William Penn, at Jordans."

"12th of 12th Month, 1750, [February 12, 1750–51] Daniel Bell and Jane Hoskins, of Pensilvania, was at yᵉ burial of Margrate Frame. There was a hearse and seven Coaches in all. They went away after Meeting from Jordans."[3]

The stone over her grave is believed to be the one (placed with the others in recent time) marked " Mary Frame."

Richard Penn and his family must be spoken of at length later. The death of Dennis Penn, the fifth of the children of William Penn by the marriage we are now describing, has been mentioned.

The apoplectic stroke which disabled William Penn occurred at Bristol on the 4th of October, 1712.[4] He was

[1] Residence of John Penn, son of Thomas (nephew of Margaret Freame, first cousin of Philadelphia Hannah), Stoke Poges, Bucks, England. To be spoken of more particularly later.

[2] J. J. Smith's address.—Pennsylvania Castle, to be hereafter referred to, was a residence of John Penn, son of Thomas, on the island of Portland, in the English Channel.

[3] These citations from Butterfield MSS. In " Jordans and the Chalfonts," pp. 248, 250.

[4] The time of this stroke is precisely fixed by the date of Penn's letter to Logan, cited in Janney's " Life of Penn " (p. 525), with Hannah's postscript to it, also dated. Maria Webb says (" Penns and Pening-

writing an earnest letter to Logan, some passages of which may be here cited. After impressively urging Logan "to move all springs that may deliver me from my present thraldom" of money troubles, he refers to a plan he had entertained of assigning his proprietary patent to trustees, for the maintenance of a government which would protect the Friends in Pennsylvania, and plaintively adds, " But I am not to be heard, either in civils or spirituals, till I am dead." Other passages follow :

" I am now to tell thee that both my daughter and son Aubrey are under the greatest uneasiness about their money, which I desire, as well as allow thee, to return per first [opportunity] . . . I have paid William Aubrey, (with a mad bullying treatment from him into the bargain), but [? about] £500, which with several hundreds paid at different times to him here makes near £1100, besides what thou hast sold and put out to interest there—which is so deep a cut to me here,—and nothing but my son's [Aubrey probably] tempestuous and most rude treatment of my wife and self too, should have forced it from me.

" I writ to thee of our great and unhappy loss and revolution at Bristol, by the death of our near and dear friends, father and mother Callowhill ; so shall only say he has left all his concerns in America to poor John, who had almost followed his grandfather, and who by his sorrow at his death and burial, and also by his behaviour since, has justified my special regards to him, as of an uncommon character and capacity. Now, through the Lord's mercy, he is

tons," p. 426, Philadelphia edition) that it occurred "on the 24th of Fifth month,"—*i. e.*, July,—and Summers has followed this ("Jordans and the Chalfonts," p. 224). And I regret to say that in the "Memorial History of Philadelphia," Vol. I., p. 173, I have said that it occurred on the 4th of August, my mistake being that I took "Eighth month," with which Penn's date begins, in its modern form. (Hannah's postscript is dated "13th 8ber," which I did not note.) Thus are errors repeated when once committed.

on the recovery, as I now likewise am, by the same Divine
goodness; for I have been most dangerously ill at London."

A few sentences followed, and then, in the midst of one,
his pen stopped: he had sustained a second stroke of apoplexy. October 13, Hannah Penn added on the other side
of her husband's letter a pathetic postscript to Logan : "The
enclosed my poor husband wrote, but had not time to finish
before he was taken ill with a second fit of his lethargic
illness, like as about six months ago, at London ; which has
been no small addition to my late most severe exercises.
But it has pleased the Lord, in the midst of judgments to
show us mercy, in the comfortable prospect of his recovery,
though as yet but weak. And I am ordered by the doctors
to keep all business from him until he is stronger. . . ."[1]

February 5, 1712–13, Hannah Penn again wrote to Logan,
from Ruscombe, where, as already mentioned, the family
home had been fixed in 1710. Her husband, she says,
recovered from the seizure at Bristol, "so as by easy journeys to reach London, and endeavored to settle some affairs,
and get some laws passed for that country's [Pennsylvania's]
case ; but finding himself unable to bear the fatigues of the
town, he just reached Ruscombe when he was seized with
the same severe illness that he has twice before labored
under. And though, by the Lord's mercy, he is much
better than he was, and in a pretty hopeful way of recovery,
yet I am forbid by his doctors to trouble him with any
business till better."

These three strokes of apoplexy—the first in London, in
the spring of 1712 ; the second at Bristol, in October ; the
third at Ruscombe, probably in January—permanently disabled Penn's mental powers, and left his physical strength
so shattered that he gradually declined until his death at
Ruscombe, July 30, 1718. The "Life" prefixed to his
"Select Works" describes the closing six years as "a con-

[1] These letters in full in Janney's "Penn," pp. 525, 526.

tinual and gradual declension." The sale of his proprietary
rights in Pennsylvania to the Crown, begun before the first
stroke, was suspended and never completed, the Crown
lawyers advising that he was incompetent for so important
an act. His will he had made in London in the early part
of 1712, at the time of a severe illness,—probably the first
stroke of apoplexy, though in the codicil to the will, added
at Ruscombe, May 27 of that year, he says it—the former
—was made " when ill of a feavour at London."

The condition of Penn's health, though year by year it declined, permitted him to go about for some time. Hannah
Penn wrote to Logan, February 16, 1713–14, that " he was at
Reading [Friends'] meeting last First-day, as also two or
three times before, and bore it very comfortably, and expressed his refreshment and satisfaction in being there." A
visitor in the spring of 1713 " found him to appearances pretty
well in health, and cheerful of disposition, but defective in
memory . . . nor could he deliver his words so readily
as heretofore." A year later the same visitor " found him
very little altered." He " accompanied him in his carriage
to Reading meeting," where he rose up "to exhort those
present," and spoke " several sensible sentences, though not
able to say much," and on leaving the meeting took " leave
of his friends with much tenderness." Thomas Story, in
the autumn of 1714, found him with " his memory almost
quite lost, the use of his understanding suspended. . . .
Nevertheless no insanity, no lunacy, at all appeared in his
actions, and his mind was in an innocent state. . . . That
he had a good sense of Truth is plain by some very clear sentences . . . he spoke in an evening meeting we had
together there ; . . . so that I was ready to think this was
a sort of sequestration of him from all the concerns of this
life which so much oppressed him, not in judgment, but in
mercy, that he might have rest, and not be oppressed thereby
to the end."

The "visitor" spoken of above again came to Ruscombe in 1715 and the two following years. In 1715 he found Penn's memory more deficient, "but his love and sense of religious enjoyments apparently continued, for he still often went in his chariot to the meeting at Reading, and there sometimes uttered short but very sound and savoury expressions. . . . This year he went to Bath, but the waters there proved of no benefit." In 1716 the visitor found him "much weaker than last year;" he could not remember the names of those· who called, "yet by his answers it appeared he knew their persons." In 1717 he "found his understanding so much weakened that he scarce knew his old acquaintances; and his bodily strength so much decayed that he could not well walk without leading, nor express himself intelligibly."

In February, 1714-15, Hannah Penn wrote to Logan that "he has had two or three little returns of his paralytic disorder, but I thank the Lord it went off, and he is now in pretty good health, not worse in his speech than for some months past, nor can I say he is better; but when I keep the thoughts of business from him he is very sweet, comfortable and easy, and is cheerfully resigned to the Lord's will, and yet takes delight in his children, his friends, and domestic comforts as formerly."

He must have been still in such condition of body and mind in 1716 as to be thought capable of signing the commission to Governor Keith, when he was sent out to supersede Governor Gookin, for the record made by the Council at Philadelphia, upon its reception, was, that it was "from the Proprietor."[1] Hannah Penn, however, in her letter of reproof to Keith, May 20, 1723, uses the expression, "As thou wert chosen in the time of my husband's weakness, by means of his friends only, to that important trust," etc. In March, 1717, about a year and a half before his death,

[1] "Colonial Records," Vol. III., p. 1.

Hannah Penn wrote to Logan that she had continued to live for three or four years at Ruscombe, which was a large house, and carried a heavy rent, solely on her husband's account, "for he has all along delighted in walking and taking the air here, and does still, when the weather allows, and at other times diverts himself from room to room," etc.

After Penn's death, about 1730, a man named Henry Pickworth, for some object (as Penn's friends thought, mere malevolence), asserted that Penn had died insane at Bath. Joseph Besse, the author subsequently of the well-known work, the "Sufferings" of the Friends, published a refutation of the story, and cited the testimony of Simon Clement (Hannah Penn's uncle, husband of her aunt Mary). Clement's statement, in brief, was that in all his illness Penn never had any symptoms of insanity. "He was indeed attacked with a kind of apoplectic fit in London, in the month of May, 1712, from which he recovered, and did go to the Bath, and from thence to Bristol, where he had a second fit about September [October ?] following ; and in about three months after he had the third fit at his own house at Rushcomb, which impaired his memory [etc.] . . . But . . . so far from any show of lunacy . . . his actions were regular and orderly, and nothing appeared in his behaviour but a loving, meek, quiet, easy temper, and a childish innocence," etc.

Penn was near the completion of his seventy-fourth year when he died. The close came between two and three o'clock in the morning of July 30, 1718. He was buried on the 5th of August at the Jordans ground, where his dust remains. Thomas Story's journal gives a few details relating to his death and funeral :

"We arrived at Ruscombe late in the evening, where we found the widow and most of the family together. Our coming occasioned a fresh remembrance of the deceased, and also a renewed flood of many tears from all eyes. . . . On the 5th I accompanied the corpse to the grave, where we had a large meeting," etc.

Rebekah Butterfield's journal says the burial was in the presence of "twenty or thirty publick Friends [*i. e.*, ministers] and a vast number of Friends and others."

The ground at Jordans has been repeatedly described by visitors, and pictures of it showing the stones that now mark the graves are numerous. One of these views is given as an illustration to Mr. George L. Harrison's report (1882) of his visit to England, by authority of Governor Hoyt, of Pennsylvania, to procure approval of the proposition to remove the remains of William Penn to Philadelphia for reinterment. The stones were, unfortunately, in several particulars wrongly lettered. That of Letitia Aubrey was marked " Letitia Penn." The death of Gulielma Maria Penn was given as 1689, that being the time of the death of the last child of Penn's first marriage. Margaret Freame was marked " Mary Frame." And, as already mentioned, the grave, marked " John Penington, 1710," is believed to be that of John Penn, " the American," who died 1746.[1]

Prince Butterfield, brother to Rebekah, whose memoranda concerning burials at Jordans and other Quaker events are esteemed a valuable source of our modern knowledge, informed the sometime vicar of Penn, the Rev. B. Anderson, that, " contrary to the rest, William Penn's head lies to the south, and the remains of his second wife, Hannah Penn, are laid upon his; also that he [P. B.] saw William Penn's leaden coffin when the grave was opened to bury his second wife."

It appears by Penn's interrupted letter, October, 1712, that Thomas Callowhill and his wife had then recently died. It is evident that Thomas Callowhill was not only a valuable friend to his son-in-law, but also a useful citizen of Bristol.

---

[1] These errors have more recently been in part, if not entirely, corrected.

An earlier letter from Penn to Logan, dated at London, January 16, 1704–5, says, " and if my wife's mother should die, who is now very ill, I believe not only my wife and our young stock, but her father too, would incline thither [Pennsylvania]. He has been a treasure to Bristol, and given his whole time to the service of the poor Friends' funds, till they made eight per cent. of their money, and next the city poor, where, by act of Parliament he has been kept in [office] beyond form, he has so managed to their advantage that the city Members gave our Friends, and my father [-in-law] in particular, an encomium much to their honor, in the House."[1]

WILLIAM PENN'S CHILDREN BY HIS SECOND MARRIAGE.

WILLIAM PENN, the Founder, married, second, at Bristol, March 5, 1695–6, HANNAH, only daughter and child of Thomas Callowhill and his wife Hannah (daughter of Dennis Hollister). HANNAH PENN was born April 18, 1664, at Bristol, and died December 20, 1726, and was buried (in the same grave with her husband) at Jordans. Her children by William Penn were :

1. John, "the American," born at Philadelphia, January 29, 1699–1700; died unmarried at Hitcham, Bucks, England, October 25, 1746; buried at Jordans, November 5.

2. Thomas, born at Bristol, England, March 9, 1701–2; married and had issue. See details later.

3. Hannah Margarita, born at Bristol, England, July 30, 1703; died at Bristol in February or March, 1707–8.

4. Margaret, born at Bristol, England, November 7, 1704; married, 1727, Thomas Freame, and had issue: (1) Thomas, buried at Jordans, 1746; (2) Philadelphia Hannah (said to have been born at Philadelphia, 1740, and to have died 1826), who married Thomas Dawson, created Viscount

---

[1] " Penn-Logan Correspondence," Vol. I. p. 355.

7

Cremorne; and perhaps others. Margaret Freame died in February, 1750–51, and was buried at Jordans on the 12th of that month.

5. Richard, born at Bristol, England, January 17, 1705–6; married and had issue. See details later.

6. Dennis, born at Ealing, Middlesex, England, February 26, 1706–7; died, unmarried, February 6 (or January?), 1722–3, and was buried at Jordans.

7. Hannah, born in Ludgate Parish, London, September 5, 1708; died at Kensington, January 24, 1708–9, and was buried at Jordans.

VII.

Family Life at Ruscombe.

FROM 1710 until after William Penn's death in 1718, the home of the family was at Ruscombe, a place in Berkshire, near Twyford. It was rented by Penn, and from an expression in a letter of Hannah Penn, already cited, the house seems to have been a large and expensive one. Like most of the houses in which the Founder had his home in the course of his life, Ruscombe has been entirely destroyed. The traveller by rail from London to Reading now passes over the spot where it stood, "in the last deep cutting between Maidenhead and Twyford, on the Great Western Railway."

The Penn papers in the collections of the Historical Society of Pennsylvania include a number of letters, mostly from Hannah Penn to her son Thomas, which have interest for us in studying the family life at this period. They disclose many details in the experience of such a family as the Penns, in the time of George I., at a country mansion in England. The letters are, it is true, quite incomplete, some of them are occupied with matters comparatively trivial, and the view they give us is but fragmentary, yet their contents, simple and without concealment, are authentic and trustworthy as far as they go, and, taken in connection with the facts which we already know, they throw a fresh and fuller light on our subject.

The family at Ruscombe, in the period we speak of, included Penn until his death, his wife and her five children (until John was sent to business at Bristol and Thomas to London), and during some of the time the wife and children of William Penn, Jr. These, with the several servants usual

in an English house like Ruscombe, made a large household,
and there were no doubt frequent visitors. The head of the
house, after her husband's paralytic stroke, was Hannah Penn.
Fortunately for them all, she brought to her hard place a
large ability. The heiress of a prosperous merchant, she had
been reared in the somewhat austere community of Friends at
Bristol to habits of business industry. Long before her day
the writer of the Hebrew Proverbs had described such a
woman :

> "She is like the merchant-ships ;
> She bringeth her food from afar.
> She riseth also while it is yet night,
> And giveth meat to her household,
> And their task to her maidens. . . .
> Her lamp goeth not out by night.
> She layeth her hands to the distaff,
> And her hands hold the spindle. . . .
> She looketh well to the ways of her household,
> And eateth not the bread of idleness."

Her situation was indeed very difficult. The deaths of
both her parents had but a short time preceded the disability
of her husband. His affairs, public and private, were sadly
embarrassed. Pennsylvania was mortgaged, and the great
movement of German settlers, by which the lands were rapidly
taken up and the financial condition of the Penns improved,
had but just begun. Besides the care of her own children,
and her concern for their future, she had also her anxieties
for the wife and children of her step-son, who were practically
abandoned to her care. William Penn, Jr., seems to have
been himself seldom at the house. In 1714 Hannah wrote,
"I have not seen him this half year, nor has he seen his
father these eighteen months."

Her Bristol relatives gave her their firm support. John
was sent, as already mentioned, to live there and become a
merchant. Simon Clement, her aunt Mary's husband, was
one of her valued advisers. Her own marriage settlement,

reserved for her private use, had been drawn upon to assist in sustaining the family fortunes.[1]

Thomas Penn went up to London late in 1715 or early in 1716, to enter a business career. He was then but a lad, —in the latter year fourteen years old,—yet his mother seems to have relied upon his services in a marked degree. It seems probable that he was his mother's own son, with her business energy and capacity, an inheritance from the Bristol merchants. Her letters to him are addressed, in 1716, "at Michael Russell's, Mercer, in White Hart court, Grace-church street," and we may presume that we have here the name, occupation, place of business, and probably also the residence of his employer,—his "master" in the terms of that day. Members of the Russell family are several times cordially referred to in the letters.[2]

[1] This may have occurred considerably earlier. Penn, in a letter to Logan, 10th of Third month, 1705, says, "They [Hannah's children] bought dearly what they had [in Pennsylvania] their mother lending her estate in land to the value of at least £3,000 or thereabouts, to answer my debts, that was raised by selling her hereditary land, or being mortgaged, which was all one."

[2] There is an allusion to Michael Russell in Joseph Smith's "Catalogue of Friends' Books," Vol. II. p. 519, referring to him as party to some legal proceeding ("Michael Russell, appellant ; John Cochran, respondent"), and to a printed document, "The Appellant's Case."

In the period following the Great Fire in London, 1666, the London Friends leased land of the Fishmongers' Company at White Hart Court, Gracious Street (as it was then commonly called), a plot near the junction of Gracechurch Street and Lombard Street, which had been occupied by the White Hart Inn, destroyed by the fire. A meeting-house and several dwelling-houses were built. Dr. John Fothergill was a tenant of one of the houses in 1748. Andrew Sowle, the bookseller, and Tace Raylton, his successor, whose names are familiar on the early Friends' imprints, also lived there. *Cf.* "The London Friends' Meetings," W. Beck and T. F. Ball. By successive leases the Friends held the property until 1862, when they surrendered it to the Fishmongers' Company.

A letter from John Penn, at Bristol, to his brother Thomas, in 1716, is as follows :

"BRISTOLL 6 Octo 1716.

"DEAR BROTHER

"I have Rec'd thine of 8 Sep'. by wch find that thou art Settled of wch I am heartyly Glad not doubting but it will be for thy advantage & all that I begrudge thee is the Conversation of So many of our Good ffr^ds & Relations & at Present my Mother a Line from whome I have not had Since she was the Last time at London, Pray to whome Give my Duty as also Respects to all our Good fr^ds & Relations wch wch my Dearest Love to Self.—

"Conclude from
"Thy affec Bro :
"PENN."

Hannah Penn's letters to Thomas, as preserved in the series in the Historical Society's collections, begin at an earlier date than the above. They have a pathetic under-tone of continual anxiety and pressure. In one she says, "After fourteen days' expectation and many disappointments I have at last drawn on thee for ten pounds, payable at sight to Edmund Hide, which take care to answer punctually. I would have return'd twenty, but could not get it done ; hope I shall to-morrow, for I never underwent the straits I have since these thy disappointments. I wrote to Henry Gould-ney, and John to thyselfe, by last post, & to no purpose, for Harry Prat says he has nothing ; so I have promis'd, but am not able to perform."

Other letters are to the same effect. December 20, 1717, she says, " No sooner one load goes off, but another goes on by the expences of a large family. I am in a great strait, having promised the butcher more than I can raise for him."

It would seem, indeed, that Thomas Penn in these years must have been almost daily concerned in some business for his mother, and that apart from the aid given her from Bris-tol she relied upon him largely, in London, to collect debts, to arrange advances or loans, to put off creditors, to meet drafts which she had been obliged to make, to purchase and forward supplies, etc.

Let us now read somewhat more at length from the mother's letters. Here is one at the beginning of 1716:

"3d of 1st Mo., 1716.

"DEAR CHILD,

"Thine with the King's speech [1] came but last post; it had two post marks, so think the neglect lay there,—perhaps the want of a fairer direction, that seeming to have been wrote in haste; however, that it brought me acct's of thy health & bro'r Aubrey's amendment, made it very acceptable to me, as was the king's speech to the family. My sister has wrote to thee, and sends it with the little things to-morrow, by Stephen; if thou can have time call at thy sister Aubrey's for it. Thy poor father has been often ill, but at present is indifferent, as is the rest of the family. Give my kind love to thy Master, to whom and in his business double thy diligence, to make amends for the lost time. I have almost forgot how thy accounts stand, which I expect at thy leisure to be informed of, but have herew'th sent thee an order on Joseph Boult for 30£; about 10 of it Judeth Fisher will call on thee for, about a week hence; 'tis for somewhat she is to buy for Mary Chandler, so pay her demand, and husband the rest well. Let me hear from thee now and then, but I will not expect much, because of thine to-day I find 'tis a very buisy time with you, I have also more writing to do, so inlarge not, but putting thee in remembrance of the mercys thou hast received, which bear in mind and endeavor to make notable returns in a watchful and circumspect life.

"I am in the best love,

"Thy truly aff'te Mother,

"H. PENN."

In a letter in the Sixth month (August) of the same year she mentions sundry family affairs, but particularly speaks of his wardrobe, over which she long continued a mother's supervision. She says, "I hope this will find thee at thy place and that thy master is well returned, to whom give my dear love. . . . I doubt I shall not be able to send thy cloathes this week, for some of thy Linnen is not yet dry,— wherefore think thou must shift this 3d day, or for fear of the worst I may send thee a suit of Linnen herewith. . . . Pray get leave to go to Joseph Boult's, to hasten me ye 20£,

[1] George I. He was scarcely warm in his seat or sure of retaining it. The Stuart rising in Scotland had just been put down.

if he has rec'd it, by Stephen[1] if possible. Give my dear
love to thy brother Aubrey, and my thanks for his fine piece
of venson, which was acceptably partook of by us all yesterday.   I also take thy cousin Lowther's care and love to
thee very kindly, in bringing thee to thy place, and was
sorry thy master happened to be from home, and [hope]
that thou will in a little time find it to thee as a home.   I
want to know what thy sister Penn does, whether she is
gone for the North, or not, or intends going soon.   .   .   .
With my dear love and best desires for thy good I close this."

The mother's anxiety that the lad should do well in the
business of his master is frequently expressed.   She is concerned also for his health.   She prescribes medicine for him,
in the medical fashion of that day.   She has many little
errands for him.   Here is a letter in the autumn of 1716.
Hannah Penn had been in London on a brief visit,—staying,
it would appear, at the Aubreys' :

" RUS[COMBE] ye 16th of 8br

" DEAR CHILD

"Give my kind love to thy Master and tell him I desire him to Give
thee Leave to Carry this Irish Letter to the post house safe, the night it
Comes to hand ; put Tom Greys also into the penny post, and deliver
that to H. G.[2] with thy own hand at his house.   Thou must also put
C'ristopher on Inquireing after the box Y[t] went in the Coach with us
from my Son Aubrey's. . . .

"We are, I bless God, all pretty well.   I think it necessary thou
should take a little moderate purge of Epsom waters, or let D. Phipps
or C. Heathcote order thee one, & Do thou pay first.   Take care of
cold ; I have left fustian to line either thy old Coat, or waistcoat, when
needful.   Ask Mary and betty at thy bro. Aubrey's after my Gold Seale,
which I cannot find since I came home, & doubt I left it on their table
or window, the night before, as I also did forgett the Lemons, and

[1] Stephen was evidently some one going frequently and regularly to
London, probably a " carrier."

[2] Henry Gouldney.   He has already been referred to in a previous
foot-note.   At his marriage, January 26, 1681, he was described as " of
Cheapside, linen-draper," son of Adam Gouldney, of Chippenham,
Wilts.

Shrimps,—if Mary got any for me,—but that's no matter now, only my
Seale and the Lemons, order Christopher to send wth the box.

" [We have now six little] pigs, one of which I would send thee, if
acceptable, & y^t Mary thinks would dress well after such a Journey,—
or I will send a goose next week. My uncle and cousin Clement are
gone for Bristoll.

" My dear Love and best wishes attend thee ; I am

" Thy aff Mo

" H. P."

The goose which the mistress of Ruscombe here suggests
went up to London presently, for a week later than this
letter there is a note from the little daughter of the household, Margaret Penn, who writes Thomas in a style which
suggests that of their father in his early and cheerful days.
She says,—

" Ruscombe, ye 23 of 8ber, 1716.

" Dear Brother

" I Rec'ved thy Letter and Kind Presant by Mary, which I thank
thee very kindly for, & like them very well. My Father is as well as
Usuall, as is my mother now, and Sister Aubrey ; they send thee their
Dear Love, as I do most indearedly, and am

" Thy very aff^{te} Sister

" Marg'tt Penn."

[This is the letter ; but here is the postscript :]

" My Mother gives her Kind Love to the Master, and has sent him
a Ruscombe Goose, and I send thee a fue Pears and appels, and if I
knew when it would be thy wedding day would send thee, too, a Chicken,
or anything that would be more acceptable."

The writer of this will be recognized as Margaret, the
younger sister of Thomas,—she who afterwards married
Thomas Freame. In this correspondence she is called
" Pegg," reviving the recollection of her aunt, the " Pegg "
of London, in the day of Pepys's Diary. Her banter of
Thomas about gifts for his wedding-day was far in advance
of that event, for he,—a prudent bachelor, with ambitions
presently for betterment of fortune and advancement in
rank,—postponed it more than thirty years.

In a letter already given in part, dated at Ruscombe, " 28th of 1ober 1716," there are these details :

" Thy poor father has been very indifferent these 2 days, which has Increas'd my Cares, but being in the same Manner as Usuall I yet live in hope of the Lord's Mercy in his Preservation to us. the rest well and send their Love both [to] y⁰ Master [and] H. & E. G."

[A postscript :]

" Delay not too long the sending some raisons, figgs, & almonds for thy poor father, also 6 lemonds & orringes. thou has I suppose baskets. If thou fail by Stephen thou may send by Ambrose 5th day till tenn from the bell savage." [1]

An undated letter, probably about this time, says,—

" DEAR CHILD

" having this opertunity by Tho Grey I let thee know thy father is midling, myselfe and the rest of us pretty well. Thy brother after being hindred severall days by the Weather is gone toward bristoll this morning wᵗʰ R. Colter & in expectation of overtaking John Cowling. I desire thee let the bearer J. G. have halfe a Guiney to buy me some Tea, and would have thee send me 5 Guineys made up safely in itˢ by Stephen of the money yet remaining in thy hands, & if thou hast opertunity by or upon the first of next Month inquire of Jo : Gurnell how the Exchange is and if he can as Usual help me to 50ᵗʰ in a bill at 30 days sight on Tho Wight and what Exchange. I hope thou had mine by last return, & will if thou had not, send me a pᵈ of Coffee. Send me also some patterns of black and white Grosett if you cut any. [On back of letter :] Give my dear love to thy Mᵗ and Mᵐ Mary Russell & H. G."

Another incompletely dated letter, probably July, 1717, is filled with requests and commissions :

[1] The Bell Savage was a famous old inn on Ludgate Hill, established at least as early as 1453. " In its later years it was a great coaching inn, but the formation of the railways destroyed its trade ; it fell into neglect and dilapidation, and was eventually [1873] demolished." The printing establishment of Cassell, Petter and Galpin was built on the site.

[2] This method of sending money seems to have been frequently used. See later ten pounds sent " in a peck of oysters." A note from Margaret to Thomas, November 3, 1717, after stating that " brother John is gott safe to Bristol," adds that " my mother received the tee, and that which was in it, safe."

" CHILD

" send down if thou can an ell of silk to match Each of these, the Lightest was bought at Collisons not long since. A Persian [*word lost*] match'd to the other Culler may do if thou cannot gett it exact.

" 4th-day morning. . . . Thou may call on Jo Boult for the money for these silks if thou need.

" 16th of 5th Mo. This was wrot a week since and intended by Bishop Vickress[1] who disapoynted me by not calling. I am sorry in thy last thou gave me no Acc[t] of Dear E. G's illness, for whose loss I am in no small Concern,[2] Greatly Pittying her poor husband & near & dear Relatives, of whose welfare lett me hear. & tell thy Sister Pen we are all near as She Left us. Guly has a little Complayn'd of her head akeing today but is better tonight, we are all else so so."

[On the back of the letter :]

" Thou may stop in Jos Boults hands, if not already sent to me 20[lb] for these things I send for, but not more than necessity requires, & desire him to send the rest & a pound of Coffee with it.

" J Penn is pretty well again.

" Put thy aunt's letter into the post house wth Care."

Joseph Boult, so frequently mentioned as one of those who were relied upon for money in time of need, appears to have been an agent of William Penn, though his precise relation to him does not clearly appear. There is a note to Thomas Penn, in 1717, from a tenant probably, written at Lewes, in which the writer says that " being with him in a barber shopp by his house I ask'd him if his name was Boult, for y[t] I thought I had Paid him money on acco[t] of thy Father, and whether [he] did Business still for him. He said he did when he had ord[r] & if I had any money to pay he would write about itt," etc.

A letter from Hannah to Thomas on the birthday of Margaret, the completion of her twelfth year, November 7, 1716, is as follows :

[1] A neighbor. See letters from him later.

[2] Probably Elizabeth Gouldney, wife of Henry Gouldney. She died " of cholick," 13th July, 1717, and was buried at the Bunhill Fields ground on the 17th. She was fifty-nine years old.

" RUS[COMBE] ye 7th of 9 mo. & Pegg's birthday.

" DEAR CHILD

" I have by Coach both thine as also one to thy sister, who is now turned from her thirteenth Year, & has helped Sukee to finish thy 6 shirts (and will help to recruite thy old ones) wch I suppose will be also wore out, by this time twel've month, if thou hast health, of wch I hope, and I therefore think I had best, if I can gett neat french Doulas, to make thee 6 or 8, which would be very Comfortable to me in ware, & to thee, I fancy, this winter.

" I have for some weeks delayd sending a goose to thy Mistress, in hopes of Wild foule, or something else valuable to send with it, but being hitherto disapoynted, and the waters at present forbidding our pursuite of any Game, I send this alone at last, to begg her acceptance ; tho am Indeed ashamed to think I have stayd so long to so little purpose. Thy poor father is rather worse, at least more uneasy, for a day or two past, but hope if the weather mends, that so he may gett out more, that he may be better again ; we are else pretty well, & all dearly salute thee.

" I am glad of Sam^n Arnolds having accepted the bill, & desire mine to Andrew Hall may be payd to Content. I would also desire ten pound by Stephen in a peck of oysters, but I would not be too often troublesome and therefore will try to shift till thou receaves ye 50^lb from Jon : Gurnell, and of which send me 20 in good Goldsmiths Notes & 20^lb in Mony, also pay betty Collison ten in part of acc^t—& send me by first some patterns of Grave Mixt Grassetts from her, till I get a Suite made I cant well adventure to London this cold weather. Nor have thou as yet told me whether the Doctor is yet gone from thy Sisters or not, but of that mention nothing to them unless he is absent.

" If thou wants Cloathing before I come up let me know what.

" if Jon. Gurnell is Unsatisfied for want of the words Vallue rec^d thou may if wth his advice Interline it, but I am always in a Strait in those words, least my letters should Miscarry or be Intercepted between me and him."

[On back of letter, in another hand :]

" My Mistress would have thee tell J. Gurnall that Shee will write to Thomas Wight by next post without faill, but desiers her bills may not be sent till ye post following, and also would have thee when opertuinity offers to goo and see thy aunt Lowther and Lett M^rs know whare Shee Lives."

Aunt Lowther's[1] house was probably in London ; she may have been moving ; her residence, it seems, was not well known at Ruscombe at this time. She had been a widow since 1692, and was now approaching the end of her days. The following, in the spring of 1717, gives a view of the different concerns that occupied the mistress of Ruscombe :

" RUS ye 4th of 1st mo 1717.

" DEAR CHILD

" I am weary, it being both Gardening and Washing time, and Expecting to morrow, on the Green, if not in the house, the familys thereof to the Buriall of Mary Blagrove. But having received thy 2 letters, I answer that part however relating to thy sister Pen ; in which let her have a guiney, besides her bill, and take for thy selfe 20£, or more if absolutely needful, but I am surrounded wth Calls and Cares ; I hope thou had and will mind the Contents of my last, & send me the money soon. Hasten this also to J. Vine ; I expect my Landlord's Call Soon, he became of age to day. Thy two letters I had to night together, also the hoods, oranges, Coffee, etc. ; tis too late to see the patterns, So say nothing, & expect to hear again from thee soon."

A letter, September 10, 1717, sends Thomas to Henry Gouldney and Joseph Boult on business, and says, " my being full of company, and thy Aunt Wharley[2] going to-

[1] This was Margaret, sister of William Penn, the Founder. There are some letters from Margaret and her husband (Anthony Lowther) to him, during his first visit to Pennsylvania, in the Friends' collections at Devonshire House, London. One of these from Margaret, dated Aug. 4, 1683, at Maske, refers to its being sent by Joshua Hoopes, (" he came just now in, and tells me he is for Pennsylvania ; a stranger to me but lives at Skilton,") and says : " Robin is now with us ; we sent for him for a month ye summer, so y^t wee are now all togather, ffor I think I shal come in ye latter end of No'ber, or ye beginning of De'ber. Y^e time makes my condytion more mellencholy." (She alludes to the execution of Lord William Russell, etc.)

[2] The extent to which the recognition of relationship was carried is exemplified here. Isaac Penington, by his marriage with the widow Mary Springett, had five children, four sons and one daughter, Mary, who married Daniel Wharley, of London. Mary Wharley was therefore a half-sister of William Penn's first wife, and her sistership to William Penn's second wife was altogether one of courtesy.

morrow hinders my writing to H. G.   Thy dear father is
full as well as thou left him ; I have been ill, but am better."
Mary Russell, who was one of the family with which Thomas
lived, perhaps the wife of his master, was then at Ruscombe,
and sent love to her relatives.

In a letter in November, 1717, Hannah writes to Thomas,
sending a letter by a " New England Friend " who has been
at Ruscombe, with whose visit, she says, we " have all been
pleased and comforted."   Thomas's wardrobe, at the beginning of winter, excites her concern once more, and is
coupled with the ever-present finance question.   " I would
not have thee," she says, " want Stockens, but get them ; or
what thou cant not well Shift without ; but for a new Coat,
if thou can spare it this winter do, by new lineing or a
thicker wastcoat but especially till R. Baker is payd.   I hope
thou have pd poor Danell Skinner, I have Walter's bill, and
others presses me hard, as also my coming to London, but
the weather and roads much discourage.   I am heartily
Afflicted at the Loss of dear Silvanus Grove, in Whom
we have all lost a Most Capable and Valuable friend.   The
Tea is come safe, & we like it pretty well.   My Dear Love
to thy M. & M., & very dearly to thee."

In a letter of about the same date, devoted mainly to instructions as to money, or drafts on Samuel Arnold and
Jonathan Gurnell, she fears she takes up too much of his
time, and intends to ask excuse of his master when she
next comes to London.   But there is this postscript :

" I had thine ; am sorry for thy Loss and Negligence in losing the
guinea ; tis wit dear bought, and I hope will last with thee for thy increase of care in time to come.[1]   Send the enclosed by first penny post.
Johne and all other our relations well at Bristol by last post.''

[1] We may believe that Thomas laid this experience and admonition
to heart.   It does not seem that he often wasted or lost a guinea, in later
life.

A letter in December, 1717, speaks of Thomas's wardrobe in some detail. Referring to the tardy receipt of some things which he was to send down from the city, she adds,—

" But [I] am now satisfied in that, as also in thy Choice of a Coat, only doubting that when thou have wore this a month or 2, Every day, 'twill be too bad for First days ; or perhaps thou dessigns thy other for every day, and the new one for best, which I think Indeed the Most Likely. I wish thou could have shifted till nearer Spring for a hatt, for I doubt to buy a good one now twill be near spoyld before the Hight of summer. I wish thou had saved thy last from spoyling, by buying one more ordinary and cheaper, & which I fancy will be thy best way still, & so postpone a good one till summer ; of which however Consider and act for the best Husbandry, & then please thy selfe ; but be sure wch ever tis, that tis Packd up in a very Frd-like way, for the fantasticall cocks in thine, and thy brother Johne's hats has burthend my spiritt much, and Indeed more than most of your dress besides ; therefore, as thou Vallues my Comfort, Regulate it more for the future. I have a Multitude of Toyls and Cares, but they would be greatly Mittigated, if I may but behold thee and thy brother, persuing hard after Vertue, & leaveing as behind your backs the Toyish allurements & snares of this uncertain world. Oh may it be so, saith my soule.

" Thy poor father is as of late, so, so ; my selfe and the rest Indifferent. Pegge, who has been at Atalls, Just come home, & sends her dear Love to thee ;· give mine to thy sister Aubrey."

[Then she adds :]

" But I will not longer detain thee than to advise thee not to faile of reading the Scriptures, and prizing the happiness of silence in meetings, when thou can get to them."

Ten days later she is concerned for Thomas's health :

" I have not wrote to thee since thy last, being Loath to Intercept thee in thy load of business, in which practice diligence, but forgett not thy own health, by overlifting or overworking, for the continuance of thy health will be for thy master's advantage, as well as my comfort. . . I only add my good wishes, tho the surfeit [etc.] thou took last year will make me in care for thee till I hear this is over."

There are two notes at this time from Gulielma Maria Penn,—the daughter of William, Jr., the "little beauty,'· as her grandfather had called her in one of his letters to

Logan fifteen years before, when she was in her infancy. They are to Thomas, and indicate that he had been doing errands for her also; they bear a slight air of mystery. It may be noted that she begins both, "Dear Uncle," and signs herself "thy very affectionate cousin." (Thomas was, of course, half-brother to her father.) She desires him, in one, "to send y⁰ inclosed to M. Knight, and y⁰ other to my mother." Then, in a postscript: "If thou hast any Letters for me send them to Cousin M. Stafford, at Margaret Wiggin's." The second note runs thus:

"December y⁰ 22 1717.

"Dear Uncle

"I desire y⁰ will Excuse me for troubleing thee so often. I rec'd both my letters & am very much obliged to y⁰ for thy kindness in Profering thy self, to do anything for me. I desire thou wilt send y⁰ inclosed to Cousin Patty Stafford. Pray dont say anything to any Body that thou heard from me; allso if anything comes for me Send it By y⁰ Aylesbery Coach, as y⁰ last Parcel was sent, and thou will very much oblidg

"Thy very aff⁰⁰ Cousin

"G. M. Penn."

Mary Penn, William, Jr.'s, wife, has been in London, and unwell; Hannah chides Thomas for making but a brief report of the case. She says,—

"Rus. y⁰ 27 of 12-mo 1717-8

"Dear Child

"Thy last letter, on acc¹ of thy sister Pen's illness a little surprisd me, & on which I wrote to H Gouldney. I hoped for a letter from some of you since, but none Came as y¹ except one from thy sister Aubrey, which however has Easd me; but When ever thou writes of illness of thy frds be not so short as not to tell the Malady, especially when thou desires anything for their care, for w⁰⁰ out knowing y⁰ Cause tis hard to study a Cure, but I hope 'tis nothing bad, if 'tis let me hear again by post. . . . I would have thee write me a line 7⁰⁰ night, to lett me know how thy sister does, & when any Ships Sayle; lett me also know whether thou have now any cash in hand, & how much, also How Irrish Exchange runs. Cousin Tho. Aubrey is got hither on his way for London & pretty well, his Horse lame or would have left us to morrow, but intends it y⁰ day after, to whom I refer for perticulars, and about y⁰ patterns to my next opertunity, and with dear Love from me and Pegge conclude; from thy

"Aff⁰⁰ Mother, H. P."

The letters which I have observed passing between the two brothers John and Thomas at this period, and later, are kindly and affectionate in tone. Thomas, perhaps, is somewhat formal and business-like, but is always regardful of the conventions of correspondence. I have noted one letter, in 1723, in which, being then at Bristol, Thomas wrote to John, in London, at "Crown Court, Aldersgate," and departed from the plain manner of the Friends, saying throughout "you," "ffebruary," "ffriday," "Monday," etc., but this is an exception ; in other letters, later, he uniformly says "thine," "thy," "thee," "First-day," etc. His letters are well written, in a fine, even, and pleasing hand, and he expresses himself clearly and definitely.

Hannah Penn's cash-book, a small, square book, showing the house-keeping expenses at Ruscombe between May 15, 1715, and November 5, 1719, is among the Penn collections of the Historical Society of Pennsylvania. The opening entries, and most of those which follow, are in the handwriting of Hannah Penn, but some are in another hand, probably that of her son John. The account begins with this entry :

"We came to Ruscomb from Bath the 9th of 5th mo : 1715,[1] then Rec'd of John Wren by bill on Joseph Boult £10."

The page upon which this is entered contains further entries of the proceeds of bills drawn upon T. Wight through Jonathan Gurnell, payments of cash by Ambrose Galloway, and others, making in all twelve entries between May 15, 1715, and Twelfth month, 1716, and covering four hundred and thirty-one pounds and fifteen shillings. Other memoranda of bills drawn, etc., appear on other pages, but most of the book is occupied with cash payments. As these throw light on the daily life at Ruscombe, I extract as follows :

[1] This was evidently Penn's visit to Bath, taken in the hope that the waters might benefit him, mentioned by the "visitor" to Ruscombe, in last chapter, and also by Simon Clement.

8

```
"1715                                      £  s  d
5th mo. 9   payd hire of yᵉ horses & to the Coach man
              yᵗ brought us up from Bath . . . . .   5  0  0
            pd Carriage of our goods fro Bristoll . .     12  6
            pd a debt to Rachell Hall . . . . . .    4  0  0
            pd Jane Grove for Tayloring work . . .   1  1  6
            pd the poors Tax ½ year . . . . . . .        9  4
       22   pd Farmer Crockford in pᵗ for Hay . . .   5  0  0
            pd Goodee Lovejoy for weeding &c. while
              we were from home . . . . . . . .           14 10
            pd Goodee Collins for her work . . . .       15  0
            pd Neighbour Burton, horse hire . . . .       9  0
            disbursements at Henly Markett . . . .        7  ½
            to my pockett 5ˢ to my husband 10ˢ . .       15  0
            to Daughter Aubrey for severall things .  3  8  0
            To Daughter Pen to pay Gilbert Tomson's
              bill . . . . . . . . . . . . . . .    17 10  0
            for 3 Lobsters . . . . . . . . . . .          2  3
            for a dosen of Cherrys . . . . . . . .        1  6
       23   pd Thomas yᵉ Butch'r in full of a former
              bill . . . . . . . . . . . . . . .     3 15  9
            pd for 7 ducks & 6 fouls . . . . . . .        9  0
            pd for a dosen of sope . . . . . . . .        5  0"
```

The entries above are nearly all those occupying the first
page of cash payments.   Other entries on subsequent pages
include the following :

"1715, 5th mo. 27, payd for a Couple of Rabets 1s, 6d.   For 4 lbs
of butter, 6s.

" 28th pd for a dish of fish, with Lobster and Crawfish 7s 6d ; John
Good, for white liming yᵉ house, 10s ; for severall things of yᵉ Pedler,
3s. 9d.; for gathering herbs and camomile flowers, 1s ; for a sythe for
yᵉ walks, 2s 6d.

" 6th mo 1, for a flitch of bacon, 39 lbs, 19s 6d.

" 19th, to Tho : Pen for his journey to Bristoll, 10s.

" 22nd, pd bringing Johnes things and a hamper from Bristoll, 5s.

" 27th, pd Margaret Chandler's son by bill on Joseph Bouk in full
for wine due to her £3 13s 6d."

Other entries, omitting dates, are extracted as follows :

" For a roasting pigg 2s 6d ; for a bushel of Potatoes 2s ; for a
goose to send to London 2s 3d ; for pins and other small things at reding

4s ; for earthen pans at twiford, 2s 4d ; pd Tho Grove y* window tax 15s ; for sweeping chimneys, etc., 2s ; y* smith at Twifords bills £1 19s ; pd Thos Grove, for landlord, y* land tax £3 11s ; mending y* side-saddle, etc., 1s ; for stuffe for an under coate for Pegge 3s 4d.''

Entries of payments of taxes and ,rent suggest with tolerable certainty that the owner of Ruscombe was a Mr. Foster. 1718, First month (March) 26, there is this entry : "pd Landlord Foster by disbursements & taxes £9 10s, and in money £10 10s in full to Decem'r last.''

The cash-book contains no entries from Fifth month (July) 21, 1718, to November of that year. Two pages were left blank, but the account has not been set down. The melancholy reflection is that this was the period in which the death of the Founder occurred.

Entries in the book about a year later, in the handwriting of one of the children (as there are occasional payments of petty cash to " my mother "), and evidently a man, suggest the work of John Penn, though it may have been Thomas's. They seem to show quite clearly that at this time, probably Michaelmas (September 29), 1719, the home at Ruscombe was broken up. The entries of cash paid out are nearly all stated to be " in full," and then appears this one :

"Balance this 26th Octo' 1719 and wch I Brought from Ruscombe to Hammersmith £4 16s 1 ½ d.''

There are three pages of charges in the book, begun by Hannah Penn, headed " Son and Daughter Penn, Dr.'' These begin in September, 1712, just after the apoplectic seizure of the Founder ; they refer, of course, to William, Jr., and his wife. They extend to Eighth month (October), 1717, and amount to about three hundred pounds. We shall more particularly refer to the subject which they represent in the chapter on William Penn, Jr.

In May, 1720, Hannah Penn was in London, and wrote from there to Rebecca Blackfan, at Pennsbury, in Pennsylvania, a letter which has already been referred to, but which is worth giving in full :

" LONDON, ye 9th of 3rd Month, 1720.

" DEAR COUSIN :

" By ye Death of my dear Husband & ye Loads of affliction that has encompass'd me thereon I have been disabled from conversing much wth my Friends, as well as from doing them or myself much service on that side y⁰ water. But as it would be my greatest pleasure to find myself in a Capacity to pay my dear Husband's Debts, & see my poor Children made capable of maintaining themselves, wch I am now struggling for, & when attained, shall be also willing to assist thee & thy Son, if you are not yet got to a Settlement, but I would hope you are in some little way and Place, for I am realy concern'd to think of thy Son's loseing so much of his time. And that it may be no longer, I have sent thee Peter Evans's Bond, for thee to advise wth my Friends upon, & use as they shall direct,—James Logan & R. Hill, in particular.

" I find sev'l of my Letters to thee & others have miscaried, & therefore know not whether they had acct of y⁰ Death of my dear Sister Lowther, who Died of a Lingering Feaver & gradual decay about 5 Months after her dear Brother. My poor Niece Poole is also since Deceas'd, of an uncommon Ayling & pain in her Head, scarce understood by any, but as was suppos'd proceeded from a Bruise on an overturn in a Coach some Months before : She has left one only Daughter, who I hope may have Comfort in Her Riches, & not become a Prey to ye World, or some Worldling. My Cousin John Lowther is maried, has one Child, (a Daughter) and Lives at Mask as yet. My Cousin Sir Thomas, the Heir of Sir William, is just return'd from his Travels in France & Flanders. He went out a very promising hopeful young Man, & I greatly hope is not worsted but improved by his journey. His two Sisters are both Living, but his younger Brother Died of the Small Pox two years since. My Daughter Aubrey is I hear well, as is my Daughter Penn & her Son & Daughter, all here in Town, & Springet wth a Merchant in Ireland.

" My Children, Three of them are in Town here, well, as are I hope my Two youngest at School. My Son Penn, after his Father's Death, came over from France to send his Commissions, as I hear, to your side, & then return'd again to France, where I think he has spent his time mostly ever since, & I doubt too fast, for I hear he is now but weakly, & 'tis doubted in a Consumptive way ; May he yet Live to see, & have a Heart given him to repent of his Follys, is what I heartily desire. My Son John gives his kind Love to thee & his Cousin William, to whome give mine, & in thy next let me know in what Condition Pensberry is & by whom Inhabited now, for I hope I am not at any charges thrre, but that it at least maintains itself and Family ; and I hope thou

hast taken Care to preserve the Goods as much as may be from damage,
an Inventory of wch I shall write to J. Logan for, as being liable to be
Call'd to an Account for it on acct of Debts, & because I am under a
necessity to prove ye Will in Chancery by the opposition my Son Penn
&c. has given me therein.

"I find by reading thy last Letter, again, per W. Watson, that thou
art still on Pen'sberry ; who will be the Inheritor of that Place at last is
yet uncertain, 'till ye Law has settled our Affairs, but ye Goods & Stock
must be valued, to help to pay Debts, of wch my Husband has paid &
engag'd for divers on his Son's Acct ; some of wch I have been oblig'd
to pay, & am call'd on for more, wch I avoid 'till our matters are determined. The young Blacks must be disposed of to prevent their
increasing Charge, I have offer'd my Daughter Aubrey one, but she does
not care for any, I would however have ye likelyest Boy reserv'd, and
bred to reading & sobriety as intending him for my Self, or one of my
Children ; about wch I design to write to J. Logan, for if Sue proves a
good Industrious Servant, & Sober, I would have her ye more tenderly
us'd in ye disposal of her Children. I have wrote more than I intended
& 'till my Head achs, so wth kind Love to thee, & my Cousin Wm &
those of my Loving Neighbours who formerly knew me in your parts, I
close & am

"Thy Loving Cousin, and Friend,

"H. PENN.

"To REBECCA BLACKFAN."

Endorsed "To Rebbecka Blackfan at Pensberry or Elswhere in Pen-
sylvania."

The statement that three of the children are in London
and the two youngest at school confirms the presumption
that the Ruscombe home was broken up in the autumn of
1719. The three in London were, of course, John, Thomas,
and Margaret. Those at school were Richard and Dennis.
Three years later, John, who had then come of age, appears
to have been settled in the country, and there is a letter to
him from Thomas in London. It suggests that Hannah's
and Margaret's home was then with John, but that a lodging
for them was being inquired for. The letter follows :

"LONDON, May 15, 1723.

"DR : BROTHER

"I had James's Letter which came just in the Nick of time to hinder
my purchasing a Natural pacer 5 yrs old and 13 Hands High for about

5 Guineas. Shal be glad to hear the Horse he mentions may please thee. I have herewith sent thee a Gallon of good French Brandy which hope will do ; also [*blank*] of Cloths, the Charge whereof have put down below.[1] My Mother was in the City last night, and is brave and well. Daniel Phillips I suppose has been with her, so that she can inform thee his opinion concerning Tunbridge & Windsor, but there's a Lodging to be let at Winchmorehill, about 1 Mile from Bushill, and Close by the Meetinghouse, which shee may have. W. Picton had it some time Since : 'tis a very pleasant Situation, and large garden, near the New river, and but about 5 miles from Wormly, where you may have fishing enough. If thou likes that side of the Country I think the place will do. I have no more to add but Love to thy Self & Peggy and am

> "Thy aff : Bro.
> "THO PENN.

" I expect to see thee first day."

In March, 1726, a letter to John Penn from one of his correspondents is addressed to him " at Thomas Penn's, in Three Kings Court, Lombard St., London." A year or two later John had established himself in Berkshire, at the place called Feens, already mentioned. It was near Maidenhead and evidently not far from Ruscombe, and letters addressed to John by Thomas and Richard show that he lived there until he came to Pennsylvania in 1734. His brother's letters allude to it as "your house." We get a glimpse of one of his friends at this period, Thomas Bishop Vickris, who had been among Hannah Penn's neighbors at Ruscombe. There are notes from him to John in 1729 ; these allude to his (Vickris's) house as " a cottage " at " Winton." John, it appears, had given him a pointer dog, and in acknowledging the present, Vickris assured the donor that the animal should " have a Liberal Education suited to his Birth !" October 22, 1729, Vickris writes from London to John, " I am eating soope and drinking your health at y George and Vulture w'th your Bro Tom."

[1] The memorandum of the "cloths" is given on the lower corner of the letter. It includes twenty-six yards "Callam," eight yards "Sarsnet," and "four yds Wide." altogether five pounds four pence.

VIII.

William Penn, Junior.

OF the children of William Penn by his marriage to
Gulielma Maria Springett, only two, as we have already seen, married, and one of these, Letitia Aubrey, had no
children. The other was William Penn, Jr., and from him is
derived one of the two existing lines of the Penn family.

William Penn, Jr., was born at Worminghurst, his
mother's estate, March 14, 1680–1, ten days after the grant
of Pennsylvania to his father. Little is known of his childhood and youth. His father's letter to him, before sailing
in the " Welcome," has been given. He was married early.
The Bristol Friends' records show the marriage of William
Penn, Jr., and Mary Jones, daughter of Charles, Jr., and
Martha, at Bristol, on the 12th of Eleventh month (January),
1698–9. He was then not quite eighteen years old. His
wife was four years older. She was born on the 11th of
Eleventh month (January) 1676–7, and was, therefore, just a
day more than twenty-two on her wedding-day.

The marriage certificate is as follows :

[The memoriall or Copy of the Certificate of Willm Penn Junr. &
Mary Jones's Marriage. The Certificate itselfe being made on double
Stampt pchment according to the late Statute.]

Whereas it doth appeare by the memorialls of the men's meeting of the people called Quakers within the Citty of Bristoll that
William Penn, son of Willm. Penn Esq and Mary Jones daughter of
Charles Jones Junr. of the same Citty, merchant, did on the four &
twentieth day of the eighth month last past manifest their intentions
of marriage. AND WHEREAS such their intentions was on the
eighteenth day of the ninth month last published in the publique

meeting house of the said people in the presence of many people there congregated AND FORASMUCH as there appeares no just cause wherefore a marriage between the said William Penn Junr. & Mary Jones should not be consumated we therefore whose names are hereunto subscribed are witnesses that on the day of the date hereof the said Willm. Penn Junr. taking the said Mary Jones by the hand did declare that he did take the said Mary to be his wife, And that the said Mary holding the said Willm. Penn Junr. by the hand did declare that she did take the said Willm. to be her husband, And that also the said Willm. Penn Junr. & Mary holding each other by the hand did mutually promise each to other to live together husband and wife in love and faithfulnes according to God's Holy ordinances as in Holy scriptures declared untill by death they shall be separated AND ALSO the said Willm. and Mary as a further testimony of such their taking each other and of such their promises each to other have hereunto with us sett their hands the Twleveth day of the eleaventh month in the year one thousand six hundred ninety eight.

WILL. PENN JUR.
MARY PENN.

The names of the Witnesses that subscribed with them to the same Certificate are—

Walter Duffield	Charles Jones	Martha Jones
Thomas Penn	Anne Jones	Eliz: Jones
J. Hampton	Margt. Lowther	Anthony Lowther
Isaac Jenings	Letitia Penn	Sarah Roath
Tho. Callowhill	Hannah Penn	Eliz: Harford
Charles Harford	Ch : Jones Jun	Jane Watkins
Richd. Snead	Edw : Hackett	William Penn
Wm. Stafford	J. Dooer	Nathll. Wade
Robt. Bound	Lidia Hacket Junr.	Ffra : Whitchurch
Paul Moore	Margret Lowther Junr.	Wm. Cluterbuck Snr.
Benj: Coole	Eliz: Corshey	Richard Codrington
	Richard Rooth	Wm. Coplin
	Marget. Rooth	Henh. Swymmer
	Jane Trahear	Richd. Taylour. Junr.
	Danll. Pill	John Corshey
	Ffra : Roath	Edw : Jones
	Peter Young	Katherne Bound

[Certified to be an Extract from the Register or Record numbered Society of Friends 116, and entitled a Register of Marriages formerly kept by the Society of Friends at the Monthly Meeting of Bristol.— From the General Register Office, Somerset House, London.]

Charles Jones, Jr., father of Mary Penn, was the son of Charles and Ann Jones, of Redcliffe Street, Bristol, who were among the early Friends in that city. The name of Charles Jones appears in Besse's record of the " Sufferings " of Bristol Friends in 1663 and later. The son, Charles, Jr., was probably born prior to 1654 ; the Friends' records show seven other children born to his parents between that year and 1664. Charles, Jr., married, 1674, Martha Wathers, and she dying First month (March) 8, 1687–8, he married again, 1695, Sarah Corsley, widow. He died, it seems, from William Penn's letters cited below, about January, 1701–2. By his first wife he had several children, including Mary (Penn), who appears to have been the second child.[1]

When William Penn sailed for Pennsylvania, in 1699, he left his son behind. " William [Junior] . . . and . . . his young wife chose to remain in England," Maria Webb says. Their first child, Gulielma Maria, and their second, Springett, were born during the two years of William Penn's absence. In the latter's correspondence with Logan, after his return to England, there are numerous allusions to William, Jr., and his family. Thus :[2]

[Kensington, 4th of Eleventh month (January), 1701–2 :] " My son and family well ; a sweet girl and a Saracen of a boy ; his wife—a good and pretty woman—at Bristol on her father's account, who is dead and buried."

[Kensington, 3d of Twelfth month (February), 1701–2 :] " Son and wife at Bristol upon C. Jones's death. I send a packet to thee that was

[1] John Jones, of Bristol, linen-draper, whose will is dated December 13, 1699, and was proved 1702, appears to have been a son of Charles Jones the elder, above, and a brother of Charles Jones, the father-in-law of William Penn, Jr. He leaves to his " cousin [niece] Mary, married to William Penn, £100."—*Cf.* will, PENNA. MAG., Vol. XVII. p. 74.

[2] The letters to and from James Logan, from which numerous citations follow, are to be found in the " Penn-Logan Correspondence," two volumes, issued by the Historical Society of Pennsylvania. It seems unnecessary to cite volume and page with each extract.

from him. . . . . The three daughters, I think, or son and wife, administer. All amicable among the relatives."

In a letter to Logan, from Worminghurst, August 18, 1702, William Penn, Jr., thanks him for informing him of some "base and scandalous reports" which had come to Logan's ears concerning him, and adds,—

"I hope you will be assured I am far different. . . . . I love my friends, keep company that is not inferior to myself, and never am anything to excess. My dress is all they can complain of, and that but decently genteel, without extravagancy ; and as for the poking-iron I never had courage enough to wear one by my side. You will oblige me if you give this character of me till I make my personal appearance among you, which shall not be long, God willing. . . . ."

[Postscript :]

"My children are, I thank God, both well, and remember to thee. The boy is a jolly fellow, able to make two of his uncle already."

William Penn's letters to Logan contain these passages :

[London, 6th of Fourth month, 1703 :] "My son has another boy, mine and his name."

[Another letter, about the same time as above :] "My son (having life) resolves to be with you per first opportunity. His wife this day week was delivered of a fine boy, as I found when I came home in the evening, and which he has called William, so we are now major, minor, and minimus . . . my grandson Springett a mere Saracen, his sister a beauty."

William Penn, Jr., came to Pennsylvania in company with Lieutenant-Governor John Evans in February, 1703–4. It had been a cherished plan of his father's to send him to the new country, to get him out of undesirable company at home, and to let him acquire the knowledge of a simpler and more moderate way of living. The young man's letter to Logan in August, 1702, already cited, shows that he was expecting to come soon, and the visit had evidently been resolved upon considerably earlier. February 4, 1701–2, W. Penn, Sen., had written to Logan, from Kensington, suggesting how he should manage the young man when he came :

" My son shall hasten ; possess him, go with him to Pennsbury, advise him, contract, and recommend his acquaintance. No rambling to New York, nor mongrel correspondence. He has promised fair ; I know he will regard thee. . . . Be discreet ; he has wit, kept the top company, and must be handled with much love and wisdom ; and urging the weakness or folly of some behaviors, and the necessity of another conduct from interest and reputation, will go far . . . he is conquered that way, pretends much to honor, and is but over-generous by half, and yet sharp enough to get to spend. He cannot well be put on. All this keep to thyself."

In a letter February 24, 1702–3, Penn spoke of his son's departure having been delayed by reports of sickness at Philadelphia, as well as his—the son's—wife's approaching confinement (expected in six weeks). And in another letter whose date is missing, but presumed to be about the same time, Penn writes to Logan,—

" Immediately take him away to Pennsbury, and there give him the true state of things, and weigh down his levities, as well as temper his resentments and inform his understandings, since all depends upon it, as well as for his future happiness, as in measure your poor country's.[1] I propose Governor Hamilton, S. Carpenter, I. Norris, young Shippen, and your easiest and most sensible and civilized for his conversation ; and I hope Col. Markham, and Cousin Ashton, and the Fairmans may come in for a share ; but the first chiefly. Watch him, outwit him, and honestly overreach him for his good ; fishing, little journeys (as to see the Indians), &c., will divert him ; and pray Friends to bear all they can, and melt toward him, at least civilly if not religiously. He will confide in thee. If S. Carpenter, R. Hill, and Is. Norris could gain his confidence, and honest and tender G. Owen not the least likely, (for he feels and sees), I should rejoice. Pennsylvania has cost me dearer in my poor child than all other considerations."[2]

[1] The underlying thought here, no doubt, was that the young man would succeed his father as Proprietor and Governor.

[2] The allusion here is not very plain, unless it means that by his absorption in Pennsylvania's affairs, and perhaps his absence from England, 1699–1701, Penn had neglected a due parental oversight of his son.

Governor Evans and young Penn left England, probably in the early autumn of 1703, and had a long voyage. A letter, dated at London, December 4, 1703, from Penn to Logan, asks him to "tell my poor boy that all his were well the last post . . . per next packet boat to Barbadoes, a month hence, he will hear from his wife." Three days later, "7th 10br," probably also from London, Penn again wrote to Logan,—

" My son's going did not cost me so little as £800, and the land he left destitute of stock at Wormingburst, with the taxes becoming due at his going off, with carpenter's [bills] etc., makes 200 more, and thou mayst imagine how hard it is for me to get it, Ireland so miserably drained and reduced as it is, an account of which I had to-night, at my lodgings from Sir Francis Brewster's own mouth. . . . Let my dear child have my endeared love. The Lord direct his ways for his honor, his father's comfort, and his own peace."

William, Jr., had been living, it is evident from this letter as well as other evidence, at Worminghurst. It is probable that he had removed there at his marriage. During his absence in Pennsylvania his father apparently went there, and may have made the place his home. He says, in a letter, 31st December, a short time after the last cited, " A Scotch plot [and other circumstances] allow me a few days at Worminghurst for my better health and refreshment."

Evans and young Penn reached Philadelphia February 2, 1703-4. A letter from Isaac Norris to Samuel Chew, dated " 12th of 12th month " (February), says, " The Governor and W. Penn, junior, caught us napping ; they arrived late at night, unheard to all the town, and at a time when we were big with the expectation of a Queen's governor." A letter from Logan to Penn, Sen., dated at Philadelphia, Twelfth month (February) 15, contains evidence that the voyage had been unusually long. He says,—

" I leave the account of the tedious voyage. . . . By thy son . . . I received thine of the 27th 6th mo. [August]. . . . . Thy son's

voyage I hope will prove to the satisfaction of all, and to his, and therefore thy happiness. It is his stock of excellent good nature that in a
measure has led him out into his youthful sallies when too easily prevailed
upon. . . . . He is very well received. . . . . 'tis his good fortune
here to be withdrawn from those temptations that have been too
successful over his natural sweetness and yielding temper."

Penn writes to Logan from London, on the 10th of First
month (March), 1703–4,—

"Tell my son I met my wife and his at young S. Tilley's marriage,
near Guilford, and then they were well ; and by two letters since their
return. Guly and Springett are well from their agues, and little Billy
so too and the spark of them all ; and my poor little ones also well, and
great love among the children."

Hannah Penn writes to Logan from Bristol, 5th of Eighth
month (October), 1704,—

"I am very glad our son likes the country [Pennsylvania] so well
and has his health so well there. 'Tis in vain to wish, or it should be,
that he had seen that country sooner (or his father not so soon). . . . .
With this comes a letter from his wife, so that I need say the less of her,
only that herself and the three pretty children are well for aught I
hear." .

Penn writes to Logan from Bristol, on the 2d of November 1704,—

"If my son prove very expensive I cannot bear it, but must place
to his account what he spends above moderation, while I lie loaded with
debt at interest here, else I shall pay dear for the advantage his going
thither might entitle me to, since the subscribers are [or ?] bondsmen
cannot make ready pay, according to what he has received, and on
his land there. So excite his return, or to send for his family to him ;
for if he brings not wherewith to pay his debts here, his creditors will
fall foul upon him most certainly."

The young man's stay in Philadelphia lasted only a few
months ; the reproaches, just or unjust, which attended it
are familiar in our local history of the time. Upon his arrival,
he and James Logan boarded a while at Isaac Norris's, and
then, in June, took William Clark's "great house," newly

built, on Chestnut Street at the southwest corner of Third, where they kept "bachelors' hall" and where later Governor Evans joined them.   Young Penn would not adjust his expenditure to the allowance—apparently very moderate—which Logan was authorized to pay him.   His outlay was, the latter reported to Penn, "much above the limits set me.   The directions given me can by no means satisfy him, nor answer what is thought suitable the presumptive heir of the Province." Logan was a clean and temperate liver ; he had, no doubt, little satisfaction in the direction which young Penn and the Governor were inclined to take,[1] but his performance of his duty in the premises was not remitted.   Like many men of his race, he was a faithful and exact administrator.

Young Penn was made, immediately upon his arrival, a member of the Provincial Council.   The minutes show [2] that at the meeting February 8, 1703-4, "William Penn, Junr., y* Propr's Son, was called to y* Board & took the affirmation of a member of Council."   He was thereafter occasionally present at the meetings, and in the list of those attending his name was placed at the top, next following that of the Lieutenant-Governor.   His last attendance appears to have been September 15, 1704.   He was promptly taken also, as his father had suggested, to Pennsbury, and a meeting with the Indians was held.   Logan says, in a letter dated 14th of First month (March), that the preceding week, Penn, Jr., himself, and Judge Mompesson "went to Pennsbury to meet one hundred Indians, of which nine were kings.   Oppewounumhook, the chief, with his neighbors who came thither to congratulate thy son's arrival, presented nine belts of wampum for a ratification of peace, &c., and had returns [of

[1] Logan writes to Penn, July 14, 1704, "The Governor is at present very ill with the *cholica pictorium*, in no wise owing, I believe, to what is commonly accounted the cause of it, intemperance."   The allusion shows the reputation which Evans had already established.

[2] "Colonial Records," Vol. II. p. 117.

presents] accordingly. He [W. P., Jr.] stayed there with
the judge, waiting Clement Plumstead's wedding with Sarah
Righton, formerly Biddle."[1]   But the social life of Philadelphia was undoubtedly dull, seen from the standpoint of a
young man who had tasted and enjoyed dissipation in England.
The hopeful experiment of reformation through exile was
doomed to failure.   In July, Isaac Norris wrote to Jonathan
Dickinson, "Our young proprietor seems to like the country,
and talks of fetching his family; but by endeavoring to sell
off all of his lands, he must give me leave to think otherwise.
He goes to no other worship [than the Friends'] and sometimes comes to meeting.   He is good-natured, and loves company, but that of Friends is too dull."   Norris was in a position to know of the young man's desire to sell his lands, for
the purchase of the manor of Williamstadt—seven thousand
four hundred and eighty acres, on the Schuylkill—had been
pressed upon him by the young man.   He and William Trent
finally bought the manor, and remembrance of Isaac Norris is
preserved in the name of the borough, Norristown, now a city
in size and population, built upon it, and also in the name,
Norriton, of the township adjoining.[2]

Two months later, Isaac Norris, writing again to Jonathan
Dickinson, reported the occurrence which put a climax upon
the young man's stay in the little Quaker town.   A sharp
conflict between Governor Evans and the Friends was already
established, and Norris says "their attempts to discourage
vice, looseness, and immorality,—which increase,—are baf-
fled by proclamations [from the Governor] making void

[1] This marriage took place March 1, 1703–4.   The bride was the
widow of William Righton and the daughter of William Biddle, of New
Jersey, ancestor of the Philadelphia family of that name.

[2] A letter of Logan's, cited in Watson, Vol. I. p. 34, says, "Last
night William Penn jun'r sold his manor on Schuylkill to William Trent
and Isaac Norris, for £850.   They were unwilling to touch it, for without a great prospect none will now meddle with land, but in his case he
was resolved to sell and leave the country."

their presentations" (from the mayor's court). Then he adds,—

"William Penn, junior, quite gone off from Friends. He, being in company with some extravagants that beat the watch at Enoch Story's, was presented with them : which unmannerly and disrespectful act, as he takes it, gives him great disgust, and seems a waited occasion. He talks of going home in the *Jersey* man-of-war, next month. I wish things had been better, or he had never come."

"Enoch Story's" was a tavern, a drinking-place, with the sign of the Pewter-Platter, in Coombe's Alley,[1] the resort, it would appear, of the "men about town." The story of the occurrence to which Isaac Norris alludes is variously told,[2] but the main facts were that a party were drinking at Story's one evening, and that a dispute arose, and a fracas followed, in which young Penn and others were involved. The watchmen (who were citizens serving on this duty a night at a time) came in, and in their effort to restore order were beaten themselves, and gave some severe blows in return.[3] The

[1] Afterwards Pewter-Platter Alley, opposite Christ Church, running from Second Street to Front.

[2] Watson's "Annals," foot-notes to the "Penn-Logan Correspondence," etc.

[3] Watson says, "Penn called for pistols to pistol them, but the lights being put out, one fell upon young Penn and gave him a severe beating." Deborah Logan (foot-note to "Penn-Logan Correspondence") cites a different tradition that Joseph Wilcox, an alderman—soon after mayor—seized the Governor, Evans, "who was one of the gentlemen's party, and the lights being out, gave him a severe drubbing, redoubling his blows upon him as a slanderer when he disclosed his quality." It is evident that two occurrences have been confused. One was late in August or very early in September, in which young Penn and "the watch" were concerned, and another on the evening of November 1, involving "the watch and some gentlemen," and also "the Mayor, [Griffith Jones] Recorder, and one Alderman." By an examination of the dates and details given in Logan's letter and the minutes in the "Colonial Records" (especially September 15 and November 2), the two affairs will be distinguished. The minutes call that of November "a great fray."

affair was "taken notice of" in the mayor's court (then comparatively young, established under the city charter of 1701), but action was suppressed before the grand jury, according to the statement of Logan in a letter to Penn, Sen., on the 28th of September, Governor Evans exerting himself to prevent any further publicity or prosecution.[1] But, as Isaac Norris said in the letter to Jonathan Dickinson, young Penn was mortally affronted. He had regarded himself evidently as the future ruler of the Colony, the prince imperial, the heir-apparent, and as entitled to indulge his humor in a performance like that at Story's, if he wished. The idea that he was to be treated as other persons was too humiliating to be endured. He accordingly broke with the Quakers at once, ceased to attend their meetings, and attached himself to the company of Lord Cornbury, Governor of New York and New Jersey, who about this time was visiting the Delaware. Logan says in the letter already cited,—

" He is just now returned from Pennsbury, where he entertained the Lord and Lady Cornbury, and what we could not believe before, though for a few days past he has discoursed of it, assures us that he is resolved to go home from York in *Jersey* man-of-war, and within a week at furthest designs to set off from this place."

The young man did so return. He sailed in the " Jersey " (some time in November, probably), and was never again seen at Philadelphia. It had been an unfortunate visit. He had injured not only himself, but his father, and added strength to the partly democratic and just, partly factional and unfair, opposition to the Proprietary interest. Logan wrote regretfully and pathetically in a letter to Penn, from New Castle, on the 8th of December,—

[1] At a meeting of the Council, September 15, young Penn was mentioned as having been proceeded against in the mayor's court. ("Colonial Records," Vol. II. p. 160. *Cf.* foot-note in " Penn-Logan Correspondence," Vol. I. p. 321.)

9

" 'Tis a pity his wife came not with him ; there is scarce any thing has a worse effect upon his mind than the belief thou hast a greater regard to thy second children than thy first, and an emulation between his own and thy younger seems too much to him in it, which, were it obviated by the best methods, might be of service, for he is and must be thy son, and thou either happy or unhappy in him. The tie is indissoluble."

The voyage in the "Jersey" was rough, as was natural for a crossing of the Atlantic in a sailing-ship of 1704, in midwinter. In a long, sad, almost sobbing letter from Penn to Logan, dated at London, on the 16th of January, these passages occur :

" . . . as for Guy no news yet ; but my son, who has come safe, though near foundering in the *Jersey*, says he believes she [Guy's brig] is lost, for after the storm they saw her no more . . . nor didst thou send me word what my son sold his manor for ; but after all he drew a bill for £10 at his arrival, to ride 200 miles home, and which he performed in two days and a night. I met him by appointment between this and Worminghurst ; stayed but three hours together."
[Earlier passage in the letter :] "The Lord uphold me under these sharp and heavy burdens. . . . I should have been glad of an account of his [W. P., Jr.'s] expenses, and more of a rent-roll, that I may know what I have to stand upon, and help myself with. He is my greatest affliction for my soul's and my posterity's or family's sake."

Upon his return to England, young Penn endeavored to begin a public career. His father, in a letter from London (dated at Hyde Park), on the 30th of April, 1705, speaks of his own troubles, and adds, "with my poor son's going into the army or navy, as well as getting into Parliament," etc. A little later, May 10, he says,—

"My son has lost his election, as also the Lord-Keeper's son-in-law, but both hope to recover it by proving bribery upon the two that have it, Lord Windsor and Squire Arsgell. I wish it might turn his face to privacy, and good husbandry, if not nearer to us."

Apparently the nearing of relation did not occur. The young man found his wings too weak for the flights he proposed, and was soon in straits for money, which his father in his own financial stress could not supply. Penn, Jr., wrote to Logan after his return, asking for help :

"You must believe I cannot live here about a court without expenses which my attendance occasions, and I must own to you I was never so pinched in my life, wherefore must beg you to endeavor all you can to send over my effects with all speed you possibly can. . . . I hear the prosecution against me still continues, and that they have outlawed me upon it.[1] I have complained to my father, who tells me he has and will now write about it, and that I shall have right done me in it, which I do expect at your hands, I mean at the Quakers', who are the people that have given me this affront . . . as my honor has been injured, I am resolved to have justice done me, or run all hazards, without consideration to relation, friend, or interest in the country.

"I desire you, if possible, to sell the remainder of my land there, before you send over, and make what returns you can. . . .

" P. S.—Pray put Isaac Norris and William Trent in mind of their promise to send me over a pipe of old Madeira, which I shall take kindly. My father has promised me to write you about my charges there. If there be any extravagant ones, I am to bear them ; but as to that of books, pocket money, and clothes, with the charges of going and returning, he will allow."

The young man apparently resumed his residence at Worminghurst upon returning to England. In a letter to Logan from London, 8th of Fifth month (July), 1707, at the time his own affairs were approaching their worst, Penn, Sen., wrote,—

" . . . Depend upon it, if God favors me and my son with life, one, if not both will come as soon as possible. Worminghurst he has at last resigned for sale ; so that having conquered himself and his wife too, who has cost me more money than she brought by her unreasonable, and for that reason imprudent obstinacy for dwelling there, to which she could have no pretence, either by family or portion, but by being my son's impetuous inclination ; and I wish she had brought more wisdom, since she brought so little money, to help the family. Worminghurst, with some land to be sold in Ireland, about £45 per annum, will lighten his load as well as mine ; for his marriage, and my

[1] This was probably not the case.

daughter's [Letitia's] too, have not helped me,—his to be sure, more
especially. We are entering, or it seems likely we should, into nearer
friendship than before, he knowing the world and duty to a father
better ; for he has been of no use, but much grief and expense to me
many ways and years too, losing him before I found him, being not of
that service and benefit to me that some sons are, and 'tis well known
I was to my father before I married. But oh, if yet he will recommend
himself, and show himself a good child and a true Friend, I shall be
pleased, and leave the world with less concern for him and the rest
also."

Isaac Norris, then in England, aiding in the settlement of
Penn's affairs, and judiciously explaining to people there the
nature of the controversies in Pennsylvania, in a letter to
" his relations," on November 4 (1707), said, " Worminghurst, that has been these many years a charge, and little
profit, is sold well, and many debts are paid off by bills on
Pennsylvania.[1] Some Friends have been industrious in this,
that if that of Ford's should go against him, his and his
friends' reputations may stand the clearer, having nothing but
that unreasonable debt against him."

And four days later, writing to Logan, Norris adds,—

" Worminghurst is sold well, and thou wilt see bills to a considerable value. I have been persuaded to negotiate one, I think the largest,
viz. : William Buckfield's for £608. I have sent it to brother [Samuel]
Preston for acceptance. I understand he [Buckfield] has been an old
servant and friend of the Governor, and the debt has been ready money
lent, and to do it [lend to Penn] has dipt into a little estate of his own
  . . . several of the Governor's friends, tho' they would have all done
honorably, yet seem to be more particularly in care for him than others
[creditors]. I request thee, therefore, to put good bonds into hand."

After his father's apoplectic seizure, in 1712, William Penn,
Jr., seems to have left his family very much—but probably

[1] Hepworth Dixon, in his Life of Penn, says (p. 321), " He sold the
Worminghurst estate to a 'Squire Butler for £6,050, just £1,550 more
than he gave for it, after having cut down £2,000 worth of timber.
This money satisfied some of his creditors, but not all ; and one of
them, a man named Churchill, was so importunate as to try to stop
Butler's payment of the purchase-money."

not altogether—to the care of Hannah Penn. The cash-book kept at Ruscombe, as has been mentioned, contains three pages of items of money advanced on their account by Hannah Penn between September, 1712, and October, 1717, the whole amount being about three hundred pounds. In Twelfth month, 1712, ten pounds was "paid Thos. Overton for their house-rent." In 1713 there are payments "for fitting the children," "expence at the Children's going to school," eight pounds "paid Alice Hays for Daughter's and Guli's board," cash "paid Gill. Thomson for Springett and Billie's board," cash paid for "Daughter's and Guly's board to December," etc., and cash to William Penn, Jr., to pay "his note due to Cousin Rooth," twenty-five pounds. Payments for board for "Daughter" and for the children continue each year down to 1717. The last entry of the account is cash paid "S. Arnold for Guly's last half year's board & necessaries at Richard Wildman's."

The will which William Penn the Founder made in 1701, at New Castle, Delaware, as he was about sailing on his return to England, and which was left behind in the care of James Logan, bestowed the Proprietorship and Governorship on William Penn., Jr.,[1] after some bequests to Letitia Aubrey, John Penn, and the expected child, Thomas. The provisions of this will were, of course, in the father's mind during the period of the son's visit to Pennsylvania, and later, and until the will of 1712 was definitely made,—the sale of the Province to the Crown not being completed,—the young man stood in succession as Proprietary and Governor. When his father died, no doubt William, Jr., was disappointed and chagrined, if not altogether surprised, to find that he was left simply the estates which had been inherited by or settled on him from his mother and his grandfather, the Admiral. This was the provision made for him in the will of 1712. This

---

[1] See the will in full in "Memoirs of the Historical Society of Pennsylvania," Vol. I. p. 222.

will has been several times printed,[1] but is worth giving here
as part of the record on which the present narrative chiefly
rests :

"I WILLIAM PENN Esqr so called Cheife proprietor & Governour
of the Province of Pensilvania and the Territoryes thereunto belonging,
being of sound mind and understanding, for which I bless God, doe
make and declare this my last Will and Testament.

"My Eldest Son being well provided for by a Settlement of his
Mothers and my ffathers Estate I give and devise the Rest of my
Estate in manner following

"The Government of my Province of Pennsilvania and Territories
thereunto belonging and all powers relateing thereunto I give and devise
to the most Hono'ble the Earle of Oxford and Earl Mortimer, and to
William Earle Powlett, so called, and their Heires, upon Trust to dispose thereof to the Queen or any other person to the best advantage
they can to be applyed in such a manner as I shall herein after direct.

"I give and devise to my dear Wife Hannah Penn and her ffather
Thomas Callowhill and to my good ffriends Margarett Lowther my dear
Sister, and to Gilbert Heathcote Physitian, Samuel Waldenfield, John
ffield, Henry Gouldney, all liveing in England, and to my friends
Samuel Carpenter, Richard Hill, Isaac Norris, Samuel Preston and
James Logan, liveing in or near Pensilvania and their heires All my
lands Tenements and Hereditamts whatsoever rents and other profitts
scituate lyeing and being in Pennsilvania and the Territores thereunto
belonging, or else where in America, upon Trust that they shall sell and
dispose of so much thereof as shall be sufficient to pay all my just debts,
and from and after paymt thereof shall convey unto each of the three
Children of my son Willm Penn, Gulielma-Maria, Springett, and
William respectively and to their respective heires 10,000 acres of land
in some proper and beneficiall places to be sett out by my Trustees
aforesaid. All the rest of my lands and Hereditamts whatsoever,
scituate lyeing and being in America, I will that my said Trustees shall
convey to and amongst Children which I have by my present Wife, in
such proporcon and for such estates as my said Wife shall think fit but
before such Conveyance shall be made to my Children I will that my
said Trustees shall convey to my daughter Aubrey whom I omitted to
name before 10,000 acres of my said Lands in such places as my said
Trustees shall think fitt.

[1] "Memoirs of the Historical Society of Pennsylvania," Vol. I. p.
219; PENNA. MAG., Vol. XIV. p. 174, etc.

"All my p'sonall estate in Pennsilvania and elsewhere and arreares of rent due there I give to my said dear Wife, whom I make my sole Executrix for the equall benefitt of her and her Children.

"In Testimony whereof I have sett my hand and seal to this my Will, which I declare to be my last Will, revoking all others formerly made by me.

"Signed Sealed and Published by the Testator William Penn in the presence of us who sett our names as Witnesses thereof in the p'sence of the said Testator after the Interlineacon of the Words above Vizt whom I make my sole Executrix.

[Signed] "WILLIAM PENN.

[Witnesses]
    "Sarah West
    "Robert West
    "Susanna Reading
    "Thomas Pyle
    "Robert Lomax

"This Will I made when ill of a feavour at London with a Clear understanding of what I did then, but because of some unworthy Expressions belying Gods goodness to me as if I knew not what I did, doe now that I am recovered through Gods goodness hereby declare that it is my last Will and Testament at Ruscomb, in Berkshire, this 27th of the 3d Month, called May, 1712.

"WM PENN

"Witnesses p'sent
    "Eliz Penn   Mary Chandler
    "Tho : Pyle   Josiah Dee
    "Tho : Penn   Mary Dee
    "Eliz : Anderson
"Postscript in my own hand

"As a further Testimony of my love to my dear Wife I of my own mind give unto her out of the rents of America vizt Pensilvania £300 a year for her naturall life and for her care and charge over my Children in their Education of which she knows my mind as also that I desire they may settle at least in good part in America where I leave them so good an Interest to be for their Inheritance from Generacon to Generacon which the Lord p'serve and prosper. Amen."

The will, when a copy was sent to Pennsylvania, did not altogether please James Logan. He wrote to Hannah Penn,[1] on the 4th of November, 1718:

[1] MS. letter in Historical Society of Pennsylvania collections.

"The sloop *Dolphin* arrived from London, bringing us divers letters, and among y⁰ rest one from Jn⁰ Page to me with a copy of our late Proprietor's will wch gives me some uneasiness as being Drawn in hast I believe by himself only, when such a settlement required a hand better acquainted with affairs of that Nature.

"The Estate in these parts is vested in so many without impowering any P'ticular or a suitable number to grant and Convey, that I fear we shall be puzzled. I hope you will take advice there what methods must be pursued in y⁰ Case. In the meantime all the Province & Lower County's are in the Trustees, till y⁰ Mortgage is Cleared, toward w'ch if our remittance by this ship come safe I hope another Large tally will be struck by them."

To this the extended letter of Simon Clement, of Bristol, the uncle of Hannah Penn, dated at London, March 6, 1718–19, addressed to Logan, replies.[1]   Among other things, Clement says,—

"The Proprietor's will may indeed be said to have been made in haste, as you guess: but it was dictated by his friend Mr. West, though the blunders committed therein could not have been expected from a man of his accuracy. The truth is that he himself had labored under a paraletick affection, from which he never recovered the use of his limbs one side, nor I believe at that time the strength of his capacity, though it was afterwards perfectly restored, and continued to the time of his death, about six months since."[2]

Clement says further in this letter that he has no fear that Penn's choice of trustees will prejudice the standing of his affairs with those now in power,—Harley, Earl of Oxford, not being in 1718 the popular man he was in 1712.[3]   "You

[1] "Memoirs of the Historical Society of Pennsylvania," Vol. I. p. 233.

[2] The meaning here is not very plain. Clement could hardly have imagined that Logan did not know fully about the physical condition of Penn, between 1712 and 1718, and he surely did not mean to say that his mental "capacity" was ever "perfectly restored" after the stroke of August, 1712.

[3] Robert Harley, minister under Queen Anne, was "at the height of his power" in 1711, when he was appointed Lord High Treasurer, and created Earl of Oxford and Earl of Mortimer. He was dismissed from

know," he says, "at that time they were the fittest that could be thought on ; and though they are since grown a little out of fashion, the using their names on this occasion can give no offence to those now in play. Great men lay no stress on such little things. I prepared a draught of a commission for those lords to confirm your Governor, [Keith] by the authority devolved upon them, which I left several weeks since with Lord Oxford, to peruse and communicate with Lord Powlet, but I can't yet get him to dispatch it. And you know we cannot be as pressing on men of their degree as we might on men of our own rank, but I shall continue my solicitation in it as I find opportunity."

William Penn, Jr., at first signified his disposition to acquiesce in the will's provisions, and to join his step-mother in carrying them out. Later he changed his mind. The will was admitted to probate in the Prerogative Court of Canterbury, "in common form," on the 4th of November, 1718, after some delay by William Penn, Jr.[1] He had several meetings with Hannah Penn, in London, and Clement says in the letter already cited, they "mutually declared themselves desirous to cultivate the former friendship in the family, and to submit all their differences to be decided by a decree in the Court of Chancery, to be obtained with as

office in 1714, impeached 1715, and sent to the Tower, and in 1717, after being brought to trial (at his own demand), discharged.   This summary indicates the ground of Logan's concern, to which Clement was replying.   It may be added that some writers on Penn's will have been confused by Harley's title, supposing that "Earl of Oxford and Earl Mortimer" must mean two persons, and that there were thus *three* trustees.

[1] Letter from Simon Clement to Logan, London, December 30, 1718. "I am very glad . . . that the country can receive no prejudice for want of renewing the present Governor's [Keith's] commission, which has been delayed principally by reason of Mr. Penn's first obstructing the proving his father's will in the Prerogative Court, which, however, he has since consented to, and 'tis done." ("Memoirs of the Historical Society of Pennsylvania," Vol. I. p. 231.)

little expense and contest as possible, and I believe they will
take that way at last, though the young gentleman seems
fickle and inconstant, and has been ready to fly out once or
twice since, and is gone again to France without putting in
his answer to the bill for proving the will, which must therefore be at a stand until his return, which he pretends shall
be in this or the next month.   His agents talk as if he believes the will has not sufficiently conveyed the power of
government from him, and that he will send over a governor.
But I should think he has more discretion than to offer it in
earnest, or that he would not find anybody fool enough to
go on such an errand; at least I am confident that your
governor will never yield up his authentick authority to any
person who should come up with a sham one."

Clement was evidently unaware, as he wrote this, that
William Penn, Jr., had already made a definite claim upon
the Governorship and Proprietorship of Pennsylvania, and
had sent out, several weeks before, a new commission in his
own name to Lieutenant-Governor Keith, accompanied by
a letter of "instructions."   The letter was dated January 14,
1718–19, and directed Keith "immediately to call together
the Council, and with them, in the most public manner,
make known my accession to the government of the said
Province and Counties [upon Delaware] and assure the
country of my great affection for them," etc.   At the meeting of the Provincial Council, April 28, 1719, Keith laid the
documents before the Council, and proposed that the Assembly be immediately (May 6) called together, "in order
to join with me and this Board in recognizing Mr. Penn's
right and title to the Government,"—to which the Council
assented, "every member present" agreeing that the Assembly should be summoned.

The Assembly, however, on the 9th of May, declined to
approve the claim of Penn, Jr., to succeed his father.   They
pointed out the provisions of the will on the subject of the

Proprietary rights. They called Keith's attention to a law passed by them, and confirmed by Queen Anne, providing that the Governor in office at the death of the Proprietary should continue until further order from the Crown, or from the heirs of the Proprietor. And they further emphasized the facts that the will devised the Proprietorship to the two earls, and that the new commission had not the royal approval. Under these circumstances they advised the Lieutenant-Governor *not* to publish the new commission or the accompanying instructions.[1]

The Council met two days later, on the 11th, and after discussion, decided by "a majority above two to one" that the Assembly's advice was good. Later, advices were received from London that the Board of Trade and Plantations recognized the validity of Keith's first commission, and regarded that from Penn, Jr., as invalid. It resulted, therefore, that the claim of the Proprietorship and Governorship by the son came to nothing, and apparently was not pressed beyond the one point of sending out the commission and letter to Keith.[2]

[1] The Council's minutes say that "by means of other letters or accounts since received by Capt. Annis, the Assembly have fallen into sentiments different from what had been expected."

[2] In the Council, upon the question of concurring in the judgment of the Assembly, there were present Richard Hill, Jasper Yeates, William Trent, Isaac Norris, Jonathan Dickinson, Samuel Preston, Anthony Palmer, Robert Assheton, John French, and James Logan. A "majority above two to one," ten members voting, would reasonably be seven to three. Of the latter three, as it appeared by proceedings at a subsequent meeting of the Council, Assheton was one. (He was the son of William Assheton, of Lancashire, whose wife was a relative in some degree of William Penn the Founder. Robert Assheton is commonly spoken of in Penn's letters as "Cousin Assheton.") At the Council meeting, November 7, 1719, Lieutenant-Governor Keith charged Assheton, in writing, with divulging the proceedings of the Board, and with writing "the latter end of August or beginning of September last," to William Penn, Jr., assuring him of his friendship,

William Penn, Jr., died about two years after his father. The time and place of his death are variously given. John Jay Smith, in his address before the Historical Society of Pennsylvania,[1] says he "died in France;" Janney says he "died in France of a consumption;" Maria Webb says he "died in the north of France, in 1720, of consumption." Upon the authority of a genealogical sketch in Lipscombe's "History of Buckinghamshire," cited for me by Rev. W. H. Summers,[2] it may be said that he died at Liége, Belgium, June 23, 1720. His wife, Mary Penn, died early in December, 1733. Rebekah Butterfield's journal, kept at Jordans,[3] contains the following entry:

"5th of 10th month, [December] 1733, Robert Jordan and John Gopsill was at y⁰ burial of Mary Pen, widow, mother of y⁰ aforesaid William Pen [3d]; they came and went with y⁰ relations."

Three children of William Penn, Jr., and Mary Penn are known. These were Gulielma Maria, Springett, and William, 3d. The dates of their births are given in the Friends' records (at London) for Surrey and Sussex. Information concerning them may be concisely stated as follows:

and attacking him (Keith) for not publishing the new commission, etc. Keith professed to give the substance of the letter from Assheton to Penn, *inter alia* that he (Assheton) "was Mr. Penn's stiff friend, and had stickl'd for him, tho' to no effect hitherto, because he had only one member of the Council to join him; that though the bearer [of the letter] was a stranger to Mr. Penn, yet being heartily recommended to his favor by these letters he might freely take an opportunity over a bottle to assure Mr. Penn that these things were unquestionably true." It resulted that Assheton, upon Keith's demand, left the Council, though later, 1722, he again became a member.

[1] "Penn-Logan Correspondence," Vol. I. p. xv.

[2] MS. letter, March 25, 1897.

[3] Cited in Mr. Summers's "Memories of Jordans and the Chalfonts," p. 242.

1. *Gulielma Maria Penn*, born Ninth month (November) 10, 1699, at Worminghurst; the "beauty" and "sweet girl" of her grandfather's letters. She married, "early in life," Awbrey Thomas. He was the son of Rees and Martha Thomas, who came from Wales to Pennsylvania and settled in Merion in 1691. Martha, his mother, was an Awbrey, the sister of William Awbrey (or Aubrey), who married Letitia Penn.[1] Awbrey Thomas was born Eleventh month (January) 30, 1694. He "visited England," and there married Gulielma Maria Penn (as above). "He did not long survive his marriage, and died . . . probably in England." He left one son, William Penn Thomas, who died unmarried about 1742. His widow married, second, Charles Fell, who was the son of Charles, son of George, son of Judge Thomas Fell, of Swarthmore Hall.[2] By her marriage with Charles Fell, Gulielma Maria (Penn) Thomas had a son, Robert Edward Fell, "who in the year 1756 was promoted to a captaincy of marines. Afterwards he became a lieutenant-colonel in the army, under which title he lodged a pedigree in the Herald's Office, and procured a confirmation of arms in the year 1770; he was then described as Robert Edward Fell of St. Martin's in the Fields, Middlesex. His will . . . was proved the 28th of February, 1787, by Thomas Brookholding, his sole executor, and the husband of his niece Philadelphia. There is no evidence of his having been a married man; but in his will he leaves his sword and pistols to his nephew, William Hawkins Newcombe."[3] There are several letters from him in the col-

[1] She was his second wife. *Cf.* article by George Vaux, PENNA. MAG., Vol. XIII. p. 294.

[2] Watson, "Annals," Vol. I. p. 121, quotes from the *London Gazette*, year 1724, a paragraph that "Mrs. Gulielma Maria Fell, granddaughter of the famous Quaker, Sir William Penn, was publicly baptized in the parish church of St. Paul, Convent Garden, in October last."

[3] Maria Webb, "The Fells of Swarthmore Hall," p. 356.

lections of the Pennsylvania Historical Society, addressed
to Thomas Penn. In July, 1770, he was an officer of Lord
Loudoun's regiment, and stationed at Limerick, Ireland.
He acknowledges the favor of Thomas Penn having paid
money for him "to Mr. Barclay" (probably John Barclay,
of Dublin), and "having been obliged to make new Regi-
mentals for the Review," he has drawn for ten pounds
more of money coming from his mother's estate,—showing that his mother, Gulielma Maria Fell, was then dead,
and indicating that Thomas Penn was the executor of her
estate.

There were two other children of Charles and Gulielma
Maria Fell, (1) Mary Margaretta, who married John Barron,
and (2) Gulielma Maria Frances, who married John Newcomb. May 26, 1750, M. M. Barron writes to Thomas Penn,
from Leeds, a cordial family letter, in which she alludes to
her husband.[1] August 24, 1750, J. Newcomb writes from
Frowlesworth to Thomas Penn. He and his wife have been
boarding, but find it "very disagreeable," and propose
housekeeping at Michaelmas. He asks for money. He
speaks of "our little girl," who is at present at Hackney.
Another letter from the same to the same, October 22,
1750, announces the birth of "a fine little boy," to "my
dear little woman," the previous day, and that "by her
particular Desire" he has been named Thomas Penn Newcomb.[2]

It seems to be commonly assumed that this line of William Penn the Founder, through his granddaughter, Gulielma Maria Penn, and Charles Fell, is now extinct.

[1] MS. Letter, Historical Society of Pennsylvania.

[2] Ibid. John Newcomb was a clergyman of the Established Church,
and at this time vicar of Leire, near Lutterworth, in Leicestershire. He
had found the vicarage in very bad order, when he was inducted, and
so went to stay with the vicar at Frowlesworth. (Information from
Mary Radley, Warwick, 1899.)

2. *Springett Penn*, born Twelfth month (February) 10, 1700–1, at Worminghurst. He was the "Saracen" of his grandfather's letters. He did not marry. It is probable that he spent much of his time in Ireland. There are a few letters from or relating to him in the collections of the Pennsylvania Historical Society. One from John Penn to him, dated London, August 3, 1727, on a business topic, is freezingly severe in tone. Springett, however, was evidently not one to permit lectures from his half-uncle—a man of very nearly his own age—to disturb his equanimity. There is a letter from him to John some time later; it is dated "Stoke, March 13, 1728–9," and begins "Dear Jack;" it ends thus:

" Perhaps Alderman Tom knows more of y° matter than either of us, for it seems he was pleased to receive y° Gentleman's Request very favorably, turned his Quidd w'ʰ great Gravity, & gave an assenting nodd. Now if you have fed y° poor Gentleman with hopes and at y° same time cautioned me, y° Devil take you & his Worship y° Ald'n; if otherwise, be free in communicating yo' thoughts to my Bro Will, & he'll save you y° trouble of writing them to

" Yo'r aff Nephew & hum Servt :
"SPRINGETT PENN."

Springett Penn joined with Hannah Penn (his step-grandmother), in 1725, in appointing Patrick Gordon Lieutenant-Governor of Pennsylvania. The chancery suit over the Founder's will was not then settled. At the meeting of the Council, at Philadelphia, June 22, 1726, the commission of Major Gordon "from Springett Penn, Esquire, with the assent of Mrs. Hannah Penn, and his Majesty's royal approbation thereof," was produced and read, and "was forthwith published at the court-house." Springett Penn died in Dublin, Ireland, 8th February, 1731.[1]

[1] This date is given in the article on the Penn Family in Appleton's "American Biography." In the Breviate in the Boundary Case (p. 444) it is stated as occurring December 30, 1730.

3. *William Penn, 3d.* He was born, as appears by the Friends' records, at Worminghurst, First month (March) 21, 1703, and made then the "minimus" of the three Williams. He was twice married, and through his first wife descends the Penn-Gaskell branch of the Founder's family. This line will be more fully spoken of in a later chapter.

IX.

Thomas Penn.

THREE children of William Penn and Hannah Callowhill,
as we have seen, were married,—Thomas, Margaret,
and Richard. Of Margaret (Freame) we have already spoken.[1]
It remains, in this branch of the Founder's family, to speak
of Thomas and Richard and their descendants. We therefore take up Thomas' and his line.

At the death of his father, Thomas was in his seventeenth
year,—an apprentice, as we have seen, with Michael Russell,
in London. Apparently he resided in the city from that
time until he came to Pennsylvania in 1732. Here he stayed
nine years, and in 1741 returned to England. In 1751 he
was married; in 1775 he died. About 1728 he appears to
have been engaged in business of some sort in London, and
to have had a partner. He writes to his brother John, April
26 of that year, and signs the letter "Thomas Penn and
Company;" in it he speaks of "my business on partnership,
of which I some time since acquainted thee."[2]

It is as the principal Proprietor of Pennsylvania for nearly
thirty years that Thomas Penn has distinction. His influential
connection with the Province was second only to that of his
father.

The will of the Founder remained in dispute for nine
years, 1718 to 1727. A summary of the several steps in the
case is given in the "Breviate in the Boundary Dispute,"[3]
and the subsequent arrangements concerning the Proprietary

[1] Some further details concerning her may be given later.
[2] MS. letter in Historical Society of Pennsylvania collections.
[3] "Pennsylvania Archives," 2d series, Vol. XVI.

estate are outlined in an article by the late Eli K. Price, in the
American Law Register for August, 1871. Probate of the
Founder's will was granted at Doctors' Commons, November
14–18, 1718. Hannah Penn then executed a "Deed Poll of
Appointment," upon her powers under the will, by which she
assigned half of Pennsylvania and the Delaware counties to
her son John, and divided the other half between Thomas,
Richard, and Dennis. In October, 1721, a suit was begun
by Hannah Penn, in the Court of Exchequer, in her own
right and for her five children (who were then all minors), to
establish the will and her and the children's rights under it
against all the other parties in interest,—the two earls to
whom the powers of government were devised; Springett
Penn, as heir-at-law of William Penn, Jr.; the surviving
trustees in Pennsylvania, named in Penn's will; and the
younger children of William Penn, Jr.[1] This suit in the Exchequer Court, after many delays, during which Dennis Penn,
Henry Gouldney (one of the mortgagees), the Earl of Oxford,
and Hannah Penn all died, was decided favorably to the will
July 4, 1727. The "family deed sextipartite," to which an
allusion has been made, was then framed, by which it was
agreed that John Penn should have half the Pennsylvania and
Delaware property, Thomas one-fourth, and Richard one-
fourth, and that John's share should be charged with certain
money payments to Margaret (Freame). In 1729–30, January 13 and 14, "Indentures of Lease and Release" were executed by the two surviving trustees of the old Ford mortgage,
Joshua Gee and John Woods, to the three brothers, in the
shares agreed on, half to John, a quarter to Thomas, and the
other quarter to John and Thomas, as trustees for Richard.
June 24, 1735, Samuel Preston and James Logan, surviving
trustees in Pennsylvania under the will, released the estates
on their part. The will of the Founder was thus established,

[1] The reference to Gulielma Maria, his daughter, in this suit, shows
that she was then the wife of Aubrey Thomas.

and the enjoyment of the Proprietary rights lodged in the possession of the three surviving sons of his second wife.

There had been some question in the minds of the young Proprietaries what use to make of their inheritance. Prior to Springett Penn's death, in 1730 (? 1731), a negotiation with him had been on foot to sell to him and his brother William a life-right in the Proprietorship, and there was another negotiation for the purchase by John, Thomas, and Richard of all Springett's claims. After his death the claims of William Penn, 3d, were extinguished by the payment to him of five thousand five hundred pounds.[1]

Thomas Penn's residence in Philadelphia covered nine years,—the later period of Governor Gordon's administration, and his death; the interval, 1736–38, in which James Logan was acting Governor; and the first three years of Governor Thomas's perturbed administration. During these nine years the State-House, now Independence Hall, was built and Christ Church was given its present dimensions, the " Indian Walk " took place, and the great Indian Council of 1736 was held in the Friends' meeting-house at Second and Market Streets. This was the period when the " Palatine " German immigration was at full height, and the Scotch-Irish were also coming freely.

Leaving England in the summer of 1732, Thomas Penn reached the Delaware in August, and landed at Chester on the 11th of that month. An express rode with a letter from him to Governor Gordon, at Philadelphia, and that official hastened to receive him with due honor. The Governor, "and all the members of the Council who were able to travel, accompanied with a very large number of gentlemen," set out next day for Chester, waited on him, and paid

---

[1] This sum was secured to him by a mortgage, and on this he borrowed two thousand five hundred pounds of Alexander Forbes, his father-in-law. The mortgage was finally extinguished by the three Proprietaries, January 29, 1740–41.

him their compliments in due form. That he was embarrassed by the ceremonial, as the story attributed to Keimer the printer, cited in Watson, avers, is not very probable; he does not appear to have been a person unequal to the demands of the station he occupied, whether it might be that of mercer's apprentice or something higher. The company dined at Chester, then set out for Philadelphia, and near the city the mayor, recorder, and aldermen, "with a great body of people," met the party and extended the civic welcome. There was general anxiety to see the visitor, for since the brief stay of William, Jr., twenty-eight years before, and his angry departure, there had been none of the family of the Founder seen here. There were crowds in the streets as the cavalcade entered, and women and children gathered on the balconies and door-stoops to see the new arrival,—"a son of William Penn!" That they found a personable man we may infer from the portraits of him.

The stories which were told afterwards of Thomas Penn, the outcome of his stay here, are preserved by the omnivorous Watson, and may be read in his "Annals." They represent his manners as cold. This may have been. I presume him to have been a self-contained and somewhat formal man, with little disposition to what in a later day has been called " gush." The democratic colonists doubtless tried him by the tradition, then still fresh among them, of his father's gracious and graceful manner, and they are said to have found his brother John, when he came two years later, a more affable person. We may take from Watson the story of that worthy Welshman, descendant of the bards of Cambria, the Reverend Hugh David, who visited Thomas Penn to read him a congratulatory poem recalling the honorable connection of the Penns with the royal house of Tudor, and who retired from the presence much disappointed. Relating his experience afterwards to Jonathan Jones, of Merion, Hugh said with great disgust, " He spoke to me but three sentences : ' How dost thou do ? '

' Farewell l ' ' The other door l ' "   It is past denial that such
brevity of speech and lack of poetic appreciation must figure
poorly in the Welsh chronicle.

Thomas Penn addressed himself with energy to the Proprietary affairs.   The situation had greatly changed since the
days of continuous outlay and no income in the first years of
the settlement, and of perpetual struggle to balance income
and outgo in the period when the Founder broke down.
There was now a large revenue from the sale of lands and
quit-rents, and the expense of the government could be sustained by the increasing numbers of the people.

In September, 1734, John Penn arrived at Philadelphia
with his sister Margaret—the " Pegg " of the Ruscombe
family life—and her husband Thomas Freame,[1] and now all
the children of Hannah Callowhill but Richard—for Dennis
had died in 1722—were gathered at Philadelphia.

The *Pennsylvania Gazette* for September 26, 1734, says,—

"An Express from New Castle having late last Thursday night
brought the agreeable News that the Honourable John Penn, Esq., the
eldest of our Proprietors, with his Brother-in-law, Mr. Freame, his Lady
and Family, were on board a ship from London standing up this River
[Thomas Penn and others hastened early next morning to Chester and]
Mr. Penn, Mr. Freame and his Lady came on shore about 4 in the
afternoon."

John Penn returned to London in a year, to carry on the
controversy with Lord Baltimore over the Maryland boundary,
but Thomas and the Freames remained at Philadelphia,
and Thomas established himself there in a residence between Bush Hill and the Schuylkill, with grounds esteemed
handsome in that day, and long known as the " Proprietor's
Garden."   A young Virginian, Daniel Fisher, who had come

[1] Thomas Freame had come over earlier, probably in 1732, and had
returned to England.   With some persuasion his wife now accompanied
him to Pennsylvania.   She finally returned to England in 1741 with
her brother Thomas.

to Philadelphia to seek his fortune, and who walked late in the afternoon of the first day of the week, in May, 1755, "two miles out of town," found the garden, though somewhat neglected, more attractive, he thought, than that of ex-Governor James Hamilton at Bush Hill. It was, he says, "laid out with more judgment." The house, of brick, was "but small," with a kitchen, etc., "justly contrived for a small rather than a numerous family,"—a bachelor's establishment, plainly. "It is pleasingly situated," says the writer, "on an eminence, with a gradual descent, over a small valley, to a handsome, level road, out through a wood, affording an agreeable vista of near two miles." The greenhouse, at that season empty, its plants and flowers disposed in the pleasure-garden, "surpassed everything of its kind" Daniel Fisher had seen in America, and he looked with pleasure on "a good many orange, lemon, and citron trees, in great perfection, loaded with abundance of fruit, and some of each sort seemingly ripe." There was also a neat little deer park, but he was told that no deer were then kept in it.

At the time of Daniel Fisher's visit to the Proprietor's Garden, Thomas Penn had been absent from Philadelphia fourteen years. He returned to England in 1741. He had taken a somewhat active part in the affairs of the Province, especially in the treaties and conferences with the Indians, and had been occasionally present at the meetings of the Governor's Council. The Council's minutes record him as present March 26, 1741, and at a meeting October 14, that year, several Cayuga chiefs being present, Governor Thomas told them that "Mr. Penn had hoped to have seen the Chief of their Nations here this summer, but being disappointed, and being obliged to go for England, he had left the Governor in his place."

The *Pennsylvania Gazette*, August 20, 1741, has this paragraph :

" This day the Honourable Thomas Penn, Esq., one of the Proprietors of this Province, attended by a Great Number of the Principal Inhabitants of this City, set out for New York, in order to embark on board his Majesty's Ship Squirrel, Capt. *Peter Warren* Commander, for *Great Britain.*"

Apparently he did not sail from New York, however, but from a port in New England, and his ship did not get away until October. The following letter to Richard Hockley,[1] who was about to sail from England for Pennsylvania, to act as agent for Thomas Penn, gives the time and circumstances of his arrival in England :

" DEAR DICKEY :

" As we have been in pain for you, hearing Privateers were off our Capes, and should have great pleasure in hearing you were safe, I conclude it has fared so with you, and that you will be glad to hear my Sister [Margaret Freame], with her children and myself are arrived, in perfect health, as wee have been ever since our departure, which was this day five weeks from New England ; wee expected after seeing the mast ship in the morning to have proceeded to Portsmouth, but the wind blowing hard at South our Captain judged propper to put in here, where it blows hard, but as soon as the wind is fair wee propose to sail for Portsmouth, from where I shall be very glad to see you. Enclosed is a letter from my Brother which put in the Post if he is not in Town, and desire Joseph Freame to get the enclosed bill for £1000 accepted and take his receipt for it. Wee all affectionately salute you, and I am

" Your Very Sincere Friend,

" THO : PENN.

" PLYMOUTH HARBOR, NOV 2ed, 1741."

The death of John Penn, in 1746, left Thomas Penn the holder of three-fourths of the Proprietary and family land in Pennsylvania and Delaware. One-fourth had come to him in fee, as we have seen, and two-fourths had been left him in life-right by John. He thus became, prospectively if not already, a rich man. Thenceforward for almost thirty years, to his death in 1775, he was the chief of the Penn family and a figure of the first importance in the public affairs of Penn-

[1] Penn MSS., Historical Society of Pennsylvania.

sylvania. Throughout the period following his return to
England he was continually in correspondence with the
Lieutenant-Governors and other officials, and with his legal
and business representatives in Pennsylvania, and the mass of
letters from and to him, in the collections now owned by the
Historical Society of Pennsylvania, is so extensive that it has
been fully examined by but few persons.

Thomas Penn's letters bear the mark of an energetic,
prudent, and capable man. His and the other Proprietary
correspondence, Mr. W. R. Shepherd says,[1] after a fuller and
more careful inspection than almost any one else has given, is
creditable to the writers. "Our real cause for surprise," he
thinks, "should be that in their voluminous correspondence
with their officers in the Province, so few harsh and unkindly
expressions appear."

The change in Thomas's financial condition made by the
inheritance of John's half of the property was important.
Down to that time, according to his own statement, in a letter
of October 9, 1749, to Richard Peters,[2] he had spent, year
by year, almost the whole of his income. "People imagine,
because we are at the head of a large province," he says,
"we must be rich; but I tell you that for fifteen years, from
1732 to 1747, I laid by [only] about £100 a year." He
had been inclined to think, as is shown in a letter from
Margaret Freame to their brother John Penn, in 1736, that
he was doing in Pennsylvania the chief work for the united
Proprietary interest, and should have corresponding compensation. He suggested, she wrote John, that he should be
paid three thousand pounds for his expenses in managing the
family affairs here,—two thousand pounds by John and one
thousand pounds by Richard.[3]

[1] "Proprietary Government in Pennsylvania," by William Robert
Shepherd. New York, 1896.

[2] Copy of letter in Historical Society of Pennsylvania collections.

[3] Extracts from this letter, dated Philadelphia, June 14, 1736:

"We [Margaret and Thomas Freame, no doubt] went up to Pennsbury, where we could not be long by ourselves; at last we got an

While in Pennsylvania Thomas Penn engaged in some commercial ventures. John Barclay—one of the sons of Robert Barclay, author of the famous Quaker book, the "Apology"—was a merchant in Dublin, Ireland, and to him Thomas consigned flaxseed and flour.[1]

After returning to England, Thomas Penn lived in London for a time. Letters in 1743 were addressed to him, " To the care of Mr. John Samuel, Merch't in Three Kings Court,

opportunity to speak to our brother.'' He was ''pretty warm'' over a proposal of John's, ''but on thinking it over became more mild.'' He would not, however, send a proposed power-of-attorney (for the sale of some property, apparently), ''for you att home [John and Richard] that dont love any trouble will dispose of it for what you can get . . . He much wonders at my brother Richard's declining to come over . . . I heartily wish all your affairs were so well settled as the Family might enjoy life rather than suffer it.''

The Freames at this time were remaining in Pennsylvania for the purpose of selling their lands, some of which appear to have been at Tulpehocken, in what is now Berks County. Thomas Freame writes to John Penn that there are plenty desiring to buy, but they want small tracts and have little ready money, while he wishes to sell in large blocks and for cash. He says, writing from Philadelphia, March 22, 1736-7, ''I met with a very great Disappointment, for those Dutchmen that I wrote you were about a large part of my Land went up with me to see it. They approved of the Land and agreed wth me for a price, so that I began to think of seeing you this Summer, I having been informed that they had sixteen hundred pounds in Gold by them, but it proved otherwise, for they would pay but £150 this summer and the rest Six years hence. This would have done very well if I could afford to let my money lay at Interest, but that is not what I want, therefore I did nothing with them.'' Later, in September, 1736, he again writes to John that as soon as he is able to ride (he had been unwell) he is going to Tulpehocken '' with some Palatines lately come in, to whom I have some expectation of disposing of half that tract.''

[1] John Barclay signs himself in his letters ''thy sincere friend and affectionate kinsman,'' but the relationship is not clear. It was John Barclay's niece, Christian Forbes, who had married William Penn, Jr.'s, son, William Penn, 3d, in 1732, but this could hardly be regarded as creating kinship with Thomas.

Lombard street," and in 1745 and 1746 "at Mr. Draper's, Apothecary, in Charles Street, Convent Garden." He was, however, much in the country with John, first at Feens, where John continued to live after returning from Pennsylvania in 1735,[1] and later at Hurley, or Hurley Place, near Maidenhead, in Berks, to which John appears to have removed from Feens a year or more before his death. John's health had not been good. There are frequent allusions in the letters to his illness, and Bishop Vickris, writing to Thomas from Bristol, in October, 1746 (near the time of John's death), much regretted the removal from Feens to Hurley.[2]

Thomas Penn had expected to return to Pennsylvania. In a letter to Richard Peters, at Philadelphia, March 13, 1744, giving him a message for the Indians, he says to tell them, "And, as for myself, that I fully expected to return before this time, but some affairs have hindered me ; how-

[1] Feens was rented during John's absence, with its furniture, etc., and "three fields" to a Walter Fisher for £32 2s. a year. The housekeeper at the place was named Hannah Roberts. John Penn, after his return to England, writes, December 2, 1735, to Thomas Penn, his steward or agent (a colored man, apparently ; there are several letters to and from him in the Historical Society's collections), "at Walgrave, near Twyford, Berks," thus : "I much want to know if the Gentleman is Returned to feen's & when he will leave it, for I should Like to come down next Week if the house is Clear, want to know also if you have gott me a man for the Garden & horses, & if you hear anything of a Person for the house that can Shave and Write pretty well. I shall likewise want a maid servt. I wish you could gett some good small beer brewed soon to be fitt to drink at Xmass. if Dick Wilkins or Underwood has a good Sober Easy troting horse, shall want one when I come down."

[2] "I find you have got him into a more healthy and dry air, but I fear my good Friend, tis too late in the day. Oh how I lament his ever putting a foot in that baneful place at Hurley, I greatly feared the Consequences and often Dissuaded him from it." A bill for repairs at "Hurley Great House," up to October 17, 1746, a few days before John's death, was paid by the executors of his estate, William Vigor, Joseph Freame, and Lascelles Metcalf.

ever, I hope to be in America some time the next year."
And in a letter a few weeks later, May 9, he says, "I can't
think of seeing Philadelphia until the latter end of summer
twelvemonth."

Thomas Penn married, August 22, 1751, Lady Juliana
Fermor, fourth daughter of Thomas, first Earl of Pomfret.
The *Gentleman's Magazine* for September, 1751, reports the
marriage :

"Aug. 22. Hon. Thos. Penn (one of the two proprietors of Pennsylvania) was married to Lady Juliana Fermor, youngest[1] daughter to
E. of Pomfret."

And the *Pennsylvania Gazette*, November 14, 1751, has the
following paragraph :

" By Capt. Hinton [ship "Philadelphia," John Hinton, from Lon-
don] there is advice that the Honourable Thomas Penn Esq ; one of
our Proprietaries, was married the 22nd of August last, to the Lady
Juliana Fermor, youngest daughter of the Right Honourable the late[2]
Earl of Pomfret."

In a letter to Richard Peters, September 29, 1751, Thomas
Penn wrote,—

"As some of your letters are of a private nature, I shal now reply
to such of them as I have not taken notice of in my letter of business,
but first I shall tell you that for some time before I met with that unfortunate, and what had like to have been fatal accident, I had determined
on a change of life, and had settled all the necessary points and made
visits to the lady, which I resumed on my return to Berkshire, and wee
consummated our marriage the 22nd of last month. This necessarily
engaged my mind as well as person til finished, that I could not sit
down to write, but as my grand business is now finished, and I am
happily settled with a companion possessed with those qualities that
must render a reasonable man happy as well as of a Family remarkable
for their affection to each other, and into which I have been received

[1] There is an error, apparently, in the statement that she was the
youngest daughter ; two others, according to the list in Burke, were
younger than she.

[2] "Late" is an error ; he was then living, and died two years after,
in 1753.

with marks of the greatest regard, I shall now sit down as a correspondent to answer all my friends' letters.

" . . . Wee are turning our thoughts toward Pennsylvania, and if
I should be prevented from embarking the very next summer, if I live
till the spring after, I make no doubt of being ready then."[1]

The " unfortunate " and nearly " fatal accident " alluded
to above, I have not found described in the Penn papers,
though it is, I am told, referred to in some of them.   It is
said that Thomas and his brother Richard were riding in a
coach out of London, and having pistols with them,—for
fear of highwaymen, probably,—one of the weapons, in
handling, was accidentally discharged, causing a peculiar
and serious wound upon Thomas's person.   Evidently this
occurrence was a few months earlier than August, 1751.

Lady Juliana Fermor was born in 1729, and was therefore much younger—some twenty-seven years—than her
husband, being, in fact, a woman in her youth at the time
of her marriage.   There are several portraits of her preserved,[2] and one of these, a small full-length, painted by
Peter Van Dyck (a descendant, it is said, of the great Van
Dyck) about the time of the marriage, represents her as
a well-looking lady, in her wedding-dress of white silk,
made in a style which illustrates strikingly the fashion of
the time, the skirt being spread out by hoops to enormous
dimensions sidewise.   She stands near the fireplace of a
handsome room, presumed to be in her father's house in
Albemarle Street, London.

This marriage was an event of high importance to Thomas
Penn and to all his family, most of whom, we may feel
sure, had theretofore regarded him as a confirmed bachelor,

[1] He never realized these expectations ; he did not again come to
Pennsylvania.

[2] Most of them in the possession of her descendant, the Earl of
Ranfurly, at Dungannon Park, Ireland.   *Cf.* article by W. M. Conway,
PENNA. MAG., Vol. VIII.

—he was nearly fifty,—and had been not inconsiderate how his valuable estate as well as his present bounties would be ultimately bestowed. An agreement had been made in 1732 between the three brothers, John, Thomas, and Richard, "to devise their shares [of the Proprietary estate] to the eldest son in tail male, remainder to other sons in like manner," and upon failure of these to other members of the family in succession ; this agreement was confirmed by Thomas and Richard in 1750, and meantime John, in his will, 1746, had left his estate to Thomas for life, with remainder to his first son, "in tail male," and then successively, in like manner, to the other sons. By this will of John, the will of Richard Penn, and the marriage agreement of Thomas, to be mentioned presently, the descent of the Proprietary estates was fixed.

The Fermors (Farmers, Farmars) were a family of greater social distinction, in the year 1751, than Thomas Penn. They accounted themselves as having had an ancestor among those Norman invaders of England who were enriched at Saxon expense in the Conqueror's time, and they had reached knighthood in 1586, baronetcy in 1641, and the peerage in 1692.

Their seat was at Easton Neston, in Northamptonshire, where Sir George Fermor (knighted by Elizabeth in 1586) had entertained James I., in 1603, so acceptably that his son. Hatton Fermor, was also made a knight by that charming and generous monarch.[1] In 1641, the family being then

[1] Robert Fermor (or in after-spelling Farmer and Farmar), a younger son of Sir George of Easton Neston, went to Ireland in the army of Elizabeth, received confiscated Irish estates in Cork and Tipperary, and was " slain " in that island in some of the fighting there. His grandson, Major Jasper Farmar, a neighbor of William Penn's at Shangarry, became a purchaser of land in Pennsylvania at the early settlement, and coming over in the ship " Bristol Merchant," in 1685, died on the voyage. Major Farmar's son, Edward Farmar, was later a prominent citizen at Whitemarsh, near Philadelphia.

staunchly royalist, Charles I. made a baronet of Sir William
Fermor, and in 1692 his son, Sir William, being then equally
in favor with William III., was made a peer, with the title of
Baron Lempster. Lord Lempster married three times, his
third wife being Sophia, daughter of Thomas, Duke of
Leeds, and one of his children by her was Thomas Penn's
father-in-law, the second Baron Lempster, who was made
by George I. Earl of Pomfret (Pontefract, in Yorkshire,
pronounced Pomfret) in 1721. He married, 1720, Henrietta
Louisa, daughter of John Lord Jeffreys, and had a large
family,—Burke gives a list of eleven children. The eldest,
George, succeeded to the peerage on the death of his father
in 1753. Four died young. One daughter, Henrietta, married, 1747, John Conyers, Esq., of Copt House, Essex;
Sophia married John Carteret, Earl Granville; Charlotte
married William Finch, Esq., and died in 1813. These were
older than Lady Juliana; the two younger, according to
Burke's list, were Louisa, who married Sir Thomas Clayton,
Bart., and Anne, who married, July 15, 1754, Thomas, first
Viscount Cremorne, the husband, later, of Philadelphia
Hannah Freame.[1]

The Earldom of Pomfret, it may be here mentioned, became extinct June 8, 1867, by the death of the fifth Earl,
George William Richard (born December 31, 1824), who
was unmarried. He was the great-grandson of Thomas, the
first Earl, father of Lady Juliana Penn.[2]

[1] Philadelphia Hannah, born at Philadelphia in 1740, was married
to Lord Cremorne, May 8, 1770, and had a son and a daughter who
both died young.

[2] John Jay Smith, in his address ("Penn-Logan Correspondence,"
Vol. I.), cites some information as to this last Earl. Granville John
Penn (Thomas Penn's grandson) had been his guardian. He left two
sisters, one married to Sir Thomas George Hesketh, M. P., of Rufford
Hall, Leicestershire, and the other to Colonel Thomas W. Ogilvy.
Portions of his property descended to these sisters and to his cousin,
Sir George William Denys, of Draycott Hall, Yorkshire.

The marriage with Lady Juliana was preceded by elaborate property arrangements. The settlement made upon her and the children whom she might have was drawn up with great care and a prodigious expenditure of legal phraseology. August 14, 1751, eight days before the marriage, the bridegroom expectant executed a "Lease for a year in order to the Settlement upon the marriage of Thomas Penn with Lady Juliana Farmor," and later the settlement was executed, quadripartite, Thomas Penn being of the first part; "the Right Honourable Thomas, Earl of Pomfret, Baron of Lempster, and Knight of the most Honourable Order of the Bath," of the second; Lady Juliana, of the third; and Messrs. Barclay[1] & Hyam, the Quaker merchants of London, of the fourth part. It can hardly be supposed that any one but the lawyers—and possibly Thomas Penn— ever read in full this latter extended document, much less followed intelligently all its repetitious details. The original, on eight skins of parchment, each twenty-six by thirty-four inches, is in the collections of the Historical Society of Pennsylvania. Printed in the private volume prepared in 1870 by the late William Henry Rawle, American counsel for the family,[2] it covers sixty-four pages octavo, in solid array, without the relief of one paragraphic break.

The effect of this settlement was to leave Thomas Penn's property, including the Proprietary estate in Pennsylvania, to (himself) the settler's use for life, with remainder to his eldest son by Lady Juliana, "in tail male," with remainder then to their second son, then to the third and every other son successively, then to his first and other sons successively by any other wife, then to his brother Richard Penn, then

[1] This was David Barclay, another son of Robert of Ury, the "Apologist," and brother to John of Dublin, already mentioned.

[2] "Articles, Wills, and Deeds creating the Entail of Pennsylvania and Three Lower Counties upon Delaware in the Penn Family." Philadelphia, 1870.

to his nephew John Penn, 2d, eldest son of Richard, then
to the first and every other son successively of John Penn,
then to Richard, 2d, son of Richard (brother of John, 2d),
then to Richard Penn, 2d's, eldest son, then to Richard,
2d's, second son, then to Richard, 2d's, third and other sons
successively,—all these being "in tail male." Finally, all
these failing,—which as a matter of fact they all did by the
year 1869, something over a century after this extended en-
tailment in the male line,—the property was to descend to
the heirs of Thomas Penn "in tail general." It is by virtue
chiefly of this last clause in the settlement that the present
and recent heirs of the Penn property in Pennsylvania, in
the line of the Founder's second marriage, are the Stuarts
of Bedfordshire (of whom we shall speak later), descendants of Thomas Penn's daughter, Sophia Margaretta.

Some idea of the presents bestowed by the bridegroom
at his marriage may be suggested by the bill of James Cox,
a London silversmith, which accompanied a letter, September 2, 1751.[1] The list of articles furnished by Mr. Cox
includes a brilliant hoop ring, a gold watch chain, a " gold
seal for Mr. Hockley," "an onyx [word illegible] in gold,
complete," a " double coat engraved," etc., all to the cost of
£56 16s. 6d., while, as the letter explains, there was some
other article of greater value preparing by artists of the
highest skill.

A complimentary letter on his marriage, addressed him
by Cossart de St. Aubin, agent in London for the Mora-
vians (from 1746 to 1755), is preserved. It is addressed to
Thomas Penn, at Hitcham, near Maidenhead, and proceeds :

"Permit me Sir to congratulate you on your happy marriage. I can
assure you it has given me great joy and also to our good Mr. Spangen-

[1] The letter apologises for delay in waiting on T. P., as the writer had
been suddenly called to attend "Mr. Whitefield," on account of his
"sudden and unexpected departure," and could not fail to respond
without disobliging him.

berg [Moravian bishop], who joynes with me in warmest wish for your
happiness . . . May you live long and happy, to the Comfort of all
that are dear to you. I flatter myself our people [the Moravians] are
included in the number, and that they desire nothing more but to enjoy
your protection, and that of your Descendants to the remotest ages.

"(P. S.) Mr. Spangenberg and Company set out for America the
end of the week. He should have been exceeding glad to wait on you.
He goes with Capt. Bryant, who falls down the river today or Monday,
bound for N. York."

What changes in his religious connections took place in
consequence of Thomas Penn's marriage, and the social
position which he now assumed, are not very clearly defined.
He had hardly considered himself one of the Friends for a
long time, and yet he had not very definitely abandoned
association with them.[1] In 1743, when Governor Thomas
was contending with the Pennsylvania Assembly, and war
with France was impending, Thomas Penn wrote him, "I
felt obliged to solicit the ministry against the Quakers, or
at least I stated that I did not hold their opinions concerning defence. I no longer continue the little distinction of
dress."[2] After his marriage he went regularly to church,
but down to 1771 certainly,[3] and probably all his life, he
never took the sacrament. A deposition made in 1758
showed that he considered himself a member of the Established Church from about that time. His son John, born

[1] His brother John, as already stated, was buried in the old ground
of the Friends, at Jordans, with his father and mother. In 1736 Margaret (Freame), writing from Philadelphia to John, says, "Your appearance among Friends was, I hear, taken very kindly, and your behaviour
just like yourself." John not only appeared among the Friends, however,
about that time, but elsewhere as well, for in the same letter Margaret
says, "I am glad to find you had so kind a reception at Court, and if
you were to go often now the ice is broken I believe it would be of
sarvis."

[2] "Letter-Book of Thomas Penn," Vol. II., in Historical Society of
Pennsylvania collections.

[3] See statement made for him, May, 1771, *post.*

11

1760, was baptized at the church of St. Martin's in the Fields. In a letter to Governor James Hamilton, 1760, alluding to the visit to England of William Logan (son of James Logan), Thomas said, " You may be assured I shall treat him with regard, and shew him I have no disregard to those of his profession [the Friends], except on their levelling republican System of Government so much adopted by them." [1]

Before his marriage Thomas Penn had settled in a town house. Letters in 1747, and perhaps earlier, were addressed to him " at his house in the New Street, Spring Gardens, near Charing Cross." This continued to be his city residence until his death. In 1750 letters were addressed to him " at Hitcham, near Maidenhead Bridge, Bucks." Nine years after his marriage (1760) he acquired the handsome and valuable estate of Stoke Poges, in Bucks, where for over eighty years the family home remained, and where the name of Penn, through himself, his sons, and grandchildren, acquired new and honorable distinction. October 18, 1760, in a letter to Governor Hamilton, at Philadelphia, he wrote,—

" You will be pleased to hear the others [children] with their mother, [are] well at Stoke, to which we are removed, I having bought it : it is a very large old house, that we passed when I went with you to see the Duke of Marlborough's, and was then my Lady Cobham's."

Stoke Poges is most famous as having the church-yard which Gray's immortal " Elegy " describes ; in this yard the poet's remains are buried. The residence, Stoke, belonged to Sir Edward Coke in Queen Elizabeth's time, and here he entertained that difficult female but vigorous monarch, his royal mistress, in 1601. Later it became the property of Anne, Viscountess Cobham, and at her death it was sold to

---

[1] He might have done well, when in this frame of mind concerning systems of government, to read some of his father's writings on the subject, of the period 1680 to 1690.

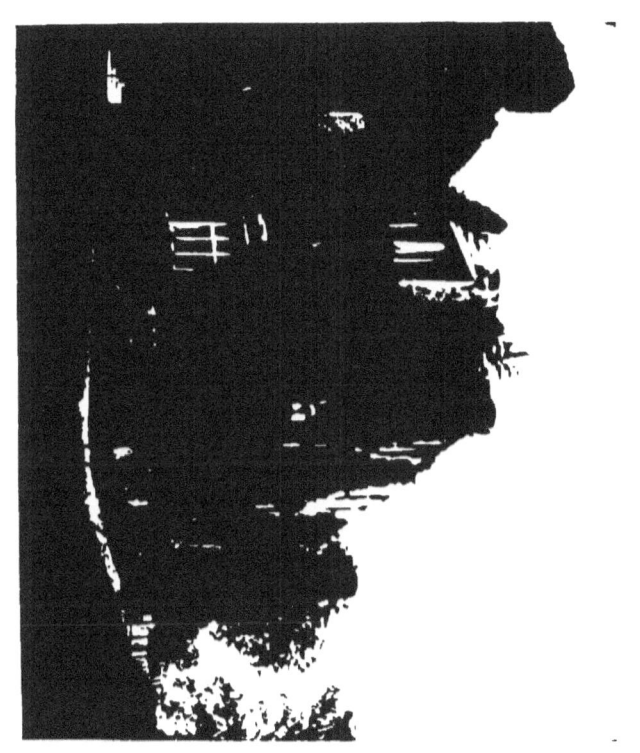

Thomas Penn.[1] The old manor-house furnished the place
and, in part, the subject for Gray's humorous poem, "The
Long Story," whose descriptions may interest us in this
connection if not in any other. Two of its stanzas afford
some description of the old house :

> " In Britain's isle, no matter where,
>   An ancient pile of building stands :
>   The Huntingdons and Hattons there
>   Employed the pow'r of fairy hands

> " To raise the ceiling's fretted height,
>   Each panel in achievements clothing,
>   Rich windows that exclude the light,
>   And passages that lead to nothing."

At Stoke Thomas Penn, with his family, continued to live,
except when in the city, and there he is buried. The alterations and new erections made by his son John have materially
changed the appearance of the place since 1775 ; but then,
as now, it was a costly and elegant residence.

The children of Thomas Penn and Lady Juliana seem to
have been eight in number, of whom four died in infancy or
youth, while four grew up, and three of these married. The

---

[1] "The estate having been seized by the Crown for a debt, James I.
granted the manor in fee to the celebrated lawyer, Sir Edward Coke,
who in 1601 (being then Attorney-General) entertained Queen Elizabeth
here very sumptuously. Upon the death of Sir E. Coke, at Stoke Poges,
in 1634, the manor came to his son-in-law, Baron Villiers, of Stoke
Poges and Viscount Purbeck. Stoke House was in 1647, for a short
time, the residence of King Charles I., when he was a prisoner in the
power of the army. Lord Purbeck died in 1656, and about 1720 the
manor was sold by his heirs to the family of Gayer. In 1724 it was
purchased by Edward Halsey, Esq., whose daughter and heir married
Sir R. Temple, afterwards Lord Cobham. This lady (then a widow)
died here in 1760, when this estate was conveyed to the son of William
Penn, Esq., founder of Pennsylvania. In 1848 the manor was purchased from the Penn family by the Right Hon. Henry Labouchere,
who was created Baron Taunton in 1859."—*Sheahan's History of Bucks.*
London, 1862.

first child was named William. He was born June 21, 1752, and died February 14, 1753. He was buried at Penn, in Bucks. A daughter, Juliana, was born May 19, 1753, and lived to grow up and marry. A second son, Thomas, was born July 17, 1754, but died September 5, 1757, and was buried at Penn. Twin children, William and Louisa Hannah, were born July 22, 1756, and both died young, the former April 24, 1760, and the latter June 10, 1766. Both are buried at Penn.

In the parish church at Penn, under the northeast corner of the nave, there is a large vault, made in the last century, in which there are six small coffins. Four of these contain the remains of the children who are named above as dying young,—William, Thomas, William, and Louisa Hannah,— one contains those of a son of Richard Penn, and the other simply marked " P," is not identified.

The grief of the parents at the loss of all but one of their first five children is expressed in letters from Thomas Penn. The death of William, the third son, who lived to be nearly four years old, especially affected him. In a letter to Richard Peters, at Philadelphia, March 8, 1760, he had mentioned the birth of "a fine boy" (John) " this day fortnight," and quickly following, in other letters, appear the following paragraphs :

To Governor Hamilton, April 10, 1760 : "I am in a very anxious state. My son William was attacked with a slow fever about two months ago ; at first it was thought intermitting, but has since been almost always upon him, and affected his Breathing, so that his situation is very doubtful."

To Richard Peters, April 11 : " [He] has slow fever, and some appearance of knots and obstructions in his flesh, which are said to be the cause of it. . . . His mother having taken him to Marybon, for the benefit of the Air, and not to be without the reach of advice, makes my journeys to and from that place several times in the day absolutely necessary."

Another letter to Governor Hamilton, May 10, announces the death of the little boy on the 24th of April, and adds, " [it is] an irreparable loss to me, as I had, from the opinion of my friends, as well as from what I myself observed in the Child, great reason to believe that both his Capacity and Disposition were such as would have rendered him a valuable and useful man." Writing to Peters the same day, he said the boy was a good scholar and had a "disposition sweet, though very lively." "My hopes now," he added, "are on a child not three months old, who very providentially came before this dreadful time, or his Mother might have suffered greatly under it." And writing also to Richard Hockley the same day, he said the death "leaves my only hope [as to a son] in one less than three months old, a very slight dependence, and yet many such have succeeded."

This child (John) lived to grow up and to attain ripe years. Two other children—Granville, born in December, 1761, and Sophia, born in December, 1764,—also grew up and died at an advanced age.

Thomas Penn was in declining health for some years preceding his death. In December, 1769, his brother Richard writes to him at "Westgate Buildings, Bath," saying he hears he is in better health than he had been. In May Thomas was again at Bath, returning to Stoke Park June 9. On July 4 Richard, writing to him, refers to "the Doctor's orders for you to proceed immediately to Tunbridge Wells." To that place Thomas went, and a little later (August) tried the coast air at Margate.

A statement filed among the Penn papers, under date of May 17, 1771, a memorandum, apparently, submitted for a legal opinion, presents a number of interesting biographical data at this point. Thomas Penn, it seems, had been nominated by the Lord Mayor of London "to be a Sheriff of the City of London and County of Middlesex." The statement thereupon says,—

"Mr. Penn was 40 years ago admitted a freeman of the City of London, and has twice voted for a Member [of Parliament], once for Sir John Barnard, and lately for Mr. Trecothick. Mr. Penn has no property whatever within the City of London, and never lived within the city, is near, if not quite 70 years old, has had a stroke of the Palsy, and cannot walk without help. Mr. Penn was originally bred a Quaker. Since his marriage, which is many years ago, he has gone to church regularly, but he has never received the Sacrament. However, having gone regularly to church, I don't think he can be looked upon as a Protestant Dissenter. Mr. Penn desires to be advised what he can do to prevent serving this disagreeable office, or being fined for not serving the same."

The opinion of "Ja : Eyre, Lincoln's Inn Fields,"—evidently the counsel consulted,—is placed upon the same sheet as the foregoing. His opinion is that nothing can be done at present. Mr. Penn will have to await the election,—he may not be elected ; then, if seventy years old or over, he might resist a suit for the fine on the ground that he is not physically a "fit and able person," as required by the law.

By the opening of 1775 Thomas Penn's strength was evidently far spent. His wife was now conducting the Pennsylvania correspondence. She writes from Stoke to Governor John Penn, January 7, of that year, "Mr. Penn is going to London for the winter." Then follow, in successive letters, same to the same, the following passages :

Stoke, January 10 : "Mr. Penn has no particular complaint, but I think the winter does not agree with him and that he is weaker, though he goes out every day."

London, February 21 : "I am sure that he rather loses than gains strength. As I know your affection for him, I cannot write without giving you some account of his health."

London, March 1 : "I think Mr. Penn is visibly worse the last two months, tho' he still looks well at times, and goes out in the Coach as usual."

Finally there comes this announcement,—

"I know the news I have to communicate will affect you, But the consideration that poor Dr Mr. Penn had long since been no Comfort to himself will I hope make the hearing it is at an end less painful to you. It pleased God to release him yesterday, March 21, in the evening. . . .

"SPRING GARDENS, March 22. "

He was taken to the country for burial. In the church at Stoke Poges is a tablet with the following inscription:

In a Vault
In this Church are
deposited the Remains of
Thomas Penn,
of Stoke Park in this Parish
(Son of William Penn
Founder of Pennsylvania),
Born 1701. Married 1751. Died 1775.
And of his wife the Rᵗ Hon. Lady Juliana Penn,
Born 1729. Married 1751. Died 1801.
Also the remains of their Sons
John Penn of Stoke Park. Born 1760. Died 1834.
And Granville Penn of Stoke Park.
Born 1761. Married 1791. Died 1844.
Also Isabella, wife of the above Granville Penn,
eldest daughter of Genˡ Gordon Forbes, Col. 29ᵗʰ Regiment.
Born 1771. Married 1791. Died 1847.
And of their Sons
Granville John, late of Stoke Park. Born 1802. Died 1867.
Thomas Gordon, in Holy Orders. Born 1803. Died 1869.
William, Born 1811. Died 1848.
Also their Daughters
Sophia, 1ˢᵗ wife of F. M. Sir Wᵐ Gomm G. C. B. Col. Coldstream Guards.
Born 1793. Married 1818. Died 1827.
Louisa Emily, Born 1795. Died 1841.
Isabella Mary, Born 1795. Died 1856.
Henrietta Ann, Born 1797. Died 1855.

The character of Thomas Penn has perhaps been sufficiently suggested. It is not easy to conclude that, on the whole, he was other than a just man, according to his light. He was undoubtedly kind and considerate to many different members of his family who desired his assistance or favor. He was guardian for William Penn, 3d's, son, Springett, the last male Penn in the elder line; he interested himself energetically to save some of her estate to the widow of his spendthrift cousin, Walter Clement; he educated and assisted his nephew John, the Governor; and from the day when we found him a lad in London, doing errands for his mother at Ruscombe, he certainly was honestly serviceable to many persons. Much severity has been bestowed upon him; these approaches to praise are no more than his due.

Thomas Penn's portrait, in the possession of the Earl of Ranfurly, painted at the time of his marriage (a copy of which was added, March, 1896, to the collections of the Pennsylvania Historical Society), is "a small full-length of a perfectly dressed and somewhat precise gentleman, in the costume of the middle of the eighteenth century. He wears an embroidered grayish lilac silk coat and breeches, and a long white satin waistcoat. He stands at the open door of a wainscoted room, with uncarpeted wooden floor. Through the doorway an antechamber can be seen, with a window opening upon a pleasant country view." [1]

A painting by Sir Joshua Reynolds, 1764, shows the four children of Thomas and Lady Juliana Penn, then living: Juliana, a girl of eleven; Louisa Hannah, eight; John, four; and Granville, three. It is a fine example of Sir Joshua's work; a criticism which might be suggested is that the two girls appear too mature for their years. This painting was in possession of William Dugald Stuart, at Tempsford Hall, Beds. A "splendid mezzotint," made by Charles Turner in 1819, dedicated to John Penn (one of those in the picture), and probably executed by his order, is described by Mr. Conway as then (1884) in the possession of the Earl of Ranfurly.

---

[1] Article by W. M. Conway, PENNA. MAG., Vol. VIII. p. 357. See it also for details as to other portraits of Thomas Penn.

1. William, born June 21, 1752 ; died February 14, 1753 ; buried in the vault at the parish church at Penn, in Bucks.

2. Juliana, born May 19, 1753. She married, May 23, 1771, William Baker, Esq., of Bayfordbury, Herts, and died April 23, 1772, and was buried at Stoke Poges. She left one child, a daughter, Juliana (surname *Baker*), who married, January 18, 1803, John Fawset Herbert Rawlins, Esq., and died *s. p.*, September 11, 1849, at Gunters Grove, Stoke Courcy, Somerset.

3. Thomas, born (*Gentleman's Magazine*) July 17, 1754 ; died (plate on coffin at Penn) September 5, 1757. The coffin-plate says his age was " 2 years and 1 month," and apparently there is an error here ; probably the figure 2 should be 3.

4. William, born July 22, 1756, and died April 24, 1760 ; buried at Penn. Details concerning him, in letters of his father, have been given.

5. Louisa Hannah (twin with William), born July 22, 1756 ; died June 10, 1766 ; buried at Penn.

6. John, born February 23, 1760 ; baptized March 21, 1760, at the church of St. Martin's in the Fields ; died unmarried June 21, 1834. Details will be given of him later.

7. Granville, born at the city residence, New Street, Spring Gardens, December 9, 1761 ; married, June 24, 1791, Isabella Forbes ; died September 28, 1844, leaving issue. See later.

8. Sophia Margaretta, born December 25 (? 21), 1764 ; married Archbishop William Stuart ; died April 29, 1847 ; buried at Luton, Beds, leaving issue. See later.

X.

The Descendants of Thomas Penn.

AT the death of Thomas Penn, three of his children were
living,—John, Granville, and Sophia Margaretta. John
the "heir," the baby whose coming just before the affecting
death of his brother William seemed providential, and served
in some measure to distract the mother's grief, was a lad of
fifteen; Granville was thirteen, and Sophia ten.

Thomas Penn left an extended and carefully drawn will.
It was dated November 18, 1771, and had three codicils, the
last being of June 23, 1774. It was admitted to probate
April 8, 1775. Though the descent of the Proprietary estate
had been strictly provided for in the family agreements and
settlements, he had a large private estate, real and personal,
to dispose of. He appointed his wife, Lady Juliana, and
his son-in-law, William Baker, executors for the personal
estate, except that in Pennsylvania. He committed to them
also the disposal of real property at Bristol and Gloucester.
His nephew, Richard Penn, and Richard Hockley, were
appointed executors in America. At Philadelphia, ex-
Governor James Hamilton, Rev. Richard Peters, and Richard
Hockley were appointed trustees to sell certain private lots
and tracts, and remit the proceeds to the executors in England. Stoke Park was devised to the English executors as
an entailed trust for five hundred years, the life use of it to
his son, John Penn, "without impeachment of waste."
The furniture at Stoke went to John. Lady Juliana received the city house, with money, plate, etc. Provision
was made for the education of the children. John was to
have an allowance of three hundred pounds a year till he

John Crull

was fifteen, and then five hundred pounds a year until twenty-one.

The son-in-law, William Baker, as previously stated, had married Juliana Penn in 1771, and she had died the following year. The widow, Lady Juliana, now found him a valuable aid in the administration of her husband's extensive affairs. She writes, April 25, 1775, to Rev. Mr. Peters, " It has pleased God to raise us up in England a most active and capable friend in Mr. Baker, who is Guardian, with me, to the children, and without whom I should not have known what to have done." Many letters at this period, on the family account, are by Mr. Baker.[1]

A letter to Edmund Physick, agent at Philadelphia, by the two executors, April 5, 1775, says that by his quarterly statement on 29th September, 1774, he had a balance of fourteen thousand pounds, and they have since received, in four remittances, thirteen thousand nine hundred pounds. They hope he will state his later accounts, and remit. " The total stop which will be put to the trade of the five Middle Colonies by the Bill now depending in Parliament, if the Association entered into by the Congress is adhered to, will make the Communication between America and Great Britain, and the opportunity for remitting, more difficult."

Writing to James Tilghman, the same date (5th), the executors said,—

" There are three great points which require much attention : the settlement of the dispute with Connecticut, the adjustment of the western boundary with Virginia, and the composition of arrears proposed with the settlers in the three lower counties."

In a letter to Governor John Penn, at Philadelphia, May 29, 1775, Lady Juliana says,—

" I am returned to Stoke with my two little girls.[2] Miss Baker has

[1] Mr. Baker was sometime member of Parliament for Hertfordshire.

[2] These were her daughter Sophia and her granddaughter, the little Juliana, who survived Mrs. Baker's death in 1772. The " boys " were, of course, John and Granville.

been innoculated this spring, but is now well, tho' she was ill enough
with it to make me very uneasy for some time, and I have the happiness
of finding my boys in perfect health ; they dined at home to-day, and
desired me to add their compliments," etc.

The two boys were no doubt receiving their education
preparatory to college.   John was entered later at Clare
Hall, Cambridge.   The entry records him as a "nobleman,"
—by virtue of his mother's rank.   He received his M. A.
degree in 1779.   When he came of age, in February, 1781,
he was at Brussels, and had been there for some time.
"About March" of that year, he says,[1] " I left my family to
return to England.   I lived between Stoke and London the
remainder of the year, and after somewhat preparing myself
for understanding the beauties and sights of Italy, and pro-
curing letters   .   .   .   set off in the winter for Calais.   By
the favor of Mr. Schutz, I obtained a permit from the Comte
de Vergennes, signed by the F. King, to land at Calais—
which the war made necessary."   He went to Lisle, thence
to Brussels, had, he says, few acquaintances, read Roman
classics, took lessons on the harpsichord ("afterward laid
aside "), and attended the Court of the Viceroy of the
Austrian Netherlands, the Prince de Saxe Teschen.   Then
he proceeded to Spa.   " I am in lodgings at a painter's
house," he says.   He hired "a little horse," at half a guinea
per week, rode through the forest, and produced an ode—
his muse inclined to odes—of fifteen stanzas of six lines
each.   He praised the

> ' Elysian views that now once more,
> Ere six revolving years are o'er,
> Entice my voluntary feet."

Proceeding to Düsseldorf, to Coblentz, and other Rhine
cities, he went to Munich and Augsburg, and reached Paris
January 31, 1783.   " One of my first things was waiting on

[1] MS. " Commonplace Book," in collections of the Historical Society of Pennsylvania.

the American Commissioners at Paris. . . . When I arrived the treaty of peace had been signed three days."

Lady Juliana Penn died November 20, 1801. A notice in the *Gentleman's Magazine* for November of that year says, "At her house at Ham, Surrey, in her 73d year, [on the 20th] closed a pattern of Christian excellence by a serene and peaceful death, Lady Juliana Penn . . . relict of the late Hon. Thomas Penn," etc.

The limitations of our present study forbid our giving as much space to John Penn as he deserves. On the whole, he is a curious and interesting personality. He inherited, apparently, traits of his father, the prudent business-man, and others of his grandfather, the idealist and reformer. He was sixteen when the American Revolution caused the collapse of the family's great colonial proprietorship, but the event does not seem to have soured or seriously shocked him. Like his uncle John, he remained a bachelor to the end of his life. He evidently enjoyed his large possessions, but probably his greatest pleasure was in the expenditure of his money,—much of it on objects which many men would not have cared for. He was an amateur in the arts, something of a poet, something of an architect, a gentle-paced reformer, a chevalier who rode without raising much dust, and an official who did not disdain routine affairs.

The return of peace permitted him to visit Pennsylvania. In June (1783) he sailed from Falmouth for New York. The voyage was long, and closed with a mild experience of shipwreck. "After seven weeks," his manuscript record says, "we were awaked at one o'clock in the morning by the noise and motions of the vessel stranded off Egg Harbour, on the Jersey coast. After firing minute guns, and being avoided by one ship in sight, we were taken up by the *Three Friends*, Capt. Anderson, a small sloop from Philadelphia, bound to New York, which carried us there. We got on board at 6 o'clock in the morning."

John Penn now took up his residence in Philadelphia, and remained here for five years. The Assembly of Pennsylvania, the single-bodied Legislature established under the Constitution of 1776, had four years before his arrival, in the throes of the Revolution, seized the Proprietary estates. The act is dated November 27, 1779. It is entitled "An Act for vesting the estates of the late Proprietaries of Pennsylvania in this Commonwealth," and this title presents the substance of what follows. A clause of the preamble declares that "the claims heretofore made by the late Proprietaries to the whole of the soil [etc.] cannot longer consist with the safety, liberty, and happiness of the good people of this Commonwealth," and section 5 enacts "that all and every the estate, right, title, [etc.] of the heirs and devisees, grantees, or others claiming as Proprietaries of Pennsylvania, whereof they or either of them stood seised, or to which they or any of them were entitled," on the 4th of July, 1776, "except as hereinafter excepted, . . . shall be, and they are hereby vested in the Commonwealth of Pennsylvania, for the use and benefit of the citizens thereof."

The property excepted was the private lands and the Proprietary tenths, or manors. Quit-rents due the Proprietaries on the public lands were to cease and determine. One hundred and thirty thousand pounds, "sterling money," was appropriated "to the devisees and legatees of Thomas Penn and Richard Penn," and "to the widow and relict of the said Thomas Penn," in such proportions as the Legislature should thereafter direct. No part of the money was to be paid until at least one year after the making of peace between England and the United States, and then not more than twenty thousand pounds, nor less than fifteen thousand, in any one year.

The estate thus appropriated by the State John Penn valued, according to an elaborate statement in his "Commonplace Book," at £1,536,545 4s. 3d. This money loss was composed of three items : (1) the arrears of current quit-rent payments ; (2) the quit-rent right, capitalized (at twelve years' purchase); (3) the value of the unsold lands. As to the last, he computed that 21,592,128 acres of land were taken. There had been 552,784 acres assigned in manors and family grants, and 4,132,976 acres had been sold on quit-rent. The unsold area, "at the lowest valuation," he estimated as worth £1,295,527 12*s*. 4¾*d.* " The loss then suffered is that of the [right of] government; three-fifths of royal, one-fifth of other mines ; and of lands and money to the value of" the sum above stated.[1]

John Penn addressed himself to the care of the remaining property. He and the other heirs petitioned the Assembly, without result, in relation to the sequestration. He felt some inclination to make his home here. His cousin John, who had been Governor when the catastrophe of 1776 occurred, had remained, and on the whole was well liked and cordially treated. John (our present subject) says, " I felt indeed the accustomed *amor patriæ* and admiration of England, but sometimes a republican enthusiasm which attached me to America, and almost wholly tempted me to stay.[2] I may date my becoming wholly an Englishman from the breaking

[1] The amount of money received by the State of Pennsylvania from the sale of the Proprietary lands, after the divestment, up to 1789, is stated at £824,094 0*s*. 7*d.* The amount of the claim made upon the British government by the heirs was £944,817 8*s*. 6*d.* *Cf.* Janney's " Penn," p. 535, foot-note.

[2] He records in his " Commonplace Book " the names of the members of "the Convention for improving the American Government," 1787. He called promptly on Dr. Franklin when the latter returned from France. The diary of General Washington, during his attendance upon the Federal Convention, contains this entry : " Thursday 19 [July, 1787] Dined at Mr. John Penn's (the younger) drank tea, and spent the evening there." The diary of John Penn, in April, 1788, of a trip on horseback from Philadelphia to Reading, Harrisburg, Carlisle, and Lancaster, appears in the " Commonplace Book," and is printed in the PENNA. MAG., Vol. III.

up of that Assembly [1784] and publication of its minutes
relative to the treatment of our memorial." He bought
fifteen acres on the west bank of the Schuylkill, for six hundred pounds sterling, in 1784,—" a dear purchase," he calls
it,—and began the erection upon it of the small mansion
which still stands there in the Zoölogical Garden, now a part
of Fairmount Park.[1] This he named " The Solitude,"—from
the Duke of Wurtemberg's, he explains. His city house
appears to have been "at the corner of Market and 6th
streets;" at any rate, it was there, Monday, May 26, 1788,
"at 9 a. m.," that his plate, furniture, etc., were sold at
auction, preparatory to his return to England.[2]

Returning to England, probably in 1788, he entered upon
a busy and indeed active career. A pension—four thousand
pounds a year—was voted by the Parliament to the Penns
in compensation for their American losses,[3] and the instal-
ments of the allowance by the State of Pennsylvania began
to be paid in 1785. John Penn, therefore, felt himself a
fairly rich man, and he began in 1789 the erection of a
large and handsome residence at Stoke. The early plans
for it were by Nasmith, but they were completed by Wyatt.[4]

[1] It continued to be a part of the Penn estate until it was taken by
the city for the Park.

[2] The gross proceeds were £564 4d. Taxes and commissions off, it
realised £539 11s. 10d.—PENNA. MAG., Vol. XV. p. 373.

[3] The Penn annuity was voted by the House of Commons May 14,
1790. The petition of Lady Juliana Penn for compensation had been
presented in that House February 8, 1788, by the Right Hon. Frederick
Montagu, who spoke of the services of Admiral Penn in adding to the
domain of England by the capture of Jamaica. Mr. Pitt consented,
"on the part of the King," that the petition be received.—*Gentleman's
Magazine.*

[4] Britton and Brayley's " History of Buckinghamshire " (London,
1801) describes Stoke as it appeared at the beginning of the present
century, and calls it "one of the most charming and magnificent residences in this part of the country." The account proceeds :

" It is built chiefly with brick, and covered with stucco, and consists

The old manor-house with its historic memories, which had been the family residence for thirty years, was partly taken down.[1] In 1798 John Penn was sheriff of Buckinghamshire. In 1802 he was member of Parliament for the borough of Helston, Cornwall. In 1805 he was appointed royal governor of the Isle of Portland, in Dorsetshire, on the Channel coast, and this place—practically a sinecure, it may be presumed—he retained for many years. He acquired here about 1815, from the Crown, "the ruins of Rufus Castle, and a few acres 'round it," paying one hundred and fifty pounds therefor, and began, upon plans by Wyatt, the erection of another costly and handsome place, known since as Pennsylvania Castle.[2]

of a large, square centre, with two wings. The north or entrance front is ornamented with a colonnade, consisting of ten Doric columns, and approached by a flight of steps, leading to the Marble Hall. The south front, 196 feet in length, is also adorned with a colonnade, consisting of twelve fluted columns of the old Doric order. Above this ascends a projecting portico, of four Ionic columns, sustaining an ornamental pediment. The Marble Hall is oval, and contains four fine marble busts, supported on scagliola pedestals. . . .

"The park, though rather flat, commands some very fine views, particularly to the south, where the eye is directed over a large sheet of water to the majestic Castle of Windsor, beyond which Cooper's Hill and the Forest Woods close the prospect. A large lake winds round the east side of the house, with a neat stone bridge thrown over it. The lake was originally formed by Richmond, but it has been considerably altered by Repton, who also directed the laying out of the Park."

[1] A portion of it, however, was preserved, and is still (1897) in use. It is of brick, ivy covered, and has decided architectural interest. Over the front door-way is the date of the original erection, 1555. The interior, among other attractions, has a beautiful old fireplace. Rooms in the second story were fitted up by the Penns "as pleasure-rooms, or resting-places, and furnished with portraits, hangings, and other decorations in keeping with the age of the erection." In this old house Sir Edward Coke wrote his famous "Institutes."

[2] November 11, 1815, writing from Portland to William Rawle, Jr., of Philadelphia, John Penn said, "I see this place is called 'Pennsyl-

12

At Stoke, besides building the new house, John Penn
erected in 1799 a cenotaph to the poet Gray. This is after
a design by Wyatt, and stands in the grounds of Stoke
Park, but near the church-yard, where the remains of Gray
are interred with those of his mother.[1] On three sides of
it are selections from the Ode to Eton and the Elegy, and on
the fourth the inscription :

> THIS MONUMENT
>
> IN HONOUR OF THOMAS GRAY
>
> WAS ERECTED IN 1799, AMONG
>
> THE SCENES CELEBRATED BY THAT
>
> GREAT LYRIC AND ELEGIAC POET.
>
> HE DIED JULY 30TH 1771 AND
>
> LIES UNNOTICED IN THE CHURCHYARD
>
> ADJOINING, UNDER THE TOMBSTONE
>
> ON WHICH HE PIOUSLY AND PATHETICALLY
>
> RECORDED THE INTERMENT OF HIS
>
> AUNT AND LAMENTED MOTHER.

John Penn also erected a memorial to Sir Edward Coke.
It stands in the park, about three hundred yards from the

vania Castle ' in the new Weymouth guide, though only christened so in
joke by the late Duch* of Bolton and Sir J. Hippesley. This therefore
seems destined to be its name.''

John Jay Smith, in his address before the Historical Society of Pennsylvania, November, 1867, described this place as he saw it in 1865. It
was, he said, ''though castellated, a modern residence, calculated for a
large family, and abounding in every comfort. On a small, mounted
brass cannon on the front lawn, with its muzzle pointed seaward, is
inscribed that it was presented by an intimate friend, a nobleman, to
John Penn, ' member of Parliament.' . . . By careful shelter and artistic
planting, John Penn succeeded in surrounding the castle with belts of
beautiful trees.''

[1] John Penn paid much attention to the fame of Gray. Besides
erecting the cenotaph, he formed a splendid collection of Gray's
works. In the library of Stoke was the original manuscript of the
Elegy and a copy of every edition then published of it and Gray's
other poems.

north front of the house. It is a fluted column sixty-eight feet high, and is surmounted by a statue, heroic size, of the famous old jurist. The column was designed by Wyatt; the statue is by Rossi.

Like many another builder of great houses, John Penn found them costly. His letters to his correspondents in Philadelphia contain at times serious complaints of poverty. Writing to Thomas Cadwalader,[1] from London, August 13, 1824, he says,—

"I am really, by the failure of remittances, obliged to make a great and heroic effort at economy. I have had no party as usual, this year, and do [not] accept invitations, as I cannot give them, besides reducing my dinners, when alone, to one or two dishes. This is to enable me to pay off a debt of between four and 5000 pounds, incurred in a great measure in consequence of my dependence on remittances, by putting in complete repair, which was found necessary, the north or entrance colonnade of Stoke."

Again to the same, from the same place, January 26, 1825,—

"I have been at length so far irritated by this tendency of my expenses to exceed my income as to have resolved to put on to the world an appearance of economy, rather singular ; as for full half a year I have confined my dinners to a single joint ; though it is little in character with the great houses I have built myself."

In 1822, July 24, he writes that he has bought a farm adjoining Stoke for five thousand seven hundred and fifty pounds. Burke (" General Armory ") says, under his notice of Granville Penn, that the family owned in Bucks the manors of Stoke Poges and Eton, "the latter purchased by the late John Penn, Esq."

Of the city house, which had been his father's residence, he writes, January 1, 1816, to Thomas Cadwalader,—

[1] General Thomas Cadwalader received the power-of-attorney of John Penn in 1815, and of Richard Penn (son of the first Richard) in 1817, then tenants in tail male, to make sale of their lands in Pennsylvania.

" This part of the town, which as a garden is represented in the elegant ' Mémoires de Grammont,' a scene of the revelry of some of Charles the Second's courtiers, and in ' The Spectator' a promenade visited by Sir R. de Coverley's water party, was built over [*i. e.*, built upon] sixty years ago, when my father fixed himself in this house ; the best in the street, and opening into St. James' Park."

Not only as a civil-life governor, but also as an avowed defender of England, John Penn appears. He was lieutenant-colonel of the First (Eton) Troop of the First (South) Regiment of the Royal Bucks Yeomanry. Two portraits of him hung in the picture-gallery at Pennsylvania Castle, one in "full court-dress," and another "in full military array, sword in hand, at the head of the Portland troop of horse, which he had organized for the defence of the English coast against the expected invasion of Napoleon."[1]

Besides his labors of authorship, one other undertaking of John Penn's requires particular notice. This was his philanthropic enterprise, begun about 1817, and named in 1818 the "Outinian Society." Its original object was to promote matrimony, and it was called at first the Matrimonial Society ; later its scope was broadened and the other name adopted.[2] The announced object was to aid social reforms which were liable to be neglected, but the marriage concern was chiefly kept in mind.[3] The Society held meetings monthly, in the season, at Mr. Penn's town house, and

[1] John Jay Smith's Address.—This portrait is by Sir William Beechey, P.R.A., and was engraved by R. Dunkeston, and published 1809. A drawing by Tendi, from a bust of John Penn, by Deare, engraved by L. Schiavonetti, was published 1801.—" Dictionary of National Biography."

[2] The name is from a line in the Odyssey, which, freely rendered, means, "*No one* is my name, *Nobody* is what my father, my mother, and my friends call me."

[3] The obituary notice in the *Gentleman's Magazine*, 1834, says, "Some years ago Mr. Penn raised many a smile by his employing more than one lecturer gravely to persuade youth of both sexes to enter into the holy bonds of matrimony."

at other times in the country, at Leamington, Cheltenham, Bristol, etc., where a lecturer, who was the secretary of the Society, delivered a lecture to the audience of genteel persons who assembled. The scheme may have been thought amusing, but at any rate considerable companies gathered to enjoy it, whose names are preserved to us in the official reports of the Society. These were printed in the best style of the art, and, as we may presume, at Mr. Penn's expense.[1] For a time it must have been quite a fashionable function. To give it a start,—which was somewhat difficult apparently, —the Marchioness of Salisbury lent her patronage, and thus encouraged others of quality to attend. In the intervals of the lecture at Mr. Penn's town house the company walked in the gardens, giving the affair something the character of a Greek philosophical academy. The frontispiece to the principal volume of the Society's Reports is a picture :

"The Portico, Spring Gardens, No. 10 New Street (the only Portico) belonging to J. Penn, Esq., with the Company assembled, as it appears during the delivery of the Outinian Lectures, every Saturday throughout the Season."

The Society was recorded as "Founded in the hundredth year after the death of the benevolent WILLIAM PENN, and in the year of the second peace of AIX-LA-CHAPELLE. For securing the advantage of benevolence and justice, with the aid of monitory suggestions, in Critical and Ethical lectures, where NO OTHER provision can easily be made for that purpose : or particularly proposing to lessen those evils incident to the pursuit of Happiness by Marriage, or otherwise, from which the complaint has sprung that 'the business of Everybody is that of Nobody.'"

[1] The list of those who attended within the first two or three years appears to make about fifteen hundred names, many of them *"passim,"* —attending more than once. There were marchionesses, countesses, viscountesses and baronesses, and other ladies, besides many gentlemen of rank and distinction.

A medal of the Society had, obverse, the bust of
William Penn with the Charter of Pennsylvania in his
arms, and the legend: "Outinian Society Founded 1818.
William Penn deceased 1718." Reverse, Ulysses assailed by
Polyphemus.

The Report announced that a "mediatrix," a "confidential
female," would serve the Society in the matrimonial movement, but to allay possible fears of the too extended scope
of her enterprising labors it was stated that she was not to
promote marriages "of young or inexperienced heirs or
heiresses of fortune;" in these cases the persuasive effort
would be to restrain their ardor until they had full opportunity to secure "suitable matches." The copy of a blank
appears in a report; this was to be sent out by the Society,
to be filled up with the description of eligible parties, under
no less than fifty-one different headings. It was called
"The True Friend, or a table shewing the Exact Situation
in Life and Personal Qualities of known Marriageable
Ladies."

The Society continued in some form of activity for several
years; by 1825 it appears to have been concerned with be-
friending new inventions,—an improved breakfast-waiter, a
lamp-label bearing street names, etc.,—and to have relaxed
its matrimonial zeal.

Apparently, John Penn regarded himself as following in
the footsteps of his grandfather the Founder; at what distance he does not make plain. In one letter he says his
Society is simply carrying on the "useful business of the
form of humanity established by William Penn." Writing
to Francis Hopkinson, at Philadelphia, from Stoke, August
14, 1820, he says,—

"If I can be said to differ observably in opinion from a grandfather
with whom I conceive that I essentially agree more than with any other
man of either past or present times, it is in the circumstance that I
would allow them [the fine arts, to which he had just previously alluded]

within the bounds of morality a larger scope than may suit the provisions of a Lycurgus. This would be, however, for the same end of a
true liberty, of which William Penn made so good a use."

His literary labors are represented in a number of works,
all of the amateur order. In 1796 he printed a tragedy,
"The Battle of Edington, or British Liberty," derived from
the history of King Alfred. This was privately produced
at the Haymarket Theatre, the critics cut it up, and the
author answered the critics. In 1798 he issued his "Critical, Poetical, and Dramatic Works," in two volumes,
octavo. In 1811 Cambridge University encouraged him
with the degree of LL.D.

Besides the portraits of John Penn already mentioned,
there is one by Pine, painted in 1787, and presented by him,
December 18 of that year, to his friend Edmund Physick,
of Philadelphia. The portrait was supposed later to be that
of his cousin John Penn the Governor, and a copy was
placed under this supposition, in the capitol at Harrisburg,[1]

At the death of John Penn, June 21, 1834, his brother
Granville succeeded. He was born at the city house, New
Street, Spring Gardens, December 9, 1761. He had matriculated at Magdalen College, Oxford, November 11, 1780,
but did not take a degree. He entered the civil service,
and became an assistant chief clerk in the War Department,
for which, upon retiring, he received a pension of five hundred and fifty pounds a year. June 24, 1791, he married
Isabella, eldest daughter of General Gordon Forbes, Colonel
of the Twenty-ninth Regiment of Foot. General Forbes
was "of the family of Forbes of Skillater, in Aberdeen-
shire ;" his wife Mary was the "eldest daughter of Benjamin Sullivan, Esq., of Cork, Ireland."

At his marriage, Granville Penn "settled in London."[2]

[1] *Cf.* PENNA. MAG., Vol. I. p. 115.

[2] In a house in Hertford Street, Mayfair, it would appear from an
allusion in John Jay Smith's Address. In 1801, the notice of his
mother's death states, he lived at Petersham.

He occupied his leisure with literary labors, the results of which remain to us in numerous substantial volumes, two of which, the "Memorials" of his great-grandfather, Sir William Penn, are of value and form one of the chief sources of knowledge concerning the Admiral. The other works are largely theological ; some, however, being classical commentary and criticism. Mr. Penn's first book, "Critical Remarks on Isaiah," appeared in 1799 ; the Life of Admiral Penn was published 1833.

Granville Penn was a justice of the peace for Buckinghamshire, presumably after his succession and residence at Stoke. He died at Stoke, September 28, 1844, and it has been observed that this was almost precisely two centuries after the birth of his grandfather, William Penn the Founder,—a remarkably long period to be covered by three succeeding generations.[1]

The children of Granville and Isabella Penn were nine in number, four sons and five daughters, as follows :

1. John William, died in infancy ; buried at Stoke Poges, December 18, 1802.

2. Granville John, born November, 1803 ; died at Stoke unmarried, March 29, 1867. See below.

3. Thomas Gordon, died unmarried, September 10, 1869. See below.

4. William, died unmarried, at Brighton, January 7, 1848. He was matriculated at Christ Church, Oxford, June 5, 1818, aged 18, and received B.A. in 1833, and M.A. in 1837, being then of Semoure Hall, Norfolk. He was a barrister-at-law, of Lincoln's Inn, 1844.

5. Juliana Margaret, died in infancy ; buried at Stoke Poges, March 21, 1804.

6. Sophia, married (first wife of) Sir William Maynard

---

[1] William Penn was fifty-eight years old when his son Thomas was born, and Thomas Penn was sixty-one when his son Granville was born.

Gomm, field-marshal, K. C. B., and died without issue, 1827.
(Her husband was an officer of high distinction in the English
military service. His father was killed at the storming of La
Pointe-à-Pitre, in Guadeloupe, 1794, and he—the son—was
gazetted an ensign before he was ten years old. His most
notable service was in the Peninsular war. After the death of
his first wife, he married Elizabeth, daughter of Robert Kerr,
but died childless. Upon his return from service in India, he
purchased the Penn mansion in London, in Spring Gardens,
and made it his residence.)

7. Louisa Emily, died unmarried, May 27, 1841.

8. Isabella Mary, died unmarried, at Brompton, January
28, 1856.

9. Henrietta Anne, died unmarried, at Brompton, June
13, 1855.

Granville Penn's will is referred to at some length in the
Gentleman's Magazine, 1845. It was proved January 16 of
that year, and was dated February 9, 1836. It left to Granville John Penn, his eldest living son, substantially the whole
of the disposable estate, including three thousand pounds a
year of the Parliamentary annuity (charged, however, with
some annuities and legacies), the premises in New Street,
Spring Gardens, and the estate at West End, Stoke Poges,
Bucks (the same, probably, purchased by John in 1822).
The entailed property passed to Granville John Penn, as
tenant in tail male, by the provisions of previous wills and
settlements.[1]

Of the nine children of Granville Penn, it will be seen
above that only one married, and she left no issue. In the

[1] The "Dictionary of National Biography," in its article on Granville Penn, states that Pennsylvania Castle, with all its historical contents, was subsequently, in 1887, purchased by J. Merrick Head, Esq.
This gentleman remains the owner of the property, 1899, his residence
being "Ardverness," Reigate, Surrey. Photographs of Pennsylvania
Castle as it now appears, kindly sent to the author by him, have been
deposited in the collections of the Historical Society of Pennsylvania.

line of Thomas Penn, therefore, this branch of the family ends here, and our account of it will be completed when we speak of Granville John and his brother Thomas Gordon. Referring first to the latter, it may be said, briefly, that he was M. A. of Christ Church College, Oxford, took orders in the English Church, and at his death, September 10, 1869, was the last male descendant of William Penn, Founder of Pennsylvania, bearing the name of Penn. With him the male entail of the Proprietary estate ended, and it passed to the heirs of his aunt Sophia, the wife of Archbishop Stuart. He was a man " of most extensive reading and research," but he was declared by a commission of lunacy incapable of managing his estates, which were consequently in Chancery until his death.

Granville John Penn maintained the ancient usage of the family by twice visiting Pennsylvania. His first visit was in 1852, his second in 1857. He presented to the Historical Society of Pennsylvania the large Indian wampum belt which is preserved among its collections, and which has come to be affectionately regarded by many as a present made by the Indian chiefs to the Founder at the " Great Treaty " of 1683. He was cordially received in Philadelphia on both visits,[1] and in 1857 was entertained at supper in the Letitia House, since removed to and now standing in Fairmount Park.[2]

[1] An invitation issued by Granville John Penn during his stay in Philadelphia, in 1852, to a party at " Solitude " is as follows :

Mr. Penn requests the pleasure of Mr. Geo. M. Justice's *Company on Tuesday the 29th June, between the hours of one and five o' Clock.*

At Solitude on the Schuylkill.

144 Walnut Street

19th June 1852

The Steamboats ply from Fairmount at every hour during the afternoon.

[The portion in *Italic* is printed ; the remainder written.]

[2] See Horatio Gates Jones's account of the supper at the Letitia House, in PENNA. MAG., Vol. IV. p. 412. "The chief dishes were

This, however, was only one among many attentions paid him.   " He was the recipient of a public dinner ; the Mayor and Councils of Philadelphia gave him a public reception, and his speeches on both occasions were remarkable for classical taste and dignified delivery.   These attentions he returned by a very elegant collation under tents at ' Solitude.'   He afterwards visited many parts of this State, and extended his tour to Washington, Ohio, etc., expressing himself everywhere delighted with our scenery and people, and highly gratified to witness so much that was beautiful, and such great prosperity. His name was a passport to many kindnesses and civilities." [1]

Granville John Penn studied at Christ Church College, Oxford, and received there his degree of M.A.   Dr. Langley, afterwards Archbishop of Canterbury, was tutor to him and his brother.   He was educated for, and became, a barrister-at-law.   His early education, as well as that of his brother, was conducted by their father ; they had never gone to school previous to their entering college.[2]   His early years were

baked and boiled shad. [It was the 29th of April.] Mr. Penn appeared to enjoy the whole affair very much. . . . Among the many jokes . . . I remember one which seemed to amuse Mr. Penn not a little. Some one said that the shad was a remarkable fish, because it always returned to the same river where it was hatched. ' Is that the case ? ' asked Mr. Penn. ' O, yes,' was the reply, ' and there is no doubt, Mr. Penn, that you are to-night eating part of a lineal descendant of one of the shad of which your great ancestor partook when he lived at Pennsbury Manor ! ' ''

[1] John Jay Smith's Address.

[2] From the same :   '' While at college he acted as one of the pages at the coronation of George the Fourth—a position much sought for by young men of family. He was fond of relating that on this great occasion, the young pages, unaccustomed to waiting on others, forgot to bring in the hot dishes ; the royal company was consequently obliged to be contented with the cold collation set out for show during the ceremony ; after which the newly-fledged servitors had the satisfaction of consuming the turtle soups, the game, and other delicacies intended for royalty ! ''

passed at his father's house, or "with Lord and Lady Cremorne, or at Stoke Park, whither the family, at the period of the Weymouth season, regularly migrated, during their uncle John's residence at the Portland Castle." [1]

Granville John Penn was a deputy lieutenant and magistrate for Bucks. Succeeding to his father at Stoke, in 1844, the family home was kept there until the sale of the property a few years later.[2] A picturesque and interesting description of the place as it appeared in 1845, before the breaking up, is given in John Jay Smith's Address, from which we are now freely citing. He says,—

"The family at Stoke Park then [1845] consisted of the widow of Granville Penn—her husband being then very recenty deceased—a very old lady, Granville John, three unmarried sisters, and the youngest brother, William, who was educated for the Bar. The mother, the three daughters, and the three sons are now [1867] all deceased, but a more happy and united family than they formed twenty-five years ago it would be difficult to describe. Their surroundings were all of the very first class, as regards a truly noble residence, an extensive and perfectly kept park, abounding in deer and other game, a library of great size and value, liveried servants, fine horses and coaches, with everything that could make life desirable. The picturesque park that has seen so many successive generations come and go, as we rambled among its beautiful and ancient trees, was as silent as any scene amid our own native forests. The servants had mowed the extensive lawns, the hot-house gardeners had set out the Italian portico with newly flowered plants, covering the pots with lycopodiums and mosses, and the attendants had all disappeared before breakfast was announced : every sound was stilled and the place was all one's own. The deer silently wandered among the ferns half as tall as themselves ; the librarian, himself a learned man and an author of merit, was at his post to hand the guests any book they required.

[1] John Jay Smith.

[2] It has already been quoted from Sheahan's "History of Bucks" that the manor was purchased by Mr. Labouchere (later Baron Taunton) in 1848. Sheahan also says that Stoke Court, the residence (1862) of Abraham Darby, Esq., was purchased of the Penns in 1850. Stoke Park is now (1899) the property of Mr. Wilberforce Bryant.

"One felt assured, on passing into the great entrance-hall, beneath a funeral hatchment in memory of the late proprietor, that he was not entering a house of consistent Quakers, for one of the first objects was a pair of small brass cannon, taken by Admiral Penn in his Dutch wars, elegantly mounted and polished ; and near by, opening on the left, was a fine billiard-room. Family prayers were not neglected ; the numerous servants were regularly assembled, as is a usual custom in England : the service of the day is reverently read, and all, from the head of the house to the humblest individual, on their knees give thanks for mercies received. The house was not wanting in memorials of Pennsylvania, a large portion of the Treaty Tree, sent by some members of the Historical Society, with a silver label on it, ornamenting the grand drawing-room of the second story, which was reached by a superb, long, and rather fatiguing marble staircase. The birds of Pennsylvania, too, were represented in elegant cases, together with Indian relics, and a finely preserved beaver, which animal was once the annual tribute of the Penns to the Crown." [1]

Granville John Penn died rather suddenly, March 29, 1867, no one but his man-servant being with him. He had, it is said, "an unsigned will" in his hand. His estate passed to his brother, Rev. Thomas Gordon Penn, already mentioned.

We return now to the last of the children of Thomas and Lady Juliana Penn, Sophia Margaretta. From her two family branches are in existence,—that of the Stuarts, present representatives of the Penn inheritance in Pennsylvania, under the entail, and that of the Earl of Ranfurly. Sophia was born in December, 1764. She married, in April (? or May), 1796, William Stuart, who subsequently became Archbishop of Armagh, in the Established Church, and consequently "Primate" of Ireland.

The father of Mr. Stuart was a famous figure in English politics,—John, third Earl of Bute,—who was the early associate and adviser of George III., and for several years his Prime Minister, the shining mark for the shafts of Wilkes and "Junius." The wife of the Earl of Bute was the only

[1] This description, in greater detail, is also given in John Jay Smith's "Recollections," (privately printed, 1892).

daughter of that even more famous person, Lady Mary
Wortley Montagu. The children of the Earl included five
sons, of whom William was the youngest, and was "designed for the church." He was prepared at Winchester
School, studied at St. John's College, Cambridge, received
his M. A. in 1774, obtained a fellowship, and later received
the vicarage of Luton, Bedfordshire.[1] This place he held
over fourteen years, faithfully performing his parish duties,
when he became, 1793, Canon of Windsor. Later he was
appointed Bishop of St. David's, and in 1800 made Archbishop of Armagh.[2] He took the degree of D.D. in 1789.
Boswell, in his "Life of Johnson," mentions him as having
been introduced to the Doctor "at his house in Bolt Court,"
and as "being, with all the advantage of high-birth, learning, travel, and elegant manners, an exemplary parish priest,
in every respect."[3]

As Archbishop for twenty-two years he filled a conspic-
uous place in the affairs of the Irish Church. Extended

[1] A thin living. "G. P." (Granville Penn, no doubt) says in the
Gentleman's Magazine for June, 1822, "with only two hundred pounds
a year, although the duty was very laborious."

[2] "G. P." earnestly refutes the idea that his elevation came from
his father, or was due to his father's influence, and points out that the
Earl of Bute died March 10, 1792, and that Mr. Stuart's promotion
from his parish work to the deanery did not come until next year.

[3] Maria Edgeworth says of Archbishop Stuart (in a letter to her aunt,
Mrs. Ruxton, of Black Castle, April 28, 1809), "The Primate was very
agreeable during the two days he spent here [Edgeworthstown]. My
father traveled with him from Dublin to Ardbraccan, and this reputed
silent man never ceased talking and telling entertaining anecdotes till
the carriage stopped at the steps at Ardbraccan. This I could hardly
credit till I myself heard his Grace burst forth in conversation. The
truth of his character gives such value to everything he says, even to
his humorous stories. He has two things in his character which I think
seldom meet—a strong taste for humor, and strong feelings of indigna-
tion. . . . He is a man of the warmest feelings, with the coldest
exterior I ever saw."

allusion is made to him in Rev. John Stuart's "History of Armagh."[1] He died May 6, 1822. The peculiar and distressing circumstances of his death have passed into the chronicle of the time, and may be given here from the obituary article (May, 1822) in the *Gentleman's Magazine*. The Archbishop was ill at his house in London. Sir Henry Halford, an eminent physician, was called in, and prescribed a "draught," which was ordered at an apothecary's near by.

"His Lordship having expressed some impatience that the draught had not arrived, Mrs. Stuart inquired of the servants if it had come; and being answered in the affirmative, she desired that it might be brought to her immediately. The under butler went to the porter, and demanded the draught for his master. The man had just before received it, together with a small vial of laudanum and camphorated spirits, which he occasionally used himself as an external embrocation. Most unluckily, in the hurry of the moment, instead of giving the draught intended for the Archbishop, he accidentally substituted the bottle which contained the embrocation. The under butler instantly carried it to Mrs. Stuart, without examination, and that lady, not having a doubt that it was the medicine which had been recommended by Sir H. Halford, poured it into a glass and gave it to her husband! In a few minutes, however, the dreadful mistake was discovered, upon which Mrs. Stuart rushed from the presence of the Archbishop into the street, with the phial in her hand, and in a state of speechless distraction. Mr. Jones, the Apothecary, having procured the usual antidote, lost not a moment in accompanying Mrs. Stuart back to Hill street, where he administered to his Lordship, now almost in a state of stupor, the strongest emetics, and used every means which his skill and ingenuity could suggest to remove the poison from his stomach, all, however, without effect. Sir Henry Halford and Dr. Baillie were sent for. These physicians added their efforts to those of Mr. Jones, but with as little success."[2]

[1] Extracts from this are given in the *Gentleman's Magazine*, Vol. XLI.

[2] Writing from London to her step-mother, in Ireland, May 10, 1822, Maria Edgeworth says, "The sudden death of the Primate, and the horrible circumstances attending it, have incapacitated me from any more home-writing at this moment. Mrs. Stuart gave him the medicine; he had twice asked for his draught, and when she saw the servant

Mrs. Stuart, widow of the Archbishop, survived her husband twenty-five years, and died April 29, 1847. She was buried at Luton, Bedfordshire, in the Stuart family vault. Her and the Archbishop's children were :

1. Mary Juliana, born May, 1797 ; married, February 28, 1815, Thomas Knox, Viscount Northland, who, succeeding his father, became second Earl of Ranfurly, of Dungannon Park, County Tyrone, Ireland. The Earl of Ranfurly was born April 19, 1786, and died March 21, 1858. His widow survived him, and died July 11, 1866. They had eight children,—three sons and five daughters.[1] The eldest son, Thomas, who became third Earl of Ranfurly, will be mentioned below. The second son, Major William Stuart Knox, was member of Parliament for Dungannon, 1851 to 1874. The third son, Granville Henry John Knox, born 1829, died 1845.

2. William, born October 31, 1798 ; married August 8, 1821, Henrietta Maria Sarah, eldest daughter of Admiral Sir Charles Morrice Pole, Bart., K. C. B., etc. (Mrs. Stuart died July 26, 1853, and he remarried 1854.) William Stuart was educated at St. John's College, Cambridge, where he received his M.A., 1820. He was a magistrate and deputy lieutenant for Bedfordshire, and high sheriff 1846. He was member of Parliament for Armagh 1820–26, and for Bedfordshire 1830–34. His seat was Aldenham Abbey, near Watford, Herts. He died July 7, 1874. He had five children—three sons and two daughters—by his first marriage.[2] The eldest son, Colonel William Stuart, will be mentioned below.

come in, she ran down, seized the bottle, and poured it out without looking at the label, which was most distinct ' for external application.' When dying, and when struggling under the power of the opium, he called for a pencil and wrote these words for a comfort to his wife : ' I could not have lived long, my dear love, at all events.' "

[1] List in Burke's "Peerage."
[2] List in Burke's "Commoners."

3. Henry, born 1804; died 1854; sometime member of Parliament for Bedfordshire.

4. Louisa, died unmarried September 29, 1823. Buried at Luton.

The third Earl of Ranfurly, Thomas, son of the second Earl, and grandson of Archbishop Stuart, was born November 13, 1816; married October 10, 1848, Harriet, daughter of James Rimington, of Broomhead Hall, County York; and died May 20, 1858. His three children included his eldest son, Thomas Granville Henry Stuart Knox, fourth Earl of Ranfurly, who was killed in 1875 while on a shooting expedition in Abyssinia, and his second son (brother to the last named), Uchter John Mark Knox, fifth Earl, who was born August 14, 1856, and succeeded to the title on the death of his brother, just mentioned. He is married and has children.[1] An article in the PENNSYLVANIA MAGAZINE, by W. M. Conway, describing some of the numerous Penn portraits and relics in his possession at Dungannon Park, 1884, has been heretofore referred to. The Knox family, of which he is representative, forms, it will be seen, one of the two existing lines descended from William Penn through Thomas Penn.

William Stuart, mentioned above, who died 1874, became, on the death of Rev. Thomas Gordon Penn, unmarried, without issue, 1869, the "tenant in tail general" to all the property which remained of that which John Penn, Thomas Penn, and Richard Penn had entailed in Pennsylvania. By the failure of the male line in every branch descended from William Penn's second marriage, it now came to him as the oldest son then living of the only daughter of Thomas Penn who had left issue. Mr. Stuart thus received not only the John Penn two-fourths, but the Thomas Penn one-fourth and the Richard Penn one-fourth of the Pennsylvania property. By two indentures, dated August 5 and

[1] Burke's "Peerage," 1891.

13

September 2, 1870, respectively, he " barred the entail," and
by another indenture, dated November 11, 1870, he confirmed
all the Penn conveyances previously made in Pennsylvania.[1]

By his will, William Stuart devised all his real estate to
his son, Colonel William Stuart. The latter was born in
London (at the house of his grandmother, widow of the
Primate, Hill Street), March 7, 1825. He was member of
Parliament for Bedfordshire 1854-57 and 1859-68, and
magistrate and deputy lieutenant. He married, September
13, 1859, Katharine, eldest daughter of John Armitage
Nicholson, Esq., of Balrath, County Meath. She died Oc-
tober 16, 1881. Colonel Stuart died December 21, 1893.
They had issue :

1. William Dugald. See below.

2. Mary Charlotte Florence, born at Kempston, Beds,
May 2, 1863.

3. Henry Esme, born at Kempston, July 15, 1865.

4. Elizabeth Frances Sybil, born at Kempston, May 20,
1867.

William Dugald Stuart thus represents now (1897) this
branch of the Penn family, descended from Thomas Penn.
He was born at Southsea, Portsmouth, October 18, 1860,
and was educated at Eton and St. John's College, Cambridge.
He is a barrister-at-law of the Inner Temple. He entered
the army and passed several years in active service in the
field as an officer of the King's Royal Rifle Corps. His
principal residence is at Tempsford Hall, Bedfordshire,
where he has in his possession the famous " portrait in
armor " of William Penn the Founder, a replica of which is
in the collection of the Historical Society of Pennsylvania,
the beautiful " Group of Four Children " (Thomas Penn's),
by Sir Joshua Reynolds, a replica of the Lely portrait of

[1] This action is highly commended by Hon. Eli K. Price, in his
pamphlet " The Proprietary Title of the Penns," as making a perfect
title for holders of land derived from the family.

Admiral Penn in the gallery of Greenwich Hospital, and
other interesting family relics. Attention has been given
by him, in recent years, to the remnants of the manor
estates of the Penns in Pennsylvania.

TABLE: DESCENDANTS OF THOMAS PENN.

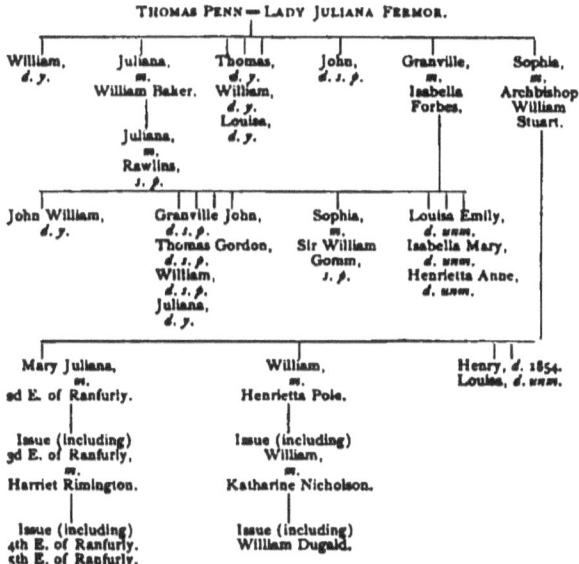

XI.

Richard Penn and His Descendants.

RICHARD PENN, son of William Penn the Founder, was the only one of the three Young Proprietaries, inheritors of the Pennsylvania property, who did not come to visit their inheritance. Richard was born, as already stated, at the house of his grandfather, Thomas Callowhill, in Bristol, January 17, 1705–6. He was named after his uncle Richard, the younger brother of the Founder, who died in his youth, more than thirty years earlier. In 1720, as appears from his mother's letter to Rebecca Blackfan, Richard was "at school." Later he was sent to business in London, and in a letter from his brother Thomas to (their brother) John, in 1728, the former speaks of him as an apprentice, and says,—

" Neither would I by any means have Dick one day more, while he is an apprentice, absent himself from business, and therefore beg you not to put it in his head, for if he does not now for two months, while all their customers are in town, constantly attend and ingratiate himself with them, it being his last Spring, I had almost as lief see him drive plow," etc.

However judicious Thomas's views may have been as to Richard's conduct, it appears that the latter, not far from the date of this letter, must have exchanged apprenticeship for matrimony. In the reconveyance to the Penns of the Pennsylvania estates by Gee and Woods, the surviving mortgagees, in January, 1728–9, one-fourth of the Proprietary right, being Richard's share, was conveyed to his brothers John and Thomas, in trust for him, the reason for this being, as stated in a note in the pleadings in the Maryland Boundary case,

194

RICHARD PENN, PROPRIETARY

" Mr. Richard Penn being then married was the reason why the legal estate was not vested in him, only the Trust thereof."[1]

Richard Penn married Hannah Lardner. She was the daughter of Dr. John Lardner, a physican of Gracechurch Street, London, and Woodford, Epping Forest, Essex, her mother, the wife of Dr. Lardner, being a Winstanley.[2]

July 11, 1729, writing to his brother John, Richard says, " My wife joyns with service to you." This was but a few days before the birth of their first child, John, who was afterwards Governor of Pennsylvania. The following letter to his uncle John ("the American") is among the Penn papers :

" LONDON, July 15, 1729.

" Dear John I hope you got well home—I got well to Town. Last night about Eleven o'clock Mrs. Penn was happily delivered of a fine Boy. He is to be named after your honour and I'm to have y* pleasure to stand Godfather. Your last Civillitys have put me so far in y' debt that I fear [I] shall never have opportunity enough to return them, but pray believe me, dear sir, you most obedient [etc.]

" GEO : STAINFORTH.

" To JOHN PENN, ESQ., at Fein's,

" near Maidenhead, Berks."

It may safely be assumed that Richard's marriage was regarded by his two elder and bachelor brothers as an " early " and not prudent one. Richard's correspondence with them in the years following discloses that John, partly, no doubt, from his larger portion, and Thomas, from his superior business sense and greater personal force, dominated the youngest member of the trio. A letter to Thomas in Pennsylvania, undated, but evidently in 1732 or 1733 (well written

[1] Presumably John and Thomas must later have conveyed his share to Richard in fee.

[2] Hannah's brother, Lynford Lardner, born 1715, came to Pennsylvania in 1740, was in the Proprietary Land Office, represented the Penns, was Receiver-General, Keeper of the Great Seal, etc., and died 1774.

for that day, in a good hand, and fairly spelled), refers to the landed interests, expresses regret for taking Thomas's time, and proceeds, "but I am sure you'd excuse me, for you know what a situation I was in when you left us, and I declare I never wanted a guinea so much as now." There is also this postscript :

" My little boy is in breeches, and I think has throve ever since ; he sends his Duty to you, my little girl is hardly old enough, but I do it for her." [1]

Richard's will shows that in 1750 he had a house, or houses, in London, and sundry references in the fragmentary family letters suggest that he must have spent some time in town, but his principal residence during most of his married life was at Stanwell, in the city suburbs, in Middlesex. He writes from there to his brother Thomas in Pennsylvania as early as January 20, 1732-3, and for many years his correspondence is usually dated there. A letter from Bishop Vickris (the old friend of the family, especially of John, heretofore repeatedly mentioned) to John Penn, dated at Wandsworth, May 2, 1736, says,—

"I got to Stanwell just at dinner time, & stay'd till 5 o'Clock Yr Bro' Dick was so good as to propose carrying me to Twitnam [Twickenham] in his Chair which I readily accepted on, & twas a great Ease to me. Yr Cosen Will Penn [1] went to Sussex last week & no body Knows when he Returns."

Richard and William Penn, 3d, seem to have been quite friendly ; at any rate, there is a note extant from the former to his brother John's housekeeper at Feens, Hannah Roberts, October 29, 1734,—during John's visit to Pennsylvania,—as follows :

"I am going the latter part of this week with my cousin William Penn into Sussex ; he wants two or three spaniels ; if all my bro's

[1] These were John, afterwards the Governor, and Hannah.

[1] This was William Penn, 3d, son of William Penn, Jr. Details concerning him will be given later.

[John's] are not disposed of I desire you will send by the bearer of this letter two or three of them, and the gun which was my cousin Springett's—it is a whole stock and steel mounted.''

Richard was apparently desired by his brothers to go to Pennsylvania. The letter, already cited, of his sister, Margaret (Penn) Freame, in June, 1736, from Philadelphia, to John Penn, in England, says, " He [Thomas] much wonders at my brother Richard's declining to come over."

By the betterment of the Pennsylvania estate Richard and his family benefited of course, and probably from about 1740 they felt themselves comfortably off. But there are traces in the letters of Richard's consciousness of his subordination to his brothers. In an earnest letter to John in January, 1745–6, a few months before the latter's death, he complains of John's having treated him like a child in regard to financial matters, etc. Other family affairs are suggested in other letters. In one from Thomas Penn, in London, to Richard Hockley, April 16, 1741, the former says,—

" My Brother Richard and Sister are gone to Bath, where she has been dangerously ill, but is recovered ; her illness so discomposed my Brother that he has not taken regularly to the waters, so that he can give me no account of the Effect they have upon him.''

Bishop Vickris, writing from Bristol, July 3, 1747, to Thomas Penn, says,—

" . . . I congratulate your Bro and Sister Penn upon their having another Son, and if he bears the Name of his Good and Honourable Grandfather I hope he will inherit his virtues, which will make him truly Rich and Great.''

Richard and Hannah Penn had four children :

1. John, Governor of Pennsylvania. We shall speak at some length of him below. He was twice married, but left no issue.

2. Hannah, who is referred to above in the letter to John, in 1732 (or 1733), as " my little girl," not old enough to send her duty message to her uncle. There is among the Penn

letters one from her to her uncle John, written in a very
formal, childish hand (though she must have been some
twelve or thirteen years old), as follows :

" TWICKENHAM, 4th Ap. 1745.
" HONOURED SIR
"I have done according to your Desire in consulting with Mrs.
Delafosse what Work I should do, and she advises me to do Cross
Stitch chairs.   I saw my Papa and Mama, last Saturday, who were very
well, as is
" Honoured Sir
" Your most dutiful Niece
" HANNAH PENN."

Hannah married, July 19, 1774, James Clayton,[1] and died
in Cavendish Square, London, without issue. She was buried
at Stoke Poges, October 2, 1791, where her husband also
had been buried January 23, 1790. Her will was proved
October 21, 1791, leaving her estate to her brothers John
and Richard Penn and the children of the latter.

3. Richard, who became Governor of Pennsylvania. See
below.

4. William. His birth is alluded to in Bishop Vickris's
letter, above, in 1747. He died in childhood, February 4,
1760. In a letter to Governor James Hamilton, at Philadelphia, February 8, 1760, Thomas Penn says, " Our family is
now under great affliction, my Brother's in particular, his
youngest son and your God Son dyed last Monday of a
lingering fever." One of the codicils to Richard Penn's
will says William was buried in Penn Church, Bucks.[2]

Richard Penn died February 4, 1771, and was buried at
Stoke Poges. His will, made in 1750, and the four codicils,
1756, 1760, 1763, 1768, convey considerable family informa-

[1] Cf. *Gentleman's Magazine.*   The groom is described as " late of
Sunbury," and the bride as " Miss Penn of Laleham, in Middlesex,
daughter of [etc.] with £30,000."

[2] See letter previously cited, from the Vicar of Penn, 1895, Rev. J.
Grainger, M.A., describing the Penn coffins in the vault of that church.

HANNAH (LARDNER) PENN

tion. The will is dated March 21, 1750, and was proved March 4, 1771. The testator describes himself as "of Stanwell, in the county of Middlesex, Esquire." He appoints William Vigor, Esq., of Taplow, Bucks, and Joseph Freame, of London, banker, his executors (but as they both died before he did, a codicil later appoints his wife Hannah in their stead), they to act as to all his personal estate in Great Britain or elsewhere, except America. For America he appoints Lynford Lardner, Richard Peters, and Richard Hockley. He says in the will proper (1750), after speaking of his eldest son, John Penn, " I have at present only three younger children, a daughter, Hannah Penn, and two sons, Richard Penn and William Penn." In the codicil, March 13, 1760, he says, " My younger son William Penn is lately dead." He directs that a family vault be made " in the body of Stoke Church, in the county of Bucks," fourteen or sixteen feet long, seven feet broad, seven feet high. He says (1750), " I am possessed of an house called Batavia House, in the parish of Sunbury, in the County of Middlesex, with the garden [etc.]. I have purchased two individual sixth parts thereof." Later in a codicil he says he has bought two-sixths more. He leaves a house in Cavendish Square to his wife.

Hannah Lardner Penn, wife of Richard, survived her husband over fourteen years. Her death is noted in the *Gentleman's Magazine* (Vol. LV., Part I., p. 326) as of date April 20, 1785 :

"At Laleham, Middlesex, Mrs. Penn, widow of the late Hon. Richard Penn, formerly proprietor and governor of Pennsylvania, in North America."

John Penn, eldest child of Richard Penn and Hannah Lardner, became, in 1763, just when the Colonial wars closed and the Revolutionary ferment began, Lieutenant-Governor of Pennsylvania for his father and uncle, and he has the distinction of being the last Proprietary Governor.

His life from 1752 to his death in 1795 was mostly spent in Pennsylvania, and at his death he seems to have left behind a good repute, thus fairly preserving, if he did not increase, the family name in the Founder's Colony.

His early life, however, had upon it a serious cloud. He married "while a school-boy," as the accounts phrase it, a wife whom his family, and perhaps more particularly his uncle Thomas, compelled him to repudiate. The right and wrong of this transaction appear to me very uncertain, but the data available are too meagre to permit intelligent discussion of it. The wife was, it seems, the daughter of James Cox, of London,—whether the silversmith who made Thomas Penn's wedding presents for Lady Juliana, I do not know. Probably the marriage occurred as early as 1747, in which year John would have been eighteen years old.

The course adopted with John was to send him off to Geneva, to pursue his studies in care of a tutor. The record of this exile in the Penn manuscripts of the Historical Society of Pennsylvania is quite extended. Thomas Penn, August 6, 1747, made an agreement with one Robert Dunant to take John to Geneva, teach him, direct his conduct, etc. A little later they set off, Thomas Penn accompanying them to the Continent. John writes to his uncle, October 2, 1747, from Basel, "After we parted, we went on," etc., and adds a postscript: "I hope you will excuse writing, as I cannot get any pen fit to write with, having left the writing box behind, it being put into your chaise, out of a mistake." Dunant and John reached Geneva October 10, and December 1 John acknowledges letters from Thomas, written at Frankfort and Rotterdam, on his return, and London after his arrival home.

The stay at Geneva continued about four years, until the autumn of 1751. The preserved letters passing between uncle and nephew are quite numerous, and it would appear that Thomas did not spare reproofs, while John at times pleads so abjectly for pardon for faults committed, especially in London,[1] as to awaken our concern as to his entire sincerity, and to show, certainly, that he very much wished the continuance of his uncle's favor. There is also a letter, without date, from James Cox to Thomas Penn, reciting John's marriage to his daughter, and pressing the inquiry, since John has now finished his studies, what is proposed to be done. It is a straightforward letter, couched in sensible language, and, so far as it goes, gives no unfavorable impression of the Cox side of the case. August 26, 1750, William Lowther[2] writes to Thomas Penn from Geneva, saying he had found John Penn there, doing well, had received many civilities from him, etc. A year later Thomas Penn was arranging for John to travel, and provided funds for him through Thomas Hyam & Son, London, merchants and bankers. In September or October, 1751, John set off; he writes from Turin, October 13, from Milan six days later, from Florence, November 6, and from Rome the 11th of December. Precisely how or when the tour concluded does not appear, but the time must have been not much later. In the summer following he came to Pennsylvania. Writing from Hitcham, England, August 26, 1752, to Richard Peters at Philadelphia, Thomas Penn says,—

" I wrote you a few lines by my nephew from Deal, who arrived just in time to take Mr. Morris's passage off his hands, as we thought it best for him to stay a little longer." [3]

[1] The manner of his allusions seems to suggest something more than a reckless marriage.

[2] This was probably Sir William Lowther, the last of the baronets in the line of Anthony Lowther and Margaret Penn,—the great-grandson of that couple. He died 1756.

[3] A further passage in this letter is of interest in connection with Thomas's expectation, at this time, of revisiting Pennsylvania. He says, " I have recommended to my Nephew to give some orders for the cleaning of my House, & desire you will give him any assistance you

The *Pennsylvania Gazette*, November 30, 1752, contains advices from New York, November 27 :

"Last Monday there arrived here Capts. Bryant and Garrison from London. John Penn, Esq., a Grand Son of the late William Penn, Esq., Proprietary of Pennsylvania, came passenger with Capt. Bryant, and is since set out on his Way for Pennsylvania."

And the same journal, December 7, adds,—

"Friday last John Penn, Esq., (son of the Honourable Richard Penn, Esq., one of our Proprietaries), arrived here from London."

Shortly after his arrival, John Penn was made a member of the Provincial Council. The minutes, Tuesday, February 6, 1753, state,—

"The Governor [James Hamilton] proposed to introduce Mr. John Penn, the Eldest son of Proprietor Richard Penn, lately arrived here, into the Council, and left it to the consideration of the Board what Place they would be pleased to offer him; Whereupon the Council, taking the Governor's Proposition into their Consideration, unanimously agreed, as he stood in so near a Relation to the Proprietaries, and was

can in it. I desire the painting may be immediately done, that the smell may be gone before the time I can possibly be there, and the papering in the spring, as I hope to embark in April or May [1753] at farthest."

Mr. Keith says (" Provincial Councillors of Pennsylvania," p. 309), "The father-in-law [Cox] wrote to him [John Penn] in 1751, after he had been away four years, to induce him to cut loose from the Penn family, as he was of age, and his uncle's recent marriage rendered it unlikely that he should be his heir ; but John Penn, after a trip to Italy, where he spent more money than his uncle thought proper, cheerfully submitted to his uncle and father, who did not scruple at sending him permanently from his wife. Lieut. Gov. Hamilton, to whom the story was confided, offered him a home in Pennsylvania. In order to see his father before crossing the Atlantic, he came as privately as possible to England. His return being discovered, he hastily withdrew to Lille, and waited until an opportunity offered to go to America. He then recrossed the Channel, took ship, and, after various delays and a voyage of seven weeks and three days, arrived in New York, Nov. 21, 1752. He reached Philadelphia on December 1st, and became the guest of [James] Hamilton at Bush Hill."

himself perfectly agreeable to them, to place him at their Head, and that when he shall have taken the legal Qualification he should be considered as the first named or Eldest Counsellor on the Death or Absence of the Governor or Lieutenant Governor.''

The minutes show him to have been moderately attentive to the Council meetings; his presence is noted after August (1753) at eight of them within six months. In 1754 he was one of the Commissioners sent to represent Pennsylvania in the conference with the Indians at Albany, New York. April 6 of that year Governor Hamilton informed the Council that he intended to appoint John Penn and Richard Peters, of the Council, and Isaac Norris and Benjamin Franklin, of the Assembly, "as Commissioners for this Province to the treaty in Albany in June next."

John's conduct here, however, did not please his uncle. Letters from the latter to Richard Peters refer to him in terms of sharp dissatisfaction. These letters especially belong to the year 1755. February 21 of that year Thomas Penn writes to Peters,—

"I write you this line to tell you in confidence that my nephew's demands have been much more than they should be on Mr. Hockley that he is ordered not to take any more than the amount of his bills. [Some bills, he complains, have been drawn by J. P. on parties in London who did not even know him, and have gone back unaccepted.] I think he had better return to Europe, and begin to fear he wants to settle in England."

Again, August 15, Thomas Penn wrote to Peters, and after further complaints of John, said,—

"Your letter . . . shows me plainly that I must never expect any assistance from him . . . I receive great pain to find after all my expense he will remain so useless a branch of my family. I could not have thought it possible that any young man would have said he could not do business, and hated a place belonging to his Family, where any man might live with the greatest satisfaction, and that he lives in a sort of exile in the place where he could live with honour, and where he would have been sent had he married the first Duke's daughter in the kingdom. . . . I have nothing to do now but to throw him off my mind,

as much as possible, and hope for a more useful member of society in
my own offspring. . . . I think it better he should return.''

Following these instructions, no doubt, in the autumn of
1755, about three years from the time of his arrival, John
Penn returned to England. His last attendance at the
Governor's Council is recorded on September 24 of that
year. What occurred in England in the following eight
years to improve the relations between himself and his
uncle must be left to surmise, but in 1763 he returned to
Pennsylvania, commissioned by his uncle and his father as
their Lieutenant-Governor. Thomas Penn writes to Richard
Peters, from London, August 31, 1763, thanking him for
remaining in Philadelphia till his nephew, by whom this
letter is sent, should arrive, and adds, '' We are very sensible Mr. John Penn will arrive at a time of great difficulty.
. . . I make no doubt all those we have experienced the
friendship of will assist him. . . . My nephew Richard
Penn accompanies his brother, to see the country. I must
desire your friendly offices to him.'' In the '' Colonial
Records '' (Vol. IX. p. 71), a memorandum, at New Castle,
on Saturday, October 29, says,—

"The Assembly sent a Verbal Message to the Governor by three
Members that the House, having understood that His Honour intended
to set off To-morrow morning for Philadelphia in order to meet the
Hon'ble John Penn, Esquire, lately appointed his Successor in the
Government, and this day arrived in the river from England, proposed
to adjourn, [etc.].''

In the Council, at Philadelphia, October 31, the commis-
sion of John Penn, signed by Thomas Penn and Richard
Penn on the 18th of June, and with the royal approval
August 31, was produced and read, and he took "the usual
oaths." Then "the Governor, attended by the Council,
Mayor, Recorder, Aldermen, and Common Council, and
preceded by the Sheriff and his officers, went to the Court
House, where his commission was published with due

solemnity in the presence of a very great concourse of people. Immediately afterwards the Battery Guns fired a Royal Salute, and the bells of Christ Church [were] rung in compliment to him."

The next day "the Governor, accompanied by the Earl of Stirling, Lynford Lardner, and Richard Penn, Esq's., and several other gentlemen, went to New Castle," where the commission was publicly read, etc., with due ceremony.[1]

The commission given John, it seemed, was for three years only, and was to expire December 1, 1766; accordingly the Council minutes show that in 1766 a new commission was sent over, extending to 1769, and in 1769 another for three years more. But in 1771, upon the death of his father, John again went back to England. In the Council, Monday, May 6, 1771, the president, James Hamilton, announced that John Penn had embarked for Great Britain on the previous Saturday. Richard Penn, his brother, produced in October following (16th) a commission as Lieutenant-Governor, and served as such until August, 1773, when John returned. On Monday, the 30th of that month, John Penn appeared in the Council and produced a revocation of Richard's commission, dated April 30, and his own commission of the same date.

The public service of John Penn, beginning in 1763 and closing thirteen years later with the final collapse of the Proprietary government, fortunately and favorably shuts from view the apparent shortcomings of his earlier life. It was, on the whole creditable to him. His position through the whole period was one of extreme difficulty, and the fact

---

[1] In a letter from George Roberts, Philadelphia, to Samuel Powel (afterwards mayor of the city), then in London, dated November 5, 1763, the writer says, "Last week we had the pleasure of hearing our new appointed Governor's proclamation read. The usual calvacade attended. . . . His honor Penn is a little gentleman, though he may govern equal to one seven foot high."

that he retained his place without alienating the good will of the people generally is a testimony to his personal qualities.

May 31, 1766, John Penn married Ann, the eldest daughter of Chief-Justice William Allen, of Philadelphia. The marriage is upon the register of Christ Church, and presumably took place there. The *Pennsylvania Gazette*, in its issue of June 6, 1766, announced,—

"On Saturday last the Honourable John Penn, Esq., our Governor, was married to Miss Ann Allen, eldest daughter of the Honourable William Allen, Esq., Chief Justice of this Province, a young Lady adorned with every Accomplishment to render the married State happy."

Of this event Thomas Penn writes to Richard Peters, July 17, 1766,—

"I have this day an account of my nephew's marriage from himself, and write to him by this opportunity to wish him joy. I think there is a good prospect of their being happy ; she has good sense, great sweetness of temper and prudence, and I think he knows how to prize qualities so amiable in so agreeable a form."

The presumption is that the first wife, the daughter of James Cox, was then deceased, but the light on that episode is very imperfect.[1] By neither marriage, so far as appears, was there issue. By his connection with the Allens John Penn's social, and for a brief time political, influence was increased. Up to 1776 the Allens were in the front rank of Colonial importance. Mrs. Penn's mother, Mrs. Allen, wife of the Chief-Justice, was the daughter of Andrew Hamilton, the distinguished lawyer, defender of the newspaper press, Speaker of the Assembly, etc., and the brothers of Mrs. Allen—uncles of Mrs. Penn—were Governor James Hamil-

[1] There is an entry in the *Gentleman's Magazine* of the death, March 17, 1760, of Mrs. Grace Penn, wife of John Penn, Esq., and my valued friend and correspondent, Joseph J. Green, of Tunbridge Wells, England, suggests that this very probably was she to whom we are here referring.

ton, of Bush Hill, and Andrew Hamilton, of The Woodlands.
Mrs. Penn's brothers, John, James, and Andrew Allen, were
active and prominent men, the last named for some time
Attorney-General of the Province.

The displacement of his brother Richard by John in 1773
seems to have been somewhat abrupt; it caused a serious
breach between them. The diary of Mrs. Penn's brother,
James Allen,[1] contains these allusions to the matter:

"August 23 [1773]. The 20th of this Month, Mr. John Penn, my
Sister, & Brother John [Allen] arrived at New York in the *Grovenor*
Mast Ship, & are daily expected here. He comes to assume the Government & to supersede his Brother; to his [Richard's] great dissatisfaction. This step, tho' highly approved by Mr. John Penn's friends,
it is thought will lay the foundation of a lasting animosity between the
brothers. Mr. John Penn's reasons for this measure are that his
Brother has set up a claim to the Proprietary Estate in reserved Lots &
Manors, & immediately on his coming to the Government entered a
Caveat in the Proprietary Offices, declaratory of his right, which he still
reserves, notwithstanding his signing Patents as Governor.

"Sept. 8, 1773. Last night at Club the Governor and his brother met
for the first time since his arrival, but they took no Notice of each other.
Mr. Penn never having visited his Brother, and being determined to
continue at variance."

A letter from Judge Yeates to Colonel Burd, October 6,
1733, says,—

"The accounts from Philadelphia tell us there is no connection between the present and later Governors, though they have dined together
twice in public. Mr. Richard Penn takes no notice of his brother, nor
even speaks to him."

And a letter the following day from Edward Shippen to
Colonel Burd says,—

"Mr. Bob. Morris, the head man at the Merchant's feast, placed
Governor Penn on his right hand, and his brother, the later Governor,
on the left; but not a word passed between the two brothers."

[1] PENNA. MAG., Vol. IX. p. 181.

14

This estrangement continued for some time, but appears to have been healed within a twelvemonth; a letter from Lady Juliana Penn to John Penn, at the end of 1774, expresses her satisfaction in learning from his letters of an earlier date that a reconciliation had been effected. She speaks most kindly of the matter, and adds that "Mr. Penn [her husband] would be sorry any [letter] went from hence without mentioning the subject, till he is sure you have received his approbation and affectionate compliments upon it."

In a letter to Lady Juliana, April 3, 1775, John said, "I have received your favor of December 31, and am obliged to you and my uncle for your kind congratulations on the reconciliation between me and my brother, which, as you observe, was happily timed, for I was then surrounded with many vexations, and I do not yet see an end to them."

In 1773, after his final return from England, John Penn purchased of Dr. William Smith a tract of one hundred and forty-two acres on the west side of the Schuylkill, and soon after built upon it a handsome mansion, giving to the place the name "Lansdowne." The estate is now a part of Fairmount Park. The house was burned in 1854. It is understood that Horticultural Hall, erected for the Centennial Exhibition of 1876, occupies nearly or exactly the site of the mansion. Its erection was completed before 1777, as it appears on a map of that year—Faden's—and is there marked as exceeding in size and distinction the other "seats" of the neighborhood. "Lansdowne" was left by John Penn's will to his wife, and she almost immediately—March 9, 1795—conveyed it to James Greenleaf, who subsequently became her niece's husband.[1]

"Lansdowne" was John Penn's principal home for the remainder of his life, though he had, probably always, a city

---

[1] James Greenleaf married (1800) Ann, daughter of James Allen (Mrs. Penn's brother). He was associated with Robert Morris, and was engulfed in the misfortunes of the great financier.

house also.[1]   In the stress of the war operations in 1777 he was sent by military authority to Union Iron-Works, in New Jersey, with Chief-Justice Chew, and remained there a prisoner on parole from August of that year until May following.[2]

The feeling towards John Penn seems to have been always kindly.   General Washington, in 1787, when in Philadelphia

[1] "After his marriage to Miss Allen, Penn resided in the house built for Col. Byrd of Westover, on the west side of Third street below Spruce." (Keith's "Provincial Councillors.") In 1793, the City Directory shows, he lived at 44 Pine Street, between Second and Third. He was buried from there 1795.

[2] Two short notes from John Penn to his business agent, Edmund Physick, are in the Friends' Collection at Devonshire House, London, and belong nearly to this period.   They are as follows :

"To Edmund Physick, Esq.

"Dear Sir :

"Mr. Bremner, the bearer, can tell you all the news, so that I have nothing to say but that I want your assistance in the money way. I have parted with three servants since you were here and if some relief does not come soon, I suppose I shall be obliged to turn off all the rest and become bankrupt.   Some think the English army will be here soon, others are of a different opinion, though I cannot help thinking they will at least attempt it, and I suppose succeed.   If you can come down I shall be glad to see you, for it will be necessary to consider how you are to get to Town when General Howe gets possession.

"I am yours sincerely,

April 16, 1777.   "John Penn.

"To Edmund Physick, Esq.

"Dear Sir :

"I have but forty shillings left, therefore I must desire you will send me one hundred pounds by the bearer.   have you heard anything of Sam Meredith ?   I am sorry to hear by John Keble that the Purchases are not completed as I am confident the money will not last much longer therefore I must beg you will dispatch this business as soon as you possibly can.

"I am yours sincerely,

"John Penn.

"Thursday."   [No place, no date.]

attending the Constitutional Convention, twice or oftener accepted his invitations to dine or drink tea.   Glimpses of the social situation are afforded by extracts from family letters. December 13, 1783, Mrs. Rebecca Shoemaker wrote to her husband from Philadelphia,—

"That set [the Tory party] have prudently determined, as they can not exist in retirement either at Lansdowne or any where else out of public places, to join the others, and Gov. [John] Penn and lady, Mrs. Allen and mother . . . and all their former intimates, are now as happy at Mrs. Stewart's formerly M'Clanachan, at the French Minister's, or in any other Whig Society, as ever they were in the select circle they once were the principals of."

Same to same, May 23, 1785 :

" Betsy Allen has been confined to her chamber six months with the Rheumatism.   Her eldest daughter is now grown up and is a very fine girl.   Perhaps if young J. Penn[1] would think so it would be agreeable ; he lives a most recluse life over Schuylkill.   He bought about 20 acres of land and is making it all a garden and has built a house in a most singular stile.   I believe he still retains that peculiarity of address and manner we thought he had in N. York."

John Penn died February 9, 1795, and was buried in Christ Church.   A tablet within the church bears this inscription :

Here lieth
The Body of
The Honorable JOHN PENN, Esq'
One of the late Proprietaries of
Pennsylvania
who died February 9th A D 1795
Aged 67 years

Two statements in reference to his death and his remains are commonly made, and both apparently are on the authority of Watson, who says[2] that he died " in Bucks county,"

[1] This, of course, was John Penn, son of Thomas, and his place here referred to "Solitude."   He remained, as we have seen, a bachelor.

[2] "Annals," Vol. I. p. 125.

and that, after interment "in Christ Church ground," his remains were "taken up and carried to England." As to the
latter statement, Mr. Thomas H. Montgomery[1] says that the
records of the church afford no evidence of such removal.
The diary of Jacob Hiltzheimer records : "February 12,
1795. Mr. John Penn, formerly Governor, when this State
was a province of Great Britain, was buried from his house on
Pine street, in Christ Church yard."[2]

Ann Penn survived her husband, and was made by his
will, dated January 2, 1795, his residuary legatee, and co-
executor with John F. Mifflin. John Penn had had, after
his father's death in 1771, the life use of that one-fourth of
the Pennsylvania Proprietary right which had come to this
branch of the family in 1729. A decision by the Supreme
Court of Pennsylvania, in 1800, in the suit of Richard Penn
against his brother John's executors, reviewed the subject
of their property relations, including an agreement which
the two brothers had made in 1787 respecting the division of
the moneys received from the estates. The decision of the
Court was for the defendants.[3]

Ann Penn died in 1830. An obituary notice from a
periodical of the time says :

"July 4, 1830, in Upper George Street [London] Anne, relict of
John Penn, formerly Governor of Pennsylvania."

Richard Penn, brother of Governor John Penn and
second son of Richard the Proprietary, was born, as his
obituary implies, in the year 1735. He was thus six years
younger than John. He entered St. John's College, Cambridge, but quitted without a degree. By the will of his
uncle, John Penn, he received a small allowance, about
eighty pounds a year, but this he found quite inadequate to
support his mode of life. Letters from him to his uncle

---

[1] PENNA. MAG., Vol. VII. p. 476. [2] Ibid., Vol. XVI. p. 418.
[3] Reported in 2 Yeates, Penna. Supreme Court Reports, p. 550.

Thomas, asking assistance, and the latter's somewhat sharp replies, are among the Penn papers. His arrival in Pennsylvania with John, in October, 1763, has been noted. John, as Governor, appointed him to a place in the Council, and he qualified January 12, 1764. He was the first president of the Jockey Club of Philadelphia, formed in November, 1766, and so continued until 1769, in the beginning of which year he returned to England. He there remained until after the death of his father, in February, 1771. He was then appointed Lieutenant-Governor by his uncle Thomas and his brother John, and came again to Pennsylvania, arriving here October 16, 1771. He served a little less than two years in the place to which he had been appointed, and was superseded, as already mentioned, by John, in August, 1773. Contemporary accounts generally represent him as more popular at that time than John. The journal of Miss Sarah Eve says,[1]—

"August 30th.—This morning . . . hearing that Mr. John Penn was to be proclaimed Governor, curiosity led Deby Mitchel and I to go to see him. For my part I had rather be his brother than he, the one possesses the hearts of the people, the other the Government. Yesterday he made a public entry into Town with a large train."

The estrangement of the brothers was apparently not of John's choice,[2] and he made overtures to Richard, intended to heal the breach. An offer from John of an allowance of five hundred pounds a year, while the latter remained Governor, Richard declined, but upon the death of Richard Hockley, John appointed him naval officer at Philadelphia, and he accepted the place with appropriate acknowledgments.

Richard married at Christ Church, May 21, 1772, during his service as Governor, Mary, the daughter of William and

[1] PENNA. MAG., Vol. V. p. 197.

[2] Though an expression in James Allen's journal seems to suggest this.

Mary Masters.[1] This marriage has a romantic interest, for
thus it came about that the daughter of Letitia Penn's un-
successful suitor of 1701 now became the wife of Letitia's
nephew.[2] William Masters had married in 1754, many
years after his failure with "Tishe," Mary, the daughter of
Thomas Lawrence, sometime mayor of the city, and had
died in 1760, leaving two daughters, Mary and Sarah, aged
respectively four and two years. It was the elder of these
whom Richard Penn now married, and the disparity of the
ages of the two may be noted. Richard was then thirty-
seven years old, and his wife, born March 3, 1756, was a
little past sixteen.

Thomas Masters, grandfather of the young bride, had had,
early in the eighteenth century, a large holding of ground in
the " Northern Liberties " of Philadelphia, and this, inherited
by William Masters, passed to his widow and little girls.[3]

---

[1] Jacob Hiltzheimer's journal, May 22, 1772 : " Richard Penn,
Governor of this Province, was married to Miss Polly Masters last
night." . . .

[2] This statement is in accord with that of other authorities, yet I
cannot forbear mentioning the element of doubt that appears in it.
The William Masters of 1701 could hardly have been under eighteen
(though Logan, in the letter cited, calls him " young William Masters ")
to have been a suitor of Letitia Penn (who was twenty-three), and if
so, he would have been a man of seventy-one in 1754, when the
person of his name married Mary Lawrence. Facts known concerning
Mary's husband, however, indicate that he was not young in 1754, but
" well on in years." Thompson Westcott, perceiving the apparent
difficulty of the matter (" Historic Mansions "), makes an effort to
solve it : " And so Richard, perhaps in ignorance that Mary's grandfather had nearly three-quarters of a century previous been a suitor for
the hand of his great-aunt," etc. This is only adding positive error to
general uncertainty. Letitia was Richard's own aunt (of half blood),
not his great-aunt, and, as already stated, the William Masters of 1701
is said to have been the father, not grandfather, of Mary Penn.

[3] Sarah, the second daughter, married Turner Camac. *Cf.* Keith's
" Provincial Councillors of Pennsylvania."

The widow Masters also received from her father, Thomas Lawrence, in 1761, a large lot on the south side of Market Street, between Fifth and Sixth, and erected there soon after a handsome house, one of the finest in Philadelphia, which became later an " historic mansion " of the city.[1]   Here she was living with her two daughters at the time of Mary's marriage to Richard Penn, and a conveyance was made to the bride, by the widow, two days before the wedding, of her interest in the property, " in consideration of natural love and affection," it being obviously a wedding present.

The Market Street house became known as " Richard Penn's," though as a matter of fact his ownership in it was only through the interest of his wife, and their married life in it extended but little beyond three years.   The house was burned January 2, 1780, while in their ownership.   Jacob Hiltzheimer's diary, that date, says,—

" Early this morning a fire broke out in Mr. Penn's house on Market street, occupied by Mr. Holker, the French consul, which destroyed all but the first floor."

And Elizabeth Drinker in her journal records,—

" 1780, January 2, Richard Penn's large house, up Market St., took fire last night, and this morning is consumed all but yᵉ lower story. A most violent snowstorm this afternoon and all night." [2]

Richard Penn bought, in April, 1775, of Andrew Doz, the " Peel Hall " estate, forty-five acres, on which Girard

[1] The house is described by Richard Rush as quite superior ; " few, if any equal to it are at present in Philadelphia," he says in his Recollections of 1790-1800.   It was the residence of General Howe during the British occupancy of the city, 1777-78, and again was selected by General Benedict Arnold when Howe departed.   After Arnold, Holker, the French consul, occupied it, and subsequently Robert Morris bought it and lived there.   General Washington stayed in it with Morris during the sitting of the Constitutional Convention, 1787, and in 1790, when the seat of government was removed to Philadelphia, he occupied it as the Presidential residence for the next seven years.

[2] The house was subsequently rebuilt by Robert Morris.

College now stands, and it was during his ownership, November, 1777 (he being then in England), that the British engineer officers burned the house, with many others, along the north side of the then city, as a supposedly necessary feature of their defensive operations. "Peel Hall" was sold February 15, 1779, by Tench Francis, attorney for Richard Penn, to Owen Biddle, and the description in the conveyance shows its condition :

" . . . with the outhouses, improvements, and gardens, being now torn down, burnt, and almost destroyed, and the tract or piece of land belonging thereto being laid waste, and opened to commons, the Fences which enclosed the same being taken away and destroyed.''

In the summer of 1775 Richard Penn, with his family, went to England.[1] He had been solicited by the Continental Congress, then sitting at Philadelphia, to take to London the second petition of the Congress, the Address to the King, called the "Olive Branch," which John Dickinson had drawn up. Penn and Arthur Lee, agent in London for the Massachusetts Colony, presented it to the Earl of Dartmouth, September 1, 1775, and in November, the petition being under consideration in the House of Lords, Richard Penn was interrogated, on motion of the Duke of Richmond, as to the condition of the American Colonies.

---

[1] The following letter from Richard Penn to Lady Juliana is among the Penn papers in the Pennsylvania Historical Society's collection :

"DEAR MADAM :

"I have just now received your letter of the 22ᵈ of March informing me of the Melancholly Event of my Uncle's Death . . . God be prais'd ! the happy & advantageous Marriage I have contracted in this Country enables me to live like a Gentleman in England for which place I intend to Embark this Summer, where I hope to find you and your family in good health.

"I am, dear Madam,

"Your Most Obedient Servant

"RICHᵈ PENN.

" PHILADELPHIA, May 10 [1775]."

His replies were intelligent and judicious ; he had had, no doubt, a sympathy with the Colonial claims, and was well qualified to give information as to the circumstances out of which they arose.

Following upon this return to England, Richard Penn spent there practically the whole of his remaining years. During the continuance of the Revolution, the receipt of funds from Pennsylvania being probably mostly cut off, he appears to have been in severe financial straits. A letter (1780) says, "My friend Richard Penn's distresses have almost drove him' to distraction. I understand from Mrs. Penn they are now kept from starving by the bounty of Mr. Barclay.[1] For aught I know Mr. Penn might long ago have been in the Fleet Prison, had not Mr. Barclay stepped forth to his relief."

With the termination of the war his own and his wife's circumstances no doubt improved. In 1785 the Masters family, Richard Penn joining, sold the Market Street house and grounds to Robert Morris. In 1787 his brother John agreed with Richard to pay him one-fourth of the sums received by him (John) as his share of the one hundred and thirty thousand pounds voted by the State of Pennsylvania as compensation under the Divesting Act, and one-third of the returns from sales of the reserved property made after the act was passed. Upon the death of John, Richard succeeded to the life-right which John had enjoyed in the Proprietary estate.

For many years Richard Penn was a member of Parliament. He was elected to the House of Commons April 9, 1784, for the borough of Appleby, Westmoreland, and represented it until December 20, 1790, when he was returned for Haslemere, Surrey. From 1796 to 1802 he sat for the borough of Lancaster, and in 1806 was again

[1] Barclay, no doubt, of the London firm of merchants and bankers, Friends, descendants of Robert Barclay the Apologist.

chosen for Haslemere. His residence is named as Queen
Anne Street West, County Middlesex. In 1808, or earlier,
he came to Philadelphia with other members of his family,
and his residence appears in the Directory of that year as at
210 Chestnut Street, between Eighth and Ninth. This visit
is commonly spoken of as not continuing more than about
a year. He returned, and died in England. The *Gentleman's Magazine* says,—

"May 27, 1811. At Richmond [Surrey] in his 76th year, R. Penn
Esq., grandson of W. P., one of the Proprietaries, and formerly Governor of Pennsylvania."

Mary Penn survived her husband eighteen years. The
Gentleman's Magazine records,—

"Aug. 16, 1829. At the house of her younger son, Richard Penn,
Esq., in Great George street, aged 73, Mary, relict of the Hon. Richard
Penn, one of the Hereditary Lords of Pennsylvania."

Richard Penn is spoken of as an attractive and genial
man. Thompson Westcott says[1] he "possessed a fine person, elegant manners, was of a social disposition, and a *bon
vivant*. He was the most popular member of his family who
visited Pennsylvania after the death of the Founder."

Of the four children of Richard and Hannah Lardner
Penn, only Richard, as has already appeared, had issue. His
children by Mary Masters Penn were :

1. William, of whom an account will be given below.

2. A daughter, mentioned but not named in the *Gentleman's Magazine*, who died June 17, 1790. (The notice
simply says, "June 17, 1790: The youngest daughter of
Richard Penn, Esq.") She was probably an infant.

3. Hannah, who died unmarried at Richmond, Surrey,
England, July 16, 1856. She accompanied her father and
brother William to Philadelphia in the visit of 1808.

4. Richard. See below.

[1] "Historic Mansions," p. 253.

5. Mary, born April 11, 1785; married 1821 (being second wife of) Samuel Paynter, Esq., of Richmond, Surrey, J. P. for Surrey and Middlesex, High Sheriff of Surrey in 1838. Her husband died July 24, 1844. She died without issue March 26, 1863.

Our consideration of the line descended from William Penn the Founder, through his son Richard, is thus narrowed to the two sons of Richard, 2d, and Mary Masters. These sons, William and Richard, 3d, left no issue, and the line thus ends. It only remains, therefore, to speak appropriately of them. The two brothers were both notable men, having remarkable talents, but William's ability was offset by serious defects and weaknesses. They have each the distinction of receiving in the *Gentleman's Magazine* an extended and appreciative obituary notice, from which we shall quote below.

William Penn was born in England, June 23, 1776. He was entered at St. John's College, Cambridge, but did not take his degree.   While there he produced (1794) a pamphlet "which attracted the particular notice of Mr. Pitt, Mr. Wyndham and the Government generally," its title being *Vindiciæ Britannicæ*. It was a reply to a pamphlet which had been published by Gilbert Wakefield, of Jesus College, Cambridge, entitled "The Spirit of Christianity compared with the Spirit of the Times in Great Britain." The pamphlet was criticised by the *Analytical Review*, and Penn rejoined with such effect that, had his habits and disposition favored, "a path was opened for him to any advancement he could possibly desire." Unfortunately, "he was too fond of that species of festive companionship in vogue at that period, and which precluded a man from standing in any other sphere." [1]

William was for a time a captain in the Surrey militia. He came to Philadelphia with his father and sister Hannah in 1808, and appears to have remained in Pennsylvania for

[1] *Gentleman's Magazine*, obituary notice.

at least four years. Letters written by him in 1810 are
dated in Dauphin County, and in 1812 he signs legal papers
as of Northampton County. The most notable event of his
visit here, if not of his life, was his marriage. This was the
occasion of much sharp comment and of some warm discussion. His wife was named Catharine Julia (or Juliana
Catharine) Balabrega, her parents being Jacob and Mary,
of Philadelphia. She was born March 13, 1785, and was
baptized in Christ Church. What her relations to William
Penn may have been is not disclosed, but his appearance at
the house of Rev. Dr. James Abercrombie, rector of Christ
Church, on the evening of August 7, 1809, to say that within
an hour he would return with Miss Balabrega to be married,
threw that worthy clergyman into extreme distress, and
when at the end of the time Penn appeared with her and
her sister, Dr. Abercrombie and an intimate friend of Penn,
who 'had been hurriedly summoned, earnestly endeavored to
dissuade him from the step. Penn insisted, however, that
he was determined upon it, and declared that if the rector
refused to officiate, he would go to an alderman near by—
naming him—at once, " and enter into a civil contract of
marriage," upon which Dr. Abercrombie yielded and married
them. Later, having been much criticised, Dr. Abercrombie
published a pamphlet,[1] in which he presented two letters from
William Penn, describing the marriage (as here stated), an
extended letter from Bishop White, and a still longer opinion
of a lawyer, justifying him (Dr. Abercrombie) in performing
the marriage.

The objection to the bride is suggested, but not positively
stated. Bishop White develops his opinion of the case by
means of a supposititious example, in which one of the couple
proposing to be married " labours under the apparently just
imputation of very faulty conduct." William appears to have

[1] " Documents Relative to the Celebration of a Late Marriage."
Printed by Smith & Maxwell, Philadelphia, 1809. Pp. 47.

been sincerely attached to his wife at least as late as August 11, 1812.   On that date he wrote from Easton, Pennsylvania, to John Penn, of Stoke Poges, proposing to sell to him all his interest in Pennsylvania, with the avails of which he wished to purchase an annuity.[1]   Having explained and urged the proposal,—which apparently was not accepted,— he says,—

"I do not think I am likely to last very long, which idea renders me doubly solicitous to place beyond the reach of inconvenience a most deserving Wife, who is indeed my only Friend on this side of the Atlantic.   I shall certainly never visit the other, and am grown so misanthropic that I protest I see no difference between the old, and the new World, except [etc.]."   He subscribes himself "your faithful, affectionate, and much obliged kinsman."[2]

He returned to England later, however, and lived there until his death.   Of his wife there is no further definite information.   They are said to have been childless.   In 1817 he is styled "of St. John st., Adelphi, Co. Middlesex."   Much of his time he spent in or near the debtors' prison in London. He wrote for sundry periodicals, his contributions to the *Gentleman's Magazine* being usually over the signature of "the Rajah of Vaneplysia," the last word being an anagram of Pennsylvania, omitting two of the *n*'s.   His learning was quite extensive, and indeed pedantic, as an example of his letters in the magazine mentioned sufficiently shows.

He died in Nelson Square, Southwark (London), September 17, 1845.   "Pursuant to his own desire," says the notice in the *Gentleman's Magazine*, "the remains of Mr. Penn were deposited in the church of St. Mary Redcliffe, Bristol, by those of his illustrious ancestor, Admiral Sir William Penn."   We cite in conclusion as to him a further paragraph from the same obituary :

[1] He had then, by the death of his father, come into the one-fourth of the Pennsylvania rights belonging in this line of the family.

[2] MS. letters in collection Historical Society of Pennsylvania.

" Extravagance and heedlessness brought him into debt, and he passed so much of his time within certain confines in Southwark, that he afterwards, when free from such restraint, declined to quit that neighborhood, and ended his days there. He was a kind, good-hearted man, and according to a common remark might truly be said to have been an enemy to no one but himself. More than this he was a man of transcendent abilities, an excellent classical scholar, and possessed of a wonderful memory, which he displayed by an extraordinary power of quotation in conversation. His talents, however, were rendered unavailable, from a recklessness and indifference to his position in society, and a turn for conviviality, which was towards the end of the last century very much in fashion. When he chose he could transfix the minds of those he associated with by the depth of his research and splendid talents. We have heard it asserted, that after a midnight excess, and being completely oppressed with wine, instead of retiring to rest, he would wrap a wet napkin round his head, and write a powerful paper for the *Anti-Jacobin.* He mixed with the highest ranks in society, and was courted in every company ; and it was of him George the Fourth (then Prince of Wales) said, ' He was a Pen often *cut* (drunk, a term now obsolete, as well as the custom, in a great degree), but never mended.' Had he improved the opportunities which came in his way towards the end of last century and beginning of this, there was probably no elevation attainable which he might not have reached."

Richard Penn, the younger brother, remained a bachelor, and appears to have been a man of estimable character. It was at his house in Great George Street, as already mentioned, that his mother died in 1817. He was for many years a trusted and useful official of the Colonial Department of the English government. He devised a cipher code for use in despatches, published 1829, with the title "On a New Mode of Secret Writing." He was elected a Fellow of the Royal Society, November 18, 1824. His portrait, by E. W. Eddis, was engraved (1834) by M. Ganci. The obituary notice in the *Gentleman's Magazine* says,—

" Mr. Richard Penn, jun., entered the Colonial Department, at the beginning of the present century, in which he remained many years successively under Lord Hobart, Viscount Castlereagh, and Earls Camden and Bathurst. He had talents admirably suited for official duties, added to a *bonhomie* and agreeable address which gained him the esteem of everyone. He had also a very profound acquaintance with the French language, and was well versed in all its difficulties of grammatical construction. Possessed of a competent fortune, he dispensed it in a manner suitable to a gentleman. His benevolence and charity were of the most extensive nature, and to be in distress was at all times a sufficient recommendation to his bounty ; but his feeling for the orphan was particularly strong. Mr. Penn possessed a rich vein of humor, with much good sense and good nature, all of which are fully evinced in a little book which he wrote, under the title of ' Maxims and Hints on Angling, Chess, Shooting, and other Matters ; also Miseries of Fishing ; by Richard Penn, Esq., F.R.S.' (London, Murray, 12mo, 1842).[1] There are very many neat woodcuts interspersed in the work, from designs by his friend Sir Francis Chantrey, and other eminent artists.''

Richard Penn died at his house at Richmond, Surrey, April 21, 1863, "aged 79." He had enjoyed after the death of his elder brother (1845) the life use of the Richard Penn fourth of the Pennsylvania rights, and upon his death they vested in his second cousin, Granville John Penn, in accordance with the limitations of the family entail, heretofore mentioned. He survived his sister, Mrs. Paynter, it will be observed, only about a month, and with his decease this line from William Penn the Founder closed.

RICHARD PENN, PROPRIETARY, AND HIS DESCENDANTS.

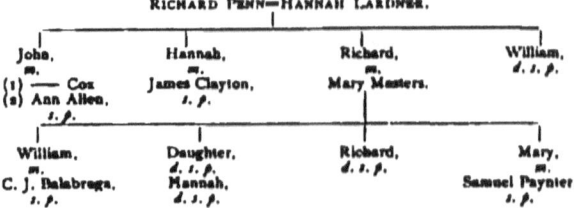

RICHARD PENN—HANNAH LARDNER.

John, *m.* (1) —— Cox (2) Ann Allen. *s. p.*	Hannah, *m.* James Clayton, *s. p.*	Richard, *m.* Mary Masters.	William, *d. s. p.*
William, *m.* C. J. Balabrega. *s. p.*	Daughter, *d. s. p.* Hannah, *d. s. p.*	Richard, *d. s. p.*	Mary, *m.* Samuel Paynter, *s. p.*

[1] The edition here mentioned is evidently only one of several. The book on Angling, with '' Maxims and Hints for a Chess Player '' added, was published in 1833, with an enlarged edition in 1839, and an edition of '' Maxims and Hints on Shooting,'' in 1855.

XII.

William Penn, Third, and His Descendants.

THE several family lines descended from William Penn the Founder have now all been traced except one,— that resulting from the marriage of his grandson, William Penn, 3d, and Christian Forbes. In the present chapter it is proposed to follow this line to existing generations.

William Penn, 3d, son of William Penn, Jr., and his wife, Mary Jones, was born at Worminghurst, March 21, 1702–3. The allusion to his birth, " we are now major, minor, and minimus," in a letter from the Founder to Logan, may be recalled. His childhood and youth were probably passed largely in the care of his mother and of his step-grand-mother, Hannah Penn. He was seventeen years old at the death of his father, 1720. When a young man he appears to have spent some time in Ireland.[1] In 1730–1 the death of his elder brother, Springett Penn, unmarried, brought to him the heirship of the remaining estates of the elder line. They included the old estate, "Shangarry," in Ireland, with which he was especially associated during the remaining years of his life, and a place in Sussex, in England, "The Rocks," which I presume to have been a remnant from the inheritance of the Founder's first wife, Gulielma Maria Springett, whose possession descended in the elder line.

Following upon his succession, the first event of import-

---

[1] A letter to him from Thomas Penn, in London, March 5, 1729–30, is addressed to " William Penn, Esq., at Thomas Griffith's, Apothecary, on the Blind Key, in Dublin, Ireland." It begins " Dear Will."

ance—and an interesting one—was his marriage, on the
7th of Tenth month (December), 1732, to Christian, daughter of Alexander and Jane Forbes. The certificate follows:

The 7th of the 10 Mo. 1732.

WILLIAM PENN of Kingston Bowrey in the County of Sussex
Esq, son of William Penn late of Worminghurst in the said County
Esq. Deceased, & Mary his wife him surviving and CHRISTIAN
FORBES daughter of Alexander Forbes of London, merchant, &
Jane his wife, Having publickly declared their intentions of taking
each other in marriage, before several meetings of the people of God
called Quakers in Wandsworth in the County of Surry according
to the good order used amongst them whose proceedings therein
after due enquiry and deliberate consideration thereof with regard
unto the righteous Law of God were allowed by the said meetings
they appearing clear of all others and having consent of Parents &
Relations concern'd. NOW THESE ARE TO CERTIFIE all
whom it may concern that for the full accomplishing of their s^d
marriage this 7th day of the month called December in the year
1732 They the s^d William Penn and Christian Forbes appeared in
a publick assembly of the aforesaid people, & others met together
for that end in their meeting house near Devonshire Square in
London. And in a solemn manner he the said William Penn taking
the s^d Christian Forbes by the hand did openly declare as followeth
Friends in the presence of God & this assembly whom I desire to
be my witnesses I take this my Dear Friend Christian Forbes to be
my wife promising by Divine Assistance to be to her a faithful &
loving husband till by death we are separated. And then & there
in the said Assembly the said Christian Forbes did in like manner
declare as followeth, Friends in the fear of God & presence of this
Assembly whom I desire to be my witnesses I take this my Friend
William Penn to be my husband & promise by the Lord's Assistance to be unto him a faithful & loving wife till by death we are
separated. And the said William Penn & Christian Forbes as a
farther confirmation thereof & in testimony thereunto, did then &
there to these Presents set their hands.

We whose names are hereunto ⎰ WILLIAM PENN.
subscribed being present.   ⎱ CHRISTIAN FORBES.

Among others at the solemnizing of the above said Marriage & subscription in manner aforesaid as witnesses hereunto have also to these presents subscribed our names the day & year above written.

Ann Forbes	Ellz Knight	Mary Penn
Alex. Forbes Jun.	Martha Stafford	Alexr Forbes
Jo. Coysgarne	Priscilla Barclay	Jane Forbes
Ellz. Coysgarne	James Barclay	Jno. Forbes
Da. Barclay	Martha Moys	Barbara Forbes
Mary Banks	Richd Moys	James Hoskins
Joseph Todd	Wm. Hughes	Jno. Trubshaw
Is. Collinson	Nat Cole	Wm. Howard
Tho. Richardson	Jesse Poole	Tho. Poole
Mary Hodges	Phil. Elliot	Tho. Zachary
Jno. Wilson	Osgood Gee	Ellz. Wells
Rt. Gerard	[and many more]	Ellz. Charter
Mary Falconer		Patience Barclay
Alex. Barclay		Jno. Falkner.
Ellz. Barclay		

[Certified to be an Extract from the Register, numbered Society of Friends 958, and entitled a Register of Marriages formerly kept by the Society of Friends at the Monthly Meeting at Kingston.—From the General Register Office, Somerset House, London.]

This was, it will be seen, strictly a Friends' wedding. The departure from the Society of William Penn, Jr., after his visit to Philadelphia in 1704, had probably influenced his wife and children also, and Gulielma Maria (Fell), as we have seen, was "publicly baptized" in St. Paul, Covent Garden, in 1723 or 1724. In the present case, however, William, deeply in love with "Chrissie" Forbes, returned, for a time at least, to the faith of his great ancestor. A letter from his uncle John Penn to Thomas Penn (then in Pennsylvania), from Feens, 1st October, 1732, makes this announcement :

"My Cos⁰ Will Penn has cutt of his buttons, Left of his Sword & Ruffles, & appears a plain Quaker, he will Certainly be marry'd very soon at Meeting to Miss Chrissie Forbes."

And a few weeks later we have another letter from John to Thomas, dated at Feens, 28th January, 1732-3, the following passage savoring, one must admit, something of levity :

"I must begin with acquainting you of the Conversion and Marriage of our Nephew Wm Penn, with the daughter of Alexander Forbes,

which was Solemnised on the 7th of Last Month at Devonshire house
Meeting before a numerous Assembly to the Consolation of Thousands
of the Righteous, who are full of the Prophecy of Robert Haddock the
last Yearly Meeting was Twelve Months, which was that in Two years
time the Young man should be made a Brave Instrument In the hand of
the Lord for the Conversion of many, therefore it is believed that in the
next Yearly Meeting he will come forth in a Powerful manner.''

The marriage, indeed, had encountered other impediments
than those which could be removed by the laying aside of
sword and ruffles. William was not clear of prior engage-
ments of marriage. He had, it seems, entered into a matrimonial contract, more or less formal, in Ireland, with a young
lady named Ann Mansell, "and his intended bride had to
listen," in the Friends' meeting at Wandsworth (near London), "to the reading of documents connected with his
former love affair, including a full release from Ann Mansell
and her family, in consideration of William Penn's having
paid £1000 in compensation for his breach of promise." [1]

The bride, Christian Forbes, is described as a lovely girl
of a notably pious character. She was quite young—in her
eighteenth year—at the time of her marriage. Her father,
Alexander Forbes, was a son of John Forbes, of Aquorthies,
near Aberdeen, in Scotland, and her mother, Jean, was a
daughter of Robert Barclay, of Ury, author of the famous
Quaker book the "Apology." Between these two families,
Forbes and Barclay, very intimate relations existed : three
sons of John Forbes (Timothy, James, and Alexander) had
married three daughters of Robert Barclay (Patience, Catharine, and Jean). Aquorthies and Ury are neighboring estates, and in the Quaker movement in the later half of the
seventeenth century both families had earnestly joined.[2]

[1] Beck and Ball's '' London Friends' Meetings,'' p. 323.

[2] In the social and ecclesiastical friction that was evolved, members
of both families had been imprisoned in the gaol at Aberdeen, and had
suffered some losses of property. The Barclays, Robert and his father
Colonel David, are well known in many ways ; Besse, in his '' Sufferings '' of the Friends, mentions John Forbes, of Aquorthies, as in
prison at Aberdeen, 1677, and as otherwise persecuted.

The young bride was descended through her mother's family, the Barclays, from the royal family of the Stuarts, Robert Barclay's mother, the wife of Colonel David Barclay, of Ury, who served under Gustavus Adolphus in the Thirty Years' War,[1] was Lady Catharine Gordon, daughter of Sir Robert Gordon, who was the second son of the Earl of Sutherland, and a cousin to King James VI. of Scotland, who became James I. of the United Kingdom.[2]

The married life of William Penn, 3d, and his young wife was, however, pathetically brief. She died inside the year (November 1, 1733) of illness following upon the birth of her child, a daughter, on the 22d of October. Her funeral occurred at Jordans ground on the 7th of the month. The journal of Rebekah Butterfield says, " 7th of 9th month, 1733. Daniel Bell and John Fallowfield was at Jordans att yᵉ burial of William Pen's wife, daughter of Alex. Forbes." The daughter, Christiana Gulielma Penn, survived, and it is through her, subsequently married to Peter Gaskell, that all the Penn descendants of the elder line are derived. There is a sketch of the mother, Christian (Forbes) Penn, in " Piety Promoted," Part X., London (1810), edited by Joseph Gurney Bevan,—a collection of Quaker memorials,—in which her religious character is highly extolled. Her age at her death is stated as eighteen years and a quarter.

Christiana Gulielma Penn, the daughter, was reared in the family of her grandfather Forbes, at Dowgate Hill, the

---

[1] Whittier's poem, " Barclay of Ury," and its lines—

" him who stood
Ankle deep in Lutzen's blood
With the brave Gustavus "—

are familiar.

[2] Through this marriage of Colonel David Barclay to Lady Catharine Gordon their descendants trace their descent back through all the English kings, beginning with Richard II., to Alfred. (Browning's "Americans of Royal Descent," edition of 1894, p. 554.)

London home, and at Aquorthies. Letters show that for
some time, at least, Alexander Forbes took a helpful interest,
as his large means enabled him to do, in his son-in-law,
John Penn, in the letter to Thomas, January 28, 1732–3,
already cited, says,—

"I am very sorry it is not in my Power to Satisfy my Cos⁰ William
Penn, but it is not, without acting very much to my disadvantage, wherefore he must Stay [wait] which I hope he can do, for some time, for he
lives now with Alexander Forbess, & is at very little Expence."

In the adjustment of the Proprietary rights in 1731 (after
the death of Springett Penn), John, Thomas, and Richard
Penn gave William Penn, 3d, five thousand five hundred
pounds for his claim, secured by a mortgage on the Pennsylvania proprietorship. On this mortgage Alexander
Forbes lent William Penn two thousand five hundred
pounds. (The mortgage was finally extinguished by the
three Proprietaries, January 29, 1740.[1]) In a letter to John
Penn, from London, April 20, 1736,[2] asking for interest due
"last midsummer," on the mortgage, Alexander Forbes mentions his need for it, as he is helping William Penn to raise
some money immediately, his affairs being in such shape
"that there is a necessity," etc. Alexander Forbes, it may be
added here, died May 25, 1740. The *Gentleman's Magazine*
records the death, under that date, of "Mr. Alex. Forbes,
London Merchant, of great Worth and Reputation." [3]

William Penn, 3d, married a second time, December 7,

[1] Breviate in the Boundary Case, pp. 447, 448, 462, 504.

[2] A letter dated a few months earlier, July 20, 1736, at Battersea,
from William Penn, 3d, to Thomas Penn, then in Pennsylvania, is
published in *The Literary Era*, Philadelphia, May, 1898. It is a well-
expressed communication, and refers mainly to the Pennsbury Manor
property in Pennsylvania.

[3] Several of the Forbes family, Mr. Summers says ("Memories of
Jordans and the Chalfonts"), lie buried at Jordans.

1736, Ann Vaux.[1] She was the daughter of Isaac Vaux, of London, and granddaughter of George Vaux, of Reigate, mentioned by Besse in his "Sufferings" of the Friends, as fined, etc., in 1683. Ann's uncle, George Vaux, a physician of Reigate, who died 1741, was a distinguished linguist and antiquarian.

This second marriage was marred, as was the first, by unlooked-for circumstances, but of a different sort. William and Ann appear to have removed to Ireland, and they were living in Cork in March, 1738, when a son was born. The Friends' records of Cork contain this entry :

"Springett Penn, son of William Penn, and Anne his wife, was born at their dwelling-house in Ballyphechane, in the South Liberties of the County of this City, between the hours of 8 and 9 in the evening, the first day of the First Month, 1738.

"N. B.—The above memorial was delivered me by the hand of William, the father of the above Springett, and desired it may be registered in this book.—JOSHUA WIGHT."

The matrimonial troubles of William and Ann must have followed soon. Apparently she left him and went to London, and he charged her with one of the gravest of offences. A letter from him, in January, 1741-2, is among the collection preserved by Thomas Penn. It is addressed to Thomas Penn, who was then in Pennsylvania :

"D⿃ UNCLE THOMAS

"I wrote thee two lettᵐ in answʳ to thine from Plymouth & Philadelphia. I hope thou hast received them both wᶜʰ I have no accᵗ of yet ; I hear that thou hast money of mine in thy hands, if so, I desire thee to let me know wᵗ yᵉ sum is that I may give thee a proper recᵗ for it and have it lodged in yᵉ hands of Freame & Barclay, in Lombard Street, because it may prevent my remitting money from here in order to carry

[1] An entry in the printed registers of St. Paul's Cathedral, published by the Harleian Society, gives the marriage there, of William Penn, of Withyam, Sussex, Esquire, widower, to Ann Vaux, of the parish of St. Diones, Backchurch, London, spinster, by license, December 7, 1736, " by me, William Reyner."

on a suit I have in Doctors' Commons for a divorce, y⁰ occasion of w⁰ʰ I presume thou hast heard of, therefore I begg a speedy answ' to this, for y⁰ Term is drawing on apace & I must supply my Proctor by a remittance from hence in case thou had no money due to me, or that should not be sufficient.   I am, wᵗʰ my d' love to you all,

"Thy very aff'ᵗᵉ kinsman,
"Wᴹ Pᴇɴɴ

" Dᴜʙʟɪɴ, Jany 18th 1741.
" I directed my former letters to y⁰ Pennsylvania coffee house."

William Penn, 3d, continued to live in Ireland until his death. Letters to Thomas Penn, in 1741, are dated at Dublin ; they represent his desire to sell his interest in the Pennsbury estate in Pennsylvania (which was not, however, accomplished), and mention " my house at the Rocks, in Sussex." A note from Thomas Penn, at Kensington, January 5, 1743, addressed " To the Housekeeper at Wm. Penn Esq.'s House at the Rocks," says,—

" I have sent the bearer Danl Chandler down to view the underwood belonging to the Rocks Farm, by order of my Nephew, and send this to desire you will provide for him and his horse at the house while he stays."[1]

Further letters from William Penn, 3d, to Thomas Penn disclose facts of interest. April 20, 1746, he writes from Cork, speaking of the death of his aunt Letitia Aubrey, and the provisions of her will ; he mentions that his own plate is in pawn " with Benn : Pike " for thirty pounds. A few days later, April 29, he again writes from Cork,—

" . . . I received yours, with a copy of the Inventory of Aunt Aubrey's Goods. I desire the Beds, Quilts, & Blankets, all of y⁰ Linen and all of y⁰ Plate[2] may be sent hither to me as soon as possible.

[1] On the back of this Ann Mercer (the housekeeper, no doubt) notes the receipt of ten shillings " for Danl. Chandler's charges at the Rock Farm."

[2] The plate belonging to Letitia Aubrey does not appear to have been divided until some time later. The following memorandum is in the Penn papers :

" An account of Plate belonging to y⁰ Estate of Mrs. Letitia Aubrey,

Burches will take yᵉ trouble of getting them shipped & Dispose of yᵉ remᵈʳ upon as good terms as possible. Yᵉ money arising thence, as well as yᵉ ready money left Chrissy [his daughter] and me I desire may be remitted into Ben : Pike's hands. [He concludes] with dear love to all yoʳ family as if named, yoʳ very affᵗᵉ kinsman & sincere friend."

August 5, 1746, he writes to Thomas Penn, asking news of his uncle John Penn (who died October 25 following), for whom he expresses affection ; nothing, he says, keeps him from going to see him "but a wicked woman, worse than all earthly things, who stands in the way and hinders me."[1] He asks Thomas to address him "at Shannagarry, near Middleton, as usual." Finally, December 24, 1746, he

deseased, & divided this seventh day of July, 1749, between William Penn Esqʳ deceased and Mrs. Christiana Gulielma Penn, the residuary legatees :

"To Mr. William Penn for his share :

"One Sawspan, a porringer, 2 candle-sticks, snuffers, and stand ; a punch ladle, 2 salts, 6 spoons, a punch straner, a purs spring and hook, a milk pott, 23 medals and coins. Weighing one hundred and twenty ounces, at 5s. 3d. £31 10s.

"To Mrs. Christiana Gulielma Penn for her share :

"One coffee pott, 3 castors, a hand candle-stick, a porringer, a soup ladle, a skimmer, 2 wax candlesticks, a tea Canister, a spoon boat, a child's sawspan, 2 salts, 1 Extinguisher, a silver cha. and frame, 1 bobin case and thimble, 1 snuff-box, 8 teaspoons, a tongs, and straner ; a nutmeg grater, 2 ink horns, a plain box, 3 small box's, a clasp, a purs spring, a watch hook, a bodkin, a pensil, 14 medals and coines. Weighing one hundred and twenty ounces.

"Gold, viz. : a Gold box, a pincushin, hoop & chaine ; 2 morning rings, 6 pieces of gold coins, a tag and mask bead. Weighing 4 ounces, 4 dwts., at £3 13s. an ounce. Val. £15 6s. 6d.

" 6 shell teaspoons garnished with silver—9.

"Weighed and valued by me, Richard Langton."

[A memorandum is appended of some articles purchased by R. L.]

[1] This suggests that in the proceedings between the pair the legal situation made it inexpedient for William to come into England. Whether the strong expression he applies to his wife was justified I do not undertake to say.

writes to Thomas Penn, presenting condolences on John's death, and says,—

" It is no time to trouble thee about business, w⁰ I shall omit. I am indeed in a very indifferent state of health myself, a Scorbutick humour attended w⁰ a Dropsical one.   I'm heartily concerned at the misfortunes of Aunt Marg⁴."

This letter very shortly preceded his own death.   The Friends' records at Cork state,—

"William Penn died at his house at Shangarry, about 15 miles from Cork, of a dropsy, 12 month [February] 6, 1746–7."

His will was dated 17th of Tenth month (December), 1743, and appears not to have been proved in England until March 15, 1760, when his son Springett presented it as executor.[1] The will appoints John Penn and Thomas Penn guardians of the children during the minority of Springett, and he to be executor when he shall attain the age of twenty-one.   To the widow William leaves one shilling, and states his reason for this with candor : " Whereas my present wife, Ann Penn, otherwise Vaux, some years ago eloped from me, and hath ever since continued without any reasonable Cause to live separate from me   .   .   .   whereby I am advised that she hath forfeited all Right to Dower and Thirds out of my Real & Personal Estate," etc.

Springett Penn, the son of William, 3d, and Ann, then a boy eight years old, appears to have been at school at Lismore, Ireland, at his father's death.   Thomas Lowder, the master, wrote, February 23, 1746–7, to Thomas Penn, asking instructions, especially in case the mother should claim the boy.   Later other letters and statements of account followed.   A letter from Lowder to Thomas Penn, August 17, 1747, says of the lad, " He is indeed a very tractable and hopeful child, with the best capacity. His dutiful respects he desires may be sent to you."   June 30, 1748, Thomas

[1] Memorandum on copy of will in Friends' collections at Devonshire House, London.

Penn sends £29 10s. 3d. to pay Lowder's bill for a year's tuition, board, clothes, etc. Replying to this, Lowder writes, July 7, and says Springett has now been two years under his care ; he cannot write much, he says, and this is pretty well evidenced by a letter of duty on the same sheet from Springett,—a very juvenile attempt, in large characters. Later Springett was sent to school to Gilbert Thompson, at "Sankey," and a letter from him, dated there November 15, 1749, is much improved in all respects. He seems, from allusions in a letter of Thompson's to the weakness of his legs, etc., not to have been in vigorous health. In November, 1750, Thompson writes to Thomas Penn that the boy set off in the stage-coach that morning for "home," and "should arrive at the Bell Inn, in Wood street, either on 6th day or 7th at the furthest, being the 23d or 24th inst., as the roads may be."

Thomas Penn no doubt had charge of Springett and of his affairs. Ann Mercer, housekeeper at "The Rocks," sends Thomas an estimate of repairs, January 4, 1749, dated "Rocks House." The brew-house and grainary, she says, need attention. "The house wants tyling, I am obliged to set many things about to catch the water, it should have been done last summer, but I suppose thee forgot it." In a note from Thomas Hyam & Son, London, November 10, 1751, to Thomas Penn, they notify him that they have bought, "according to thy order," a lottery ticket, No. 14,242, "for which we were obliged to give £12 11s. 'Tis an extravagant price, but they have been at £12 14s. this afternoon ; the Eagerness of People after them is quite surprizing." On the letter a memorandum in another hand, doubtless that of Thomas Penn, says,—

> "This ticket is for the benefit of
> Springet Penn
> Philadelphia Hannah Freame
> William Branson Hockley, &
> his sister Mary Hockley."

Whether it drew a prize is not stated ; we fear not.

The relations later of Springett Penn and his uncle Thomas were not uniformly cordial. April 25, 1760, Springett writes to Thomas, from Ealing, and after a brief condolence on "your great loss" (Thomas's son William had died only the day before), quickly turns to business, and concludes, " Therefore, sir, must desire that you let me have in three days at the farthest, all my papers without exception, that there may be no more troubles, delays, or mistakes whatsoever." To this Thomas sent an indignant, brief answer, from " Marybone, April 26 ; " he charges Springett with " ingratitude " and " inhumanity : " " am now," he says, " attending the body of my son, and cannot think of any business of my own till he is interred," nor that of any one. He desires to break off all further communication, and directs Springett to send to Mr. Heaton, his attorney. Later, May 6, Springett writes from " Broad Street Buildings " that his attorney is Mr. Thomas Life, at that address. " I hope," he says, " my Aunt and Cousins are well, and I am y' dutiful Nephew." To this Thomas replied that he had sent the deeds to Mr. Heaton, " this morning and have desired he will confer with Mr. Life about your affairs." Again, May 27, Springett writes from Great Ealing, desiring an interview, and this Thomas writes declining, referring him to his attorney, " as I have met with a Treatment from you I think very improper, and that it is owing to your being under an influence which I think is not for your honour or service."[1]

---

[1] There is a letter from Benjamin Franklin, in London, May 9, 1761, to Edward Penington, Philadelphia, in which the writer—who would have much regretted to overlook any serious defects of Thomas Penn— explains at length the representations made to him by " Mr. Springett Penn," who he says is " a very sensible, discreet young man, with excellent dispositions. The substance of the letter is that Springett believes his uncle Thomas has tried to keep him ignorant of his property rights, in order, he intimates, to defraud him. Springett particularly wants to know about a manor of seventy-five thousand acres on the Sus-

Later correspondence indicates an improvement of relations. A letter from Springett at Dublin, June 16, 1764, speaks of an offer from Thomas for his interest in Pennsbury. Finally, this last male bearing the name of Penn, descended from William Penn and Gulielma Maria Springett, died unmarried, at Dublin, in November, 1766. His mother wrote from that city on the 11th of that month to Thomas Penn,—

"SIR :

" I have taken the earliest opportunity my present Indisposition would admitt of acquainting you with the Irreparable loss I have sustained by the Death of my Son. He had for a considerable time a most violent cough, attended with symptoms of a Decay, which ultimately terminated in Consumption that nothing the Physicians of this Kingdom could Prescribe would stop. His Will has been opened, whereby he has left me all his Reall and Personall Fortune in Ireland and America. Nothing

quehanna, said to have been surveyed for his uncle Springett, 2d, by Sir William Keith, and he wishes to know the value of Pennsbury, the full title to which Uncle Thomas is desirous to acquire. The following passage from the letter may be given in full :

" There has by his account been something very mysterious in the conduct of his uncle, Mr. Thomas Penn, towards him. He was his guardian ; but instead of endeavoring to educate him at home, under his eye, in a manner becoming the elder branch of their house, has from his infancy been endeavoring to get rid of him. He first proposed sending him to the East Indies. When that was declined he had a scheme of sending him to Russia ; but the young gentleman's mother absolutely refusing to let him go out of the kingdom, unless to Pennsylvania, to be educated at the college there, he would by no means hear of his going thither, but bound him an apprentice to a country attorney, in an obscure part of Sussex, which, after two years' stay, finding that he was taught nothing valuable, nor could see any company that might improve him he left, and returned to his mother, with whom he has been ever since, much neglected by his uncle." etc.

These statements bear all the marks of being inspired by Ann Penn. It is very likely that Thomas had suggested plans to get the boy away from her, which she thwarted. That Thomas wished to defraud his ward, I do not suppose. (The letter is in Bigelow's " Franklin," Vol. I. p. 422.—It seems more appropriate for the date to be 1760.)

could Induce me to write in my Present afflicted Situation but the Respect I shall allways Endeavor to shew to his Relations that is in the power of

    " Sir, Y' Humble Serv'

                                    " ANN PENN."

Same to same, Dublin, November 29, 1766,—

[She is obliged by his letter of the 20th] "particularly by your proffers of information and services respecting affairs in Pennsylvania. I must take y* liberty of setting you right in regard to Pennsbury, for all remainders to that Estate were barred by my son, by a recovery suffered by him under the directions and conduct of Mr. Life and Mr. Penington ; y* former can give you full satisfaction in those particulars. I lodge at Mrs. Keson's, in York street, where," etc.

Same to same, February 18, 1767, acknowledging one from Thomas Penn of January 31,—

" I always considered Mr. Life as Mr. Penn's adviser in business. [He is the proper person to advise T. P. of the steps taken to cut off the entail of the American estates. Mr. Penington had written (from Pennsylvania) that] every matter was completed. [She will sell her estate in America] for the purpose of discharging a large debt contracted by my son, as well as the heavy one due Mr. Gaskell, with which the Irish estate is encumbered." [She wishes to be on a good footing with her son's family, but complains much of " Mr. Gaskell," and goes at length into details.]

Same to same, Dublin, March 14, 1767,—

"Since my last to you I have been married to Mr. Alexander Durdin, an attorney of this City." [She now does not wish to sell the Pennsylvania property. She had given Mr. Penington power of attorney to sell it. Mr. Durdin has gone on circuit, and will be back by the middle of April. He is not himself inclined to go to Pennsylvania ; he is busy, and his business profitable.]

And this closes Mrs. Vaux-Penn-Durdin's letters. Inside a month she had quitted the scene. Edward Scriven (probably a lawyer) writes from Dublin, April 16, 1767, to Thomas Penn, saying her marriage was unknown in advance to him or others conversant with her son's affairs, and that it was formed with a person she scarcely knew. It occurred "the latter end of February." Then she continued "in a bad state of health," and "as her Physician informed me, Dyed the 13 Instant."

Alexander Durdin was, it is stated, of a family "originally from the county of Norfolk." Ann Vaux Penn was his third wife. In the brief time between her marriage to him and her death, something less than two months, she had made her will in his favor, thus carrying to him that part of the Penn property in Ireland and America which her first husband, William Penn, 3d, had left to their son, Springett, 3d, and which the latter, at his death, had left to her. Her will was dated March 11, 1767, and Alexander Durdin was by it "devisee and residuary legatee." The will also created a trusteeship, the precise nature of which I have not investigated, James Duncan (who died before March 16, 1784) and Joseph Hoare, "of Dublin, Esquire," being trustees.

Mr. Durdin promptly entered into correspondence with Thomas Penn. He writes him from Dublin, August 13, 1767. He has received a letter "from Mr. Ben: Pike in Corke," about the cutting off the entail. Mr. Penington has since sent him a "copy of the Recovery suffered by Mr. Springett Penn." He has consulted counsel, and is informed as to his rights. He will sell the Pennsylvania interest to Thomas Penn sooner than any one else; he will act fairly. His letter reads as though candid and reasonable, though it may have been neither.[1]

[1] In 1784 Mr. Durdin gave letters of attorney (in which Hoare, the surviving trustee, joined) to Richard Durdin, "of the city of Dublin, gentleman, eldest son of Alexander Durdin," empowering him to take charge of the property in Pennsylvania and Delaware which had come to Alexander from his wife. One of these letters was dated March 16, 1784, and acknowledged before the Lord Mayor of Dublin, and a subsequent one, September 17, 1784, was acknowledged before the Lord Mayor of Cork. Richard Durdin, no doubt, then came to this country. He was, it is stated, a son of Alexander by his second wife, and married

We need not, however, dwell on this branch of the subject.   The second marriage episode of William Penn, 3d,
closes here, with the single exception—not an unimportant
one to the lawyers—that a lawsuit followed between Alexander Durdin and Christiana Gulielma (Penn) Gaskell, the
half-sister of Springett Penn, which lasted out the eighteenth
century.   "Christiana Gulielma's fortune was never paid,"
Maria Webb says,[1] "and Durdin resisted the claims made
upon him to obtain it.   The result was a long suit in chancery, which did not terminate till the year 1800, when the
Shangarry estate was divided between the heirs-at-law of
Peter Gaskell and Alexander Durdin."   Springett's will, it
appears, was executed December 21, 1762, but the "recovery" suffered by him to bar the entail was not completed
until April, 1764.   An opinion by Henry Wilmot, counsel
for Thomas Penn, remaining in the Penn papers, says, therefore, that as to the Pennsbury Manor Springett died intestate.
In England, intestate property could not go to heirs of the
half-blood,—i. e., the Gaskells; it would go to the Crown
first; but Wilmot says he does not know the Pennsylvania
law as to this.

We return, now, to pursue the line from Christiana Gulielma Penn, the daughter of William Penn, 3d, by his first
wife, Christian Forbes.   She was born, as already stated,
October 22, 1733.   She married Peter Gaskell, of Bath,
England.   From the similarity of their arms it is inferred
that his family was related to the Gaskells of Lancashire, a
representative of which was the family of that name at

___

a Miss Esmonde, daughter and co-heiress of Sir John Esmonde, of
Huntington Castle, near Ferris, Ireland.   Members of the Durdin
family, Miss Fanny Durdin and her brother, died in Philadelphia 1812
and 1809.   (Cf. PENNA. MAG., Vol. V. p. 364.)

[1] "Penns and Peningtons," p. 437, American edition.

CHRISTIANA CULELUM CASKLL

Beaumont Hall in that county, and Kiddington Hall, Oxford.[1]
The home of some of his immediate ancestors, it has been
stated, was Macclesfield, Cheshire.[2] His marriage to Christiana Gulielma Penn took place in 1761. Thomas Penn, in
England, writing to William Peters, at Philadelphia, October
9 of that year, says, " Miss Penn's and Miss Freame's accounts I shall expect soon ; the former is married to one
Mr. Gaskell ; I suppose he and his wife must send over a joint
power-of-attorney." And later, December 12, same year,
he writes, " Miss Christiana Penn is married to Mr. Gaskel ;
they send a power-of-attorney by a ship that is expected to
go soon for Philadelphia to you and Mr. Hockley, to finish
the sale of her land."

Peters and Hockley had been Miss Penn's agents before
her marriage ; she had given them her letter of attorney,
March 5, 1755, some months after she came of age. She
describes herself in the letter as "of London, spinster."
From her great-aunt, Letitia Aubrey, she had inherited
valuable lots and lands in the city of Philadelphia, the old
Manor of Mount Joy (Upper Merion Township), and Fagg's
Manor.[3] These several properties continued to be objects

[1] *Cf.* Burke, "County Families," edition of 1868.

[2] Statement of Peter Penn-Gaskell Hall to the author.—A member
of the family, writing late in the last century, describes a visit to the
grave of Peter Gaskell's grandfather, at or near Macclesfield.—Martin,
"History of Chester" (Pennsylvania), in connection with remarks on
the Penn-Gaskells, refers to "the Gaskells of Rolfe's Hold, Bucks."

[3] Fagg's Manor was created by William Penn in 1682, being a grant
of fifty thousand acres to Sir John Fagg, as trustee for his (W. P.'s)
wife and children. It was not laid out until 1700, when Penn was in
Pennsylvania the second time. A survey was made of about 30,000
acres, including in Chester County all the present township of New
Garden, and most of Kennett, with much more in New Castle County,
Delaware. This was divided between William and Letitia, and formed
the two manors of Staning, (or Stansing, as given in Letitia's patent.)
Two other tracts were surveyed to the westward of these, one for William

16

of concern and attention by her several agents from the time stated, 1755, down to her death in 1803. Space cannot be afforded here to go into the subject, but a complete examination of the record offices for Philadelphia and Chester Counties would develop a vast mass of business and legal details of some interest, as showing the connection of the Penn family, in its elder branch, with the soil of Pennsylvania. Besides William Peters and Richard Hockley, other agents were Miers Fisher, Thomas Clifford, and John Abraham de Normandie, who were constituted in 1785, on the death of Peter Gaskell; Edward Edwards, constituted 1794; Israel Morris, of Harford County, Maryland; and Christiana Gulielma's son, Peter Gaskell (afterwards Peter Penn-Gaskell), who came to this country about 1785, probably upon his father's decease.

In 1774 proceedings were begun to effect a "common recovery" of entailed family property in Philadelphia, in which the Gaskells represented a three-fourths interest (derived two-fourths from Christiana Gulielma's uncle Springett and one-fourth from her father), while the other one-fourth was the share of the Fell-Thomas branch, represented at that time by "Charles Hurst and others," with whom a partition was effected in 1775. A suit for damages brought by Hurst and John Barron against Christiana Gulielma Gaskell resulted in a judgment for the plaintiffs, in the Court of Common Pleas of Philadelphia County, at the June Term, 1786, for four thousand five hundred and thirty-six pounds, with costs, and a number of the defendant's city properties were levied on by

and one for Letitia, and it was to the latter that the name Fagg's Manor was distinctively applied. Peters and Hockley sold in 1758 for C. G. Penn several tracts in this manor, one of which, it is stated,—one hundred and eighty-two and a half acres, sold to Thomas Charlton,—remains (1897) partly or entirely in the ownership of his grandson of the same name. Sir John Fagg was a cousin of William Penn the Founder's first wife; the mother of Mary Proude (Springett-Penington) was Ann Fagg. (Cf. brief table, ante.)

the sheriff, and some sold, before a settlement was effected, January 1, 1790.

In 1785 Peter Gaskell died. The children of himself and wife are stated as five in number, as follows :[1]

1. Thomas Penn-Gaskell, who inherited the Irish and other property. He is described as of Shangarry (or Shannagarry), and died at Dublin, Ireland, in 1823, without living issue. A contemporary obituary notice says,—

"Died at his house, in Fitzwilliam-Square, Dublin, on the 19th of October, 1823, aged 61, Thomas Penn Gaskell, of Shanagarry, in the county of Cork, Esq. This gentleman was the heir-general of the celebrated legislator William Penn. . . . His estate in the county of Cork Mr. Gaskell inherited by lineal succession from his illustrious ancestor, Vice-Admiral Sir William Penn. . . . After being engaged forty years in a suit in the Irish Chancery, and expending upward of £20,000, he obtained a decree to possess his estate.[1] He married in the year 1794, a daughter of the Dowager Countess of Glandore, who lived but a few years ; they had only one son, who died an infant. After so much affliction he retired from the world and lived a very secluded life."

His Irish property descended to his brother next named.

2. Peter Penn-Gaskell. See below.

3. Alexander Forbes Gaskell (or Penn-Gaskell), *d. s. p.*

4. William Gaskell (or Penn-Gaskell), of London, who had two children : (1) William Penn-Gaskell, born February 20, 1808 ; (2) Elizabeth, *d. s. p.* Of these, William married and had ten children, the youngest of whom is George Penn-Gaskell, of (1898) No. 12, Nicoll Road, Willesden, S. W., London.

[1] Browning, "Americans of Royal Descent ;" Thomas Gilpin's "Chart of Penn Family ;" MS. sketch, by C. R. Hildeburn, in collections of the Historical Society of Pennsylvania. *Cf.* also Burke's "Landed Gentry," edition of 1879.

[2] This allusion refers, perhaps, to the litigation between the Gaskells and Alexander Durdin rather than to a lawsuit by Thomas Penn-Gaskell.

5. Jane Gaskell (or Penn-Gaskell) *d. s. p.*[1]

Christiana Gulielma Gaskell survived her husband eighteen years. Her mother's memorial in " Piety Promoted," already cited, says she " died a widow at Bath, in 1803." The place named is an error. She continued her residence at Bath for several years after her husband's death, and is so described in legal papers ; but in 1795, and perhaps earlier, she is described as " of Thornhaugh street, in the parish of St. Giles in the Fields, in the county of Middlesex, England," and she there died. The *Gentleman's Magazine* contains the following notice :   •

[March, 1803]   " 24. At her house in Thornhaugh-street, Bedford-square [London] aged 69, Mrs. Gaskell, relict of Peter G., esq., of the city of Bath, and only daughter of W'm. Penn, esq., late of Shannagarry, co. Cork, Ireland, the grandson and heir of William Penn. . . "

Peter Penn-Gaskell, son of Peter Gaskell and Christiana Gulielma Penn, came, as stated, to this country about 1785. He married, 1793, Elizabeth, daughter of Nathan Edwards, of Radnor, Delaware County, Pennsylvania. He died July 16, 1831, as stated by the inscription on his tombstone in the Baptist Church of Lower Merion, Pennsylvania, which adds that his age was sixty-eight years, thus fixing his birth as in 1763. He purchased, 1796, three years after his marriage, of John Bewley, a tract of land and residence in Radnor (near the present railway station, Villa Nova), which he called "Ashwood," and which remained in the family possession until 1888. In 1823, upon the decease of his brother Thomas Penn-Gaskell, he came into succession as owner of the Irish property, and he was thereafter known as " of Shangarry." He assumed, " by royal license," May 31, 1824, " in compliance with the testamentary injunction of his brother," the

[1] The names of Nos. 3, 4, and 5 are placed according to the order of a MS. pedigree by C. R. Hildeburn ; the statement that Nos. 3 and 5 *d. s. p.* is given on the authority of Browning, "Americans of Royal Descent."

additional surname of Penn,[1] and the family name has since so continued.

Elizabeth (Edwards) Penn-Gaskell, widow of Peter, died July 19, 1834, "aged 62 years." In her will, dated June 21, and proved September 12, 1834, she leaves three thousand dollars for tombstones to be placed over the remains of her husband, herself, and their children, in the Baptist burial-ground at Lower Merion.[2]

The children of Peter Penn-Gaskell and Elizabeth Edwards were eight in number, as follows :

1. William, born 1794 ; died unmarried October 12, 1817. Buried at Lower Merion Baptist Church.

2. Thomas, whom Burke ("Landed Gentry," edition of 1879) describes "of Ballymaloe, county Cork, Ireland, and Penn Hall, Montgomery county, Pa., born 1796." He was married, December 22, 1825, by Right Rev. Bishop White, to Mary, daughter of George McClenachan. He died at his home, "Penn Cottage," in Lower Merion, near Philadelphia, "at 5 o'clock," on the morning of Sunday, October 18, 1846, "in the 52nd year of his age." He was buried "in his vault," at St. John's R. C. Church, Thirteenth Street, above Chestnut, Philadelphia, on the 20th.[3] His wife Mary died December 21, 1867, "at Penn Cottage, Lower Merion," and was buried on the 24th, in the vault at St. John's, with her husband. They appear to have had no children.

3. Eliza, died unmarried, at "Ashwood," November 23, 1865, "aged 67 years," and was buried at Lower Merion. She had been resident at "Ashwood" all her life, and by her will (1861, codicil 1862) she made elaborate provision

---

[1] Burke's "Landed Gentry," edition of 1879.

[2] They were so placed, and the inscriptions upon them have been used for this work.

[3] Funeral notice in *Pennsylvania Inquirer ;* "History of the Friendly Sons of St. Patrick," etc., Philadelphia, 1892. The latter mentions that Thomas Penn-Gaskell became a member of the Hibernian Society, 1835.

designed to preserve the ownership in the family; after partition, however, the last part of it, about fifty acres, was sold, 1888, to Dr. J. M. Da Costa, of Philadelphia.

4. Alexander Forbes, died unmarried, at "Ashwood," September 8, 1829, "aged 27 years," and was buried at Lower Merion.

5. Peter, married Louisa Adelaide Heath, and had issue. See below.

6. Christiana Gulielma, married William Swabric Hall, and had issue. See below.

7. Jane, died unmarried, July 7, 1852, "aged 24 years," and was buried at Lower Merion.

8. Isaac, died unmarried, without issue, October 24, 1842, "aged 32 years," and was buried at Lower Merion. His will, dated October 23, 1842, was probated May 16, 1843, his brother, Thomas Penn-Gaskell, to whom letters of administration had previously been granted, withdrawing them and consenting to the probate, "though," the record says, "his belief of the mental incapacity of the [deceased] to make a will remains unaltered." Browning ("Americans of Royal Descent") designates Isaac Penn-Gaskell as "Dr.," and adds "of Paris."

Peter Penn-Gaskell, "of Shangarry," second of that name, son of Peter and Elizabeth, was born April 3, 1803, and married, February 15, 1825, Louisa Adelaide, daughter of Charles P. Heath. She was descended through her mother, Esther Keeley, from Captain Anthony Wayne, the grandfather of General Anthony Wayne, her great-grandmother being Esther Wayne, a first cousin of the general. Peter Penn-Gaskell, 2d, died April 6, 1866. He describes himself in his will as "of No. 1613 Chestnut street, in the City of Philadelphia," and "of Shangarry, in the county of Cork, in Ireland." His will is very long. He leaves Shangarry to his son William, and then to Peter, who received it by William's decease.

Louisa, wife of Peter Penn-Gaskell, 2d, survived him. Her will, dated June 29, 1869, was made in London, and describes her as " of Philadelphia, in the United States of America, but now residing at Eastbourne Terrace, Hyde Park, London, widow." It had three codicils added, the latest March 27, 1877, and was proved in Philadelphia July 30, 1878. The last codicil mentions her son Peter as " now living in London."

The children of Peter Penn-Gaskell, 2d, and· Louisa Heath were ten in number, as follows :

1. Elizabeth, born 1828 ; died 1869 ; married Samuel Ruff Skillern, M. D., of Huntsville, Alabama. By this marriage there were two children. The younger was Louella, who died aged three years ; the other was Penn-Gaskell Skillern, M.D., of Philadelphia, born April 28, 1856 ; married October 17, 1878, Anna Dorsey, and has issue : (1) Violet Skillern, born November 13, 1879; (2) Peter Penn-Gaskell Skillern, Jr., born March 26, 1882.

2. Louisa, married, May 15, 1845, at St. Stephen's P. E. Church, Philadelphia, by Rev. H. W. Ducachet, D. D., William Gerald Fitzgerald, of New York. (Burke's " Landed Gentry," describes him as " of Waterford.") She died 1853, without issue.

3. Mary Gulielma, died young.

4. Gulielma, died unmarried, 1852. ("A beautiful girl, who died young."—Martin, " History of Chester, Pennsylvania.")

5. Hetty, died unmarried.

6. Mary, married, 1855, Dr. Isaac T. Coates, of Chester, Pennsylvania, and died August 22, 1877. Dr. Coates died June 23, 1883. They had one son, Harold Penn-Gaskell Coates, who married Miss Jarvis, of Philadelphia.

7. William, died unmarried, December 6, 1865, "aged 29 years." He was the oldest son, and would have inherited the family property in Great Britain. He served with credit in the

national army in the war for the Union. The record[1] shows
him to have been mustered into the United States service,
August 9, 1862, at Camp Struthers, Philadelphia, as second
lieutenant of the Independent Company of Acting Engi-
neers (authority for recruiting which was given by the Secretary of War June 2, 1862). He was promoted to first
lieutenant December 16, 1862; to captain March 30, 1863;
and discharged on surgeon's certificate July 5, 1864. "His
death was caused by consumption, after a lingering and
distressingly painful illness." An extended obituary, signed
I. T. C. (Dr. Isaac T. Coates, his brother-in-law, no doubt),
published in a New Orleans newspaper, January 13, 1866,
mentions the cause of his death, as stated above, and says
he " breathed his last in the bosom of his family, and surrounded by every member of it . . . father . . .
mother . . . sisters, and . . . brother." The notice
speaks highly of his scholarship; " his acquirements for one
so young were very great." Science, metaphysics, history,
romance, are mentioned as familiar to him. In standard
poetry he has read everything "from the Edda of the icy
North to the sweet lyrics of sunny Italy." His modest and
retiring character is especially dwelt on, "yet when his sweet
voice was heard, dignity of speech, good sense, and social
eloquence always accompanied it."

8. Jane, who married Washington Irving, U. S. N. (a
nephew, it is stated, of the eminent author), and died 1863,
without issue.

9. Emily, married, 1864, John Paul Quinn, M. D., surgeon
U. S. N., and had one son, Granville Penn-Gaskell Quinn,
who died 1893, aged twenty-two.

10. Peter, born October 24, 1843, who succeeded to the
family property on the death of his father, 1866, and has
since resided abroad, mostly in London. He served with
distinction on the national side in the American civil war.

[1] Bates's "History of Pennsylvania Volunteers," Vol. V. p. 919.

He was commissioned second lieutenant in the First Regiment New Jersey Cavalry April 7, 1862, and first lieutenant November 7, 1862; was promoted to captain October 23, 1863, and resigned February 3, 1864, to become major of the Second Louisiana Cavalry, in which position he served until September 7, 1864. He married, July 6, 1869, Mary Kathleen, eldest daughter of Charles Edward Stubbs, Esq., of Sussex Square, Hyde Park, London, formerly of Lima, Peru. Some time after his marriage Mr. Penn-Gaskell visited this country. The portrait of William Penn (following the painting in armor), engraved by W. G. Armstrong, and placed as the frontispiece to the first volume of the PENNSYLVANIA MAGAZINE, was inscribed to him, 1877, by the Historical Society of Pennsylvania. Accompanying this engraving are the arms of Penn-Gaskell of Shangarry. As described by Burke they are :

"Quarterly : 1st and 4th, or, three bars engrailed vert, in chief a rose gu. barbed and seeded ppr., between two trefoils slipped of the second, for GASKELL ; 2d and 3d the arms of PENN, viz., arg., on a fess sa. three plates a canton, gu., thereon a crown, ppr., representing the royal crown of King Charles II. Crests for *Gaskell :* A sinister arm embowed with an anchor erect with cable sa. *Motto* over, ' Spes.' Of *Penn :* a demi-lion arg., gorged with a collar sa., charged with three plates. *Motto* over, ' Pennsylvania.' "

The children of Peter and Mary Kathleen Penn-Gaskell are three in number : William, Winifred, Percy.

Christiana Gulielma Penn-Gaskell, daughter of Peter Penn-Gaskell and Elizabeth Edwards, married, January 2, 1827, William Swabric Hall, and died March 29, 1830, "aged 24 years ; " she was buried in the Baptist church-yard at Lower Merion. William Swabric Hall, born in England, near Liverpool, 1799, came to Philadelphia about 1825. He died September 26, 1862, "aged 63 years," and was buried at Lower Merion. They had two children : William Penn-Gaskell Hall, who died unmarried, May 2, 1862, aged thirty-five years, and was buried at Lower Merion, and Peter Penn-Gaskell Hall, of Philadelphia, of whom below.

Peter Penn-Gaskell Hall, second son of William S. Hall and Christiana Gulielma Penn-Gaskell, is a graduate of Princeton College (now University), New Jersey, and studied law and was admitted to the bar of Philadelphia. At the outbreak of the war against the Union, 1861, he entered the national service. He was commissioned second lieutenant of the Twenty-sixth Pennsylvania Infantry May 31, 1861, and first lieutenant August 25, 1861; was honorably mustered out February 16, 1863; and was appointed additional paymaster, with the rank of major, November 6, 1863. On November 15, 1865, he was honorably mustered out. January 17, 1867, he was commissioned paymaster of the regular army of the United States, with the rank of major, and continued in that position until July 2, 1891, when he was honorably retired, having served over twenty years. He is President of the Colonial Society of Pennsylvania. He married, December 24, 1861, Annie M. Mixsell, daughter of Philip Mixsell, of Easton, Pennsylvania; she died at Vicksburg, Mississippi, February 14, 1869, and was buried at the Baptist Church, Lower Merion. Secondly, he married, at San Antonio, Texas, November, 1871, Amelia Mixsell. Issue by both marriages, eight children, as below:

1. Christiana Gulielma, born at "Ashwood" April 19, 1863.

2. Eliza, born at Baltimore, Maryland, February 1, 1865; married, July 1, 1892, Henry J. Hancock, member of the Philadelphia bar, son of George W. and Elizabeth (James) Hancock. They have issue, a daughter, Jean Barclay Penn-Gaskell, born March 24, 1893.

3. Edward Swabric, born at "Ashwood" January, 1867; died at Vicksburg, Mississippi, January, 1869.

4. Amelia, born at Vicksburg, Mississippi, January, 1869; died at Holly Springs, Mississippi, May, 1869.

5. William, born at San Antonio, Texas, January 16, 1873.
6. Peter, born at New York City, March 14, 1875.
7. Amelia, born at New York City, February 9, 1877.
8. Philip, born at "Ashwood," September 10, 1878.

TABLE: LINE OF WILLIAM PENN, THIRD.

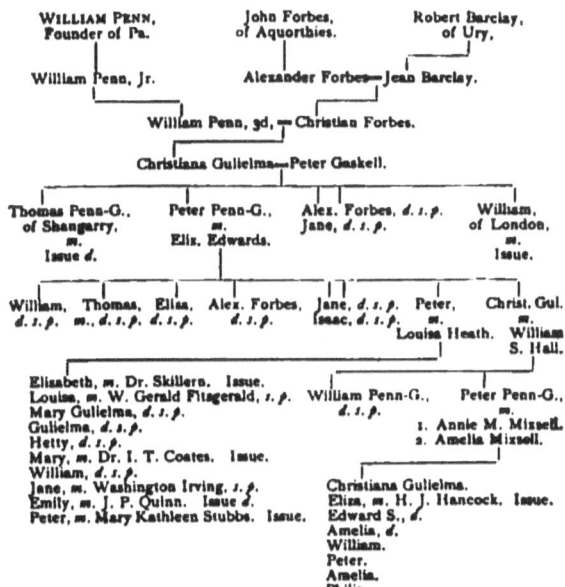

WILLIAM PENN,   John Forbes,   Robert Barclay,
Founder of Pa.   of Aquorthies.   of Ury,

William Penn, Jr.   Alexander Forbes—Jean Barclay.

William Penn, 3d, — Christian Forbes.

Christiana Gulielma—Peter Gaskell.

Thomas Penn-G.,   Peter Penn-G.,   Alex. Forbes, *d. s. p.*   William,
of Shangarry,   *m.*   Jane, *d. s. p.*   of London,
m.   Eliz. Edwards.   *m.*
Issue *d.*   Issue.

William,   Thomas,   Eliza,   Alex. Forbes,   Jane, *d. s. p.*   Peter,   Christ. Gul.
d. s. p.   *m., d. s. p.*   *d. s. p.*   *d. s. p.*   Isaac, *d. s. p.*   *m.*   *m.*
                                               Louisa Heath.   William
                                                                 S. Hall.

Elizabeth, *m.* Dr. Skillern. Issue.
Louisa, *m.* W. Gerald Fitzgerald, *s. p.*   William Penn-G.,   Peter Penn-G.,
Mary Gulielma, *d. s. p.*   *d. s. p.*   *m.*
Gulielma, *d. s. p.*   1. Annie M. Mixsell.
Hetty, *d. s. p.*   2. Amelia Mixsell.
Mary, *m.* Dr. I. T. Coates. Issue.
William, *d. s. p.*
Jane, *m.* Washington Irving, *s. p.*   Christiana Gulielma.
Emily, *m.* J. P. Quinn. Issue *d.*   Eliza, *m.* H. J. Hancock. Issue.
Peter, *m.* Mary Kathleen Stubbs. Issue.   Edward S., *d.*
                                                           Amelia, *d.*
                                                            William.
                                                            Peter.
                                                            Amelia.
                                                            Philip.

XIII.

Supplementary and Concluding Chapter.

THOUGH it was my plan to state all the facts suitable for
this essay in their appropriate connection, in the development of the family narrative, it has proved that a number
of additional data have accumulated, whose interest, if not
importance, makes a supplementary chapter appropriate.

ADMIRAL PENN'S PROGENITORS.

The investigations of Mr. J. Henry Lea in England, in
1899, have added some further data of value to our slender
store concerning the ancestry of Admiral Penn. He shows
that Giles Penn, father of the Admiral, was apprenticed, May
1, 1593, to John Horte, of the City of Bristol, draper, and
Juliana his wife, and that in April, 1600, "Gylles Penne,
draper," was "admitted into the liberties" of the city, "because he was the Prentice of Mr. John Horte, Alderman,
Deceased." An entry in 1602 shows that Robert Green, son
of Marmaduke, of Ballincham, was apprenticed to Giles Penn,
of the city of Bristol, draper, and Joane his wife.

These entries make it plain that the occupation of Giles
Penn was primarily that of a draper, and Mr. Lea thinks he
could not have been, as stated on the tablet to his son the
Admiral, a "Captain," and "several years Consul for the
English in the Mediterranean."

Mr. Lea is able to construct a fuller table of the family
line preceding the Admiral than I have given at the close of
Chapter II. of this work. Those interested in the subject will
find it in the *New England Historic and Genealogical Register*

X

for July, 1900. The children of Giles and Joan Penn he gives as follows :

GILES PENN=JOAN GILBERT.

George, who suffered in Spain, etc., d. 1664.
Giles, bapt. 4 Oct., 1603.
Henry, bapt. 26 Jan., 1604, d. unm., circa 1632.
Rachel, bapt. 24 Feb., 1607.
Eleanor, bapt. 26 May, 1610, bu. 24 Nov., 1612.
Ann, bapt. 21 Jan., 1618, bu. 23 Feb., 1651.
William, (the Admiral), bapt. 1621, d. 1670.

I may introduce, at this point, a letter from Rev. John Dempster Hammond, D. D., of San Francisco, Cal., dated Nov. 23, 1898. Dr. Hammond says :

" I have an old record, which reads as follows :

" ' William Hammond, born in the city of London, and there married Elizabeth Penn, sister of Sir William Penn ; had children Benjamin, their son, born 1621, Elizabeth, Martha, and Rachel, their daughters, all born in London. William Hammond died there and was buried. Elizabeth Hammond, with her son Benjamin and three daughters left a good estate in London, and with several godly people came over to New England in troublesome times, in 1634, out of a conscious desire to have the liberty to serve God in the way of his appointment. They had with them the Rev. Mr. Lothrop, their minister, 1634. Settled in Boston, and there died 1640 ; had an honorable burial, and the character of a very godly woman.'

" This record was made by John, son of the above-named Benjamin, and grandson of William and Elizabeth, not later than 1700 ; my copy was made 1737."

As to which I can only say that so far there is no record evidence that Sir William Penn had a sister Elizabeth. The list of his sisters, above, names only Rachel, Eleanor, and Ann ; it may, however, be incomplete.

ADMIRAL PENN'S TABLET AND ARMS.

The question, if there really was any, as to the wording upon Admiral Penn's memorial tablet in the church of St.

Mary Redcliffe, at Bristol, may be regarded as entirely settled.
Inspection and photography show with sufficient clearness
the presence of the words, "and those Penns of Penn, in the
county of Bucks," and this record evidence, whatever its value
may be, is definitely established.

An article in *Notes and Queries*, London (Fifth Series, Vol.
XI. p. 457), describes the Admiral's armor accompanying
the tablet. It "consists of the entire suit, with helmet, said
to have been worn by the gallant knight, 'admiral and
general,' during his last expedition, and it is attached to one
of the columns of the church, together with his sword,
spurs, gauntlets, and pennons, now consisting of a few fragments only."

The same article adds some details of interest in connection with the opening of the Admiral's tomb for the burial
of the last William Penn (grandson of Richard) in 1845.
It says, "In September, 1845, the family vault was opened
to admit the remains of a descendant, when it was found
that the mahogany outer coffin was completely decayed,
and the leaden one containing the Admiral had given way
at the sides. Upon lifting the lid to have the sides properly
secured, the cerecloth covering the body appeared quite
perfect; the face and hands, which had become of a brown
color, were alone uncovered, and they were well preserved,
the pointed Vandyke beard and mustaches remarkably so.
The next day, the coffin, having been carefully repaired, was
re-deposited in the vault." [1]

THE PENN-LOWTHER MARRIAGE.

In the record of the marriage licenses issued by the Archbishop of Canterbury there is this, February 12, 1666–7 :

[1] St. Mary Redcliffe, it may be worth noting, was the church under
whose shadow the marvellous boy Chatterton was reared, and in whose
"muniment room" he pretended to have found the old chest of manuscripts, "Canynge's Coffer."

"Anthony Lowther, of Moske, co. York, Esq., Bach', 24, and Margaret Pen, Sp', 15, dau of Sir William Pen, K', of St. Olave, Hart street, London, who consents ; at St. Olave's afsd, Barking, co. Essex, or Clapham, co. Surrey."

The marriage took place, as Pepys's Diary has already stated, February 14, two days after the issue of the license. Margaret was, it appears, but fifteen years old, the bridegroom being nine years her senior.

PENN'S IMPRISONMENT IN THE TOWER.

A very intelligent and careful inquiry into the imprisonment of William Penn in the Tower of London, in 1668–9, was published in *Archæologia*, London, Vol. xxxv., pp. 72–90, it being a paper read, March 17, 1853, before the Society of Antiquaries, London, by John Bruce, Esq., treasurer of the society. The value of the paper consists chiefly in its clear explanation of the manner of Penn's imprisonment, and its citation of the minutes of several sittings of the Privy Council in which the case was considered.

Mr. Bruce explains that the printing and publishing of books at the time Penn issued his "Sandy Foundation Shaken" were strictly regulated by the severe statute, 14 Car. II., cap. 33. While it is true that this could not have been very rigidly enforced, since there are many books extant printed in the period after the law was enacted, without the license which it required, it was yet available for use when the authorities might choose to employ it.

The minutes of the Privy Council show that Penn, upon search being made for the printer of his book, John Derby, came forward, avowed himself the author, and surrendered himself to Lord Arlington, principal Secretary of State, who, of his own authority,[1] sent Penn a "close prisoner" to the Tower, and Derby to the Gate-House prison.

---

[1] The statute does not seem to have been followed ; Mr. Bruce calls the proceedings "Star Chamber" throughout.

At the Council, Whitehall, December 16, 1668, the King present, Lord Arlington reported what he had done ; his action was approved, and he was directed to give orders to continue Penn and Derby in confinement. Two days later, at another council, a warrant was issued to the lieutenant of the Tower, directing that Penn be kept a "close prisoner" until the King's pleasure should be further signified, the warrant being signed by the Duke of Ormond, the Lord Chamberlain (Earl of Manchester), the Earl of Sandwich, the Earl of Carbery, Lord Ashley, Lord Berkeley, and Sir John Trevor (Secretary of State).

January 29, 1668-9, at a council, the petition of Joane Derby, wife of John Derby, the printer, was presented, asking his release on bail. It was ordered that he might enjoy such liberty of the prison as other prisoners had, but should still be kept in safe custody. May 7, 1669, the Council ordered him released.

March 31, 1669, a petition of Sir William Penn was presented to the Council in behalf of his son, and it was directed that the Bishop of London (Dr. Humphrey Henchman, appointed to that see in 1663) should examine and judge of the "heretical views" in "The Sandy Foundation Shaken," and that Sir John Robinson, the lieutenant of the Tower, should allow citations and processes issued by the Bishop to be served on Penn ; also, he should allow Penn, in charge of "a keeper and sufficient guard," to appear in the Bishop's consistory.

The action taken by the Bishop, under this order, Mr. Bruce says, was to send Dr. Stillingfleet (afterwards Bishop) to visit the prisoner.[1] At any rate, at the Council, July 28, 1669, about three months after the previous action, the King being present, his Majesty expressed himself as satisfied by Dr. Stillingfleet's report, and by what Penn "hath

[1] Penn himself says that Stillingfleet came to see him "at the King's command."

since published" (the explanatory pamphlet, "Innocency with her Open Face"), that he was sensible of his former "error." Sir John Robinson was therefore ordered forthwith to set him at liberty and deliver him "to his father, Sir William Pen." [1]

THE SHANGARRY ESTATE.

If we except Jordans graveyard, no other place seems more identified now with the Penn name than the old Irish estate of Shangarry. And this is in spite of the fact that the Founder, after the days of his youth, and his departure to Oxford, could have been there very little, while his descendants, other than William Penn, 3d, down to Thomas Penn-Gaskell, were hardly resident there at all.

The Shangarry estate, as already mentioned, was divided at the conclusion of the long lawsuit between the heirs of Peter Gaskell and those of Alexander Durdin. The two portions remain in those families, the present Penn owner being Peter Penn-Gaskell. A curious feature of the division is that the old castle from which the estate takes its name is on the Durdin portion. Possibly Admiral Penn, could he be witness to this consequence of the sixty days' nominal marriage relation of his great-grandson's widow, would think it an unsatisfactory sequel to the schemes and ambitions by which Shangarry was acquired as a war grant by the favor of Protector and King.

The Shangarry estates cover an area of about four miles by two miles (English). They lie on the extreme southern coast of Ireland, between Cork and Youghal ; [2] so close, indeed, to the Atlantic that a wide estuary in which the

---

[1] Mr. Bruce's paper is a fair and candid one, apparently with the disposition, if not the purpose, to show that Penn was not persecuted by the Bishop of London.

[2] This is the region of Captain William Penn's naval operations, for the Parliament, in 1644 and later.

17

ocean tides ebb and flow is but three-fourths of a mile from
the castle.   The region is substantially a peninsula, the
ocean on the south, Cork Harbor on the west, and the
estuary already mentioned on the east nearly enclosing it.
The place seems secluded and remote; four miles northwest
is the town of Cloyne, famous as the home for eighteen
years (1734–1752) of Bishop Berkeley,[1] and about five miles
farther northwest is Midleton, a station and post-town on
the Great Southern and Western Railway,[2] which is the
nearest point of access to the great outside world.

The " Castle " (Shangarry=Celtic, old garden) is now a
mere heap of ruins.   It receives no notice in any of the
descriptions—not even the minute studies of Mr. and Mrs.
S. C. Hall—of the picturesque remains of the region, and
the name Shangarry[3] will be sought in vain in gazetteers
and local guide-books.   There is, however, a village of
Shangarry, this being on the Penn-Gaskell portion of the
estate, and near by, " on a strip of land " which belongs to
the Durdin owner, the ruins are.   Immediately opposite
them stands what formerly was Shangarry House,—" the
House,"—now altered into stables and offices, while a newer
house (" built about 1841 "), a " gentleman's residence " of
the present century, has been erected " about five hundred

---

[1] The time of the Bishop's residence at Cloyne coincides pretty
nearly with the period of William Penn, 3d's residence at Cork and
Shangarry, but I find no trace of their acquaintanceship.   One would
have thought that at least the invalid of Shangarry might have had the
advantage of the Bishop's tar-water remedy, which at that particular
period much occupied his attention.

[2] The place is the "middle town" on the road from Cork to
Youghal.   The Post-Office Department spells it with one *d*,—*Midleton*.

[3] The spelling used locally, and by Mr. Penn-Gaskell and others of
my correspondents, is Shanagarry.   I have followed, to avoid change,
the spelling which seems to have been used originally, and which was
therefore employed in the early part of this essay.

yards farther back from the main road." [1] This main road leads from Midleton down through Cloyne, past Shangarry, to Ballycotton, on the ocean shore,—a seaside resort of some note.

The old castle had a history beginning at least as early as the time of Elizabeth. In her reign it was successfully defended against her troops by the Earl of Desmond. Walter Raleigh, at Youghal, was doubtless well acquainted with the place. In 1641 it was held by the Irish for Charles, but was taken later by Parliamentary troops, and by Cromwell's order was dismantled. Maria Webb ("Penns and Peningtons") describes it (1867) as having then some attractiveness. It is, she says, "an ivy-covered ruin ; but its tall tower, rising above the bright green foliage, gives a commanding and picturesque air to the remains." A photograph of the ruins in 1898 makes this description quite unsuitable. The ruins appear to be of no great size, and to have hardly any architectural form remaining.[2]

A Roman Catholic chapel, built about 1830, stands near the castle ruins ; the Episcopal Protestant Church of Kilmahon, of much older date, is also in the vicinity. About two miles southwest, and on the Shangarry estate, stands an old dwelling-house in tolerable repair, and still occupied as a residence, called "Sunville," and it was in this, the "old people " of the neighborhood insist, that William Penn lived when at Shangarry.

---

[1] "It has always seemed to me a pity that the new House was ever built, the old one being so much more massive and solid, but its close proximity to the high road and the village was no doubt an objection." —*Letter, 1898.*

[2] I am indebted for the photograph and for information of value in this connection to the kindness of T. Wilson Strangman, whose house, "Kinoith," stands on the Penn-Gaskell portion of the Shangarry estate. (Kinoith, which, Celtic, means "The Place of Friendship," is, he states, "an old name revived, which has been applied to this district probably since the days of William Penn.")

By the will of Peter Penn-Gaskell, 2d (who died 1866), the Penn-Gaskell portion of the Shangarry estate was charged with payments of annuities, etc., in addition to an encumbrance which already lay upon it. The diminished values of Irish estates in recent years have borne heavily upon Shangarry, and the revenues from it are probably more than absorbed in the charges upon it.

JOHN PENN'S RESIDENCE AT FEENS.

Allusion is made at several places in this essay to the residence of John Penn,' "the American," at Feens, near Twyford, in Berks, and in a foot-note to Chapter IX., besides some other details, an extract is given from a letter written by him to his servant, named Thomas Penn,¹ directing him to get Feens ready for occupancy. This letter was dated December 2, 1735, immediately after John's return to England from his Pennsylvania visit. To this, Thomas, who wrote a tolerable letter, though evidently a person of very limited education, replied, his letter undated,—

" . . . I rec'd yours of yᵉ 2d. I should have wrote sooner, had I any other news but yᵉ rejoicing of yᵉ people for your safe landing, and their wishing for you a safe arrival here. . . . Hannah gives her duty, every evening the House hath a spy to watch your coming, for they are resolved to make our church steaple rock for joy."

John, it seems, lost no time in forming plans for spending his Christmas at Feens. Tom writes to him, December 9, thus :²

" Mr. Griffin is com to feens & hath begun packing up this day & sayeth he intends to clear yᵉ hous yᵉ latter end of nexte weeke or soonor, if soonor I shall let you know. I have inquird for a man to

¹ This Thomas Penn appears to have been a colored man, and he seems to have been advanced in years. In one of his letters to John Penn, 1735, he says that if his "legs were as good as they once were" he would attend himself to some business that was under consideration.

² The letter is endorsed, " Black Tom's Letters, 1735."

shave, write and waite at table, but can heare of none about. I have set Aran to work for 12d per day, small bear and loging, and finds himself till you com to feens. Hannah hath agreede with a maide, if you like. I have wrote to [name not plain] about a horse. Hannah sayeth there wants cover sheets, if youle please to send a pece of cloth she could make y^m now shee hath time. please send word what provishhon you would have laid in. I believe I have planted Sallery a nuf. I have not yet seen any wine. . . .   "T P

"please to let me know when a ship sailes, for I muste send sum strawberries and [word torn] roots or Mrs¹ will chide."

Upon the same date as Tom's letter (and apparently in reply to it) John Penn writes to Tom. The letter is addressed to him, "att Feens, near Maidenhead, Berks, pr Maidenhead bagg," and runs thus:

" Honest Tom

"I have rec'd yours I am sorry the gentleman has not Left the house. I desire you'l Gett 2 Leggs of Pork, & a Bullock or two of Beafe, as Soon as you Can to be Ready against Christmass, also 3 or 4 good hen Turkeys, fouls, & Geese. I should be glad to know what youl want from Town that [I] may Send it Down. we shall want some Good hay & oats which pray gett for Shall have a Good Deal of Company down with me. As you cannot gett the Person that lived with Mr. Griffen, I believe Shall keep Sam, who Seems Better Since he has been on Shore ; hope you'll have Somebody in the Garden and stable by Xmass, & as we Shall want some person to go out a Shooting, perhaps Aaron may do, or if T. Skinner Could be gott for a few days. I could not Send wine Last week but Design you some on fryday p^r Waggon, wherefore desire you'l not be out of the Way. a Doz of Wood pidgeons Potted & Some Potted Beafe or Collard would be acceptable, also a hogs head in a Collar. . . . "

Same to same, December 16, 1735 :

" . . . I design to send down some Coals p^r Rounds Barge with Severall other things. I sent yesterday a hamper of Sugar, Tea, & Coffee, which hope came safe & that you Rec'd last week p^r Waggon a hhead of Red Wine. Youl have a pipe of Madeira Fryday, & a hogshead [of] fine Rum if it can be landed by that time."

¹ "Mrs." was evidently Margaret Freame, then in Pennsylvania. Letters from her, at Philadelphia, to Tom, on garden seeds, etc., are in the Penn collections.

Tom to John Penn, December 19, 1735:

" HON Sᵃ

"Yᵉ gentlemen left Feens yesterday. here is only one sarvant, we
are washing scrubing and giting Every stoole in its place as you left it
yᵗ Nothing should appeare strange to you att your returne, but feare yᵉ
rooms will scarce be dry and well air'd before Munday. please to send
a line what you would please to have got for Supper or Dinner when
you come, here will be potted befe, Collared ditto, hoggs hed brand
[?brained] wood piggons potted and so forth. People would Meete
you on yᵉ rode to congratulate youre safe returne and conducte you to
your old set did they but know ye day and way you would com

.   " from your humble sv't

                                         " T P
" feens, Fryday morning "

"Feens" is a property in the parish of Whit-Waltham,
about 3 miles from Maidenhead, and 4 from Ruscombe. It
derived its name from the family of Fiennes, to whom it
formerly belonged. Hurley, where John Penn died, is a
village on the Thames, about 4 miles north of Feens. Its
low lying situation may account for the bad effect it apparently
had on John's health. The "Great House" would be, no
doubt, Lady Place, an historic mansion where the Whig
nobles are said to have drawn up the invitation to William of
Orange, in 1688.

THE GRAVESTONES OF JORDANS GROUND.

The several reflections upon the errors in the lettering
placed upon the gravestones in the Friends' burial-ground
at Jordans make it necessary now to state that these errors
have been mostly corrected. A letter from Joseph J. Green,
the distinguished Quaker antiquarian and genealogist, October
12, 1897, from Tunbridge Wells, England, says, referring
first to the grave marked Letitia Penn,—

"The stone is now correct, 'Letitia Aubrey,' as I have drawn the
attention of the local monthly-meeting to these defects, and new stones
are now put down where errors existed. The stone 'Mary Frame' has

been taken up, or altered to ' Margaret Freame, and I think also 'Thomas Freame ; ' both are buried in one grave. The stone at John Penn's grave is also correctly marked.''

MARGARET FREAME AND HER FAMILY.

A thorough examination of the Penn correspondence would yield much further information concerning Margaret Freame, daughter of the Founder, and her family. Her husband, Thomas Freame, was the son of Robert Freame, of London, "grocer," a Friend, who married Ann Vice, at the Friends' meeting at Bull-and-Mouth, March 21, 1694–5. This Robert Freame—who was apparently of a Gloucester-shire family; his father is described as "late of Cirences-ter"—had a brother John, "citizen and grocer," of Lom-bard Street, London, who, August 19, 1697, married, at the Friends' meeting at Devonshire House, Priscilla Gould. Priscilla Freame, daughter of the latter couple, married David Barclay, "citizen and draper," son of Robert Bar-clay, author of the "Apology," and brother, therefore, to Jean Forbes, the mother of Christian Forbes, who was the first wife of William Penn, 3d. Thus :

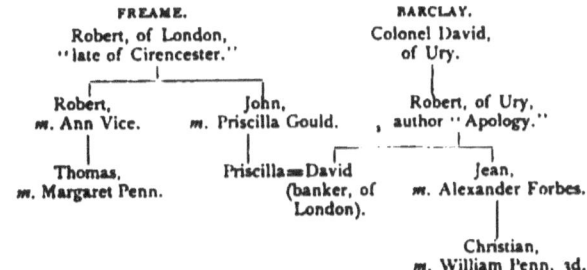

John Freame, who was "citizen and grocer" in 1697, formed later, with his son-in-law, David Barclay, the firm of Freame & Barclay, which became a very successful and

quite important London banking-house. Numerous allusions have been made to them and to " Mr. Barclay " in
the correspondence cited in this essay. David Barclay was
a rich, respected, and influential citizen of London. His
house " enjoyed a larger share of the confidence and trade
of the mercantile community of Philadelphia, during the
middle of the last century, than any other firm in London." [1]   The name of Freame appeared at the head of the
firm until 1771 ; in 1775 that of Barclay was placed first,
and has so remained. (The house has been made, within a
few years, a company, under the name of Barclay & Company, Limited.[2])

Thomas Freame, the husband of Margaret Penn, was
thus the cousin of Priscilla Barclay. The date of his marriage to Margaret Penn is definitely given in the Friends'
records at London. It is thus, in brief :

" Thomas Freame, citizen and grocer, of London, son of Robert,
to Margaret Penn, dau. of William and Hannah, late of Ruscombe,
county of Berks, at Hammersmith, 6th of 5th month [July], 1727."

Thomas Freame came to Pennsylvania in advance of his
wife. A letter from her brother, John Penn, dated at
Feens, October 1, 1732, and addressed to his brother Thomas
in Pennsylvania, says,—

" My sister Freame & her little Boy are perfectly well, & Desire to
be p'ticularly Remembered to you & my Brother Freame, whose
letter She rec'd yesterday with great Pleasure . . . I desire to be

[1] Prof. G. B. Keen in *Penna. Mag.*, Vol. V. p. 96.
[2] Not unnaturally, the Friends gave a large patronage to Freame &
Barclay. From at least as early as 1741—probably earlier—the
" stock " account of London Yearly Meeting (*i. e.*, the general fund,
contributed by the membership and sent up by the subordinate meetings) was banked with this house, and it so continues to be, 1898, a
persistency of business relations certainly not often occurring. "As
early as 1736," says my valued friend, Isaac Sharp, of London, " I
find mention of a loan from Freame & Barclay," for Friends' account.

Remembered to my Bro Freame, who I hope will be able to settle his affairs on Such a foot that he will be with us in the Spring."

Thomas Freame probably did not, as here suggested by John Penn, return to England in the spring of 1733; he stayed for several years in Pennsylvania. His wife and the "little Boy," Thomas, Jr., came over with John Penn to Philadelphia in 1734, and remained here until 1741, when they accompanied Thomas Penn on his return to England. Thomas Penn's letter (already cited) to Richard Hockley, written upon landing in England, speaks of "my sister and her children" as then with him,—the term "children" being explained by the birth in Philadelphia, in 1740, of her daughter, Philadelphia Hannah Freame, afterwards Lady Cremorne.

After John had returned to England, in 1735, Margaret wrote numerous letters to him. One or two of these have been cited. Letters also from her husband, from the little boy, and from Thomas Penn, referring to the Freames,—all addressed to John,—are preserved. They throw light on the family relations, and are of interest besides. I cite some below.

One from Thomas Freame to John Penn, from Philadelphia, October 6, 1735:

" . . . My fever continued a week after you went, wthout the Doctors being able to Turn it. at Last he got it to intermit, & then plyed me Close wth ye Bark wch has quite conquered the distemper. I want nothing now but to gain Strength wch will come by degrees. Yesterday I went out wth Peggy & Little Tom in ye Chariot. I was glad to hear you got to Sea so soon, we were afraid you wo^d have been windbound a week longer."

Margaret Freame to John Penn, from Philadelphia, November 20, 1735:

" The Governour [Gordon] is but Very poorly, and in my Opinion is not likely to hold it Long. the rest of our Acquaintance are Pretty Well, as We all are here, tho its cold Weather & We begin to freese by

266   THE FAMILY OF WILLIAM PENN.

the fireside. I forgot to tell you we have Lost Poor Miss Bettey Gordon,
who was Ship't of for Scotland about 3 weeks ago attended by only a
liitle Black Girl and no womenkind besides themselves on bord, I think
to the shame of the Governour's Family.   Since your departure I have
been Very little abroad, Except in the garden, which is my Chief
amusement.   What there I view I am sure is Natural and Sincere. . . .

  "Mr. Freame is not yet well enough to go up and dispose of his
land, but hope he will soon ; as to the Brewhouse I believe it would turn
out Very well, yet Mr. Norris is so much in the Country my Brother has
advis'd my Husband, if he could part with it on good terms to do it
. . . little Tom is very Well, has rode as far as Cousin Ashton's today,
Since which he has wrot you a letter, Without any help, and I hope he
will come to write pretty well.   he is often setting out to Feen's, and
desires his love to Black Tom and Hannah, Farmer Dell, and all the
Neighbors, to whom mine also.   if att any time you should send anything from Feen's here pray don't forget a few Horse beans.   I should
be glad to know if your Limes kept over good & if the Cranberrys I
sent Sisters Aubrey and Jackson, or which was best, one being Se
[torn] in water and one without.   I have sent you a few Water Mellon
seeds, which if not good to eat will make fine Mangos, also some
Indian corn that will be ripe in three months.   Hope you will have
some good roasting ears. . . . "

The letter from the little boy, Thomas Freame, Jr., to his
uncle, John Penn, alluded to in the letter above as prepared "without any help," is in a childish hand, and runs
as follows :

" DEAR UNCLE

  " I think in Duty I ought to wait on you wth my first Letter, which I
hope will plead excuse for all faults.   I remember what you told me,
and write or go to school every day.   I am very much obliged to you
for you kind present of tickets, and hope I shall have good success.
Pray give my duty to Uncle and Aunt Penn, and all my cousins.   My
love to Mr. Philops, Mr. Service, and Farmer Dell, with all my friends.
So conclude, Dear uncle
                              " Your affec^t nep
                                   " THOMAS FREAME

PHIL No^br 21 1735 "

A few days later, December 8, 1735, Thomas Freame
wrote John Penn, a passage in the letter being as follows :

" We have no material news worth Sending unless of y° melancholly state the Governour [Gordon] is in. His distemper at times
seizes him in such a manner that it is my opinion He cannot get over it.
He is reduced very much and is exceeding weak, Tho' still heart whole,
and at times very cheerfull."

Margaret Freame to John Penn, from Philadelphia,
March 21, 1735–6 :

" . . . The Governour, who was so bad when I last Wrot I thought
he could not Live one week is now as Well as ever he was. what cur'd
him of his Lax was so fine a Receipt I think for the good of Mankind
it should be known.—take a handfull of the Raspings of Logwood, and
Poure Boiling water on it, let it infuse by the fire till it Look of a deep
Red, Drink a teacup of this two or three times a day, and att night
going to bed.—

" We have had a very hard Winter, no appearance of Spring yet,
but Cold hard frosts so that little busness could be done. Mr. Freame
talks of going into the country next week."

Several letters from Thomas Freame to John Penn, from
Philadelphia, in 1736, disclose that the latter thought the
little boy should be sent back to England, in order to be
suitably educated, but that his parents felt unwilling to part
with him. His father earnestly assured John of the suf-
ficiency of the educational opportunities in Philadelphia,
and of the boy's studious efforts.[1]

Other letters from Margaret to John discuss the propriety of appointing Thomas Penn to be Governor on Major
Gordon's death, and the appointment of Thomas Freame to
be naval officer. Margaret seemed to think that John did
not fairly weigh the propriety of Thomas's elevation. Other
letters, some of which are cited below, refer to domestic
and other matters.

Margaret Freame to John Penn, from Philadelphia, December 10, 1736 :

[1] Some interesting details are given in the letters of the system of
education in that day.

" . . . [I] find Bro: Tom sent you word of our att last consenting to have him [Thomas Freame, Jr.] inoculated. The small-pox has and doth rage Very much in this Citty, Numbers of Persons Dying of it. at last seeing It Prove so fatal in the Common way, that by a computation one dy'd in four, and not one in fifty by Inoculation, Mr. Till concluded to have his wife and his 2 children, Mr. Taylor his little Boy, and divers others that has succeeded very well. Poor Tom had it full, but is now, I thank God Bravely recover'd, they are all turn'd, and most shell'd off. he begins to call for a Cook instead of a Doctor. he bore it all with much Patience. Doctor Dover's Regimen is drink coole tankard and small beer, but no Gascoin's powders or Slops. Loyd Zacray was his Doctor, who if he was his own child could not have more tenderly attended him. . . . Poor Mr. Allen has lost his only Son in this fatal Distemper, and too many in this Citty are under the same Affliction ; the Church bell is not suffer'd to ring but once for six [deaths] and it has rung twice a day sometimes. I hope the Cold Weather will Put a Stop to this Contagion."

Margaret Freame to John Penn, from Philadelphia, April 18, 1737 :

" Mr. fishborn's Son, who came from London by way of Maryland arriv'd here yesterday, having a Passage of thirty Days, brings little news (and no letters) but that Cousin Will⁴ Penn is married to Doct' Vaux's Daughter. Could I wonder at his Conduct in anything I should that his Pride should stoop so low."

The service of Thomas Freame as captain of one of the companies raised at Philadelphia in 1740 for the expedition under Admiral Vernon, which made a futile attack on Carthagena in 1741, has been mentioned. In a letter, September 10, 1740, from Thomas Penn at Philadelphia to Ferdinand John Paris (legal adviser of the Penns) at London, this passage occurs :

" You will find the scheme for raising men in America has had a very good effect, and I believe about 4600 will be carried from these Colonys ; and though this Province cannot furnish the number my Lord Monson proposed, yet the eight companys are a considerable number, and are now compleat. Mr. Freame has turned soldier and has the command of one. We have eight ships ready for their imbarkation, and they are to go on Board in a few days."

WORMINGHURST.

The derivation and disposition of the Worminghurst estate have been variously alluded to in different works relating to Penn. His own letters, already cited, show that it was sold in the autumn of 1707, and that William Penn, Jr., was a party to the sale. The purchaser was a Squire Butler, and the property remained in his family until 1789, when it was allotted to Ann Jemima Clough,[1] wife of Roger Clough, and by her it was sold in 1805 to Charles, Duke of Norfolk.

The house in which William Penn lived appears to have been torn down by Squire Butler. (The tradition is that he "expressed the determination not to leave a trace of the old Quaker.") He built on its site, it is said, not long after his purchase, a large brick mansion, "and enclosed a considerable part of the parish in a deer park." But this mansion was itself pulled down by the Duke of Norfolk, "the lake dried up, the timber leveled, and the park converted into a farm. A Spanish chestnut tree of great magnitude, the last remains of the former grandeur of the place, was grubbed up in the year 1825; it measured, six feet from the ground, twenty-nine feet in circumference."[2]

Worminghurst stood in view of "the South Downs." It was four miles south of the Friends' meeting-house in Thakeham Parish, and five and a half miles northwest of the meet-house at Steyning."[3]

WILLIAM PENN, JR.'S MARRIAGE SETTLEMENT.

The marriage settlement made upon the occasion of William Penn, Jr.'s marriage in 1698 was deposited later, apparently, with Messrs. Freame and Barclay, and in July

---

[1] She is called the "eldest daughter" of Butler, but with the separation of eighty-two years this appears rather unlikely.

[2] Paragraphs cited in "Some Records of the Early Friends in Surrey and Sussex," by Thomas W. and Anne Warner Marsh. London, 1886.

[3] Marsh's "Early Friends in Surrey and Sussex."

last (1898), a little more than two centuries after its making,
the document was handed over by the representatives of the
late Joseph Gurney Barclay, of London, to be deposited in
the Penn Papers Collection of the Friends at Devonshire
House. It is an "indenture quadripartite," and endorsed :
"Mr. Penn, his settlement on his sonn's intermarriage with
Mrs. Mary Jones." The signers are William Penn, Laetitia
Penn, William Penn, Jr., Mary Jones, Charles Jones, Jr., and
Nathaniel Wade.

PENN MARRIAGES IN HORSHAM RECORDS.

The proceedings in the Friends' meeting prior to Penn's
marriage with Hannah Callowhill are partly recorded in the
minutes of Horsham Monthly Meeting, in Sussex. These
show, January, 1695–6, that "William Penn, of Worminghurst, Sussex, did the first time Declare his Intentions of
taking Hannah Callowhill, of the City of Bristol, to be his
wife," and that Thomas Wright and five others were appointed
"to enquire concerning his Clearness on the Account of
Marriage." Next month these Friends "Did signifie that
they find nothing but that he is very cleare in that matter, soe
this meeting hath ordred a Certificate to be sent to the Friends
of the City of Bristol to which the said Hannah Callowhill
doth belong."

At Horsham Monthly Meeting also, in July, 1702, "William Aubrey, of White Lyon Courte, in Cornhill, London,
Marchant, and Leatitia Penn, of Wormenghurst, in Sussex,
Did the first time Declare their Intentions of taking each other
to be husband and wife. The said William brought a Certificate from his father, giveing his free Consent under his hand,
and the said Leatitia's father being present gave his free
Consent. Also the said William Aubry produced a Certificat
from the Two weeks meeting in London, signifying his
Clearnes from all others relateing to marriage, allso Laetitia

produced a Certificat from Friends in Pensilvania Signifying her Clearnes on that Accounte." [1]

THE FELL BRANCH.

The mention in Chapter VIII. of Gulielma Maria Penn, daughter of William Penn, Jr., who became the wife of Aubrey (Awbrey?) Thomas, and of Charles Fell, may be somewhat expanded. The following family record, furnished by Gilbert Cope, is derived (he thinks) from a certified copy of a parish register :

> "Gulielma Maria Fell, d. 17 Jan., 1739–40.
> "Charles Fell, her (2nd) husband, d. 1 Oct., 1748.
> [Children of the above :]
> " Mary Margaretta, bapt. 23 Aug., 1724.
> "Gulielma Maria Frances, bapt. 10 Aug., 1725.
> " Robert Edward, bapt. 29 Nov., 1726."

There are numerous deeds, etc., made by and on behalf of these children of Charles and Gulielma Maria (Penn) Fell, on record, which clearly explain many points in the family account. In 1770 Robert Edward Fell was in Philadelphia attending to their interests and engaged in the sale of their real property. In a deed, May 10, 1770, by him to Timothy Hurst, of New York, merchant, for a lot on South Street, Philadelphia, for fifty-four pounds purchase-money, a power of attorney to him (Fell), dated in March, 1769, from his sister, Gulielma Maria Frances Newcomb, "of Shrewsbury, co. Salop, Great Britain, widow," is recited, she being "one of the daughters of Gulielma Maria Fell, deceased, who was the daughter of William Penn, Jr., deceased." The deed is " by Robert Edward Fell, now residing in the City of Phila-delphia, Esquire." Another deed, May 10, 1770, same to same, for one-eighth interest in a lot on South Street, price three thousand pounds, describes R. E. Fell as the " eldest son " of Gulielma Maria Fell, deceased.[2]

[1] Entries cited in " Early Friends in Surrey and Sussex."
[2] He was her eldest son, but her third child.

A Pennsylvania land warrant, dated October 21, 1774, signed by (Governor) John Penn, in favor of Timothy Hurst, of New York, merchant, and John Barron and Israel Morris, of Philadelphia, for twelve hundred and fifty acres of land in any part of the Province, states in its extended recitals much of the family record of the Fell branch, the essential facts of which have been given. The origin of the title to the twelve hundred and fifty acres lay in the trust grant (lease and release) made by William Penn to Sir John Fagg, September 4 and 5, 1682, for fifty thousand acres, one-half being for the use of William Penn, Jr. By a lease and release in 1731, Thomas and Richard Penn confirmed unto William Penn, 3d, five thousand acres, part of the fifty thousand; and this tract William Penn, 3d, sold in 1742 to William Allen, of Philadelphia. The recital proceeds that one-fourth of the five thousand acres belonged to the sister of William Penn, 3d, Gulielma Maria Fell, who afterwards died intestate in the lifetime of her husband, leaving issue by her first husband, Aubrey Thomas, one son, William Penn Thomas, and by her second husband, Charles Fell, three children, Robert Edward, Mary Margaretta (Barron), and Gulielma Maria Frances (Newcomb). It is further particularly mentioned that William Penn Thomas died intestate without issue in the lifetime of Charles Fell.

A lease and release, February, 1768, the parties being John Barron, "of York Buildings, in the county of Middlesex, gentleman," and Mary Margaretta, his wife, of one part, and Robert Crispin, "of Chancery Lane, in said county, gentleman," of the other, recites that Mary Margaretta is one of the surviving children of Charles Fell and Gulielma Maria Penn. A deed of later date is by Barron, then "of Philadelphia," to Charles Hurst, of the same city, gentleman, and recites that Barron, "in company with" Hurst, "is entitled to sundry lands, warrants, and rights in Pennsylvania, and especially to certain 5,000 acres in right of William and

Gulielma Maria Penn, . . . under which last they have located and caused to be surveyed several tracts of land." Barron conveys all his interest in the five thousand acres to Hurst for five hundred pounds.

A letter in the Penn collections of the Historical Society of Pennsylvania, from Charles Fell to John Penn, is dated January 8, 1739–40. The writer speaks of his wife as then very ill. She is in care of Dr. Dover, and can only take "thin caudle through the spout of a teapot." The letter gives no place of address, but appears from later allusions to have been written from Westminster. Other letters immediately following disclose a pathetic story.

Same to same, Thursday, January 17, 1739–40 :

"This morning at one o'clock my Dearest Guly left me for ever . . begg the continuance of yo' Friendship to me and her Children."

Same to same, January 22, 1739–40 :

"My poor Dear Guly is this night to be buried in a private but as decent a manner as I am able in a Vault in Saint Margaret's Church, Westminster."

Same to same, January 29, 1739–40 :

". . . I am most unhappy, left greatly in debt, and am oblig'd to dispose of all my Goods, w⁶ will be sold next Thursday, to satisfy as many as the poor amount of them will come to, but what to do afterwards God only knows. My poor Dear Girls are gone this day w⁶ their Grandmother¹ to Hampton Court, in order to have their Cloaths a little righted up before they go to a School w⁶ she has recommended. [The little boy, he adds, is taken by one of the ushers of Westminster School to board with him. The writer himself has taken a sleeping-room at the coffee-house ; he is very anxious for some employment.]"

A Fell pedigree is given in *Quakeriana* (London), June, 1895. It describes Charles Fell as "an officer in the army,"

¹ This must have been Charles Fell's mother, as Mary Penn, widow of William Penn, Jr., and mother of Gulielma Maria Fell, had died in 1733.

and says he died, 1748, "at Windsor." It gives some further data concerning his (and Gulielma Maria Penn's) children, adding the name of a fourth, who "died young."

1. Mary Margaretta, married John Barron, of Leeds, co. York, afterwards of Philadelphia, and died 1769.

2. Gulielma Maria Frances, married John Newcombe, of Leir, co. Leicester, and had issue: Gulielma Maria, Susanna Margaretta, Philadelphia (married Thomas Brookholding), John Springett, William Hawkins.

3. Robert Edward, a lieutenant-colonel in the army.

4. Springett, died young.

The assumption that this line of descent from William Penn is extinct has been mentioned; if there are any descendants living, they appear to be from John Newcombe and his wife.

TABLE: FELL BRANCH PENN FAMILY.

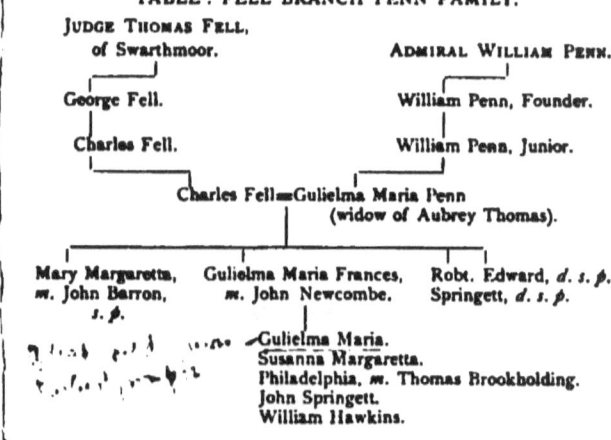

JUDGE THOMAS FELL, of Swarthmoor.
ADMIRAL WILLIAM PENN.

George Fell.
William Penn, Founder.

Charles Fell.
William Penn, Junior.

Charles Fell═Gulielma Maria Penn (widow of Aubrey Thomas).

Mary Margaretta, m. John Barron, s. p.
Gulielma Maria Frances, m. John Newcombe.
Robt. Edward, d. s. p.
Springett, d. s. p.

Gulielma Maria.
Susanna Margaretta.
Philadelphia, m. Thomas Brookholding.
John Springett.
William Hawkins.

THE CHURCH AT PENN IN BUCKS.

The venerable parish church at Penn, in Buckinghamshire, Holy Trinity, where several children of Thomas and Richard

Penn were buried, has some interest on that account, and because of the connection stated by the Founder with "those Penns of Penn in Bucks." The western limit of the village in which it stands is on the borders of Wycombe Heath, and distant some three miles from Beaconsfield. The church building is irregular, with a low square tower. It dates from 1213, and is built of rubble and flint. The chancel was added in 1736. One of its brasses contains the following inscription :

> Here lyeth the bodye of John Pen, Esquire,
> who married Sarah, the daughter of Sir Hy.
> Drury Knt, by whom he had issue five sonnes
> and five daughters. He departed this life the
> second day of July, A. D., 1641.

At the end of the slab there are representations of the sons and daughters, in devotional attitude.

Another brass, upon a coffin, found under the floor of the church, in 1899, has this inscription :

> Here lyeth buried the bodyes of William Pen
> Esq. and of Martha his wife, by whom he had
> issue one sonne and two daughters. Shee
> dyed the 19th day of November Anno Dni
> 1635. Hee dyed the 19th day of January Anno
> Dni 1638.

These two men, John Penn and William Penn, were, it will be seen, contemporary with the Admiral. What the kinship between them was I do not undertake to suggest.

WILL OF RICHARD PENN, IST.

The will of Richard Penn, son of the Admiral, and younger brother of the Founder, who died unmarried in 1673, has been summarised as below by Mr. J. Henry Lea, and printed in the *New England Hist. and Gen. Register,* July, 1900 :

Will of Richard Penn of Walthamstow, Co. Essex, younger son of Sir William Penn, late of Wanstead in Essex, Knt., deceased. Dated 4 April 1673. To be buried in Walthamstow and to poor of that place £10. To mother Dame Margaret Penn £40 yearly for life. To sister Margaret Lowther, wife of Anthony Lowther, Esq., £50, and to said Anthony Lowther £30, 2 guns and a pair of pistols at the selection of my brother William Penn. To servant George Homond £10. Mourning for mother, brother and sister Anthony and Margaret Lowther and their children, servant George, and mother and sister's servants. To sister Gulielma Maria Penn £50 in token of love. My mother Dame Margaret Extrx, Witn : — Richard Newman, George Haman (*sic*), Michaell Lee. Pro. 11 April 1673 by Extrx. named in will.

P. C. C.   Pye, 49.

RICHARD PENN, THE LAST.

A correspondent in London, Mr. Philip Norman,[1] has very kindly given me some interesting recollections of Richard Penn, the great-grandson of the Founder, who died in 1863. "He was," Mr. Norman says, "a frequent visitor at my father's house, and they belonged to the same fishing club, called the Houghton Fishing Club, whose headquarters are at Stockbridge, in Hampshire. When a boy I often stayed there with my father and met Mr. Penn. The fishing book was full of amusing sketches, some by Chantrey, the sculptor, who had been a member.

"He was fond of mechanics, and had been, I think, a good turner. He presented one of my brothers with a turning lathe. I have one or two books which he gave me, also a copy of ' Pilgrim's Progress ' with his bookplate in it. He had made his will, and after some legacies made his housekeeper (a very respectable woman), his residuary legatee. When his sister Mrs. Paynter died, he came into her property, which amounted to something like £30,000. He was very fond of her and was much affected at the news of her

---

[1] Mr. Norman is Treasurer of the Society of Antiquaries, of London, whose headquarters are at Burlington House.

death. Shortly afterward he became ill and sent for a lawyer to alter his will, but when he arrived Mr. Penn was so much worse that this was impossible ; so the housekeeper came in for the £30,000, in addition to what he had intended to leave her."

MAJOR STUART, OF TEMPSFORD HALL.

Major William Dugald Stuart, now the representative of his line of the family, descended from the Founder's second marriage, the present owner of all the general estate in Pennsylvania of the Penn family, visited this State in 1894, and again in 1898. Some further facts concerning him should be added. Though educated at Eton, he did not go (as stated in Chapter X.) to St. John's College, Cambridge, nor is he a barrister-at-law of the Inner Temple.

He entered the British army as second lieutenant in the King's Royal Rifles, June 23, 1880. He was promoted to lieutenant July 1, 1881, and captain November 13, 1889. In 1891 he served with the Manipore expedition in Burmah against the Dacoits (for which he received a medal and clasp), and subsequently in the expedition against the Chins and Lushais, in Upper Burmah. He continued serving in India until 1893, when he was placed on the Reserve of Officers. He is now (1898) major in the Third (Militia) Battalion of the Bedfordshire Regiment. He married Millicent Helen Olivia Bulkeley-Hughes, and has issue one son, William Esme Montague.

At Tempsford Hall, among the "interesting family relics" alluded to in Chapter X., Major Stuart has the gold chain and medal of Admiral Penn, voted him by the Naval Council in August, 1653. He also has the walking-staff which King Charles I. carried to the scaffold, and handed, just before his execution, to Bishop Juxon, who accompanied him. The Bishop presented the staff afterwards to William Penn the Founder, and it has thus descended to Major Stuart.

OTHER FAMILIES NAMED PENN.

There are evidently a number of persons in the United States and elsewhere, named Penn, who believe themselves connected with the family of William Penn the Founder, if not directly descended from him. So far as the record evidence goes, his living descendants appear to be in the three lines stated in the preceding chapters of this essay :

1. The line from Peter Gaskell and Christiana Gulielma Penn, daughter of William Penn, 3d.

2. The line from Archbishop William Stuart and Sophia Penn, daughter of• Thomas Penn, represented by Major William Dugald Stuart.

3. The line from the same parentage as No. 2, represented by the Earl of Ranfurly.

Except through the adoption of the additional name Penn by the Gaskell branch, no living person named Penn, so far as appears, is a descendant of William Penn the Founder, or —it may be added—Admiral Sir William Penn.

An example of many curious and also interesting inquiries made by persons who believe themselves descended from William Penn or his father is afforded by the following letter, addressed " To the Chief Justice of Pennsylvania " :

"VIRGIN ISLANDS, TORTOLA, April 11, 1871.

" HONORABLE SIR,

" I herewith respectfully beg your kind attention to the following facts, hoping you will not consider it taking too great liberty &c. that you will do me the favor of causing an answer to be sent to me.

" I am a native of these Islands and a descendant of the brother of the celebrated William Penn of Pennsylvania, which brother settled in these Islands some time in the eighteenth century. I cannot be certain as to the exact date by reason of the frequent hurricanes in these Islands, as all old papers have been destroyed.

" My object for writing to you sir, is to request that you will cause inquiry to be made as to one Richard Penn who is stated to have died last year, & who was the last descendant of the celebrated Quaker, & that he also left large property, both in specie & land, & that in the event of no descendant of the Penn family such property will revert to the Government of the United States, & if such is the case I will most respectfully request that you will communicate with me and I will be ready to pay any expenses attendant thereon as also to prove my descent before the proper authorities in these islands.

    " I have the honor to be

        " Honble Sir

          " Your most obdt. Servt,

            " WM. BENJAMIN PENN."

    This letter was delivered to Justice James Thompson, then Chief-Justice of the Supreme Court of Pennsylvania, who forwarded it to William Henry Rawle, of Philadelphia, who was counsel for the Penn heirs. May 1, 1871, Mr. Rawle wrote William Benjamin Penn, stating the facts of the case, explaining the devolution of the estate, and the vesting of it in William Stuart, then owner, and nothing further appears to have been heard from the writer of the letter.

SUNDRY NOTES.

    The old farm-house, King's Farm, Chorley Wood, where William Penn and Gulielma Maria Springett were married, is still standing, 1898.

    It is the tradition, Joseph J. Green says, that Gulielma Maria Penn, wife of the Founder, died at Rawdon House, at Hoddesdon, Herts. This was the seat of Marmaduke Rawdon, Esquire, but it had passed at the time referred to from the Rawdons to the Quaker family of the Dimsdales, one of whom became in the next century physician to the Empress Catherine II., of Russia. The old mansion is still standing. That she died at Hoddesdon has been already definitely stated, and it may have been at Rawdon House.

    The Bristol (England), apprentice records show " John Penn, son of William Penn, of Rushcombe, co. Berks, gent. apprenticed to Brice Webb, Linnendraper and Phebe his wife," under date of 17 August, 1715.

Richard Dawson, Earl of Dartrey, great-nephew of Baron Cremorne, who married Philadelphia Hannah Freame, died 1897, aged eighty years. He was succeeded in the peerage by his son, Lord Cremorne, who was formerly an officer of the Coldstream Guards, and sat as a Liberal in Parliament for Monaghan, 1865–68. " The family," a newspaper paragraph says, " is one of the great landlords of the United Kingdom, owning about 30,000 acres."

CHILDREN OF WILLIAM PENN THE FOUNDER.

BY FIRST WIFE, GULIELMA MARIA SPRINGETT.

	BORN.	DIED.	BURIED.	MARRIED.
1. Gulielma Maria.	Jan. 23, 1672–3.	Mar. 17,1672–3	Jordans.	D. unmarried.
2. William.	Feb. 28, 1673–4.	May 15, 1674.	Jordans.	D. unmarried.
3. Mary (? Margaret).	Feb. 28, 1673–4.	Feb. 24,1674–5	Jordans.	D. unmarried.
4. Springett.	Jan. 25, 1675.	April 10, 1696.	Jordans.	D. unmarried.
5. Letitia, m. William Aubrey *j.p.*	Mar. 6, 1678.	April —, 1746.	Jordans.	Aug. 20, 1702.
6. William, Jr., m. Mary Jones (issue, three children).	Mar. 14, 1680.	June 23, 1720.	? Liege.	Jan. 10, 1698–9
7. Gulielma Maria.	Nov. 17, 1685.	Nov. 20, 1689.	Jordans.	D. unmarried.

BY SECOND WIFE, HANNAH CALLOWHILL.

	BORN.	DIED.	BURIED.	MARRIED.
8. John.	Jan. 29, 1699–1700	Oct. 25, 1746.	Jordans.	D. unmarried.
9. Thomas, m. Lady J. Fermor (issue, eight children).	Mar. 9, 1701–2.	Mar. 21, 1775.	Stoke.	Aug. 20, 1751.
10. Hannah Margarita.	July 30, 1703.	Feb. 5, 1707–8.	Bristol.	D. unmarried.
11. Margaret, m. Thomas Freame (issue, two children).	Nov. 7, 1704.	Feb.—,1750–1.	Jordans.	July 6, 1727.
12. Richard, m. Hannah Lardner (issue, four children).	Jan. 17, 1705–6.	Feb. 4, 1771.	Stoke.	—, 1728.
13. Dennis.	Feb. 26, 1706–7.	Jan. 6, 1722–3.	Jordans.	D. unmarried.
14. Hannah.	Sept. 5, 1708.	Jan. 25, 1708–9	Jordans.	D. unmarried.